The Immortal King

Part One of the Godyear Saga

By Jason Malone

This edition first published in 2021

Cover design by Lena Yang
Map illustrated by Elizabeth Barlow-Hall

ISBN 978-0-473-56420-9 (paperback)
ISBN 978-0-473-56422-3 (ebook)
ISBN 978-0-473-56421-6 (hardcover)
ISBN 978-0-473-56423-0 (Kindle)
ISBN 978-0-473-56424-7 (audiobook)

Published by Jason Malone
www.talesfromardonn.com
authorjcmalone@gmail.com

This tale is for Sophie,
who showed me dreams can indeed come true.

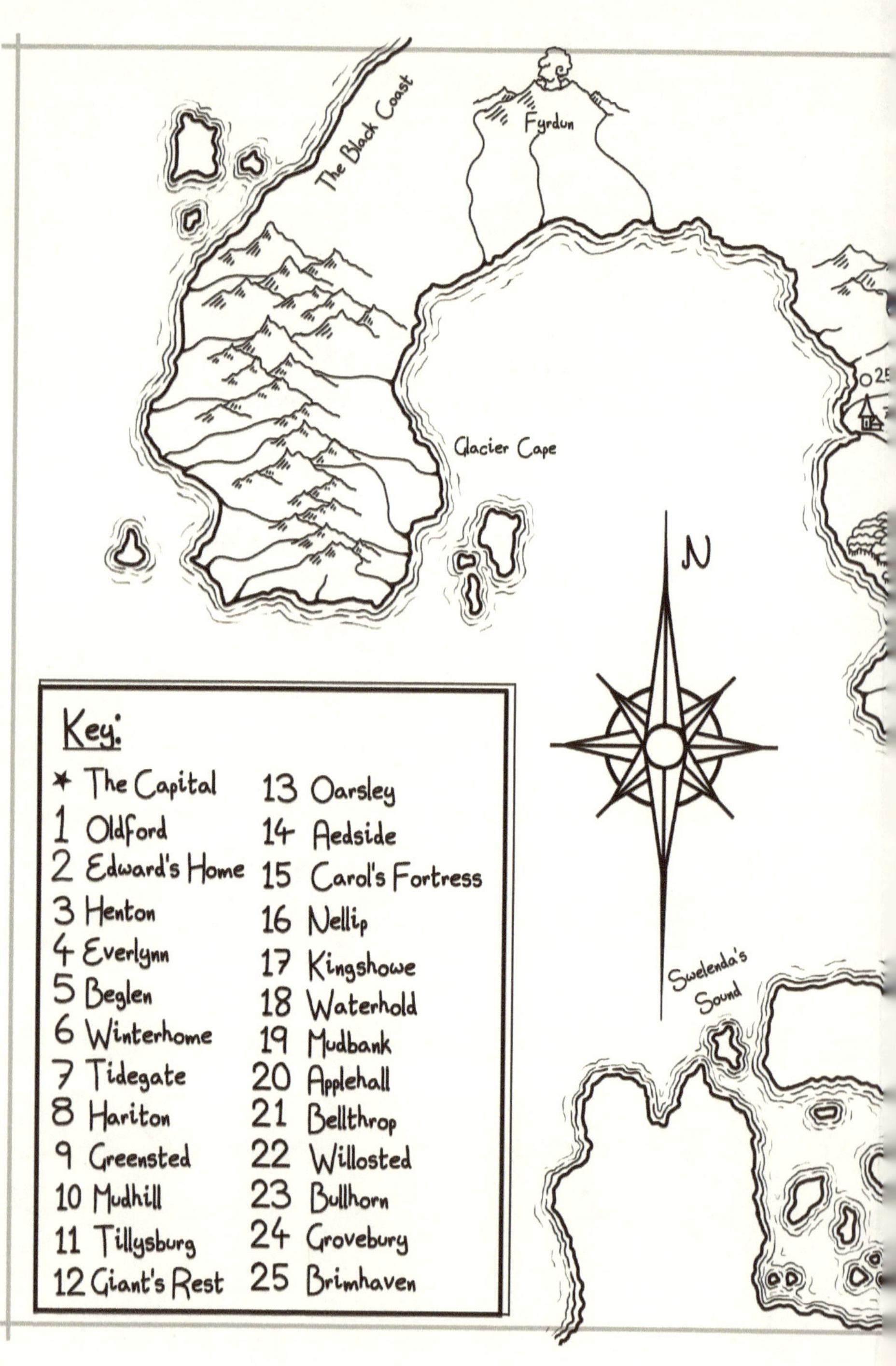

The Black Coast
Fyrdun
Glacier Cape
N
Swelenda's Sound
Key:
* The Capital
1 Oldford
2 Edward's Home
3 Henton
4 Everlynn
5 Beglen
6 Winterhome
7 Tidegate
8 Hariton
9 Greensted
10 Mudhill
11 Tillysburg
12 Giant's Rest
13 Oarsley
14 Aedside
15 Carol's Fortress
16 Nellip
17 Kingshowe
18 Waterhold
19 Mudbank
20 Applehall
21 Bellthrop
22 Willosted
23 Bullhorn
24 Grovebury
25 Brimhaven

Prologue

I will never see a return to the days of light.

I used to believe the darkness that engulfed our world was passing. I was optimistic. I was young. Foolish. Only now have I come to understand that the story of my life takes place during the dusk rather than the dawn. I am merely a character in the closing chapters of Fate's great tale.

You see, for each of us, our life in this world is like a story. We are the protagonists in our own tales, yet each of our tales constitutes the saga that is time — the Godyear, as some are wont to call it.

And like the characters in every tale, we do not realise we are merely a part of a story. We believe we can choose, that we can change lives and set events in motion, or even save the world. When we yield a successful harvest, we think it was our own labour that grew those bountiful crops; when we find victory in battle, we think it was our skill with a blade and the superiority of our strategy; when we love, we think it is because we allow our hearts to do so.

But like the heroes in those tales we tell by the fire or over a pot of ale, or those we read to our children when we tuck them in at night, we are entirely at the mercy of the storyteller.

It is ludicrous to believe we write our own stories. They are written by the greatest author of all: Fate, that cruel mistress. So powerful is she that even the Gods are subject to her pen.

And like every story, that which is written by Fate has a beginning, and, ultimately, an end. There will eventually be a closing line. A final word. The last drop of ink on the page that leaves the reader wondering, "What next?" On to the next tale, of course.

All mere mortals can do is try to understand our place in that tale. Does our story take place at the beginning of that saga, in the spring of the Godyear, or are we seeing its end? It was not until I was asked by my daughter, my little Edith, to tell her the tale of the Immortal King Emrys that I began to understand the answer to that question.

Emrys was a king cursed by a dwarf many centuries ago; I fought him in my youth. My daughter was about seven years old when she asked about him. I remember it now. I was sitting in a chair by the hearth during a cold winter, much colder than the winter before. The fire was blazing, and Edith was lying on her belly right in front of it, wrapped in furs and playing with some wooden toys an old friend of mine had made for her. She was singing softly to herself, and I was lost deep in thought.

Edith is grown now, but even then, when she was so young, she reminded me so much of her mother. She has her eyes, a deep ocean blue, and the same raven-black hair. Edith sang like her mother too.

"Da?" she asked, still watching her toys. I snapped out of my daze and looked down at her. "Can you tell me about your fight with the king that lived forever?"

"Your mother would not like me telling you that story," I said.

"Then don't tell Ma you told me," she said. She looked up at me and grinned, putting a finger over her mouth. I could not help but smirk.

"All right. But before I tell you about my part in that story, we must go back to where it all began."

And so I told Edith the legend of Emrys, as far as I understood it. As I told the tale, I began to realise the events that took place nearly a thousand years ago set in motion the beginning of the end of our age. The final chapters of our world's story. Since that day, Man has wandered deeper and deeper into the dark. I did not tell little Edith that. Not yet.

I told her this: long ago, in the days before our people conquered these lands, there were many small kingdoms. One of those kingdoms was ruled by a king named Emrys. He was part of a long and proud line of monarchs, and feeling outshone by those who came before him, he wanted to live up to his ancestors' glory by waging war against his neighbours.

As the legend says, while on campaign Emrys came across a dwarven lord, and that dwarf invited Emrys and his horde of horsemen into his hall. Time goes differently in the Otherworld, however. For three nights, Emrys and his horde feasted and drank with the dwarves, indulging in all kinds of pleasures. After the third night, Emrys and his army bade their hosts farewell, and the dwarves gave them gifts aplenty — food, wine, and wealth — to send them on their way.

But the lord of the dwarves had one final gift: a puppy with fur as grey as the sky during a storm. "Now, Lord King," the dwarf said to Emrys, "that puppy shall sit with you atop your saddle, and so long as it sits with you, you shall sit with it. Should you and your men leave their saddles, time shall catch up to them. But should the grey dog dismount, or should you wear your crown once more, this curse shall be broken."

Emrys did not know it in that moment, but while he and his army were feasting with the dwarves, three centuries had passed in our world. In that time, Emrys's descendants ruled his kingdom until our people came from the north. We conquered all the little kingdoms here and made them our own. A king from among our people married the daughter of one of Emrys's descendants, and born through that marriage was the dynasty that would rule Ardonn for generations, before they were usurped.

Emrys roamed the land seeking aid, but the people spoke a language he did not know. Food and drink turned to dust in his mouth. He forgot what it was to love. He was immortal. You see, for Emrys and his men timed flowed as if they were still with the dwarves, but he felt dead.

He grew angry and bitter and began ravaging the kingdom that once was his. He toppled lords and turned whole countries to ash, but he could never regain his crown, for it was safe behind the tall walls of Ardonn's capital. He brought chaos to the land but was eventually defeated by Ardonn's king, and he disappeared. For a century he was gone, and the kingdoms in this land prospered.

But a century later, he returned. He pillaged, he burned, he sought the crown, claiming that it was his by right, that he had never died and so the succession to his son was illegitimate. Many mortals supported him, either out of fear or lust for wealth and power, but they were once again defeated. After the next century passed he returned, only to be defeated once more.

Then, another century later and three before now, Emrys returned yet again, but this time the king who wore his crown was expecting him. He was ready. A war lasting three years was waged between Emrys and the king of Ardonn, who we now know as Carol the Great. Carol had a close friend and companion named Godwin, who was a Godspeaker, like I am. Godwin specialised in dealing with Otherworldly beings and thus knew how to defeat Emrys for good.

Together, King Carol and Godwin led Emrys into the mountains. They laid a trap, and Emrys rode right into it. Deep within the northern mountain ranges, Carol had found a wide underground passage, which led to an enormous tomb built by ancient men. That tomb would be Emrys's prison — for if he could not be killed, he could at least be bound. With a sacrifice of Emrys's blood, which flowed through Carol's veins and which was cut from Carol with Godwin's sword, Emrys was entombed within the mountain.

By defeating Emrys, Carol won the favour of many lords and kings among our people, and they swore oaths to him, though they did not know exactly how Emrys was defeated. With his newfound allies, Carol was able to unite the divided, warring petty-kingdoms and create the single, united Kingdom of Ardonn. An age of peace and prosperity came to Ardonn. Carol ruled for sixty-seven years and built his kingdom into something to rival the Heavens!

"If Emrys was trapped in the mountain, why did you fight him?" my daughter asked.

"It was supposed to be forever," I explained. "And to ensure Emrys could never be freed again, Carol, Godwin, and the few other men present swore an oath of secrecy. They swore never to share what happened beneath that mountain, for fear that someone, someday, may attempt to release him."

"Why would someone want to do that?" Edith said.

I ignored the question. "One of those men failed to hold true to their oaths, so someone did end up releasing him."

"*Now* will you tell me about your fight with Emrys, Da?" Edith sat up, her toys long forgotten. She was smiling, excited to hear about her father's adventures. She was so innocent. So naïve. She understood nothing of the world, but one day, she would come to know the things a child should never know. So why not now?

I sat back in my seat and groaned. My legs still ached back then, and even now they are not completely healed. "Soon, little one," I said. "But the beginning of my story does not start with Emrys. It begins with your mother and the night I first met her."

And so I told Edith my story. The story of my life, and my small part in Fate's saga. A story that had once been written in the pages of our world was, after many years, finally being told.

1

Moth

Bards and poets have told me that I should never start a story by talking about the weather. "Nobody cares about the weather," they say. But by the Gods, if there was one thing that defined the night I met Matilda, it was the weather.

In fact, the weather was what drove me to meet her on that bitter midwinter night in the final weeks of the 1,118th year of the Third Age of Man, just over a month before Winterlow. Indeed, the weather that night set in motion the chain of events that would make up my life's story.

There was a blizzard. I hate blizzards, and this one was particularly vicious. I could hear nothing but the awful howl of wind and the sound of ice tearing across my face. I was travelling back home through the woods of eastern Ardonn, the large forest at the base of the foreboding mountain range that separates our kingdom from our neighbours farther east. I could see the snowstorm coming from the north a few days before it hit, but I thought I could outrun it.

I could not. Each day it crept closer and closer, until finally I was enveloped in a storm of snow, hail, and wind. I probably do not need to mention that it was horribly cold. My poor horse could not bear it, and by late afternoon the frost had taken her.

I had to travel the rest of the way on foot, following a narrow dirt path in the hopes of finding some sort of hospitality. Roads typically lead *somewhere*. Usually when travelling in the wilds, I would camp out under the stars, because the night air was often warmer than the welcome people like me received from the superstitious folk in the more isolated parts of the kingdom, but in this weather I would freeze to death overnight if I could not find a fire.

It was not until nightfall that I found somewhere. I saw the thin rays of light seeping through the shutters of the village's little houses first. In fact, that was all I could see. It was so dark, and there was so much snow, that I could see nothing else except those lights. When I was but a few yards away from the village, I could at last make out the shadows of houses. I passed a rundown signpost, but it was too dark to read it. I shouted into the wind, hoping someone would hear me.

"Hello." I could barely hear myself, for the rushing wind carried my voice away the moment it passed my lips. I hugged myself tighter, wrapping my thick fur cloak around me. My bones were aching from the cold.

I ran, or at least I tried to run, to the nearest house and thumped my fist on the door, shouting for someone to let me in. There was no answer, but candlelight filtered through the cracks in the shoddy wooden door. I tried the next house along and was only answered by the bark of a dog.

I squinted off to the east. I could only just make out the silhouette of a hall, taller than the rest of the homes here and surrounded by a wooden palisade. A dim glow radiated from it, so I headed there, hoping for a kinder welcome.

The palisade's gate hung open, and no one guarded it. No surprises there. Standing guard in this weather was a death sentence. I walked through the gate, hunched over as hail pelted my back, and finally came to the double door of this modest hall. I knocked — no, hammered — on the hall's door, calling out.

There was no answer.

I pounded on the door again then stood back and swore. I was just about to try for a third time when the door swung open and a dark figure quickly gestured for me to come in. I did not hesitate and almost flew inside with the wind and snow. The man shouted something at me, and although I could barely hear him over the harsh whistling as wind rushed through the doorway, I knew he wanted me to help him close the door.

We both pushed it shut with all our strength, then he barred it and fell back against the wall with a sigh. It was a lot quieter now, and I could see the man who in that moment was my saviour. He looked to be in his early twenties, a few years older than me, and he had hair as black as night. He was wrapped in a thick fur cloak.

"Who are you, wanderer, and can I trust you?" he asked. I removed a glove from my cold hand and held it out for him. He hesitated and then shook it.

"My name is Edward, from near Oldford. You can trust me," I said.

The man frowned. "Not the right season to be in the woods this far from home," he said. "I am Gunn. My father is the earl of this lonely village." He sniffed and jerked his head, indicating I should follow him, and then walked over to the large fireplace at the other end of the hall.

I followed past the hall's long feasting table to the dying fire behind the table's high seat. The low roof was held up by oak columns, which were beautifully carved but had clearly seen better days. Gunn poured himself a horn of ale from a barrel. "You want a drink?" he asked, but he poured another horn before I could answer and handed it to me. It was too sour, but it warmed my belly.

"Thank you, Gunn," I said. He sat down on the rug right in front of the fireplace and started to revive the flames, then gestured for me to join him. I kicked off my boots, removed my belt, and sat huddled in my furs. We sat in silence for a few moments, sipping our sour ale and watching the fire grow. I could already feel the cold melting from my bones.

"Nice blade," Gunn said. He nodded to my sword.

"It was my master's," I said. "Now it's mine."

"Your master's? What is your trade?"

I stared into the fire for a few seconds. I was — am — one of the Gifted; what the nobility call a 'Godspeaker' and what the commoners call 'Elfmen,' 'Wightmen,' or 'Death-Whisperers,' among other things. You see, I have a gift that gives me senses most men do not possess. I can hear things, see things, and feel things that others cannot, and I can even communicate with beings from the Otherworld.

In days of old, every lord worth something had a Godspeaker in his court, advising him on matters his priests dare not speak of. We were respected once, but as we grew rarer, the nobles stopped hiring us and the superstitious and fearful grew to hate us. The kings of the old Eomundson dynasty still kept Godspeakers right up until the last one, King Edwin the Fifth, was overthrown nearly a decade ago. Now there are only a few of us left that are trained to use our gift. "I am one of the Gifted," I said.

Gunn raised his eyebrows and then looked as though something had clicked in his mind. "Ah, you are *the* Edward of Oldford. I have heard of you," he said. "Well, welcome to Henton, Edward Godspeaker." He raised his horn and took a big gulp.

At that, the door at the side of the hall opened, and a tall, bearded man with long black hair entered the room. He looked to

be in his forties, but the dark bags under his eyes made him look
sixty. He was fully clothed, wearing a rich green tunic belted
with thick black leather and a bearskin cloak draped over his
shoulders.

Behind him followed a young girl with similar black hair and
deep blue eyes, with skin as pale as snow, dressed in her
nightgown. She looked a few years younger than me and carried
a tray with a bowl and a piece of bread.

The man came over to us and sat in the high seat, facing the
fire. I got up onto one knee and bowed my head before him, for I
could tell he was the earl. The girl stood beside him, shuffling
her feet. "I thought I heard a guest. Welcome to Henton. My
name is Harold. I am the lord of this manor," said the man. "This
is my second daughter, Matilda." He nodded to the girl, who
placed the tray at my feet. We made eye contact for a second and
then she curtsied before leaving the room.

I did not know it at the time, but that young lady would change
my life.

Harold gave me a wave to indicate I could sit back down.
Gunn introduced me before I could, and Harold seemed intrigued
when he heard I was a Godspeaker. He asked why I was there, in
the middle of nowhere during one of the harshest periods of the
year.

I told him I had a job a few days to the north — some villagers
were having problems with a ghost — and I was heading back
home through the hidden paths in the woods to avoid paying the

tolls along the main roads. Godspeakers were once believed to be above all other men, but now those of us remaining either sell our gift to whoever pays or become outlaws.

Harold offered to let me stay for as long as the snowstorm persisted. He had a couple of spare bedrooms, he said, and plenty of food stockpiled to last us the whole season if need be. I thanked him for his hospitality, and he and Gunn left me alone to finish the cold stew and stale bread his daughter had brought me. It was not the best meal I had ever eaten, but it sufficed.

Once I had finished, I sat cross-legged in front of the fire and meditated, emptying my mind and detaching myself from the dark and bitter night. Harold's dog — a big, slobbery bloodhound — came to join me after a while, curling up by the fire with its head resting on my leg.

I closed my eyes and thought of home. I hated travelling during winter. This season was a time to remain indoors, after the harvest had been brought in and the weakest animals slaughtered for meat. It is a time to celebrate the closing of the year and take shelter from the darkness and the cold as the god Alcyn rides through the land with his host of souls. Winter, and Winterlow, is the time to remember the dead and honour our ancestors who reside with the Lord of the Otherworld. I preferred to be under my own roof in my own home — the home my master had passed on to me.

But instead I was here, out in the wilderness under a stranger's roof, trapped in a snowstorm. Because of that blizzard, I would never spend Winterlow in my old master's hall again. That Gods-damned blizzard both ruined and made my life, you will see, which was why I began my tale with it despite what the storytellers say.

If it were not for that snowstorm, I think I would never have met the Immortal King from the legends — or perhaps I would have, because Fate always gets her way.

I do not remember for how long I was meditating, but sometime after my hosts left me alone, a servant came and showed me to my room. The hall was two storeys high, surprising for a village this deep in the woods, and my room was upstairs. I immediately sank into the soft bed and feather pillows, wrapped in thick furs, and only then did I realise how tired I was.

I entered a dreamless sleep and awoke the next morning to the wind screaming outside my window. I stared up at the rafters and sighed. I knew I would not be going home that day.

I spent about a week in that house, so I took the time to get to know the family hosting me. Harold had a wife called Eloise, and they had three children: Gunn, their eldest and only son; Matilda, whom I had met on my first night; and Alia, Harold's eldest daughter.

Alia was the friendliest, and she greeted me cheerfully my first morning in Henton, but Gunn was also enthusiastic to entertain a guest. Eloise was somewhat timid, and her youngest daughter even more so. Harold was polite and welcoming, but it seemed like his hosting was more out of duty than pleasure.

Still, I grew to like the whole family. They were certainly good hosts and made every effort to make my stay as pleasant as possible, all things considered. Harold and Eloise served a hearty breakfast each morning and a modest supper to finish the day. Harold also opened a barrel of his finest wine, which we enjoyed in the evenings as we sat near the big fire in the main hall, trying to keep warm.

At night I told them stories of my past journeys, which I admit grew more embellished with each cup of wine, but the family did not seem to notice. They enjoyed hearing tales of ghosts, elves, and other Otherworldly beings. Harold also talked about his time during the Usurper's War, during which he fought for King Edwin and earned a damaged arm for his troubles. Despite fighting on the losing side, Harold gained his pardon by swearing loyalty to Lord Wim after the war, like most other nobles in the land.

As the nights grew late, Harold and Eloise would retire to bed, but Alia, Gunn, and I would stay up by the fire in the main hall, drinking and playing draughts or dice games. Matilda did not join in but would sit with us and watch. She would grin whenever I won a game, though, and would sometimes tease her sister when she lost. The two of them looked so alike, but they were of very different character.

On the second night and all the nights following, once

everyone had gone to bed, Alia would visit my room, and we would enjoy each other before falling asleep in each other's arms. Alia would wake up before the rest of her family and sneak back to her room to avoid her parents suspecting her nightly rendezvous.

Matilda was shy, but of the whole family it was she who seemed most interested in the tales I told. Her siblings preferred tales of action and struggle, but Matilda preferred the ones that meant the most to me — those of the Otherworld.

Her favourite story was of the time my old master took me to meet the Lord of the Forest and two unusual young lovers at an Otherworldly wedding. I was eight winters old at the time, afraid of the world I had been suddenly thrown into, but it was an encounter that filled me with hope.

Those tales laid the foundations for the bond that formed between us. She told me the occasional monk or merchant would come through bringing news, but most of what she knew of the outside world came from books. "I very rarely get to hear stories from a real traveller," she said on one of the occasions we were alone together. "Especially not from someone as different as you."

I took that as a compliment. I had been called far worse than *different* in my lifetime, and besides, Matilda was a little different herself. Even in those first few days I already felt we could understand each other. She sometimes bumped into the hall's columns and doorframes, or into furniture, because she would walk around with her eyes on the pages of a book. There were also a few moments when I caught her on her hands and knees or jumping in an attempt to capture some kind of insect and put it in a jar. She would blush when she noticed me watching, mumble an apology, and hurry off to another part of the hall.

Her odd behaviour made me curious, and so I decided to ask her about it. I knocked on her bedroom door one day, hoping that if I talked to her there, she would not be able to escape should she become embarrassed.

"Come in," she said after I tapped the door. I pushed it open to find a small but homey bedroom. A bed was pushed up against the wall away from the window, with fur covers and a feather pillow; three bookshelves stood against another wall stocked with a wide array of tomes.

Beside the bookshelves was a desk littered with more books, various jars and trays containing insects both dead and alive, and several half-melted candles. Above that, more shelves were nailed to the wall, holding even more jars. A worn rug lay in the centre of the room — an attempt to bring warmth to the hard wooden floor, I assumed.

Beside the open window was an armchair, and sitting in that chair, with her face buried in a book, was Matilda. "Good afternoon, My Lady," I said.

Matilda looked up from her book, wide-eyed, and threw it onto her bed. Her black hair fell loose on her shoulders, and she was wearing a white blouse underneath a dark purple dress. Matilda stood, brushed off her dress, and then curtsied a little. "Sorry. A lady does not read," she said. She blushed.

"You must not have met many ladies," I said. "All proper and respectable noblewomen are very well educated. I once met an earl who needed his wife to read him his letters!" Matilda smiled at that. "May I sit?" She nodded, so I took a seat on the bed and picked up her book. "*Comparing Moths with the Human Soul,*" I said, reading the spine. I looked up at Matilda.

"I like insects," she said.

"I can see that. So, are there any similarities between the soul and the moth?"

She nodded and sat back down. "Yes. The caterpillar is like our mortal lives," she explained. "It crawls around, never straying far from its plant, and seeks only to eat. It eats and eats until it is big, and then it goes into a cocoon, from which emerges the moth. To us, the cocoon is our grave, and when the moth emerges, that is our soul breaking free of its mortal bonds." Matilda blushed and looked down at the floor.

I smiled. "A theologian who likes insects. You sure are full of surprises."

"I am sorry," she said.

I frowned but ignored the apology. Why was she sorry? "Well, I came to ask you why you keep chasing insects, but looking at your room, I can see why."

Matilda opened her mouth to speak, but she was interrupted by a loud wail, followed by the shutters rattling and then bursting open. Snow poured in through the now open window, and the room was filled with the sound of howling winds.

Matilda jumped from her chair to push the shutters closed again, and I went over to help her, holding them shut while she bolted them in place. She was panting, her hair now a wild mess. She looked around the room. The floor was littered with patches of snow and hail, and she scratched her head. I looked down at the base of her desk, where a jar had been shattered.

"That's no coincidence," I said. A large moth stood amongst the broken pieces of glass and began to beat its wings, shaking off flakes of snow before taking flight and doing circles around a candle. Matilda saw the moth too and looked back to me for an explanation. I shrugged. "Or maybe it is."

Matilda caught the moth in her hands, spun around, and then went over to her shelf to put it inside an empty jar. "I need your help," she said, her back to me. She shuffled her feet.

"Oh?"

"For my whole life, I have read about the world. I have learned of amazing places and different insects and interesting people, but I barely get to see any of it. I want to see the world. You are a traveller, and you have told me your tales. You can take me with you," she said.

"I think you have the wrong idea," I said. "I'm not a hermit. I do have a home, and I have only seen a fraction of the world."

"Of course. But even a fraction of the world is enough for me.

If I do not leave here, I am destined to be shut away in this boring hall for a few more winters before being married to some boring lord who will only lock me away in his boring house for the rest of my life. You are my only chance of getting away from here."

I frowned. "The world is dangerous, Matilda. They do not talk about the frequent decapitations, dismemberments, diseases, and curses in those stories you read. And besides, what about your collection?"

Matilda looked desperate. "I can get a new collection. Please, Edward. I can clean your house and cook for you. I can wash your linens and clothes and sharpen your sword and scrub your mail. I can warm your bed, I am a vir—"

I stopped her there. She was beginning to make me uncomfortable. I could not just take this girl away from her family, let alone take her with me when I wandered. I walked the wilds, and the wilds are no place for a woman.

"That will not be necessary," I said. "I already have servants who are paid to do those things."

"I can do it for free."

I looked down at Matilda for a long moment. My Gift is a powerful one. I can see things that most people cannot see: elves, dwarves, ghosts, Thorns, and sometimes even gods. I can sense when the restless dead are near. I can understand the conversations between birds. But the most useful of all these things is my ability to see a person's soul. And as I looked into

Matilda's deep blue eyes, I saw a soul crippled by loneliness and longing. It was like staring into a mirror. How could I say no to her?

"In my line of work, you learn to trust your gut," I told Matilda. "And my gut is telling me it would be unwise to leave you here, but I do not think your father will be pleased to see you go."

Matilda smiled, and it seemed as though she was about to leap for joy, but she maintained her composure. "Yes, well, you will talk to him, will you not? He only really cares about Alia anyway," she said. I nodded, and she smiled even wider.

"I will try. I must go for now, but I promise I shall do what I can to get you away from here. I expect I will see you at supper?" I asked.

"Yes, yes. Thank you, Edward," said Matilda.

And so I left Matilda to her books and her bugs, wondering if I had made the right choice to promise. Where had that come from? How long had she been waiting to say that? Could I really just take her away with me and give her the adventure she wanted?

I do not know why, but something inside me told me I could not ignore her request. Something prevented me from saying no. Perhaps I only said that to escape her room and keep her happy for the moment, or perhaps in that moment I genuinely wanted to help her.

I spent the rest of the day meditating in my room, but I could not focus. My mind was constantly harassed by the thought of what to do next. Should I keep my word and help Matilda, or should I find some way to let her down gently? Her father gave me his hospitality, and it would be an incredible insult to take his daughter from him after that, for I would be breaking the sacred bond between guest and host.

Nevertheless, my intuition was telling me to take her. *Get her away from here*, it told me. *She has a far greater purpose outside of Henton.*

And so she did.

I did not talk to Matilda's father about taking her away. I thought about it. I ran through different reasons and excuses in my head, but none of them were enough to justify Harold sending his daughter away with a man she was not to marry, let alone with a Godspeaker. I thought about lying and saying that I could make her my apprentice, but she showed little signs of having the Gift, and besides, Godspeakers have always been men. It would not be believable.

I could have offered to take her hand in marriage but soon tossed that idea aside. I was not a lord, but I owned land, and being a Godspeaker does carry a certain level of prestige among the nobility, so it would not have been an unreasonable match.

However, I was not ready for that kind of commitment. In those days, I imagined I would remain unmarried, like my master, and pass my possessions on to an apprentice. I was not going to marry a girl just to free her from her boring woodland village.

No, I needed to take her away in secret. Her family would only be able to know *after* she had left. What I was planning would be seen as little more than a kidnapping, the only difference being that my victim was willing. Gods help me, but I made a promise, and honour demanded I keep it.

The blizzard began to let up on the seventh day, and the following morning the skies were clear once more and the air was almost still. It seemed as though there had been no storm at all.

"You may stay for another night, if you wish," Harold told me that morning. "It will be difficult to travel today, with all the snow on the ground."

"I'll accept that offer," I said. I felt a pang of guilt, for Harold was offering me more hospitality than he needed to, and I was planning on betraying him.

"Good. We will have a little farewell feast in the main hall tonight, for we have truly enjoyed having you. Wanderers as interesting as yourself do not usually come this way," he said. I smiled, and he went off to do his tasks for the day. He was overseeing the repairs being made around the village, but he declined my offer of help.

I decided instead to explore Henton a little, now that I could go outside and see it. Unsurprisingly, there was not much to see.

The village consisted of several dozen homes, with a little marketplace in the centre. Henton's well was dug in the middle of that marketplace, where some people had erected stalls and were busy selling wares they had crafted while locked up during the storm.

At the southern end of the marketplace was a tavern, already lively with laughter and song, while at the northern end was a small temple. I headed to the north to visit Henton's priest.

"Edward Godspeaker," he said as I entered. I shut the temple's door behind me, leaving the sounds of the marketplace outside.

"How did you know?" I asked, looking around the room. It was dark, the only light coming from a brazier that sat in the temple's centre, and by the wall opposite the door was an idol dedicated to Hefenstea, the goddess of vengeance, omens, dreams, and the stars. The priest knelt before it.

"I cannot remember the last time someone who wasn't Lady Matilda came to my temple. When I heard Oldford's famous Godspeaker was in Henton, I knew I would have a visitor soon enough," he said.

"No one cares for Hefenstea anymore?"

The priest shook his head. "Not in Henton, although the young lady is quite fond of her. Why have you come?" He turned to face me and slowly climbed to his feet. He was old, and in the brazier's light I could now see he was also blind.

"Someone still has to honour the Gods," I said.

The priest grunted. "I know why you have come, but you do

not. Hefenstea has brought you here."

"The goddess?"

"Who do you think conjured that blizzard?"

I did not reply. I washed my hands in the icy water that filled the basin by the door before splashing some on my face. I approached the idol and knelt before it, pressed my hands together, and bowed. Behind me, I heard the priest filling a horn with wine, which he blessed, then handed to me. I said some prayers to the goddess, poured the contents of the horn into the large bowl at Hefenstea's feet, then bowed again.

"Hefenstea has sent you here to help her exact vengeance against Vylan, the fallen god who defiled her. Do you know the myth?" the priest said.

"I know the myth," I said. I watched as the wine slowly drained through the small hole in the bottom of the bowl.

"Good. Hefenstea has revealed to me in a dream that a Godspeaker would come alone but would not leave alone, and this shall be the first step in Hefenstea's revenge."

I looked up at the wooden idol. Hefenstea was a fearsome goddess. She was once the fairest of all the Gods, and during a great betrayal she was raped by the fallen god Vylan. Hefenstea swore that she would avenge herself and slay Vylan and would not return to the Heavens until she had fulfilled her vow.

Thus, Hefenstea became the goddess of vengeance and now wanders the Mirror Worlds hunting down the Defiler. She is almost always depicted with a basket of heads in her left hand

and a sword in her right, which is stabbed into the chest of a Thorn — a servant of Vylan — lying at her feet. She wears a torn dress, with one breast exposed, and her face is a wild mess of fury. Her most striking feature, however, is the large set of moth's wings growing from her back.

"Why me? I do not understand," I said.

"Nor do I, Godspeaker. Nor do I." The priest went over to a small chair in the corner of the room and slumped down into it with a groan. "Hefenstea thanks you for your offering. You may go now."

I bowed one last time, thanked the priest, and then headed back outside. I remember thinking how eerie that encounter was, but at the time I thought little of it. Only later did I begin to understand.

I decided to browse the stalls for a little while to pass the time, and that was when I saw a man selling jewellery. He had a small but pretty collection.

"Are these all handcrafted?" I asked the merchant. The man behind the stall was short but stocky. He had a large red beard, and his head had been shaved — he was probably balding and wished to hide the fact by shaving his hair off.

"They are," said the merchant, hands on his hips. "Any you like?"

I browsed his stock. They were well crafted, and it did not take me long to find the perfect piece. "How much for this?" I asked, picking up a small silver necklace. The pendant was in the shape of a moth.

"Five silvers," he said.

We haggled for a bit, of course, before we agreed on a final price. Reaching into my purse, I pulled out three silvers and dropped them into the craftsman's hand. One, two, three. I pocketed the necklace and carried on through the market. I had gone to that stall intending to buy a gift for Matilda to honour our new friendship. After all, if I was taking her out into the world, we would need to be friends. When I saw that moth, I knew it would be the perfect gift for a girl who loved insects and the goddess Hefenstea.

I spent the rest of the day wandering the town and the woods around it. Most of the locals avoided speaking with me, but I was pleased enough with that. The solitude is nice sometimes, especially when I need to think.

I had devised a plan to help Matilda get away from Henton, and I told her about it once I returned to the hall just before sundown. She seemed to think it would work. We would need to sneak away in the night, and Matilda said it would be best to leave through the cellar. But before I left her to prepare her things for the journey, I made sure one last time that she was certain this was what she wanted.

"I am sure about this, Edward," Matilda said. "I have wanted this for a long time, and now is my chance."

"I really think you should consider telling your father. You are his daughter, and if you tell him what you told me, he may change his mind," I said.

"I know, but what if he refuses? Any chance I did have would be gone in an instant."

"Think it over, Matilda. I will keep your secret, if that is what you think is best, but consider how your family will feel if you disappear in the night."

I left Matilda alone and headed to the main hall, where I waited for Harold's feast. I was concerned about him being unaware of his daughter running away — not just because I would be betraying his hospitality, but also because it would break his and Eloise's hearts.

Still, I had made a promise to Matilda.

The feast began after sunset. Some of the villagers filled the hall and crowded around the long table, including the priest, who appeared to stare at me, despite being unable to see. Harold sat in his high seat at the end closest to the fire, of course, and his wife sat on his left. Alia sat beside Eloise, and Matilda beside Alia, while Gunn sat on the opposite side of the table to his father's right.

I sat between Gunn and a fat man called Merewald, the commander of Harold's two-dozen oathmen — warriors who are bound by oath to defend a lord and his family. Venison was served, along with various other meats and wild fruits and vegetables, mushrooms, and breads. A barrel of some imported wine from the south was also opened, and servants regularly refilled everyone's horns. Songs were sung, tales were told, and everyone seemed genuinely happy. I almost forgot about my plan to take Matilda away.

Matilda seemed glad too, but she barely spoke and drank not a drop of wine.

Sometime during the night, Harold began to talk of Winterlow and the coming year. I kept glancing over at Matilda while Harold spoke of his plans, and she looked uncomfortable. She stared down at her plate and picked at a piece of bread. I assumed she could not keep a secret any longer, because while Harold was talking, she looked up from her plate to her father and said, "I am going away with Edward." The sound of cheerful chatter died down to a murmur before the whole hall went silent.

"Excuse me?" Harold said. He looked from Matilda to me and then back to Matilda, his mouth half open.

"I want to see the world, so I am going with Edward tomorrow. It is my decision," Matilda said.

A flicker of anger appeared in Harold's eyes, but he held his composure in front of his guests. "Did you not think to consult me about this first? What if I want you to stay here?"

"This is my sixteenth winter, Da. I am old enough to make my own decisions."

"Old enough?" Harold sat back in his chair and shook his head. "This is not about age, Matilda. I cannot let my own daughter go wandering through the woods. Would any of you?"

Harold held out his arms, addressing his question to all of his guests. Many of them shook their heads or murmured in agreement. Harold was right, of course. It would be irresponsible to let his daughter go travelling with someone whose job is as dangerous as mine. I dealt with death, and no man wants his children involved in that.

Harold then turned to me and sighed. "And what part do you have in all this?"

I opened my mouth to speak, to admit my betrayal and offer my apologies, but Matilda interrupted before I could say anything. "Do not blame him, Da. This was my idea. Edward knew nothing of it until now."

I shut my mouth, thinking it wise to let Matilda handle this. Harold was her father, after all. He stood and waved to his guests, forcing a smile. "My apologies, friends. Continue your feast! Enjoy the food and wine," he said. "Matilda, come with me."

The guests resumed their conversations as if nothing had happened. Matilda stood and brushed the crumbs off her lap then dutifully followed her father out of the main hall. I watched them leave, then Gunn gave me a gentle nudge.

"Matilda is his favourite daughter, you know. He is not going to be happy about this," he said. Alia overheard and tossed a piece of venison at him, and they both laughed. Eloise just stared off at nothing in particular. "She has wanted to go travelling for a while now, ever since that old wanderer and his wives came through a few years back."

"That wanderer was Alcyn," said Alia.

Gunn grunted. "The girls think the man was a god, but I doubt it. Just a crazy old hermit, even said he came from Winterhome. He told us that old legend about King Emrys, and ever since then Matilda has wanted to travel in the hopes she can make some stories of her own."

I said nothing, so Gunn turned his attention back to his food. I had lost my appetite. I now just wanted the night to be over so I could go to sleep and leave early the next morning. I did not want to cause any more trouble than I already had. What was I thinking? I should never have told Matilda I would take her away. I should have said no from the start and forgotten about her. But Fate had other plans.

Matilda and Harold came back into the hall and took their seats back at the table. Harold slumped into his chair, nodded to me, and said, "Forgive us." That was the last thing he said that night, except to whisper some things to his wife every so often. He spent the rest of the feast emptying horns of wine into his belly.

Matilda played with her food for a while, her eyes wet, and avoided looking at me. I do not know what was said between Harold and Matilda, but he was clearly not going to allow his daughter to wander into the world with a stranger.

Alia and Matilda left the feast early and went upstairs, and so I spent the rest of the night talking with Gunn and Merewald about hunting. I tried my best to forget about the embarrassment of the earlier scene. After most of the guests had left, I too decided to return to my room for one last night in Henton. I felt sorry for

Matilda and wished I could help, but it seemed there was no chance for her to leave with me.

Or so I thought.

I lay awake for a while that night, wondering how I would apologise properly to Harold the next day. However, I would not get that chance, for my door opened without warning and Matilda hurried in.

"We must go soon," she whispered. "The guards are changing over."

I sat up, dumbfounded. Matilda was wearing a plainer dress than before, a cloak, and some riding boots. She set two large bags down on the floor then came and knelt before me.

"Please, Edward. This could be my only chance."

I did not know what to say. The Gods teach us that we must keep our word and stay true to the promises we make. But they also teach that we must respect our hosts.

I do not know why I did what I did next. I hurried to pack my things, helped Matilda with one of her bags, and then crept out of the room. The hall was silent, and the way was clear. Matilda stayed close behind me. We had little time to waste.

Then we heard footsteps. I held my breath and froze.

Eloise appeared ahead of us. She stopped for a moment then marched towards me. It was over.

"Does your bed not suit you, Godspeaker?" she asked. She

glanced behind me at her daughter.

"It does, My Lady. Forgive me, I—"

She raised her hand. "Quiet. The guards have retired, and a new set will arrive soon. They have been told to watch for you."

"My Lady?"

"Do not think I approve of this. Far from it. But I wish only for my daughter to be happy, and if that happiness can only be found outside of Henton, then I must accept that, even if my husband does not. But you must be far from here before the break of dawn."

"Oh, Ma. Thank you," whispered Matilda. She pushed past me and threw her arms around Eloise.

"Be safe, little one, and trust your guide," said Eloise. "The Gifted possess wisdom far greater than they may show."

I let them say their farewells, but it was brief, for we had to make haste. After one last hug, Eloise let her daughter go, and the two of us made our way to the cellar and out into the courtyard.

As Eloise had promised, the guards were nowhere in sight, but how long till others arrived, I did not know. Even so, we stuck to the shadows, and under cover of darkness we hurried for the stables where Matilda could finally put her bag down. She sighed, stretched her back, and then leant against the stable door.

"What in the Heavens do you have in these bags?" I asked.

"Everything I need," she said.

I grinned and doubted she would actually *need* most of it.

Regardless, I quickly attached our bags to a brown mare named Lilly. She was Matilda's favourite horse, and she insisted that we take her. I was racked with guilt for stealing not only Harold's daughter from him, but also one of his horses. I knew I could never show my face in Henton again.

"This is frightening," Matilda said as I helped her into Lilly's saddle.

"This is your last chance to change your mind," I said.

Matilda shook her head. "This is also the most excitement I have ever had."

I smiled, but behind that smile I was nervous. I did not want to think about what would happen to me if I were caught.

With Matilda in the saddle, I led Lilly slowly by the reins out into the courtyard towards the palisade's gate. We moved as quietly as we could, and I was grateful for the layer of snow that muffled Lilly's hooves. I was tempted to jump into the saddle with Matilda and race off into the night, but that would surely alert someone, and Lilly probably would have struggled to run with the weight of those bags.

I did not notice I was holding my breath. Only once we reached the gate did I let out an exhale. Matilda turned in the saddle, and then I heard voices behind me.

"Guards," Matilda hissed.

I kept going. They had neither seen nor heard us, so perhaps the Gods favoured us, or we were just lucky. I took Lilly slowly through the streets of Henton, hooded and cloaked. Matilda had her hood up as well. If anyone saw us now, hopefully they would think we were strangers.

A dog barked as we passed a home, its chain rattling. An owl hooted. A cat mewed as we passed through the market. My heart was pounding, pushing me onward.

The Gods were with us. We made it unnoticed to the edge of town, where the homes bordered the trees. The grim, dark winter woods were ahead.

"My father will send men come morning," Matilda said.

"Then we must be long gone by then." I climbed up into the saddle with Matilda, put my arms around her, and took the reins. She was shivering.

"They will have trackers."

"I think we can lose them if we beat them to Oldford." I reached into my pocket, pulled out the silver moth pendant I had bought, and handed it to Matilda. "Here. This is for you, for luck."

Matilda wiped her eyes with her sleeve and then took the pendant from me.

"I have slain witches and banished ghosts. I can lose a few old warriors no problem."

And so onward we went. Matilda's childhood was behind her, and as we rode off into those dead, dark woods, our adventure — our story — began.

2

Oldford

We could not ride swiftly from Henton due to the snow and the weight on Lilly's back, but Harold's trackers would not have the same problem, and I supposed that by the time the earl woke and his men set off to find his daughter, we would be about half a day ahead of them.

We rode all night. It was bitterly cold, but we needed to put some distance between us and Henton before daybreak, so we wrapped up in furs and huddled close in the saddle. Matilda fell asleep eventually, but I rode on.

She woke to the sound of the morning chorus. She spoke little that day, and I let her be with her thoughts while I pushed Lilly on. I could tell Matilda was nervous and had a lot on her mind. That was understandable, even without considering the men on our trail.

The perpetual riding made Matilda sore, and she wanted to rest for a moment. I told her we could not stop until sundown, or her father's men might catch up. To compromise, I occasionally walked beside the horse, allowing her to have both her legs to one side. That made her a bit more comfortable, but it did slow us somewhat.

We rode for hours that day, making the most of the clear weather while it lasted, and I told Matilda about my home and the world in an attempt to lift her spirits and distract her from her fears. She smiled often, but when she spoke, it was only a few words at a time. We both kept one eye looking over our shoulders for signs of our pursuers. We saw none. Much to Lilly's discontent, we had to travel off-road but made sure the path south remained not too far away, lest we get lost.

We were riding south to Oldford — and my home. The ground was easy and flat for a few miles, but the forest thickened as we moved farther from Henton and the terrain grew hilly. Henton's economy revolved around lumber, so the woods near the village were thin, but by mid-afternoon we were deep in the wilds. There were more evergreens here, so there was less snow at our feet and the forest was darker.

Matilda insisted we stop as the day grew colder and the light dimmed. I would have preferred to ride for another hour or so, but I too was growing tired, and I supposed there would be no harm in stopping now that the woods were thicker. I found a well-hidden grove where we could make camp.

"When I was little," she mumbled to me as I helped her down from the horse, "I used to play in the woods behind the manor. My sister and I would play witch hunters. One of us would be the hunter and the other would be the witch, and we would chase each other around with sticks. I was often the witch. I was never afraid of the woods, but here I am terrified." She brushed off her dress and looked up at me, wide-eyed.

"What are you afraid of?"

"I have heard stories of things that lurk in the wild parts of the land. Bogeys, dwarves, ghosts…"

I laughed. "You needn't worry about them with me, Matilda. I make a living keeping those at bay."

She nodded, her eyes to the ground. "What about robbers? And the rebels?"

"In these parts? I doubt many travel this road," I said. "Bandits plague roads where they're likely to catch a decent haul. That includes the rebels."

Matilda half smiled and then began pacing to stretch her legs. I was right about the robbers — they only patrol the main roads, and the road from Henton to Oldford was little more than a dirt path — but the rebels were another thing.

In truth, the pretender to the throne and his men rarely left their fortress in the Northern Alps, only emerging for the occasional raid or to scout. The rebels wished to overthrow King Stephan and restore the Eomundson dynasty, but their efforts caused little stir beyond the lands at the base of the Alps, and they lived in a fortress too strong for the king to bother with.

There were many tales of their supporters making camps and hiding out in the wilds across the kingdom, waiting for their captain to raise the banner of the rebellion and call his men to service, and it was said that on that day they would strike out in many places and force the king to spread his armies thin. King Stephan paid well for the heads of these men, but their existence was doubtful. Many young, foolish men travelled into the wilderness to seek them out, and few returned.

Matilda wandered about the small grove we had stopped in. This was a holy place, I felt, untouched by civilisation. Birches surrounded the area, looking like they had been caked in icing, but in the middle of the grove was an enormous, ancient oak. The trees around us were covered in snow, but this oak wore not a single speck of it. A boulder lay beside the tree, hugged by the oak's wide roots, and green grass grew sheltered from the weather at the tree's base. My worries seemed to pass away in that place.

"Matilda, this is an excellent spot to camp tonight," I said. Matilda was exploring the grove, taking care not to stray into the dense parts of the wood. I tied the horse to a tree and approached the oak. It was a thing of beauty, planted by the Gods themselves. This tree must have been as old as the world. I placed my hand on the trunk and rested my forehead against it, whispering a prayer.

"What are you doing?" Matilda asked. She had come to stand

behind me.

"This oak tree is sacred," I replied. "I was just letting this grove's guardians know we would be staying here for the night." Matilda looked confused, but I just grinned. The old ways are often strange to people these days. "You might see some odd things tonight, but do not be alarmed. The spirits of the wild are only a threat to the man of today because the man of today has forgotten how to befriend them."

Matilda only nodded and went back to the horse to unpack her things. I felt bad for the poor beast. It was being used more as a pack mule than as a horse, made to carry all the things Matilda wished to bring with her: clothes, books, bug jars, not to mention all our camping supplies and food.

When I travelled alone, I would need little more than my weapons and my tinderbox. The land provided me with food, and I would sleep on the ground using my cloak as a blanket, but Matilda insisted on bringing a cooking pot, bowls, cutlery, bedrolls, pillows, and food to last several days. Yet Lilly was a sturdy beast and did not complain.

I helped Matilda unpack and removed everything from the saddle to give Lilly a break from her burden. I was right to choose this place. The winter days were short, and already night was drawing near. Had we continued, we might not have found a better place than this. Or a safer one, for that matter.

"Are you certain we will not be discovered here?" Matilda asked.

"I am certain," I said. "Your father's men will need to rest too, and I feel they are far behind us."

Matilda sighed. She had no choice but to trust me.

"The first night away from home is the hardest," I said. "But it won't be long before we arrive at my hall, and you can sleep in a warm bed under a hard roof once more."

Matilda smiled at that. "We should make camp," she said.

"Aye." I nodded. "Give me your flask. I'll try find a stream nearby to refill it. I will also fill the pot. Perhaps we can have a stew tonight."

"Yes, sir," Matilda said.

I left the grove to go deeper into the woods, taking our flasks and the pot with me. I was in luck. There was a pond fed by a small waterfall a short walk from where we made camp. I decided to scout the area a bit to check for any signs of potential danger and to look for food.

I found some wild berries then filled our flasks and pot back at the waterfall. Just as I was about to return to our camp, I heard Matilda scream.

My heart skipped a beat. I sprinted back to the grove, bursting through shrubbery and spilling water everywhere. Matilda stood by the oak, stunned with fear.

"What is *that*?" she cried, pointing to the ground.

I sighed, and a wave of relief washed over me. "It's called a mole, Matilda." The creature was digging through the snow, sniffing about, and appeared to take no notice of her.

"It's hideous. It has no eyes," she said.

"It has eyes, they're just small. Leave the thing alone. And please, try to be more quiet."

She kicked snow at it, and it shuffled away into the bushes. I shook my head, but then we both laughed. The sun was setting now, so we set up camp. Matilda laid out the bedrolls under the oak and made a circle of stones while I searched for deadwood, and just as the sun fell behind the trees, I made a fire.

Matilda prepared a stew with the water I had collected using vegetables and herbs she had brought from Henton. It grew dark. Soon the two of us were eating a delicious meal by a fire under the holy oak. Matilda brought extra blankets in which she wrapped herself. "What was your first night away from home like?" she asked.

I smiled and looked up at the stars. "Well," I began. "It was cold, and it rained, I believe. The man who would be my master came to my family's farm when I was, um, eight years old. Gods, that was twelve years ago, now. Anyway, when he left, I went with him. We camped out in a cave for shelter, on a hill above a vast meadow. We had been riding all day long, and my arse — pardon my tongue — was killing me. I was cold and wet, but it felt good to be able to lie down."

Matilda was staring at me as I told my story, eating slowly, as if I would stop talking once she finished. I continued.

"My master and I — his name was Brendan — built a big fire in this cave and warmed ourselves, and he told me all kinds of stories about his life. I'll admit, I was terrified at first. I was heading out into the unknown, set to train for a career I did not understand but which I knew was a dangerous one. Then he pulled out this." I unsheathed my sword and held it up in the light. The orange reflection of the firelight danced on the blade, and the glow of the moon made it shine. "The blade's beauty still amazes me to this day."

"It is pretty," Matilda said.

"Brendan told me it would be mine one day, and now here it is. I did not understand why back then, but a few years later I figured it out. Brendan had no sons, no heirs to pass on his possessions and his lands, so he adopted me, his apprentice, and left me everything he owned in his will."

Matilda's eyes widened a little. "You are a nobleman?"

I laughed. "No, no, far from it. My master's ancestors served the kings once upon a time. The old dynasty. They grew rich from their trade and were granted some lands and a house. They passed these down from generation to generation till they came to my master. Then he passed them on to me. But I am neither noble, priest, nor commoner. The Gifted are often called 'casteless,' but whether that means we are above the castes or below them depends on who you ask."

"But you were born a commoner?"

"Yes. My ancestors have been free peasants for generations."

"Well, you may be casteless, but you definitely have a noble soul," said Matilda. She blushed and stared at her stew.

"Thank you, I suppose. Anyway, after that we went to sleep, and that was my first night in the wilds. I was afraid at first, but after that I realised it wasn't so bad to be away from home."

"Why did you leave in the first place?" Matilda asked. The question brought a memory to the surface, but I pushed it aside.

"A story for another time," I told her. We both went still when we heard a noise coming from beyond the grove, and Matilda looked terrified. Something was moving in the bushes, crushing snow and twigs.

Then it squeaked.

"It's just that mole again," I said with a sigh. Matilda let out a deep breath and put her hand on her heart.

"I was preparing myself for death," she said and then let out a nervous laugh.

"I told you that robbers won't bother us out here," I said.

"I fear the rebels more. I have heard stories about how they live in the wilds and that they are ruthless. Supposedly they starve you, then cut off your fingers and force you to eat them, or else die from hunger." She tightened the blankets around her.

"Who did you hear that from?"

Matilda thought for a moment, frowning. "One of the king's tax collectors," she said at last. I let out a sharp exhale.

"Do not worry about them, Matilda," I said. "Should the rebels be near, which I doubt they will be, I will talk them out of harming us. Besides, I scouted the area earlier and found nothing."

"Thank you, Edward," she said. "For all you have done for me."

I half smiled and finished my stew. I still felt the weight of guilt on my shoulders for betraying Harold's hospitality.

Matilda and I talked for a couple more hours. I was glad to have finally cheered her up and have her talking at last. As the night went on, she became friendlier and happier, and I discovered her sense of humour and her passion for tales of adventure and romance. She was a charming young lady, and I admit that on that night I already felt we were becoming friends.

Around midnight, Matilda fell asleep while I was halfway through telling a story of how I once aided a family haunted by a supernatural seal that raided their wine cellar on a nightly basis. She was resting against the oak, and her eyes slowly closed as she drifted off to sleep. I laid her down on her bedroll all wrapped in blankets and then sat up against the trunk of the oak, lost in thought, before I too was embraced by sleep.

I woke to the sound of singing. Our fire had gone out, but the area was illuminated by a strange glow. At the edge of the grove, not far from us, were lights bouncing and making circles. I thought I was dreaming. A beautiful melody sung in a language I did not know filled the grove, but at the same time it seemed distant and quiet.

The lights danced around in a circle, moving back and forth

around the grove, and I blinked. This was not a dream, and these were not lights. I realised they were people, all women with white hair and pale skin, wearing white dresses, and they were glowing, as if the light of the moon radiated from them. The women danced with each other, moving in perfect harmony with their song. Their bodies moved with a sort of gentleness but filled with energy.

"Elves," I whispered. I watched them for a few moments, awestruck. They appeared not to notice us. I reached over and shook Matilda awake.

"Edward?" she groaned.

"Matilda, do you see that?" I said.

Matilda rubbed her eyes and sat up, then her jaw dropped. "What is that?" she whispered.

I nodded at them. "Look closer," I said.

She shuffled closer to me. "They're people," she said. She was frightened.

"They are elves. Aren't they beautiful?"

They were indeed things of beauty, and I had not seen elves in this manner before. We were both mesmerised as we watched their small bare feet tread softly on the snow as they twirled and swayed and made the grove sparkle. Matilda held my arm.

"I have never seen elves before," she said. At that moment, one of the elves broke away from the circle and danced over to us. She left no footprints, and once she came close to us, I noticed her true beauty. Her snow-white hair flowed over her shoulder, falling all the way down her back. Her dress was thin, and through it could be seen every detail of her perfect form. She had flawless skin and eyes of the deepest blue.

The elf approached Matilda, her hand outstretched, accompanied by a small smile. Matilda looked up at her and slowly lifted her hand.

I took Matilda's hand instead and pushed it back to her chest. The elf frowned at me.

"Not this one," I said.

The elf smiled and then bowed her head. She then knelt, took my face in her hands, and kissed me. Her hands were softer than anything I had felt before, but her lips were as cold as ice. The elf stood back up, curtsied, then glided back to her group. Matilda looked both amazed and confused.

"What…?" she said. I stared at the performance before us, and Matilda gripped my arm tighter.

"She wanted you to join them," I said, my eyes still fixed on the elves.

"Why did you stop me?"

"Because," I explained, "you would dance with them for the rest of the night, experiencing the purest ecstasy, and at dawn the elves would bid you farewell. The sun would rise, you would feel the warmth on your skin, but you would find that many years had passed. You would have aged less than a day, yet all those you know would be long dead."

Matilda said nothing. She only stared at the elves. We watched them for a while, too awestruck to sleep, and as the first rays of light crept over the horizon, the elves wandered off into the woods and disappeared.

"Where are they going?" Matilda asked.

"Back to their world, I suppose."

"That one who came to us," Matilda said. "Why did she kiss you?"

"Because she could understand me. She was showing me that we were friends, and we needn't be afraid," I said.

Matilda frowned. "Bit strange, is it not? Kissing someone to show friendship."

I laughed. "Not to the elves. They do it down south, too."

"Have you ever been to the southern lands?"

"Yes, once, when I was fifteen. It was there I had my first…"

"Your first what?" asked Matilda.

"Never mind," I said with a grin. "We should go. We will make the most of today and travel a fair distance before sundown."

So Matilda and I packed up our camp and loaded the horse. I thanked the grove's spirits for their hospitality, helped Matilda onto the horse, and led her back to the road. We were on our way once more.

Matilda was much more talkative that day, though the saddle still made her sore. She complained that she had only ever ridden for short periods around Henton's thin woods, never over long distances like this.

Still, she tried to enjoy the journey and asked more questions than I had answers to. She seemed very intrigued by our encounter the night before, and I told her what I could of elves and the Otherworld. We almost forgot about the men tracking us, and without the burden that Lilly carried, their horses were probably swifter.

We rode through the forest for most of that day, but towards midday the woods began to grow thinner, and we emerged mid-afternoon into a wide, rolling pasture. The livestock had all been brought indoors, of course, and the fields were covered with snow, but someone had ploughed the road so we could travel swiftly and make good distance that afternoon during the last few hours of sunlight.

We found a roadside inn just as the sun was falling behind the hill and darkness descended on the land, and Matilda was the happiest she had been the whole journey. The innkeeper was wary of me, but Matilda used her name and title to get us good service. We ate and drank well that night and had a warm, soft bed to sleep in. At least, Matilda did. I slept on the floor.

We rode off at dawn the next day through the beautiful countryside. We passed many homesteads, the dwellings of free peasants — called churls — who owned their own land and their own homes, but who were still poor, with just enough land and livestock to keep their bellies full. The recent civil war had made life hard for many churls throughout the kingdom. There were still many people that lived like this, which pleased me, for it was a natural and simple lifestyle and one I wished I could live. But that was not my fate.

We camped in a cluster of trees atop a hill that night, and in the morning it was only a short ride till we came to the Royal Way, an ancient, paved road guarded and maintained by the king and his men, though in recent years parts of it had fallen into disrepair. Matilda and Lilly were pleased to reach this because it meant a fast and easy journey. I promised Matilda that if we rode without interruption, we should reach Oldford before nightfall. And reach it we did.

The Royal Way ran straight through Oldford, but as we approached we passed an ancient and formidable castle that sat on top of a hill beside the road. The castle was home to Adalbert, the lord of this part of the kingdom.

Aside from the king, Adalbert was the wealthiest nobleman in Ardonn due to the trade that flowed through Oldford along the Royal Way as merchants from the south travelled north along this route. Perpendicular to the road was the River Aed, and Oldford sat right where the road crossed the river. There, Adalbert watched over the crossing and his jewel of a town from his ancient towers atop the hill.

Matilda stared at the castle as we trotted past. Soldiers were pacing along the ramparts and a group of horsemen rode up the hill towards the gate, which was being opened to let them pass.

As we neared Oldford's own gates, merchants approached us, offering bargains for their goods, and beggars harassed us for spare change.

I felt Matilda tense up, but she was silent. I realised she had never seen a town this large before or been in the presence of so many people. It was busy outside the town walls, and it would be even busier inside.

We rode along the road through the newer parts of the town, past houses that had been built outside the walls as the population grew. Although they were newer, these parts were the slums of the city and attached themselves to the walls like barnacles. Only the wealthiest could afford to live within the walls, and with each generation the villages outside grew ever larger and ever poorer.

"The buildings are so tall," Matilda mumbled as we approached the town gates. "And I have never seen walls this big before."

We rode through the gates, and the guards gave us a nod. I knew them, having travelled through here many times, and they smiled as we passed. We would be safe from Harold's men here, at least for a night. Oldford's gates were locked after sundown, so our pursuers would have to stay outside the city's walls.

Matilda could not stop staring around at the town, agape. Oldford was a beautiful place. It was cramped, but it had a cosy atmosphere, if you could ignore the smell. The Royal Way that cut through the town was wide enough for eight horses riding side-by-side, and there were pavements on which people could erect stalls or avoid passing carts and carriages.

Above us it was narrower. Most of the buildings were jettied on each floor, and many rose four or even five storeys high. Small bridges crossed from one building to another above us, as did clothes lines and pipes, and some houses even sat on arches above the road. The street was wide but not open, and it felt as though we were passing through a tunnel. Other streets in the town were not as wide as this, and in many alleys and lanes the buildings were jostled so close together that two people could kiss from across the street.

We stopped outside a tavern, the Black Rose. The tavern had a stable attached to it, so I led Lilly there and handed her over to the stable-master who was tending the other horses. He greeted me, welcoming me back from my journey. I was a regular at this place. Laughter and chatter could be heard inside. Dusk was beginning to fall, and so some of Oldford's working men were already at the tavern for a drink after a hard day.

"Forgive me if this is not to your liking," I said to Matilda outside. "There are other places we can stay in Oldford, but a friend owns the Rose, and I get good prices here."

Matilda nodded but said nothing.

We entered the Rose, and I could tell Matilda hated it right away. It was crowded, noisy, and smelled of smoke, sweat, and ale. Men who were fat, old, ugly, or dirty — or all four — huddled around the bar and the tables, sat on window sills, or just stood around, beer dripping from their beards and food staining their clothes. Women flirted with some of the men, and a few lucky ones were taken by the hand to the rooms upstairs.

As we entered, some men turned and glanced at Matilda, their eyes flicking up and down, but when they noticed me they bowed their heads and turned their attention back to their talk and their games.

I led Matilda through the crowd as we pushed past the patrons. Some greeted me, others whistled at Matilda, and I could tell she was uncomfortable. Her face was red, and she glared at me. I admit, I regretted bringing her there, but I was low on coin and could not afford a place with better beds. We arrived at a door at the back of the tavern, and I began fumbling through my pockets. Matilda dug her shoulder into my chest, trying to get as close to me as possible to avoid the crowd. I pulled a key from my pouch.

"Here is it," I said. I slid the key into the lock on the door, turned it, and pushed it open. "Special patrons only. After you." I gestured for Matilda to enter, and I followed.

I led her up a staircase and through another doorway until we found ourselves in a gallery that looked out over the main part of the tavern. This section was much nicer. It smelled only of incense and good food; the patrons here were wealthier and better dressed than those below, and they played polite and quiet games of cards or chatted at reasonable volumes, and better still, it was not crowded. There were perhaps no more than a dozen guests up here. I sat us down at a round table.

"Sorry about all that," I said.

Matilda forced a smile. "I asked to see the world, did I not?"

"The beds here are good, and so is the food. Mildred runs a good tavern," I told her.

"Who is Mildred?"

"She's a friend. I knew her back when she bought this building."

Matilda nodded. "I am just happy to be out of that Gods-forsaken saddle."

I laughed, and at that a plump middle-aged woman with a pretty round face and blonde hair worn in a tight bun entered the gallery. She wore a blue dress with a stained brown apron.

"Edward!" she said and opened her arms. She walked over to us, and I stood, embracing her with a smile. She smelled of roast pork and happiness.

"It's good to see you, Mildred," I said. I pulled out a seat for her, and we sat down.

"Mildred, this is my companion, Matilda. She's the Earl of Henton's daughter."

A great smile appeared on Mildred's face, and she held out a hand for Matilda. "I'm Mildred, and it's an absolute pleasure to meet you, My Lady," she said. Matilda put her had in Mildred's, and then the woman immediately pulled it to her face and kissed it. "Welcome to the Black Rose."

"Thank you," Matilda said.

Mildred turned to me and folded her arms on the table. Her sleeves were rolled up, exposing her pale, chubby forearms.

"She's a fetching lass, isn't she? What'd you have to do to pick this one up?" she asked with a chuckle. Matilda turned bright red.

"It's not like that, Mildred. She wanted to see the world, so I am showing it to her," I explained.

"Thank the Gods, I was about to be jealous," she said. She punched me on the arm. "She's too young for you anyway. And certainly too good for you. How old are you, lass? Fourteen? Fifteen?"

"Sixteen," Matilda said and half-smiled. Mildred let out a roar of laughter, which made the patrons in the gallery turn and frown, and some of the patrons below hoorayed in response.

"Oh, you keep a close eye on this one, My Lady," Mildred said. "You're just his type, and it's only a matter of time before he starts making moves."

"I do not have a type," I said.

"Bollocks. Every man has his type," she said. "I run a brothel, and I have come to learn that each man has certain tastes. You, Edward, like 'em thin, with sharp faces and firm arses." Mildred cackled again.

"Could we have something to eat, Mildred?" I asked.

She turned serious and straightened her back. "Right away, sir. Roast pork pie and vegetables tonight. And I'll open a new barrel of ale, just for you two." Mildred stood and put her hands on her hips. "Would you like a girl tonight?"

I shook my head. "You know the answer, Mildred. It's the same every time."

"You're a boring old miser, aren't you? Very well, I'll get you both your meal."

Mildred marched away, and Matilda stared at me.

"What?" I asked.

"You did not tell me this was a brothel," Matilda said, frowning.

"It's not. At least, that is not its main function. It's a tavern, but Mildred lets whores work here, so I suppose it doubles as a brothel," I explained. It was probably rude of me to bring a noblewoman to the Rose, but there was nowhere better in Oldford.

Matilda only shook her head and changed the subject. "How far is it to your hall?"

"Not far, only a day if we leave before sun-up. I often make trips to and from Oldford to run errands." Matilda nodded and picked at her fingers. "Do you not like it here?" I asked.

Matilda shook her head. "It is crowded and smells awful. And men won't stop looking at me."

"We will be at my home soon, and the men there won't dare look at you the way these ones do."

"What is it like? Your home?"

"It is beautiful. In summer, you step outside to see fields of golden wheat nestled in a lush, green valley, surrounded by wide pastures stretching for miles and hills dotted with sheep. Now, however, the fields are a pristine white, but my hall remains warm and shields our bones from the bitter air. A cosy fire will be burning in the hearth right now, kept alive by my servants, while my oathmen will be huddled sharing tales and laughter. My steward, Alfred, will probably be playing his harp." I chuckled. "He's terrible, and my hounds always bark when he plays, but we love his songs all the same."

"That sounds lovely," Matilda said with a smile. "I cannot wait to see it."

I grinned and stared at Matilda in that moment, reminded of the necklace I had bought her. The moth sat in the middle of her chest, resting on the bust of her dark purple dress. It complimented her black hair, which fell gently on her shoulders, and made her deep blue eyes even sharper.

"So, here's your food. Nice and hot. Gave my cooks a good beating to make sure they did it just right," Mildred said, stealing me from my trance. She placed our plates and drinks in front of us.

"Thank you, Mildred. Though I am sure beating them was a bit excessive," I said.

She clapped me over the head. "It was a joke, you humourless dolt." She laughed. "I've also made sure your rooms are ready. I've given you your usual one, Edward, and the Lady of Henton will be in the one a few doors down from you."

Matilda frowned. "If you do not mind, Mildred, I would prefer to share a room with Edward. This city scares me, and I do not want to be alone."

Mildred glanced at me, winked, then turned back to Matilda and bowed. "Of course you can, My Lady. Means I get more customers," she said. She then placed a key down on the table. "Now, I'll leave you two in peace. If there are any problems, just give me a yell."

"Thank you, Mildred. You're a good friend," I said. She nodded, then turned and left us alone.

"I like her," Matilda said.

"I think it's impossible to dislike her," I said, digging into my meal. Matilda began to pick at her food, eating slowly. She sipped her ale and then grimaced.

"Gods, that's hideous," she said. I laughed, and she laughed with me. Matilda's mood had brightened, and soon we were chatting over our food. It was delicious, as usual, but Matilda was right about the ale. It was incredibly bitter and strong — good for a cold winter's night but terrible if you were used to mulled wine in your noble father's feasting hall. It tasted like piss, but despite that, Matilda finished her jug. She got drunk, and we talked at the table long after we finished eating.

I had called for another round of ale, which Matilda also finished, and after that she would not stop giggling. I told the occasional joke, all of which sent Matilda into a fit of giggles. She calmed down at one point, and her wide, watery eyes looked into mine and for a moment — just a moment — I caught a glimpse into her soul again.

Days ago, when I looked through her eyes as she begged me to take her away from Henton, I saw loneliness and longing, but now not a trace of that seemed to remain.

3

Home

Matilda was in a sorry state. She sat up in bed, beads of sweat decorating her forehead while she hugged a wooden bucket. Her eyes were watering, her cheeks were flushed, and her hair was a mess. She groaned again, dropped her head, and made an awful choking noise. What remained of last night's meal dribbled from the back of her throat.

We had retired late the night before. I offered to sleep on the floor so Matilda could have the bed to herself, but Matilda insisted on sharing so we did not get cold. She fell asleep the moment her head hit the pillow while I lay awkwardly on the edge of the bed as I tried to sleep.

I was woken a few hours later by Matilda throwing open the shutters and heaving her dinner out onto the streets. I found her a bucket, and now here we were.

"This is what happens when you drink too much," I said. She was gagging, with nothing left for her to throw up. She looked up from her bucket and scowled at me. "It will pass in a few hours."

Matilda put the bucket to the side, put her face in her hands, and began to cry. I rolled my eyes. I was cold and grumpy, had little sleep, and now I had to deal with this. Matilda was proving to be more of a burden than I initially thought, and in that moment, I wished I had never agreed to take her away from Henton. All I could think of was how I would be home by now if not for that damned blizzard. I pulled on my boots, buckled my belt, and put on my cloak.

"I will be back shortly," I said.

Matilda looked up at me with teary eyes. "Please stay."

"No. Just keep gagging into the bucket until you fall asleep." I headed for the door, and Matilda just lay on her side, looking hopeless. She curled up and pulled the blankets to her chin. I left her alone and went. Looking back now, I realise that I probably encouraged her by ordering more ale, but even so, she was a handful and I needed to be alone.

The Black Rose in the morning was entirely different to what it was in the evening. There were only half a dozen patrons here now, probably overnight guests who had woken for Mildred's breakfast. The room was quiet except for murmurs and the occasional clink of cutlery. I was approached by a servant girl who offered me food, I accepted, and she hurried off to the kitchen while I found a seat. I sat at a small table by the window in the corner of the tavern, and a few moments later, I had company.

"You are Edward, yes?" A man came to sit opposite me, his gloved hands clasped together. He had dark hair and even darker eyes, but his skin was incredibly pale. He was a very tidy and well-presented man. His hair was pulled back tight and his beard was neatly trimmed, and he wore an expensive leather tunic and a thick woollen cloak falling over his shoulders. The cloak was pinned together by a silver brooch in the shape of a snake coiled around itself. His garments were all dyed black. He was tall and handsome, in his mid-thirties I guessed, but despite his respectable appearance, there was a slightly menacing look in his eyes. He smiled at me.

"I am," I responded. Had I known then the amount of trouble this man would cause me, I would have said no.

"Good, good. I was passing through town yesterday, and I heard you were staying here, so I thought I would come wait for you in the morning. And here you are." He waved his hands as if he were presenting royalty. "There are other men looking for you, by the way. You are fortunate that I found you first. My name is Hakon," he said.

"How may I help you, Hakon?" I asked. I was hoping to eat my breakfast in peace, so I wanted to get what I assumed would be a boring conversation over with. Hakon folded his arms, and I knew my hopes were in vain.

"You are quite famous around these parts, are you not? I have heard many tales of your deeds. You once saved this town from a vampire, correct?"

"She was a witch," I corrected him. "People just like to exaggerate the story. What do you want?"

Hakon seemed offended by my abruptness, but he smiled. "I have a lot of coin to offer you, if you want it."

"Depends on what you want in return," I said. I stared out the window, waiting for the man to tell me about scratching sounds in his walls or an odd dream he had.

"You have heard of the legendary King Emrys, I assume. What do you know of him? Ah, here is your food," he said and nodded to the servant girl carrying a tray towards my table. He watched her, hunger in his eyes.

The girl placed the tray before me, presenting me with a steaming hot pie and a piece of fresh-baked bread. A cup of milk sat beside the plate. "Thank you," I said to the girl. She curtsied and then hurried off.

Hakon watched her for a moment and then turned back to me and smiled.

I started eating. "King Emrys?" I said. "I confess, my knowledge of that man is lacking. But I know he ruled about a thousand years ago. He was cursed with immortality and spent centuries roaming the land, leaving only devastation in his wake. That is, before he was sealed away in a tomb by a man named Godwin."

Hakon raised his eyebrows and gave me a slow nod, evidently impressed by my limited knowledge of the legend. I continued eating, waiting for him to enlighten me on the subject. "You know only the core of the legend," he said. "But that is understandable. The tale has been lost to time. Emrys was sealed away three centuries ago, after all. Fortunately, my ancestors wrote it down and stored it in their library. According to them, Emrys was king of the lands to the northwest before our people conquered this country. One day, while campaigning, he disappeared with his entire army! Ten thousand horsemen, it is said. He was thought to have died, and so was succeeded by his son.

"For three hundred years no trace of Emrys or his army was found, and he was forgotten. Then, one day, he emerged from the hills. He marched through the land with his army, all of them on horseback. Supposedly, neither Emrys nor his men could set foot on the ground until Emrys became king once more.

"So they rode for days, and the days turned to weeks, and the weeks turned to months, and Emrys grew impatient. I guess he hoped the curse would be lifted on its own. The army began to raid and eventually went to war with the king at that time — our people now ruled his lands, by the way. Emrys lost that war, and that winter he retreated to the hills and disappeared for another hundred years."

Hakon shrugged, as if he did not believe what he was telling me, but the passion with which he spoke told me he did. I listened while I ate, and he continued.

"Anyway, after a hundred years Emrys returned to devastate the land. He waged war against the king, attempting to reclaim his throne and lift his curse. He was defeated again, and so disappeared for another hundred years. Every century, Emrys would reappear, war against whomever the king was, and then disappear for another century after being defeated.

"Finally, people began to see a pattern, and the next time Emrys came the king was ready. In the year 822 of the Third Age of Man, Emrys and King Carol the Great warred for control over Ardonn's throne, and three years later, King Carol and his champion Godwin managed to seal Emrys and his men away in a hidden mountain tomb. If the legends are true, Emrys remains in that mountain to this day."

Hakon sat back in his seat. He watched me eat my pie in silence for a few moments. I was thinking. Hakon's tale intrigued me, but I did not want to show him that.

"Charming story," I said. A flicker of anger appeared in Hakon's eyes, but he just smiled. "What does that have to do with your offer?"

"Godwin was one of the Gifted. And so are you," he said.

I knew about Godwin. He was the most famous of all the Gifted, a legendary warrior-poet and close friend and champion to King Carol the Great. Carol rewarded Godwin's services with a title, an official royal position, and a large house with some land in the rich countries around Oldford.

The descendants of Godwin's second-born son sat beside the kings as Royal Godspeakers for generations until the position was abolished by the Usurper eight years ago, while Godwin's descendants from his first-born lived in that home for centuries. That home was passed down to my master, and now it belonged to me.

"My master was a direct descendant of Godwin," I said to Hakon.

"So I have heard," he said. "At any rate, I need the sword Godwin wielded when he helped Carol seal Emrys away. My sources tell me that sword was passed down to your master, and I assume you now have it. Am I correct? I would like to buy that sword from you."

I almost choked on my food. Did this man want to release Emrys from his tomb? Why would anyone want to do that? If the legends were true, Emrys would lay waste to these lands, and trapping him would not be easy a second time.

"I refuse your offer," I said and stood up to leave.

"Wait," he growled. He pulled back his cloak to reveal a long blade at his belt and gestured for me to sit. I noticed then that under the sleeves of his woollen shirt were steel chain links. Hakon was wearing mail under his clothes and was prepared for a fight. I had left my weapons up in the room with Matilda, so I sat back down.

"I want us to be friends," Hakon said, smiling again. "I know I cannot force you to help me, but know this: me and my people only want what is best for this kingdom." He leaned forward and lowered his voice. "You and I both know that the 'good King Stephan' is far from deserving of the throne. His father was a usurper, and he is nothing more than a puppet."

He almost spat that name out, and there was disgust in his voice that had not been there before. Hakon's motivations were political, it seemed, and I began to understand. Hakon wanted to support Emrys in overthrowing King Stephan, probably hoping to be rewarded for it. Hakon had no claim to the throne himself, but with Emrys, his cause might have some merit. Hakon would not be the only man to prefer a strong warlord from legend on the throne to a half-foreign bastard like Stephan.

"I am well-liked by the guards in this town," I said. "I could have you arrested for treason with talk like that."

"We both know you would not do that."

I shrugged. "I do have the sword, though it is locked away in a safe place at home. But even if I had it here, it is not for sale and never will be." I lied, of course. Godwin's sword was up in the room with Matilda — I took it with me wherever I went.

"Never? It could make you very wealthy," Hakon said.

"How wealthy?"

"I can offer you twice its weight in gold, and some more. Plus, you will have your name inscribed in the Hall of Legends once Emrys reclaims his kingdom."

"If he even exists…"

"He exists, Edward. Sell me your sword, and I shall prove it."

I shook my head. "I am sorry, Hakon. That sword is worth more to me than all the gold in the world."

"A sentimental man, I see." Hakon stood up. "Very well. Thank you for your time, Edward Godspeaker, but now I must return home for Winterlow. I bid you farewell." Hakon quickly bowed and headed off into the streets.

I pushed my plate away. I had lost my appetite, and my mind was now racing with all kinds of thoughts. The Gods had sent that man to me for a reason, but what that reason was I did not yet know. Selling Godwin's sword to Hakon and his people, whoever they were, would border on treason, but it was true that Stephan's claim to his throne was weak.

These days, my trade was becoming less and less lucrative, and I was beginning to run low on the wealth I had saved from a well-paying job several years back. On top of that, the new dynasty was not exactly kind to people like me. My trade was tolerated, but how long before we were outlawed entirely? I might have had a lot to gain from helping Hakon.

On the other hand, freeing Emrys would mean unleashing devastation on the kingdom. Would I want that on my conscience?

At any rate, King Stephan's army was probably strong enough to defeat Emrys, but it was more likely that he did not even exist. He was only a legend, after all. I sat at that table and stared out the window at the snowflakes falling lightly against the glass, and then I had that feeling in my gut — like my stomach was tied into a knot. Outside, I saw Hakon approach a group of about two dozen men, all dressed in black. He spoke to one of them, a large man, and pointed down the street.

The big man mounted his horse and, wasting no time, galloped south with about half of the darkly dressed men. I could not make out what Hakon had said, but I felt a sense of impending doom. Something was wrong.

Gods damn that blizzard.

I sat downstairs for some time, thinking, before bringing a small tray of food upstairs for Matilda. I found her asleep. I wanted to head home that morning before Harold's men arrived in town, but because of Matilda I would now have to wait till the next. She was in no state to travel. Besides, it seemed that our pursuers were already here.

I left the tray with her, collected my things, and headed out into the streets hoping to pass the time by wandering Oldford. I wanted to see if I could find any information about the men who hunted us.

I liked Oldford. It was indeed a pretty town. It had grown naturally over time as more and more trade headed north from the south, or from the sea in the west upriver towards the east. As such, it had a long and interesting history, and it had been built sporadically. It was a cramped, chaotic mess of buildings, both old and new, and I thought that made it beautiful.

Apart from the Lord of Oldford's castle, which sat atop the hill outside the city, Oldford had two prominent buildings. On the north side of the river, which ran east-to-west through Oldford, was an old temple. The temple had existed longer than anyone could remember, and it was dedicated to the god of freshwater and commerce, Brim.

Brim was said to be Oldford's patron, and according to legend he founded the town himself when he sailed down the River Aed on his voyage from Lakeland in the northeast to the ocean. It is said that Brim came across a caravan of traders who wished to sell their goods in the kingdoms to the south, but they could not cross the deep, wide river.

They saw Brim sailing downstream, called out to him, and asked him to ferry them across. He did, and once they had reached the river's south side, they gave Brim a wagon-load of rich gifts. He rewarded them by raising the riverbed in the spot they had crossed so that they would never have trouble crossing the river again.

Thus, Oldford earned its name from the ford that Brim had created. Nowadays there is a large stone bridge in the place where the ford used to be. Unfortunately, the temple is used by few these days, and its priests are unable to afford the maintenance they need to fix the growing number of chips and cracks in the building's masonry, or replace the fading paint on its walls. Even the great statue of Brim now only has eight fingers and no nose.

On the south side of the river is Oldford's town hall. Unlike the temple, this building is new, and whenever I have been in Oldford I have seen scaffold attached to some part of it, as if it is in a constant state of maintenance and renovation.

The town hall, as well as being the centre of Oldford's administration, is also the residence of the town's mayor, chosen from among Oldford's wealthy merchant families every year and who is advised by a body of elected officials. Lord Adalbert is the ruler of Oldford only in name. In reality, all military, economic, and political power rests in the hands of the mayor and his council.

Because of the location of the town hall, the wealthiest part of Oldford is that on the south side of the river — the north side is a much poorer district, though still richer than the districts outside the walls.

I spoke to some of the townsfolk, and a few told me they had seen a group of five warriors poking around the city. One man, a fishmonger I knew who sold his catch in the marketplace each day told me the men, led by one called Merewald, had asked about me earlier that morning.

He told them nothing, fortunately.

I returned to the Black Rose late in the afternoon as the sun was setting. Matilda was feeling better, but it was too late to travel, for we would be riding through the cold night. Matilda and I supped together, but this time she had not a drop of ale. She could sense my anxiety and frustration and did not talk much.

We ate in silence, listening only to the sounds of the tavern's chatter and laughter and the cheery songs played by the bard. Matilda wanted her own room that night, and I admit I was relieved. Instead of lying awkwardly beside Matilda, unable to sleep, I kept my bed warm with the girl who served me that morning. She was much better company than Matilda, especially on that cold winter night.

The skies had cleared overnight, and so without wasting any time, we bid Mildred farewell and left the Rose before sunup the next morning. She was sorry to see us go and gave Matilda a parting gift: a batch of small cakes she had baked the night before. We packed our things, saddled Lilly, and rode south through Oldford. I took care that we were not being followed, but I reckoned I knew those streets better than Harold's men.

Matilda did not speak except to say "yes" or "no," and I figured she was angry at me for some reason. I did not bother to ask why. As we rode through the busy streets of Oldford, Matilda and I shared only one conversation.

"Was that girl better or worse than my sister?" There was a touch of bitterness in her voice.

"Sorry?" I was taken aback.

"You heard me."

"Is there a problem?"

"Never mind."

I did not reply and wondered what made Matilda so upset. As

far as I was concerned, I had done nothing wrong. It was *she* who had delayed my journey home.

We approached the south gates of Oldford, and as we passed under the arch Matilda stared up at the grates the town's defenders would use to pour boiling liquids on top of any attackers.

"For oil," I told her.

She said nothing.

We passed through the dilapidated villages clinging to the town's southern walls and out into a flat, swampy country. There was little chance Harold's men could find us now; their hounds would have lost our scent in Oldford, and the tracks leading in and out of the south gate could have been anyone's. They would need to discover where I lived, but by the time they could do that, we would be safe in my hall with my oathmen ready to deter them.

Dirt tracks led us through parts of the swamp while in the wetter parts we had to cross boardwalks. Around us we could see small settlements dotting the marsh, each several miles apart. There were barely more than a few houses in each village. I explained to Matilda that the larger settlements were home mostly to eelers and that the smaller ones were merely stations that were not permanently occupied but acted as temporary homes for workers to gather peat.

She ignored me.

"Matilda," I said as we rode. "Whatever I have done to upset you, I am sorry."

She did not respond for a few moments but eventually gave up on ignoring me.

"I forgive you," she mumbled.

"We will be past this swamp soon," I assured her. "You see those hills in the distance? That's all farmland. My house sits in a valley among those hills, backed by a forest. It is much more beautiful than this place."

Matilda shuffled in the saddle, pressing her back against me. She had been sitting far forward in the saddle, evidently trying to forget I was there. "I do not understand why anyone would want to live out here," Matilda said.

"Well, I suppose you would get used to the smell. You can make good money selling peat, and in times of war an army is not likely to march through a swamp, so these people are safe," I explained. I may have lied about the smell. I rode through here frequently and never got used to it. It was an awful stench.

As we rode on through the swamp, Matilda did not seem as upset anymore, but she still spoke little. Perhaps it was the swamp smell? Or maybe my apology did not work after all. I tried to spark a conversation.

"Have you ever met the lord?"

"Lord Adalbert?" Matilda said. "I have not."

"I am not surprised. He rarely leaves his castle," I said. "I've only met him twice. He's a good man but not a very likeable one, if you get my meaning."

"How can a man govern such an important part of the kingdom if he stays in his castle?" Matilda asked.

"The mayor runs the town and the surrounding settlements, but anyone living outside of a day's ride from Oldford governs themselves, more or less. Your father would have his own laws and administer his own justice, correct?"

"Yes, he does. I never really felt like we were ruled by anyone else."

"I thought as much."

"Why does Adalbert not rule instead of the mayors?"

"The mayor would not let him even if he wanted to. King Stephan's father, the Usurper, issued a law allowing cities to have their own armies. Oldford's army is loyal to the mayor because the mayor pays their wages. Adalbert still has his own retinue, of course, but the mayor pays his soldiers more, so free men are more willing to serve him than the lord. Relations between the two are tense, to say the least," I told Matilda.

"Your tone suggests you dislike the mayors," Matilda said.

I said nothing.

At around noon, we reached the edge of the swamp and were finally on hard ground again. Lilly was a much happier horse now, and we could ride much faster. We passed a country of gentle hills coated with a thick layer of snow, but the peasants here had already made efforts to clear the road.

We came across the occasional wooded area, but the trees were always thin, and we were never in the shade for too long. That was a blessing. The sun gave us enough warmth to ride in relative comfort, and after a small stop for lunch, Matilda was happy once again.

After a few more hours of riding, she insisted on taking another break, despite the fact my home was not far. I helped her down from Lilly's saddle, and she went off to do her business behind a tree.

I looked away. The sky was thick with clouds, so I did not notice it at first, but as I stared off eastward I noticed what appeared to be a dark plume of smoke rising into the sky from behind the hills in the distance. I squinted, wondering if my eyes were deceiving me.

"Matilda," I called without taking my eyes off the cloud.

"Yes?" Matilda said as she came over to me.

"Is that smoke?" I asked.

Matilda put her hand above her eyes and then nodded slowly. "It looks like it. Is something burning?"

"Well, that is usually the case when smoke appears," I turned and went back to Lilly. "We should keep going. I have a bad feeling about this."

Matilda hurried back to the horse, and I helped her up into the saddle. "Could it be rebels?"

"This far south?" I said. I kicked Lilly into a canter. "That's unlikely. It would be difficult for a force to cross the Aed without controlling Oldford first."

"Are there no crossings?"

"There are. There is a small ford not far upriver, actually, but Carol's men would be blocked at every attempt to cross."

"Unless he could beat the river's defenders."

"True," I said.

We continued riding, and the smoke grew ever closer. By late afternoon we entered a valley and came to a low stone wall that stretched from either side of the road to the forests on the hilltops. It was not a steep valley, but a valley nonetheless, and I told Matilda that we were home at last.

"My master's great-grandfather had these walls built," I explained. "Apparently his neighbours kept moving the boundary markers, so he built a wall of stone to ensure his lands could never change."

We rode on, and eventually the road twisted. In the distance I could see my home. I owned miles upon miles of land, but most of it was for grazing livestock, which I did not have, and so I only used the hundred or so acres around my house.

Still, it was a rich and beautiful patch of country. My house was flanked by two hills and was backed to the south by a large evergreen forest that stretched for miles to the River Aed. In the warmer months, the north side of my house would be surrounded by a golden forest of wheat, and on the hills around those fields one could see my sheep, specks of white dotting the lush green pastures.

But at this time of year, the wheat was harvested, the animals were brought indoors, and the hills were completely white with snow. A very small village sat atop the hill to the west of the house, and another in the middle of the wheat fields. These villages were occupied by my tenants, who called me Earl, though I did not officially have that title, and by my small retinue of oathmen.

Except now it was all a ruin. The fields were scorched bare, and the houses, including my hall, were burned to the foundations. Thick black smoke rose from the embers, and the snow was grey with ash. The corpses of livestock lay strewn across the fields, black and bloodied, and the burned, unrecognisable bodies of men and women were propped up by stakes outside my home — or what was left of it, at least. There was nothing living in sight.

"Is this…?" Matilda began.

"Yes," I said. I galloped as hard as I could towards my hall, where I threw myself from the horse. I looked around in horror and disbelief.

It was all gone. Everything I owned, except that which I had taken with me on my recent travels, was now ash. My home, which had belonged to my master and his ancestors for three centuries, was now a ruin. I had no money, no animals, and all my people were dead. People I had sworn to protect.

I drew my sword and climbed over the remnants of my hall's doorway into what was left of the building. The scorched, shrivelled remains of my two hounds lay by the door, and I shook my head.

But what horrified me most was the display in the centre of my hall. A pile of cremated bodies stood in front of me, which would have touched my hall's roof were it still there. Smoke still billowed from it, and the embers were still hot. This destruction had happened recently.

"By all the Gods," Matilda said. She stood in the doorway, her hands over her mouth. "My father's men would never do something like this."

"No, this was not their work. Stay outside," I demanded. "Go tie Lilly to a tree, but not too far away."

Matilda did not hesitate to do as I asked.

I approached the pile, pulling my cloak over my face to block out the awful stench of burned flesh. I poked one of the bodies with my sword.

"Mail," I mumbled. This body, and many others on the pile, wore mail and steel helmets. There were blackened swords and axes and the remnants of wooden shields. "I am so sorry," I said.

I fell to my knees. The bodies in this pile were not only those of my servants and tenants, but also my oathmen — loyal housecarls who had sworn to fight for me and defend me and my own to the death, but who were also my closest friends and companions. These men were like brothers to me, and I had failed them. They had given their lives defending my home, but I was not even there to die with them.

I began to weep. Not out of grief or pity, but out of anger. I felt rage boiling up inside me. I wanted to scream, but I wept instead.

This was no mere raid carried out by bandits or robbers looking for an easy haul. This was an attack on *me*. It was personal, and whoever had killed my men and placed their burned bodies here intended for me to find them.

I stood up and swung my sword at a scorched post. It crumbled from the blow, and the fresh embers hissed. I swore and kicked what was left of it. "Oh Gods, why have you done this?" I shouted at the sky. "Why?"

Light snow began to fall. Or was it ash? I cannot remember. Perhaps it was both. But I remember hearing my name echo on the wind, and my heart skipped a beat. *Were the Gods replying?* I heard my name again, but this time it came from the doorway. I turned and saw a man standing there, with Matilda behind him.

"Edward..." he said. I collapsed again, tears falling down my cheeks. The man ran over to me and grabbed my shoulders, shaking me to my senses. "Edward, thank the Gods in all the Heavens."

"Dughlas, what happened?" I said. This man was one of my oathmen, and my best friend. I had thought his body was on the pile with the others, all burned up, but here he was. Alive.

"We can talk outside," he said. "Get up, the others wish to see you."

And so Dughlas helped me up, and I wiped my eyes with my sleeve. We went outside of what was left of my hall — my home — and there they were. Survivors. I breathed a sigh of relief, but then dizziness washed over me.

My vision blurred, and everything went black.

I woke by a small fire under a canopy of evergreens. Matilda was sitting beside me, as was Dughlas. I blinked and looked around.

"What happened? Where are we?" I asked, yawning. I had passed out, Dughlas told me, and when I returned to my senses I was tired and weak, so he and the others brought me back to a camp they had made in the wooded hills behind my hall, about an hour's walk away, where I promptly fell asleep. It was dark now.

I asked Dughlas what had happened at the house. He did not witness the full event because he and three of my other oathmen were on their way back from a hunting trip, but one of the servant girls who managed to escape the slaughter filled him in with what he had missed.

Apparently, late in the night before this, about thirty or so men dressed all in black and riding black horses came to the hall and demanded to see whoever was in charge. My steward was woken up and went outside to see them.

The servant girl did not hear the conversation, but it did not last long, for my steward and the leader of the horsemen began shouting at one another, and the latter then drew his sword and gutted my steward in one swift motion.

Chaos and panic followed, and the servant girl rightly decided to escape through the back of the hall and into the woods. Someone was smart enough to sound the horn, which was what woke Dughlas and his companions, who went as swiftly as they could back to the hall.

But they were too late. They arrived just before dawn, saw the hall alight with flames, and watched from the trees in hiding as the black-dressed men pushed into the burning building those of my servants and tenants who were not lucky enough to escape. Some of the women, and even a few of the young girls, were raped. It was brutal, senseless savagery.

Dughlas admitted he and the other three warriors felt like cowards as they watched, but I assured him they did the right thing by waiting instead of throwing their lives away meaninglessly.

After the sun came up, the men threw most of the bodies onto a pile in the middle of the hall, then they mounted their horses and rode off westwards, leaving the ruin and taking nothing with them.

When they felt it was safe, Dughlas and the others emerged from the woods and began to search for survivors. They found some hiding, and some others returned from where they had run over the course of the morning. They took these survivors back into the woods, where they made a camp while deciding what to do.

Later that day, Dughlas heard hoofbeats off in the distance, so he and my surviving warriors went back to the house to investigate. That was when they found Matilda and me.

"What happened to my other oathmen?" I asked him. I was sitting up now, warming my hands by the fire.

Dughlas shook his head. "I didn't see, but one of the servants told me they saw your warriors make a shield wall in the doorway shortly after Alfred was killed. They bravely made their stand there but were all slain to the last man."

"Did they take any of the bandits with them?" I asked.

Dughlas grinned. "Apparently each man killed two before being killed himself."

I smiled at that and found comfort in the fact they had died as warriors. They were feasting with the Gods now. Before then, I had only thirteen oathmen, but they were all loyal warriors and strong, skilled fighters. Now I had four, plus half a dozen servants.

"Edward," said another of my oathmen, coming to stand before me. I nodded to him. It was Osmund, a man near the age of fifty with a thick grey beard and numerous battle scars. Osmund had served my master Brendan for as long as he could remember, but when the usurper Wim of Tidegate rose against King Edwin in 1104, Osmund was given leave to fight under Edwin's banner. He returned after Edwin's death in 1110, which was when I first met him. I never stopped feeling intimidated by that man.

"Osmund, come sit," I said.

He shook his head. "Where were you? You were supposed to have returned a week ago."

"I was caught in a blizzard, and then I was held up in Oldford."
I glanced at Matilda, and she stared at the ground.

Osmund grunted, then nodded at Matilda. "Sticking your poker
in this new toy of yours, I bet."

"Watch your tongue, Osmund," Dughlas said. Osmund glared
at him and then grabbed me by the throat and hauled me to my
feet. His fist was raised and his eyes were burning red. I heard
Dughlas draw his sword behind me, followed by the others.
Osmund hesitated and glanced around at the men.

"Forgive me," he said. His hands fell to his sides. "I lost my
wife and two sons in that attack. I only wish you were there at
least to die for them, if nothing else."

"Edward was away, as were you. Go mourn," said Dughlas.
Osmund shook his head and then turned to go sit by his own fire
with the other two oathmen. The three of them looked back to
me and murmured to each other. They were angry with me, and
they were right to be. I should have been with them, defending
the lives of those who relied on me, but we cannot choose what
Fate decides for us.

"Get some sleep, you two," I said to Dughlas and Matilda. I
lay down, looking up at the cloudy, starless sky. We were several
miles away from the hall, but I could still smell it.

I could not sleep that night, of course. Whenever I tried,
images of my people being gutted, burned, and raped flashed
before my eyes. Was it my imagination, or was my gift giving
me visions of the dead?

I tried to push the thoughts out of my mind, but it was all I could think about. I knew exactly who was behind this. I just knew it. I kept that fact to myself, however, because I did not want to be blamed any further for this mess.

One thing was certain. The Gods were growing bored again, and for the first time in nearly a decade, they were beginning to cast their dice.

4

Hazeling

We left our woodland camp before dawn. There were twelve of us in total, and we were all miserable. Aside from Matilda and I, there were my oathmen Dughlas, Osmund, Egil, Cubert, and what remained of my servants.

We reached my house shortly after sunup, and my heart sank once again. The embers had cooled now, and the smoke dissipated, so all that remained was the gloomy skeleton of what was once my home.

Matilda tried to comfort me. She climbed down from the horse, came over to me, then lightly rested her hand on my forearm. She began to speak, but I pushed her hand away and ignored her. I wished to be alone with my thoughts.

The group waited while I went back into the ruin. I wanted to see if I could salvage anything and maybe retrieve the silver I had hidden away. Dughlas insisted on helping. He was handsome, around twenty-five, he estimated, had long blonde hair that he tied into a thick braid and a short beard with streaks of black. His shoulders were broad, his arms wide, and he stood taller than most men.

Dughlas was orphaned as a baby, and like me he was taken in by Brendan and trained in the ways of a warrior so that he could serve as Brendan's housecarl and oathman. We grew into men together, and we were like brothers. If I had to choose one man to defend me against any onslaught, it would be Dughlas.

"It's a real pity," he said.

"This was personal," I said.

"Aye, I can see that. So can the others," he said, jerking his head back to the group.

I glanced over and saw Osmund standing by his horse, watching us. "They blame me."

"You aren't the only one to have lost everything in this attack. They regret that they could do nothing to stop it but don't want to blame themselves."

I kicked through the rubble and found a few valuables. There was some jewellery and a few books that had survived the blaze more or less in good condition. Dughlas helped me lift the stone slab inside the fireplace, which hid my wealth. The iron chest was still within.

"They really did take nothing of value," Dughlas said. "It seems like they didn't even bother to look."

"That just adds insult to injury," I said. I lifted the chest out of
its hole and opened it. It was still filled with all my silver and
gold, and I scooped out two handfuls of coins. "Give these to the
other three and take some for yourself."

"What about the servants?"

"They're free to go, if they choose. But I need my warriors.
Some gold should keep them happier for now."

Dughlas nodded and took the coins to my men. I watched him
divide them up and then went back to searching through the
ruins. I found a few more items worth keeping but stopped when
Dughlas called my name.

I turned to see what he wanted and saw him pointing up at the
hill to the south, where the ruins of my tenants' homes sat. A
man was up there, watching us. He sat on a black horse.

"We should go," I mouthed to Dughlas. He nodded, then
readied the horses and helped the servant girls mount up.

I returned to the group and we carried on westwards. Matilda
asked me where we would go, evidently concerned she no longer
had any place to live, so I told her I planned to return to Oldford,
but from there I did not know.

I was hoping Lord Adalbert would provide us with hospitality
for a while, though the more I thought about that, the more I
doubted its likelihood. Adalbert was on good terms with my
master, and I had known him years ago when I was an
apprentice, but he had grown increasingly paranoid in recent
times and was notorious for turning away those he did not trust.

I also thought about going back to Henton, even if it was just to return Matilda to her family, but I could not face the humiliation. I was prideful back then. Besides, Matilda did not want to return, so we both agreed that she would stay with us unless Adalbert denied us asylum.

I told Dughlas of how I had come to meet Matilda and why she was with me. He thought I was a fool, but a kind fool nonetheless. I also told him we had been followed by Harold's men, but we both agreed that they were no longer our immediate concern.

We travelled slowly through the day because the servants wanted to keep stopping to rest, but my men and I had to hasten everyone along as fast as possible, for the man from before was following us. He kept at a distance, but every now and then he would appear on a hilltop or at the edge of the woods, as if he did not care that we could see him.

"Who is he?" Dughlas asked at one point.

I ignored the question. "When we get to the wall, I want you to keep going and take everyone to Oldford," I said.

"Where are you going?"

"I need to seek advice."

"Ah, you're going to see *her*."

I nodded. "When you get to the edge of Oldford's swamp, set up camp and wait for me there. But do not camp by the road, and make sure you are not seen."

"Aye, Boss. Don't be gone for too long."

"I will only be a few days," I said.

And so we kept moving until we reached the low stone wall that marked the edge of my land. I suppose it still was my land, even though it was no longer my home. I bid farewell to everyone, and Matilda begged to be allowed to come with me. "You do not know what it is like to be a young lady in the company of strange men."

"No, but these men have sworn to me. They will not hurt you."

I felt for Matilda and wished I could bring her with me, but there was something I needed to do alone. I did not tell her where or why I was going, only that it was important.

I then turned south and rode Lilly along the stone wall built by my master's predecessor, through empty fields and paddocks. Lilly struggled through the snow, but I pushed her on up the hill.

We came to a forest about a mile away from the road. The canopy was thick here, and it grew dark very quickly. I rode for about an hour, and just as the sun was setting, I found it at last.

This place had been almost completely untouched by humanity. I was unsure if anyone had ever visited this place before me. It was a grove in the forest where the canopy was thinner, and so needles of light from the setting sun filtered through the branches. The ground here had little snow, just patches here and there and a thin layer of frost. At the centre of the grove was a stone fountain. A fountain built by no man.

It was small and bland, nothing more than a stone basin with a pillar in the centre spouting water from the top. Yet it had a kind of peaceful tranquillity. This grove was somehow sheltered from all wind, so there was absolute silence aside from the birdsong and the trickle of water pouring into the fountain's basin.

And sitting in that basin was a woman. She was naked, washing her hair under the water. I did not know her age, but she looked to be young. Her impeccable skin was as pale as snow, and her hair was almost as white, though it had a slight orange glow. She had a face of absolute beauty, and to look upon her was like being put under a spell.

She was singing softly to herself in a strange language. The water must have been freezing, but she did not mind. She sensed my presence, and her eyes opened. They were big and round; her left eye was a gorgeous green, whereas her right was a pale blue. Her eyes fell on me, and a soft smile appeared on her lips.

"Edward," she sang. "The birds told me you were coming. I wanted to wash for you." She looked down at herself and then back up at me. "It would seem I am too slow."

I said nothing, only stared. The woman stood, shook her hair, then pulled it over her shoulder. It was very long, and the tips rested at her belly button. Water flowed down her chest and over her breasts. She had a perfect waist, which curved out to form her perfect hips, which then curved back inwards towards her feet.

"You told me you would not come here again," she said. Her head tilted slightly to the side, as if teasing me.

"You are poison to me," I replied.

She giggled and bit her lip. "My offer still stands. You could join me, and we could live here among these trees forever."

"Every night I consider it," I said. The woman stepped out of the basin and walked over to me. "I have brought you something."

"Oh?"

I pulled a silver torc from my belt, which I had taken from my hoard under the fireplace. I held it out to her.

"Come put it in the fountain," she said. I put my hand in hers, and she guided me over to the water. I dropped the torc, and it sank to the bottom. She took my other hand. "I have missed you, Edward. Will you love me?" When she spoke, it was almost like she was reciting poetry.

"Yes, but this will be the last time," I said.

She moved her face close to mine, and we kissed. "That is the seventh time you have said that, Edward."

I grinned. "And I am sure it won't be the last."

She laughed at that. We kissed again, and as promised, I loved her that night. When I touched her, the cold disappeared, and so we were able to roll around on the frosty pine needles late into that dark winter's night. For Aoife, as this woman called herself, was an elf.

I stayed with Aoife for three nights. We slept in the open under the stars, holding each other close. Her warmth protected me from the cold, and although light snow fell through the trees, I did not feel it.

She was not always naked. She wore a plain white dress, which was really just a piece of fabric she had wrapped around herself. She wore a variety of jewellery, including the torc I had brought for her. Some of it I had brought her in the past, but many other pieces came from elsewhere. All of it was silver. Aoife would often wear a crown of wildflowers in her hair, and she walked everywhere barefoot.

During the day, Aoife would bring me fruits and animals — mostly apples, rabbits, and pheasants — that she had found in the woods. She was the guardian of this forest, after all, and so its inhabitants gave their lives willingly if she commanded it. Being a creature of the Otherworld, Aoife did not need to eat, but my horse and I did.

We lay on the ground together on my final morning with her, watching the snow fall through the trees. Her head rested on my shoulder, and an arm rested on my chest.

"You will leave me today," she said, reading my mind.

"Yes," I replied.

"You do not have to go back."

"I do."

"Why?"

"Justice," I said.

Aoife rolled her eyes. "Vengeance, you mean."

"Is there a difference?"

"Yes. Are you certain it was this character called Hakon that scorched your home?"

I nodded. It was Hakon. There was no doubt about that. The description Dughlas gave me of the raiders was similar to the men that Hakon spoke to in Oldford. They came for my sword, but when they could not find it, they destroyed my home instead. I could think of no one else that would raid my lands without taking any wealth or captives with them.

"Nothing is certain," Aoife said "They could have been bandits. Your vengeance is misguided."

"Even if that were true, I cannot stay here with you. I have duties. The Gods have a purpose for me," I said.

Aoife sat up and frowned. "What do you know of the Gods? What do you know of Fate?" I blinked at her, and she shrugged and lay back down. "You are very naïve, Edward. You know little of matters that occur outside of your plane. Tell me — if your fate is already decided, why do *you* need to fulfil it?"

I thought about her question for a moment, and she spoke again before I could. "If a man dies and returns as a revenant, is that his fate?" she asked. "For a man to come back from the dead, he must fulfil certain conditions in life, but if that is so, does that not mean his fate is decided by his own actions? If his return from the dead was already decided at birth, then he could live how he wanted and still become a revenant, but the fact all revenants share certain characteristics is no mere coincidence."

I stared up at the forest canopy. "Our choices and our actions are fated. A person is already fated to act in such a way that he would become a revenant."

Aoife giggled. "No, Edward, no. If that is the case, then you have no free will. But I know for a fact that you are choosing to leave me. Just as you chose to come here."

"So there is no such thing as Fate? The future is based entirely on mere chance?"

"Fate exists. But you also have free will. You determine your own fate, based on your actions, yet at the same time your fate is unavoidable." Aoife moved her head to look up at me and smiled, while I lay there in confusion.

"That is a contradiction," I said.

"Is that a bad thing?" she asked. "You mortals are simple beings. You think that because one thing is so, the opposite cannot be so. But is it not true that you can also be dead, but alive? Can you not love a person but feel anger towards them? Can your happiness not be combined with sadness? Can you not lie in the snow but still be warm?"

I did not respond.

"What your senses perceive is based entirely on how you view the world," she continued. "The Gods originally created our worlds as one, but after the Split, the Mirror World became the Mirror Worlds: the World and the Otherworld. Mundane and arcane. Body and soul. Yet because of their shared origin our worlds, although distinct, are not wholly separate. We are proof of that."

"You have given me a lot to think about, and none of the advice I wanted," I said.

She smiled. "Go now, Edward. Your fate awaits you. But know that this is a fate you have chosen."

At that, Aoife moved up to kiss me, and the moment our lips locked, she disappeared. I found myself alone, lying in the cold snow.

The fountain stopped spouting water, but the basin was still full. I washed myself, filled my flask, and then started a fire. I cooked a rabbit for breakfast, and after eating I headed back through the trees with Lilly, then made my way back to the stone wall.

A fresh, thick layer of snow had covered the fields while I was in the forest, so Lilly had to trudge through it again. She managed, and after following the wall, we found the road again. I turned west towards Oldford.

I rode Lilly alone along the road westwards for some time. I checked the hills for that man who had been following us, but he appeared to have given up. Or perhaps he was stalking the others and had no interest in me. Whatever the case may have been, I did not encounter him again.

I did encounter someone, though. Two people, in fact. As I rode along the road, I spotted two others heading eastwards on foot. They were wrapped in thick cloaks and appeared to be hermits, but one can never be too careful. Especially in those days. I drew my sword.

"Hold," I called as I neared them. The pair stopped, and I noticed it was a man and a child. I pointed my sword in their direction.

"Hello, warrior," the man said. He held out his hands, so I lowered my blade.

"Who are you?" I asked. The man bowed his head. He had dark, curly hair and an olive complexion. These people were foreign to this land.

"Humble travellers, lord. We seek the man called Edward. He has fame in these parts," the man said. He spoke with a thick southern accent, confirming my suspicions. These two were from the kingdoms in the land beyond the River Cris, where the sun is always warm and everyone meets the day with a smile on their face. But these two looked cold and miserable.

"You have come far, and to dangerous lands. There is talk of growing tensions between the lords of Ardonn. What is your business with Edward?"

"I wish for my son here to be apprenticed by him."

"Why?"

"He has…strange senses."

I nodded, sheathed my sword, then dismounted. "What are your names?"

"My name is Livi," said the man. "This is my son, Philip." His son nodded, and I held up a hand in greeting. Philip had the same curly hair as his father, except it was longer, and he lacked the beard.

"A strong name. A king's name," I said to him and then turned back to his father. "You both have good luck, but also ill luck. You have found Edward — for I am him — but unfortunately, I cannot apprentice your son."

"Why not?"

"Half a day's ride east along this road is my home, but I assume you already knew that. However, my home is now a smouldering ruin, and most of my tenants are dead. I have barely enough money to feed myself and the survivors, and I do not know how long it will be till we have a place to live. An additional mouth to feed is the least of my concerns." I bowed my head and then turned back to Lilly.

"Wait," Livi said. He grabbed my arm, and I turned back to him. "I have nine children, and another is on its way. My family is poor, and we are struggling to get by. I hoped I could put my son into your care and that you could help him to be like you so that perhaps he may become more than a poor farmer." I turned to look down at Philip, and he looked at his feet.

"What have you seen?" I asked the child. Philip did not answer.

"He tells me he can talk to things that we cannot see. Last winter he went missing, and when he returned the next day, he told me… Philip, tell him what you told me," said Livi. He patted his son on the shoulder, and Philip glanced up at me nervously.

"I visited the home of the silvans," said Philip.

I stared at him for a second and blinked. "How long did you stay with them?"

"I stayed for supper," he said.

I put a hand to my mouth, curious. Silvans were what the southerners called elves, and if the average person had supper in their world, he should have been gone for years. I turned back to Livi.

"Why did you not seek out the Gifted in your lands?" I asked.

"We did, but all turned us away. Is my son unwell?"

"No. How old is he?"

"Eleven. My sixth son."

"I was once the son of a farmer," I said, turning to Philip. "When I was a few years younger than you, I left that farm to become the apprentice of a Godspeaker from these lands. Would you like to leave your farm, and your family, to live the life of the Gifted?"

"Yes, lord," Philip said.

"It is a hard and often lonely life. Is that well with you?"

"Yes."

I smiled a little and then looked back to his father. "Very well, Livi. I will apprentice your son. But I warn you, you are putting him on a tough road. Should you part with him now, he will face many trials in the future."

"Will he at least have food in his belly?" Livi asked.

"Yes. So long as he is under my tutelage, I will ensure he is always fed. And I shall do all in my power to defend him. You have my oath on that. I swear it."

At that Livi grinned, and then he hugged me. "Oh thank you, thank the Gods. You are a kind man."

"I will take your son in and train him. But if he proves useless, I will send him back home," I said.

He smiled even wider and then shook my hands. "He is a strong boy. He will not let you down. Philip has been very excited about becoming like you. He shall be happy."

"These are harsh times. You should make haste and return to your farm before the winter grows harsher."

Livi nodded, and tears began to form in his eyes. I do not know why I changed my mind and decided to take Philip in. Something inside me gave me the feeling that I should accept. There were few Godspeakers left in our world, and the fact that Philip was able to have supper with elves and remain unharmed was curious. For most, hundreds of years would have passed, but clearly not for him.

I sensed he had a lot of potential, and a lot of power, and in that moment I thought this must have been how my master felt when he took me in.

I walked a few paces along the road and waited for Livi and Philip to say their farewells. It would be a long time before they saw each other again, if at all. Livi thanked me once more, and I gave him some coins for the journey home. He was happy that he had found a future for his son but sorrowful at the same time.

I bid Livi safe travels, and we parted ways. Then I turned to Philip, who watched his father leave with tears in his eyes.

"Wipe your eyes," I said.

He looked up at me for a few moments and then wiped his face with his sleeve and sniffed. "Sorry, lord."

"Call me Edward." I held a gloved hand out to him, and he shook it.

"Edward. Where will you take me, if you have no home?"

"Oldford. It is a town not far from here. Come, hop on my horse. We will ride together and meet up with the rest of my people."

I helped Philip up onto my horse and mounted as well, then kicked Lilly into a trot. We rode for a few more hours, over hills and paddocks, until at last we had reached the edge of Oldford's swamp.

Philip spoke little that day, as I had when I first left my family to enter a strange world. I pointed northwards across the marsh to where the roofs of Oldford rose up in the distance and explained to Philip where we were in relation to the southern kingdoms. He told me he came from a kingdom called Luria, which was ruled by an old king called Miron. I asked him if Miron was a good king, and he said he was.

It was not long before Dughlas found us, having kept lookout over the road to Oldford. I introduced him to Philip, and then Dughlas took us to the camp he and the others had made. It was on a low ridge that hugged the edge of the swamp, and the camp sat amongst a bunch of dead willows and beeches. Matilda greeted both me and Philip enthusiastically, probably glad that she was no longer the only newcomer among strange men, but the others were less happy to see me.

Especially Osmund. "Late again," he said when I arrived at the camp.

I ignored him.

There was still light in the day, and after thinking about it for a few moments, I decided we should pack up the camp and try to cross the marsh with the hope of reaching Oldford before nightfall.

I thought we could make it, but I was wrong. The servants were even slower through the marsh, and as the sun set behind the hills, we were still far from Oldford's gate.

"We will have to spend the night in the swamp," I said to Dughlas. We both travelled on foot so the slower walkers could ride. "The town locks its gates at night to keep out the undesirables."

"We could find one of the old peat settlements," he suggested.

I agreed that would probably be a good idea, and so we all turned away from the road and followed a forgotten track that I thought would lead to one of the clusters of huts the peasants would sometimes use to gather peat from the marsh. It was growing darker by the second. I thought we would become lost in the night, but to my relief I was right, and we found a settlement.

It was a shabby place and looked to have been unused for at least a decade. The dozen wooden huts that surrounded what looked to be a communal sitting area were rotten and full of holes. We could hear the sounds of scratching and squeaking when we arrived at that poor excuse for a village. As I predicted, it was completely empty, aside from insects and its animal inhabitants.

And something else — something neither human nor animal. I should have trusted my instincts and moved on, but we were tired, hungry, wet, and cold. We had been wading through mud and water for up to an hour, and in some places, it went up to our knees. The huts were concealed by tall reeds, so we had stumbled upon the place almost by accident.

I felt uneasy, but the others were relieved to have found somewhere they could lie down and eat. The air was still and damp, but there was something else about it that put me off.

We tied our horses to a post in the centre of the village and dismounted. The food we had managed to forage would be enough to last us the night, but I would have to restock once we were in Oldford, should Adalbert deny us rest.

"There's enough room for everyone. Go and pick a shack for the night," I said. I approached the pit in the middle of the little communal area and started to light a fire. There was already enough dead wood in the pit to get one going.

"What about you?" Dughlas asked, coming over to squat

beside me. Philip lingered not far from me, unsure of what to do or where to go, and Matilda stood by the horses, hugging herself with her cloak.

"I'll stay out here," I said to Dughlas, then leant in close to whisper. "I feel something."

Dughlas stared at me for a second and then looked into the fire I had just started. "I'll trust you. Let me know if you need anything." He patted me on the shoulder and went to inspect one of the empty huts.

They were sorry things. Most were single-roomed shacks, while one had a small second room attached to the main one, which I assumed was a kitchen. That one was also taller than the others and had a loft. I noticed Philip make his way towards it.

"Philip, not that one," I shouted. "Be a gentleman and let Matilda have the big one. You have that one over there." I pointed to one of the smaller huts with a large hole in its roof and side. He nodded, but before he could go into his hut, I beckoned him over.

"What is it, lord?"

I warmed my hands on the fire, which was blazing full now. "How do you feel?"

"I feel like we are not alone," he said.

"I feel it too. Something does not want us here."

"What will we do?"

"Nothing," I responded. "You go have some food and get some sleep. I'll try to contact whatever it is later on." I turned my head to look over my shoulder and saw Matilda standing by the horses, staring at her hands. "Go on, go have a look at your new home," I said to Philip. He got up and went inside his hut while I sat gazing into the flames, trying to feel what lived here.

We were definitely being watched now.

Dughlas came back out from his hut and took some food from the horses. He chatted to Matilda while she showed him some kind of insect she had found. I did not pay attention to what they were saying, but there was something odd about the way they talked to each other. Dughlas was being his usual charismatic self, and Matilda was smiling as they talked, but then I realised what was wrong.

They were only a dozen or so feet away from me, but I could barely hear them.

The air was still, so there was no wind to carry the sound away, but their voices were so muffled, I could not make out what they were saying. I could tell Matilda was laughing, but it sounded as though she was miles away.

"Matilda! Dughlas!" I shouted.

They ignored me, so I yelled again, and this time they turned to me. Their eyes widened, and they froze, suddenly realising that something was wrong. They must have heard my voice was muffled too. I pointed to the huts and shouted for them to go inside, but they did nothing.

"Go. Inside," I yelled.

They heard me that time, and both quickly rushed to the

nearest hut. As they ran, a huge gust blasted through the settlement, causing the reeds to hiss. A deathly howl accompanied the gale, and I was almost certain it was not just the wind that screamed.

Dughlas did not hesitate to get inside the hut, but Matilda stopped at the door and turned. There was fear in her eyes. No, not fear. Terror. Horror. She felt death kiss her cheek.

"Edward," she mouthed.

"Inside!" I said. She backed into the hut — the bigger one with the kitchen and loft — and slammed the door behind her. I could not hear it shut.

I slowly approached Lilly. The horses were growing restless, stamping and snorting. I calmed them and then pulled my sword from Lilly's saddle.

"Who are you?" I yelled into the air. No response. The reeds had stopped hissing. The water was still again. The marsh went to sleep.

I sighed, hooked my sword to my belt, and went to sit by the fire. I stared into it, watching the flames jump and the wood crack. Behind me, I could hear the horses breathing. Sound had returned back to normal, it seemed, but we still had company. The reeds that surrounded us were filled with many creatures, but I felt that one — just one — was watching me intently.

"What was that?"

I turned and saw Osmund standing over me. He had a hard look on his face. A look of anger. Even so, I could see the fear in his eyes. Egil and Cubert stood behind him.

"No idea," I said. I turned back to the fire, but Osmund grabbed me by the arm and hauled me up to face him. I stared at him, dumbfounded.

"No idea? That sort of thing is supposed to be your speciality," said Osmund.

"I will need to investigate first. There is no point in making assumptions."

"Y'know what I think?" Osmund said. I raised my eyebrows, inviting him to speak. "I think you're cursed, Edward. Ever since Brendan died, ill luck has found us. All of us. Our crops have yielded less and less every year, and sickness seems to come over us more often. Now, our homes have been burned and our families slaughtered, and we are being stalked by some...*thing*."

Osmund was beginning to raise his voice, and I could see the hatred in his scowl. Egil and Cubert stood behind him, avoiding my eyes. Osmund had always been forward with me and was always willing to speak his mind, but never like this. I opened my mouth to retort as Dughlas came up behind me.

"What's wrong?" he said. Philip and Matilda were with him, and when Osmund noticed Matilda, he turned his attention away from me and pointed at her.

"That child is what's wrong," Osmund said. He turned back to me, glaring. "She told us why you weren't able to defend our homes. Oh, sure, you were caught in a blizzard. But she also told us that you stayed in Oldford with her on the day you planned to come home. If you had a shred of honour and followed your oaths instead of your prick, you would have arrived home before those bandits attacked."

"And what difference would that have made?" I asked. There was anger in my voice now, too.

Osmund spat. "None, 'cause you're a rubbish fighter. You ever been in a proper battle? During the war, I saw men worth four of you shit themselves on the field."

"But you swore an oath to us," Egil said. "You promised that in exchange for our service, you would do all you can to defend us."

"Has he not done that?" Dughlas said.

"He has, until that night." Osmund and Cubert nodded in agreement, and Egil continued.

"That is why we ask Edward to now release us from our oaths. How can we be expected to defend him, if he cannot defend us?"

"We won't follow a cursed man," Osmund said.

I thought about it for a moment. These three men were some of my best fighters, and aside from Dughlas, they were all I had left. The servants that had survived were no warriors, nor was Matilda. But those men had given their oaths freely, and it would not be right for me to deny them release from those oaths. Oaths are supposed to be maintained with mutual respect, and if they had lost that respect for me, then I was partly to blame. But I needed them.

"No," I said. "You swore those oaths as a bond for life. Only death can release you."

Egil and Cubert nodded, disappointment lining their faces. Oathbreaking was a sinister crime, and they knew that. They may not have liked my decision, but honour demanded they respect it. Osmund, however, shook his head and drew his sword.

"Our deaths or yours?" he said. He rested the point of his heavy blade on my chest. I stared at him, heard Matilda gasp, and Dughlas drew his sword.

"Do it," I said. Osmund looked down at my chest for a moment and then back up to my face. I felt him press the point against me slightly, but then he stepped back three paces and held out his arms.

"Draw your sword," Osmund demanded. I paused and then slowly pulled my sword from its sheath. "I challenge you to a hazeling, Edward Godspeaker."

From the moment Egil requested I release my men from their oaths, I feared this would happen. Osmund was proud—too proud. By now, everyone had gathered round to watch the confrontation, and Osmund would never have been pleased with anyone witnessing me denying him release from his oath.

And so I was challenged to a hazeling.

Hazeling was an ancient custom, outlawed by the usurper Wim nearly a decade ago. Even so, it was still widely practiced, and noblemen did little to enforce its ban. Hazeling was a way for men to settle disputes in a simple manner. It was a test of arms, a duel, traditionally fought within a circle of hazel branches, in which the victor was proven to be in the right. The Gods would guide the blades of the duellists, and they would choose the winner. In many cases, the duel was fought until first blood, but tonight Osmund and I would fight to the death. I could decline Osmund's challenge if I wanted, but it would bring great dishonour to me and mean Osmund would win by default.

I had to accept, and accept I did.

"You're going to die," Dughlas mumbled to me.

There were no hazel trees about, so Egil and Cubert had taken reeds from the swamp and laid them out in a circle nine yards wide, marking the ring in which the duel would take place, and Osmund was pacing within it. Dughlas, Philip, and Matilda stood beside me.

"No, he is not," Matilda snapped.

"Yes, he is, My Lady."

"Dughlas, if you are right, take Matilda back to Henton tomorrow," I said without taking my eyes off Osmund. He glared at me, pacing back and forth.

"What about me?" asked Philip.

"You do whatever Dughlas tells you. Swear to him. You will be his oathman should I die." I glanced at Dughlas, and he nodded.

Matilda grabbed my arm, and I turned to look at her. "You told me you would show me the world," she said. There was fear in her eyes and desperation in her voice. "Let me talk to Osmund. I cannot let you die here."

"The challenge has already been made. Only the Gods can decide who lives or dies now," I said. I tried to remain calm and gave the impression that I would happily accept whatever Fate had in store for me.

But behind that façade, I was afraid. Dughlas was probably right. I would die tonight. Osmund was arguably my best warrior, and I had never seen him bested in a fight. He fought for the king in the Usurper's War and returned from that war with over a dozen scars — scars that attested to his skill and experience. Osmund was faster than me, stronger than me, heavier than me, and taller than me. He knew how to fight, and he knew how to kill. He had every advantage over me.

I sighed, gripped the hilt of my sword, and kissed the blade. I stepped slowly into the ring of reeds, and Osmund stopped pacing.

The hazeling had begun.

5

Prophecy

The air was silent as Osmund and I fought. None watching uttered a word. The animals of the swamp were quiet, and the marsh reeds were still. The only sounds were the blow of steel on wood and steel on steel.

Dughlas was right. I was going to die. I had borrowed his shield so that Osmund and I would be evenly matched, and the moment I stepped into the ring, Osmund swung at me. I held the shield up to block and heard the thud of his sword as it splintered wood. I fell back, but the shield held strong, and before I could get back up, Osmund swung his blade down upon me again. I rolled to the side, Osmund's sword sliced the air, and I blocked once more. I stumbled, but this time I stood my ground. Osmund was panting already.

"I was a far better warrior than you are when I was your age,"

Osmund said. He jabbed at me before I could respond, but I knocked his sword sideways. "I was in my prime when you were still sucking your ma's tit."

Osmund made another swing at me from above, but I caught it with the shield and lunged at his gut. He jumped backwards and grinned. "Oh, that's right," he said. He thrust his blade, I dodged, and he swung. I blocked and heard the shield crack, but it did not break.

"You killed your mother when you crawled from her filthy northern cunt."

My blood boiled, and anger filled my heart. I lost my temper. I yelled and swung at Osmund, but he blocked with his own shield. I swung again, and he blocked. I hacked at his shield, again and again and again as little splinters flew from the wood.

Osmund was laughing as I drove him back. I made another slice at Osmund, but this time he thrust his shield forward and pushed me back. I lost my footing and tumbled backwards.

"Get up!" Dughlas shouted. Osmund stood over me, smiling. I watched him for a moment and saw the fire in his eyes. There was frost on his heavy breath.

"What's wrong?" Osmund said. "Did I hurt your feelings?"

"Oathbreaker," I said. Osmund's smile faded, and his anger returned. He lunged his blade downwards at my chest with a roar, but I rolled again, and in one swift movement I smashed the rim of the shield into Osmund's sword, knocking it out of his hands and sending it sliding across the dirt. I threw myself up and rammed into Osmund's side with the shield, and both of us tumbled to the ground. I climbed to my feet and stood over Osmund, who scrambled for his blade.

I stepped back and let him take it, watching as he struggled to his feet, gasping for air. He moved his mouth to speak, but no words came out. I waited. He bent over, leaning on his sword, then stood up straight and smiled at me.

"You'd be eel-food without that shield," he said. He tossed his shield away and took his blade in both hands. He stood there, inviting me to do the same. I had no choice. In hazeling, the duellists must be evenly matched.

I dropped the shield.

"Edward," Matilda cried. She stepped forward, but Dughlas hissed at her and pulled her back. Osmund and I stood opposite each other for what seemed like forever, each daring the other to strike. One wrong move now, and one of us would die.

Osmund was puffing. He was faster than me, stronger than me, heavier than me, and taller than me. He knew how to fight, and he knew how to kill. He had every advantage over me.

But he was tired.

He may have been a great warrior in his prime — and was even a great warrior now — but I was young, and he was old. I had seen Osmund fight before, but I had never noticed how quickly he tired until I fought him myself. Age had stolen his energy.

Now it was my turn to taunt.

"You tired, old man?" I jeered. I glanced at Egil and Cubert, standing together outside the ring. They were frowning. Osmund said nothing, only stood there. "Do you know why they call the Gifted 'Godspeakers'?"

"You can talk to the Gods," Osmund said.

I nodded and smirked. "Do you know what the god Alcyn told me last night in my dreams?" Fear flashed across Osmund's face. "Alcyn told me that he was waiting for you to join his host of souls. You will ride in the ranks of the dishonourable dead and take your place alongside oathbreakers, murderers, and rapists. He is excited to hunt with such a great warrior."

"You're a liar, boy." Osmund was right, of course, but I could tell he believed what I said.

"Alcyn also told me that you would die by my blade. Why else would I have so willingly accepted this fight?"

Osmund ignored me and instead threw himself forward, swinging his blade with both hands. He was fast but tired. I stepped back and parried his sword downwards with my own.

"I am sorry I could not save your family," I said. He roared and sliced his sword up towards my head. I parried again, steel rang, and the shock rippled through my arms. He stepped back and paused to catch his breath, then lunged at me.

This time I dodged the jab and stepped to his side. Osmund stumbled forward, and I slashed at his leg. The blade cut through cloth and leather. He fell on his face, but I let him climb back to his feet. It was dark, though in the firelight I could see blood dribbling from the gash in his pants.

"I've had worse," he grunted. He lunged forward again — I knew he would — and this time I dodged and struck him on the back of his head with the pommel of my sword. He collapsed to his knees and dropped his sword. I kicked it to the side and held the tip of my blade at the back of his neck.

"You asked me a question before this fight. What was it?" I said. I had won, I knew, and that made me prideful.

Osmund spat. "You don't have the balls to kill me."

"You asked me if your oath bound you to me until my death, or your death. Do you want the answer?"

"Let him live, Edward. You've won," Dughlas said. I glanced at him, and he nodded. Matilda had her hands over her mouth, and she shook her head. I turned back to Osmund, who looked up at the night sky.

"Do you want to live, Osmund?" I asked.

"My life is not yours to give or take."

And those were Osmund's last words. He would not beg and would not accept mercy. He was proud, and so was I. It was pride, not anger or bloodlust, that caused me to drive steel through Osmund's spine. Blood poured over his mail coat and onto the dirt, then Osmund's body fell to the side with a thump.

I looked up at Egil and Cubert. "Anyone else?" I yelled. They stared at me but made no challenge. "Bury him then."

I strode off into the reeds without another word, away from the abandoned village. No one tried to stop me, and no one said a word. I was angry now. Angry that Osmund had forced me to kill him. He was my best fighter, and now I feared the others would leave me too, but they would not challenge me. Not after I had killed Osmund.

I doubted I would see Egil, Cubert, and Dughlas after sun-up the next day.

I do not know when I did, but I fell asleep among the reeds, beneath the silver light of the moon. It was the night of the festival of Middlewinter, I realised, and folk across the kingdom would be celebrating the prelude to Winterlow. Efenled was bright and full that night.

I had originally gone to meditate, but I must have been exhausted, for I woke slumped against a tree stump with an aching back. I was shivering. I then remembered my fight with Osmund and sighed. Osmund was not a bad man. Was I right to kill him?

I looked up at the sky as if seeking answers, but then I had to do a double take. Was my mind playing tricks on me? The sky was pitch-black, starless, and empty. Earlier, the land had been illuminated by the light of a million stars, but now the world appeared to be encased in a big black dome. Whatever had disturbed us before was now playing tricks on me.

I put a hand around the hilt of my sword and went back to the village to check that my companions were all right. The fire was still burning in the pit at the centre of the settlement, but it had died down to a whisper. The circle of reeds was still there, but I could not see Osmund's body, so I assumed the others had buried him. Or thrown him into the marsh. I hoped they had done the former. He died like a warrior and did not deserve to be a meal for whatever creatures lurked in this swamp.

A sense of unease crept up my spine, so I gripped the hilt of my sword and went around each house to make sure everyone was well. I counted the servants, who were all sleeping in one hut together, huddled under their fur cloaks. Egil and Cubert were still there, asleep and snoring, and they shared a hut. Dughlas was there too, and he slept on the floor in a hut with Philip, who had managed to fall asleep in a dirty old bed under some holey rags and a fur coat. Everything was quiet. Peaceful.

But *wrong*.

I checked Matilda's hut and found her awake. She was in the kitchen — if you could call it that. It was nothing more than a tiny room with a stone oven. Matilda had started a fire in that oven and was warming herself. She flinched when I entered but then stood up and rushed over to me.

"Oh, Edward," she said. She threw her arms around me. "I feared I would lose my guide."

"I did not mean for all that. Forgive me," I said.

She pulled away and looked into my eyes. "What happened out there?"

"Osmund decided he was discontent with being my oathman,

so he tried to kill me."

"No, not that. That was not a lady's business. I am talking about before the fight."

"Oh, that. I am sure it's nothing."

She shivered. "I just want to be in a proper house again. Not…this."

"Well, you did ask me to take you from Henton so you could see the world. This is the world," I said. Despite the darkness, she noticed me smile, and that made her grin too, but only for a second before a frown appeared again.

"Will you stay with me tonight?"

"Not yet. I need to make sure that whatever is out there does not wish us harm."

Matilda squeezed my arms. "Take me with you then. Just please, do not leave me here alone."

I thought about it and almost said no, but I admit I wanted her company. "All right, but stay close," I said.

She smiled and then took my arm. I led her back out of the house, where I made a torch out of some materials lying about.

"Hold this," I said, handing the torch to Matilda. She carried it in her right hand and held my arm close with her other. "Just do as I say, okay?"

"Okay," she said. And so we went off into the marsh, away from the village, traipsing through the wet mixture of water and earth.

"What are we looking for?" Matilda whispered.

"A mound. Or a large rock, an odd tree, or something like that. Something that looks out of place," I replied. My head darted left and right as I scanned the landscape for any signs of Otherworldly activity, but it was so dark, I could barely see in front of me. The sky was still empty and black.

"Where are the stars?" Matilda said. I ignored her, and she changed the subject. "I am sorry about your man."

"He was a good man. He was like an uncle. But I suppose Fate did not want our paths to align," I said. The anger had gone now. I was just sad. I had lost my home and many of my people, and tonight I had been forced to kill a friend. What else would I lose?

"I did not know you could fight like that. It was astonishing," she said.

"Admittedly, I owe my skill to my sword, Godwin's sword. It was supposedly forged by an Edin before they left the World many millennia ago, and blessed by the power of their race. It is said to give its wielder the luck of all its past wielders." I chuckled. "Perhaps it isn't true, but I keep it with me always just in case."

Matilda smiled and pulled herself closer to me. "Is it true what you said about Alcyn?"

"No. I just wanted him to do something careless."

"He is with his family now, I suppose."

I nodded, but I doubted that. The souls of oathbreakers did not join the halls of their ancestors — they were cast out and doomed to ride with Alcyn, the god of death. If they were lucky, that is.

And then Matilda screamed. In one swift motion, I pulled away from her and drew my sword. Then I sighed. Matilda was frozen in shock. She had walked into the hanging leaves of a willow tree.

"Just a tree," she said, and then we both laughed. She took my arm again, and we carried on. But we had only walked a few steps when Matilda stopped me. "Wait, look, Edward. There are more."

She held the torch out as far as she could, and its light shimmered off a large pool of water. Matilda was right; there were more willow trees. They appeared to be surrounding the pool, acting like a curtain to conceal it, although I could not see to the other side because in the centre of the pond was a tall mound.

"A barrow," I muttered. "Well done, Matilda."

She smiled, but I could feel her shaking and see the nervousness in her eyes.

"The question is, can we cross over to it?"

"Maybe there is a boat," Matilda suggested.

"I doubt it. Come on, let's walk around this pool and see if we can find somewhere shallow to cross."

But in that moment, Matilda and I stopped in our tracks and stood motionless. For a voice, as if shouted to all the world from the Heavens, boomed loud and deep across the land. It only said one word, but that word filled our hearts with dread.

"No."

Matilda tried to run, but I grabbed her arm. She slipped over and fell to her knee, but I pulled her back up again.

"Who are you?" I shouted. I let go of Matilda to draw my sword, and she just stood there in fear.

"Go away," the voice howled. The branches in the willow trees whispered.

"I come as a friend," I said.

"I have…no friends," the voice called back. I sheathed my sword and held up my hands.

"You do now. My name is Edward. Why do you have no friends?"

"All…are dead. All betrayed me." The voice echoed through the marsh, but I had a feeling only Matilda and I could hear it. It was a woman's voice, deep and menacing, but tormented.

"Is that your barrow over there?" I asked.

"Yes…"

"Who built it?"

"My sons… They feared my wrath."

"Is that why you rest in this marsh?"

"Yes."

"Why have you haunted me and my friends? We seek only rest for the night."

"I wish to warn you, Edward of Winterhome."

I stepped back. How did it know my name? "Warn me of what?"

"Your triumph and your doom. The Immortal King and his…unholy horde shall return for the last time. This is…unavoidable. A chain of events has already been set in motion by a man in black…you know of whom I speak."

"Hakon," I mumbled.

"Who?" Matilda hissed. I ignored her, and the voice continued its warning.

"The Grey Dog will be awoken by you and you alone…child of Winterhome. The man in black is naught but a tool that you shall use…and you are naught but a tool of Fate. This is my warning to you," said the voice. Its harsh, hissing sound sent shivers down my spine.

I glanced back at Matilda. She was frozen, and her knuckles were white as she clutched the torch. "How do you know this?" I asked the voice.

"The dead are allowed truths withheld from the living… The Gods have allowed me to know this, for I was there when Godwin bound the king." I heard the water move but saw nothing. There was something in there watching us.

"You were there? Who are you?"

"I am the queen betrayed… Godwin listened not to my advice, and now his heir shall release the Horde once more. Kneel, Edward, and let me spare your world its fate." The water moved again, louder this time, but the willows went still.

"Matilda," I said. "Give me the torch."

She did as I asked, saying nothing. In the light, I noticed she was deathly pale, and her jaw was clenched. The feeling — that sense of unease — had welled up inside me and grown into one of pure dread. It was neither instinct nor fear giving me this feeling, but my gift.

"Get back to the village. Now," I said.

Without hesitation, she began to run, and after taking only three strides, she slipped and fell forward into the mud, falling onto her hands and knees, and I drew my sword and swung back around to the lake, from whence came a loud splash. The willows hissed again — or at least I thought they did.

But only for a second, because in the torchlight I saw it. An enormous snake had emerged from the water. Its eyes were white, its fangs dripped with venom, and its wet, black scales reflected the flames. It reared its head and hissed, jaw wide open. I froze. It was as tall as me, but that was only the part it had raised off the ground. The rest of its body sat in the mud, and its tail trailed off back into the pond.

I waved my torch at it. "Back, creature," I snarled.

It spat at me and hissed, then it pulled its head back.

"Die…" the voice boomed.

As if on command, the snake lunged at me, and I twisted to avoid it and waved the torch in its direction, but it was too fast. A searing pain shot through me as the snake buried its fangs in my arm, and within seconds my whole body felt as though it was on fire.

My hand went numb, and I dropped the torch, but I raised my other arm and swept down, my sword making contact. I sliced its body from its head in one swift motion, and it fell lifeless into the mud with a loud splash, then slid back into the water. Its head went limp and broke away from the fangs, falling to the ground.

I dropped my sword and tried to pull the fangs free from my arm, but they were stuck deep. I felt no pain, only the intense urge to vomit, but nothing would come up. My mouth was dry, my head heavy, and I felt incredibly dizzy. I looked up and saw the stars had returned, felt a thud, and suddenly my back was soaked with mud. I tried to get back up, but I was too weak. I tried to call out, but my lips were swollen, and my tongue felt like feathers.

I looked down at my arm where the snake had bitten me, and maggots were beginning to eat at the wounds. The world was pulsating, throbbing. A hundred drums beat and beat and beat deep within my ears. The willows danced. The sky spun around me. I heard my name. I heard drums.

I heard my name again.

Matilda. Matilda was there.

I heard drums, I heard my name, and then the world went dark.

I watched myself standing out in the fields. It was winter — my seventh winter. I was out there in the middle of a snowstorm wearing nothing but a pair of woollen trousers. Blood dripped down from my nose and my forehead. I had a hoe in my hands, and I was scraping at the hard, cold soil.

I was trying to turn it over for the next season's harvest, but it was nigh impossible. The snow was falling too heavily, and if I did not dig fast enough, a new layer of the stuff would replace the old. My arms were weak and cold to the bone, but I persisted, determined to turn every inch of soil. I could not go back inside until I had finished, I knew, but the snow beat at my bare back and chest and tore cuts across my face, the blood from which would only freeze within seconds.

Across the field was a small cottage. My house. My childhood home. A man sat inside by the window. He was drinking. He had a long brown beard, a tight face, dark eyes, and short brown hair. He looked like an older version of myself. He was my father, after all.

He watched me work while he sat by the window, near the fire, wrapped in blankets. I watched myself look at him and lean against the hoe. He stood up, and I immediately began digging again.

I shivered uncontrollably, and my teeth chattered. My hair, which fell to my shoulders, was frozen; the sweat had been hardened by the chill wind. I looked to the house. The back door burst open, and a girl ran out from inside. She waved at me but seemed afraid. Her hair and eyes were brown like mine, and she had the same hard jawline. She waved and called my name. "Edward! Edward! Edward!"

I ignored it at first, but she kept shouting. The door was thrown open again, and my father — a big, towering man — appeared in the doorway. He grabbed my sister by the hair, and I watched myself shouting at him to stop. She called my name again, the world went black, then I opened my eyes.

"Edward," Matilda said, shaking me. I looked up at her, confused, and then came to my senses. I was in the hut back in the peat-gatherers' village. The small stone oven had a fire burning inside, providing little heat, and I was lying in the bed in the main room attached to the kitchen. A fur blanket lay over me. I was drenched in sweat but freezing cold. Matilda sat beside me. Her clothes, her hair, and her face were all covered in mud.

"Edith," I mumbled. My arm was throbbing with pain.

Matilda frowned. "Who?"

"My sister," I said. I tried to sit up but felt faint, so I lay back down. "Where is she?"

"I do not know what you are talking about," Matilda said. I rubbed my eyes and groaned.

"She was here. I heard her voice," I muttered.

"Edward," Matilda said, putting a hand on my shoulder. "You passed out by the pond. Do you remember?"

I blinked and looked up at the rutted ceiling. I could not make sense of what had happened.

"We found a barrow in a pond out in the marsh. A voice spoke

to us, and you told me to come back here so I ran, but I fell over
and you started swinging your sword around at nothing. I
thought you had gone mad. Then you screamed, dropped your
sword in the mud, and started clawing at your arm. Then you
blacked out. Do you not remember?" There was a look of real
concern on Matilda's face.

My memories began to come back. I lifted my arm to look at
it, but there were no scars. No blood. Nothing. "But the snake…
What happened?"

"Snake? There was no snake. I ran back here and woke
Dughlas, and then he came, and we carried you back. I started a
fire in the oven and put you in the bed because you were
shivering," she said.

"Thank you, Matilda. I think you saved my life."

I looked at my arm again and rubbed it to make sure my eyes
were not deceiving me. I did not feel the unease I had felt when
we first arrived here, and my head was feeling better, so I sat up.

"You should get some rest," I said.

"But I am covered in mud," she complained.

I chuckled a bit. "I can see that. I don't think you need to
worry about dirtying this bed. We can wash properly once we get
to the castle."

"You are right, I should sleep. I am exhausted."

"As am I. I'll go sleep up in the loft there, and you can have
this bed." I started to stand, but Matilda gripped my arm.

"No," she said. "Please stay with me."

I looked into her eyes and sighed. She seemed afraid, but I knew there was no longer anything to worry about. Whatever had happened when I thought I killed that snake seemed to destroy the evil that haunted this place, at least for a time. But I could not leave Matilda alone and frightened. I nodded, and she smiled.

We both lay on our backs under the covers. There was space between us, and it was a bit awkward, but eventually Matilda fell asleep. I had trouble sleeping, as usual, so I lay staring up at the ceiling as the fire in the oven slowly died and the light dimmed to nothing. Matilda lay beside me, breathing slowly and deeply, at peace. She mumbled and hummed every so often as she slept, and eventually she rolled over and lay on her side, right next to me. I felt her soft breath against my neck, and her hand came to rest on my chest, and not long after that I too went to sleep.

We left the village behind at dawn the next morning. Philip had apparently slept the entire night without trouble, though he complained of a sore back for the rest of the day. Dughlas asked if I was all right, but he had learned not to pry too deeply into the strange things that happened to me.

As I predicted, Egil and Cubert were gone when we woke the next day. They had taken both their horses with them, some food, and the two servant men. The servant girls all stayed behind, either because they did not want to go or because Egil and Cubert considered them to be a burden. I did not ask.

The journey back through the marsh was much easier during the day, since we could see the dry patches and trails. We travelled past the barrow, and in the sunlight it was much less foreboding. The willows, the pond, and the mound were still there, and atop the mound was a tall standing stone I could have sworn was not there the previous night. It looked peaceful now.

I halted by the pond and told the others to go ahead. I was still puzzled about that snake. Was it all a vision? A dream? I scanned the ground for signs of the beast. The mud was churned up, but that was probably just from my struggle. I could see nothing, so I looked back up at the stone to try to make out its carvings.

Queen Aelda the Cruel of Aedonn lies here, the stone read. *This tomb is now her home. May she be cursed for eternity. May she wander this marshland forever, tormented by grief and regret. May she...* They were faded after that, so I could not read the rest.

I had read about Queen Aelda. She ruled these lands before the Unification, and the pages of history had painted her as a cruel, deceitful, and cowardly woman. Supposedly, she tormented her subjects, instituting harsh laws, imprisoning people for the smallest insults, serving her prisoners and slaves as the main course at feasts, and even burning her own husband alive as a sacrifice to Vylan the Defiler, Lord of Thorns.

According to legend, Aelda's three sons avenged their father by gutting Aelda in her sleep and throwing her mangled corpse into the river. But if this standing stone was correct, she was not thrown into the river, but buried in this marsh instead. Aelda's sons must have known how to prevent their mother returning from the dead.

Legend becomes history after Aelda's death. There are no scholarly texts that prove Aelda's cruelty, only songs and poems, but there are many writings surviving that talk of how Aelda's sons divided their mother's kingdom equally between them and the three reigned in relative peace for a time before turning on each other. The older of the three brothers eventually defeated the other two, and then his kingdom was absorbed into Ardonn.

Lord Adalbert, the man who sat in Oldford Castle, is a direct descendant of Aelda's victorious son, but there are rumours that their mighty line will end at Adalbert's death.

It was Lord Adalbert we were on our way to see. When we first left my ruined home days ago, I wanted to seek out Adalbert's hospitality so we would have somewhere to stay until I could afford new land, but after thinking over the words of Queen Aelda's ghost — or whatever that thing was — I became curious about Emrys, the legendary king Hakon told me about in the Black Rose. The Gods only knew why Hakon wished to release Emrys from his prison, but that warning haunted me. I had no desire to release Emrys, so perhaps when the voice spoke of *me* releasing him, she meant that my inaction would allow Hakon to do so.

I was naïve in those days and thought Fate's whims could be avoided.

I decided I should do all in my power to prevent Hakon from releasing Emrys, and the first step to doing that was to discover where Emrys was entombed, if he even existed. The answers to that puzzle might be found in Oldford Castle's library, I thought.

I turned away from the pond and the willows and caught up with my companions. We went onward through snow-covered marsh and came to Oldford's gates. We rode through those crowded streets, and Matilda grew gloomy again. She hated this town.

"I need your help," I said to her while the others were out of earshot.

"Help?"

"Yes. Aside from me, you are the only one among us who can read. When we arrive at the castle, I want you to help me search the library for information on a man called Emrys."

"Emrys," Matilda repeated. She had heard the name before and nodded. "May I ask why?"

"Do not tell the others, but I believe the man who burned my home did so in order to find my sword. I spoke to him that morning in Oldford, when you were unwell, and he told me he needed my master's sword in order to free Emrys from his imprisonment."

"But you had your sword with you. I remember, you showed me in the elf-grove," Matilda said.

"Yes, but I lied to him. His name is Hakon."

"Ah." The look of confusion disappeared from Matilda's face, and I could tell the pieces were falling into place. "So, you wish to find information about Emrys to prevent this Hakon — or if what that voice said was true, yourself — from freeing him?"

"Yes."

"All right, I will try to help," Matilda said. She gave me a warm smile.

We passed under the north gate, and as we had done about a week earlier, we rode through the slums on the outside of the city. The snow was melting in the streets and mixing with mud, piss, and dung, and that foul mixture flowed through the gutters. Beggars came to our horses asking for money or food, and the guards pushed them away. Merchants also approached us, but we had to turn them away ourselves.

I rode beside Philip and gave him a smile. "How are you, Philip?"

"I am well," he said. "Though I miss my family."

"I felt the same when I first left home. It can be hard, but know that you will see them again someday," I said. He smiled, and I ruffled his hair. I could not stop seeing myself in that boy.

At last, we reached the fork in the road. To our left, it went up the steep hill to Oldford Castle, and to our right, the Royal Way ran farther north. We went left and made the slow journey up the hill.

The castle was an impressive beast, surrounded by a steep,

grassy slope on all sides that frequently muddied, except for the west side, which was a cliff face instead of a hill. The hill was high and could only be comfortably ascended by following a narrow, winding path that took seemingly forever to climb. The castle's high, thick stone walls were almost unnecessary due to the steepness of the slope, but they added extra defence. The castle itself was circular, with three towers, one looking out to the northwest, attached to a keep, and two others on either side of the castle's only gate. It was a small but high fortress, and I could recall no army in history that had managed to conquer it. Two dozen men could easily hold off ten thousand for years.

After our horses made the difficult journey uphill, we arrived at the massive iron gate. It was shut, as usual. We found ourselves faced with five bowmen who stood on the ramparts above the gate, their bows all drawn and pointed at us. A spearman stood beside them.

"State your business or leave," the spearman called down. "Failure to do either will result in instant death. The choice is yours."

"We are here to see your lord," I called back.

"Do you have an appointment?" the man shouted.

"No. We are unexpected and uninvited. My homestead has been burned and my lands raided, and my friends and I need a roof to sleep under and some food for our bellies. We also wish to view your lord's library."

"Who are you?"

"My name is Edward, and these are my servants, my apprentice, my oathman, and Lady Matilda of Henton."

"Henton? You there," the man shouted, his voice slightly friendlier now. "I know Earl Harold. Are you his daughter?"

"I am," Matilda called back. The man raised his hand, and the bowmen lowered their bows.

"Very well. I will tell My Lord that he has visitors. But do not expect a warm welcome." The man turned away and hurried off along the ramparts to the keep. The bowmen stared down at us like statues while we waited before the gate.

"I'm glad I stole you from Henton after all," I muttered to Matilda. She just smiled.

Minutes later, there was a loud cranking noise and the gate began to slowly rise. The spearman was behind it, and he gestured for us to enter. We followed him into the castle's main yard.

"Welcome to Oldford Castle, home of Lord Adalbert," he said, taking the reins of our horses. He handed them to a stable boy, who took them away to be fed.

"Thank you. I am eager to see the lord," I replied.

He nodded. "Follow me, please, all of you."

And so the man led us across the yard and into the keep. He pushed the large wooden doors open, and we found ourselves within a small throne room. There were beautifully carved stone columns holding up the high roof on either side of the room, and from the walls hung exquisite tapestries. There were windows, but they were tinted and let in little sunlight due to the high walls that surrounded the place, so the room was mostly illuminated by the sconces attached to the columns and the large firepit in the middle.

Surrounding that firepit were four long tables forming a square. There was a tall dais at the end of the room opposite us, and on that dais sat a grand throne. On that throne was a thin middle-aged man with greying blonde hair, a shaven face, and white, wrinkled skin. He wore a fine cloak and an expensive silk tunic, and on his head he wore an iron diadem with a single ruby embedded in its centre. A spearman stood at the base of each column, staring straight ahead.

"My Lord Adalbert, your guests," our escort said. He bowed, as did the rest of us. Matilda gave a low curtsy.

"Thank you, Karl. You may return to your post," said the man on the throne. He had a croaky voice and coughed every so often.

He nodded at Matilda. "So, you are from Henton. And you… Ah, I know you. Edward, Brendan's apprentice."

I smiled and bowed my head. "I am, My Lord. We met five years ago."

Adalbert leaned back in his seat and grunted. "I remember now. Brendan stayed for several months to solve the business with the well. You befriended my daughter, if I recall correctly."

"That is correct, My Lord."

"I hear Brendan's old house has been destroyed, and you seek my hospitality. Very well, you shall have it. It is always an honour to host a lady and a Godspeaker."

"Thank you, My Lord. We are in your debt."

Adalbert coughed. "Yes, yes. I trust you will stay for Winterlow? You may take advantage of my hospitality for as long as you wish, though in exchange I hope you shall provide the services of your Gift, should I require them."

"Of course," I said.

I bowed, and Adalbert waved his hand. Some servants came and showed us to our rooms, which had already been prepared as if Adalbert were expecting guests. I was led away from the others and down a long, dark hallway into a big bedroom. It had a large red rug on the stone floor and a canopied double bed pushed with its back to the wall. There was a fireplace, with another rug by the hearth, and a small table with two chairs sat beside it. A draught board was set up on the table. By the fire was a large wooden tub, already filled with water. Bookshelves lined the walls, and close to the bed was a large cupboard and a set of drawers.

The servant who had escorted me curtsied as we entered the room. "His Lordship has told me that you are welcome to his hospitality indefinitely, should you wish it, lord," she said. "His Lordship has said that you should bathe, lord, and you have a fresh change of clothes in the wardrobe. Your current clothes will be cleaned. This will be your room for the duration of your stay." She bowed her head, and I thanked her. She left the room, and I began to undress. I was aching for a wash.

I threw my filthy clothes on the floor at the bottom of the bed and hopped into the tub. The water was hot, but not too hot, and I slid down into it and sighed. I pulled my head underwater, then back out again, and tipped it back. Closing my eyes, I rested my head against the edge of the tub, enjoying the warm embrace of this water. I always bathed in cold water at home, so it was nice to enjoy the comfort of a warm bath whenever I stayed in the home of a nobleman.

I let my mind wander as I sat in the bath. I thought about my home, which was now lost to me, and my oathmen, who were all dead or gone — aside from Dughlas, of course. I thought about Hakon and Emrys. Why had Hakon torched my home? Did he do it out of spite?

I wondered if Emrys even existed at all. If he did not, it would all have been for nothing.

But if he did, then the consequences, were Hakon to release him, would be far worse. If the legends were true, Emrys would devastate Ardonn until he was finally defeated by King Stephan's army. There were rumours that folk were arming themselves for when the fragile peace within Ardonn inevitably broke, but none would be prepared for the war Emrys would bring.

I needed to stop Hakon. But I was a fool. I thought I could escape the fate that Aelda's ghost had warned me about.

Little did I know I was walking right into it.

6

Blood

Lord Adalbert's library was underwhelming. I admit I expected something grander, but now I had my doubts about finding any information at all about Emrys. It was tidy, at least. The door looked like it had been fitted only a few months before, the stone floor had recently been polished, and the rugs and curtains were of high quality. The servant girl from before escorted me to the library not long after I had settled in, and I had been here searching for the last hour.

"I apologise that our library is…somewhat small. I do hope you have not come all this way for nothing," a woman said from behind me.

She had taken me off guard as I browsed one of the shelves, and I turned to see a young noblewoman watching me. She was tall — almost as tall as me — and slender. She wore a deep blue and white dress with flowing skirts, which tightened around the torso. Pearls were strung around her neck, and her curly blonde hair was tied into two thick braids, which fell past her shoulders and down her back. Her face was pointed, with a sharp chin, long nose, and a mouth that appeared too small for her face. Her skin was incredibly white, and that whiteness only emphasised her bright blue eyes, which were round and large and seemed to pop right out of their sockets. She had an odd look about her, but she was an unconventional beauty. I bowed to her.

"My Lady," I said, for I was addressing Ecwyn, Lord Adalbert's beloved daughter.

"It is good to see you again, Edward. How long has it been? Four years?" She approached and held out her hand for me to kiss. She had about half a dozen rings on her fingers.

I put her hand in mine and lifted it to my lips. "Five years, Lady Ecwyn," I replied.

She smiled and nodded. "Why have you not visited? I was under the impression we were friends." She came to stand beside me and pretended to look at the bookshelves.

"My master Brendan died not long after my last visit, and since then I have been busy," I said.

"A pity."

"You could always have visited me. You know where my home is…was."

"Yes, but I have heard it smells like peasant." She turned to me and smiled, but that smile became a frown when she saw the sorrow in my eyes. "Was?"

"My home has been destroyed, My Lady."

"By whom?"

"Bandits," I lied.

Ecwyn touched my cheek then took both my hands in hers. "I am sorry to hear that, Edward. Truly. Father told me you were here, but he neglected to tell me why. I do wish you were visiting on happier terms."

"As do I, My Lady."

Ecwyn nodded and made her way across the room. I followed. "Perhaps I should have invented a ghost so that you would have reason to come here. Anyway, what need have you of our library?" Ecwyn ran her fingers along a row of books.

"I seek information about the old King Emrys," I said.

"Why?"

"I want to kill him."

Ecwyn laughed. "Edward, my dear old friend, you have a very interesting vocation." She turned to face the books for a few moments before pulling one from the shelf. "Here. This one contains poems from the pre-Unification era. I used to read it as a child, but now they are all up here." She tapped the side of her head and then handed me the book. It was dusty, with a plain leather cover and a few scorch marks, but it was intact.

"Thank you, Lady Ecwyn," I said. She nodded and glided to another set of shelves.

"A good friend of mine, the girl who served you here, seems to be quite fond of you," Ecwyn said, scanning the shelves.

"Why? We barely spoke."

"One look at you, Edward, is enough to make any lady swoon. But I know your reputation, and I pray for your own sake you do not take that girl into your bed." She pulled a book from the shelf, held it under her arm, then continued searching.

"I cannot make any promises," I said.

Ecwyn sighed and then turned to me. "Let me tell you a secret. My father trains all his servants to be spies. They spy on the guests, the guards, and even his own oathmen. They gather information and then pass them on to His Lordship. When my father is satisfied with their talents, he sends them to Oldford to spy on the merchants."

"That seems…"

"Excessive? Paranoid? I agree," she said. "My father believes that the nobility and the merchantry are at war, and thus he is constantly on guard. He thinks that the merchants are spying on him and plotting to overthrow him, so he hides in his castle and gathers intelligence as if they will attack at any moment. Gods bless him."

Ecwyn turned back to the shelves and reached for a book, but her arm was a hand too short. She pointed, I pulled it down, then she handed me the other book. "Those contain histories of the kings around Emrys's time, including Emrys himself. They may be helpful."

"Thank you, My Lady," I said. "I will read these."

"Of course. If you have further questions after reading those, do come visit me in my quarters. I know much about the past, and it would be nice to spend some time together and rekindle our friendship," Ecwyn said. She held out her hand, I kissed it, and watched as she left the room. She turned in the doorway, gave me one last smile, and then was gone.

I examined the books she had given me. They were old. Very old. I had expected to find nothing useful here, but it seemed the few books Adalbert did have were histories. Just as I was about to leave for my own room, Matilda entered the library, and she immediately screwed up her face.

"This is the library?" she said.

I laughed. "The Lords of Oldford must have had little interest in assembling a collection. I have some books that might help us. Do you prefer poems, or histories?"

"Poems, of course," she said. Matilda, like me, had been given some new clothes by Adalbert and was now wearing a modest brown woollen dress. It had little sailboats sewn into the hem with a slightly darker brown wool.

"Here you go, then. Read this, and see if you can find anything useful," I said.

Matilda opened the book. "Are these about Emrys?"

"Some of them."

"I will let you know if I find anything."

"I see Adalbert has given you some new clothes. That dress looks good on you, My Lady." I gave Matilda a smile, and she only blushed. "Take care with what you say around those servants, by the way. They spy for the lord."

"How rude."

"Lord Adalbert is holding a small feast for us this evening," I said.

"For all of us?"

"No, just you and me. Shall we get started on these books beforehand?"

Matilda nodded, and the two of us went to our separate rooms to begin reading. Light still streamed in through the windows in my quarters, but it was cold, so I sat by the fire and opened one of the books.

The text was ancient. I could barely make sense of the words on the page, and the archaic language did not make it any easier. I wondered how Matilda would fare with her tome. I tried to find the sections regarding Emrys, sifting through many tales of his ancestors — all interesting — until I eventually found writings about the legendary king.

As I expected, not much was helpful. I wanted to find where Emrys was locked away and the nature of his imprisonment. I also hoped to find clues as to where he went during the hundred-year gaps between his military campaigns, though I expected to find nothing but speculation. All the information in these books told of his deeds during his reign, and there was nothing about him after his disappearance. These tales told of how he had gone into the hills one day and never returned, and every story of

Emrys in these books ended in a similar way.

The second book was much more helpful. It had new entries towards the end regarding the struggle between Godwin and Emrys, and there was a piece of information that I found useful. A line in the legend told of how King Carol the Great, Godwin, and Emrys all met atop a mountain and fought a battle lasting nine days, and realising that Emrys could not be defeated, Godwin outsmarted Emrys and led him into the mountain. Before Emrys could realise he had been tricked, he was sealed inside by Godwin's magic. Was that why Hakon needed my sword?

There was also another interesting line. After Emrys was defeated, this chronicler tells of how Godwin and Carol "went back south" to the Capital. So, this mountain in which Emrys was sealed stood somewhere north of the capital. I was interrupted by a knock at my door.

"Yes?" I called.

"My Lord wishes to invite you to supper," the servant girl called. I had lost track of time, and evening was already upon us.

"Oh. Give me a few moments," I said. I searched the large wardrobe for some more suitable clothes and changed into them. They were nothing too fancy, but the fabric was of an incredibly high quality, likely imported from the south.

I greeted the girl outside my door, and she escorted me through the keep to a small, private dining hall. Tapestries and banners hung from the walls, and a small fireplace sat at one end of the room. A table large enough for no more than a dozen people sat on a fine red rug in the room's centre. Matilda and Ecwyn were already seated and were chatting when I came in. I took a seat opposite them. Ecwyn greeted me before scolding me for failing to visit her.

"I was too engrossed in the books you gave me, My Lady," I explained. Ecwyn tutted. "Did you find anything useful, Matilda?"

"The poems said something about Emrys being sealed in a mountain somewhere to the north, with Alcyn's aid," she said. I nodded.

"Matilda explained to me that you wanted to find out where Emrys was imprisoned," Ecwyn said. "If you had only come to my room, Edward, you could have saved yourself a lot of reading."

"Do you know where he is?" I asked.

"Where who is?" Adalbert said. The Lord of Oldford took a seat at the head of the table and tapped three times. Servants began to enter the room with plates of food and bottles of wine.

"Have you heard the legend of King Emrys, My Lord?" I asked.

Adalbert coughed. "I have. Please, help yourself to the food."

We all began to fill out plates, and I poured an aromatic white wine into my goblet. I opened my mouth to speak, but Ecwyn interrupted me.

"Edward is seeking his burial place, Da. He is going to finish what Godwin could not," she said.

Adalbert raised an eyebrow and then shrugged. "Emrys is a legend. You would do well not to chase legends." He tucked into the meat on his plate.

"I make a living chasing legends, My Lord," I said.

Adalbert grunted.

"And I know where you can find him," said Ecwyn.

"How do you know that, my dear?" Adalbert asked.

"Since you do not allow me to leave this castle, Father, and since you will not have me married, even though I am seeing my eighteenth winter, I spend my time reading." She popped a piece of carrot into her mouth, and Adalbert's jaw clenched.

"We will not start this in front of our guests, Daughter. You are too young to remember when our castle was besieged by Edwin's men because I refused to pick a side in his damned war, and thus you are ignorant of the horrors of the world beyond these walls." Adalbert then smiled at me. "Please, enjoy your meal."

"Thank you, My Lord," I said.

"I know what the siege was like, Da. I am forced to relive it each day," said Ecwyn.

"Ecwyn!" said Adalbert. He went into a fit of coughing before he could scold his daughter further, then downed his cup. We sat for a few moments in silence.

"Lady Ecwyn," I eventually said. "You know where Emrys is?"

"Well, no," she said. "But I do know how you can find him. There is a man — his name is Ward — who used to be the Godspeaker for King Edwin before he was usurped. He supposedly died during the siege of the Capital in 1109, but there are rumours that he escaped and lives as an outlaw."

"And how would that be helpful?" Adalbert asked.

"It is a lead, Da. The Royal Godspeakers were said to know everything about the deeds of their predecessors. If you can find this Ward, Edward, he may be able to point you to the location of Emrys."

"Thank you, Lady Ecwyn," I said.

I had heard of Ward, but I had not heard the rumours that he survived. The siege of the Capital was a bloody affair, and after the usurper Wim defeated the Capital's defenders, he put them all to the sword, along with anyone else who supported or conspired with King Edwin. The Royal Godspeaker, Ward, was definitely in the Capital while it was besieged, but if he escaped then he might still be alive.

And Ecwyn was right. If I could find Ward, I could possibly find Emrys. The Royal Godspeakers are said to have held many secrets that only they and the king know, and the truth about Emrys could have been one of those secrets. It was not much to go by, but it could be my best lead.

"Where will you begin your search?" Adalbert asked.

I thought about it for a moment. "The Capital. If Ward did escape, his trail will start there."

"Yes, if anyone can discover the truth about the last Royal Godspeaker, it is Edward," Ecwyn said.

"Very well," Adalbert said. "I will provide you with provisions for your journey north when you decide to leave. Now, Matilda, is it? Tell me about Henton. It has been a while since Earl Harold has visited me."

And so Matilda told Adalbert of Henton and her father. Adalbert reminded Matilda and I that we were welcome to stay for as long as we liked. I thanked him and said that I would stay for Winterlow but that it would be best if I left as soon as I could, though I did not tell him about Hakon. I asked that he take in my servants as his own, because they would be a burden on the road north. He accepted.

After the meal, we all wished each other goodnight and headed to our rooms. Matilda told me she had her quarters in the opposite wing of the keep to where I was staying, at the top of one of the towers, and she said I could visit her there if I needed help finding information about Emrys.

I bid her goodnight, and once I arrived at my room, I found the servant girl from before waiting for me. She sat on my bed in nothing but her shift, with her hair down. She had obviously bathed while I was eating.

"Did you have a good meal, lord?" she asked.

I closed the door behind me. "Yes," I said. "What have you been doing in here?"

"Making myself ready."

"What is your name?"

"Eida, lord."

"A pretty name."

Eida smiled. "Thank you, lord. Will you join me?"

And so I went to join Adalbert's spy on the bed. We slept little that night.

Winterlow is the most important time of the year for the people of Ardonn. It is a tradition that reenacts the formation and eventual end of the world, and it reminds us of the cycles of death and rebirth. Of creation and destruction. Winterlow is the name we give to the final month of the year, when the days are coldest and the nights longest, before the arrival of spring and a new dawn.

Sacrifices are made and feasts are had on each of the nights of Winterlow, and peasants, warriors, and priests all come together and forsake their differences to celebrate the turning of the year. We make prayers, give offerings to our ancestors, and placate the god Alcyn so that we may avoid the wrath of his hunting horde, and on the final night of the month, a horse or a cow is given to ensure that we may see the sun once more.

The Last Night's feast is always the greatest. The special Winterlow mead is rolled out and everyone gets roaring drunk and stays up until sunrise the next day, when we all shout at the sky and pour our drinks in honour of the god Hefencyn and his consort Morenlea. The new year begins that day, since from then on the days get warmer and longer and the worst of winter has passed. It is great fun.

Adalbert's servants began preparing for Winterlow shortly after my companions and I arrived, though the lord himself took little interest in the arrangements. What he did in his spare time I did not know, but Ecwyn took charge of the preparations and made sure everything was running smoothly.

I told my servants that they would work for Adalbert now, at least until I could rebuild my home, and while disappointed, they did not protest. They helped with the Winterlow decorations, and Matilda and I helped where we could, but I spent most of my time with her in the library looking for information about Emrys or Ward, the last Royal Godspeaker.

Ecwyn would often visit us in her spare time, and she would sometimes even help us with our search. When she did, however, she and Matilda would spend more time gossiping than reading.

"Ecwyn, did you know that according to this lawbook, the very first edict of King Wim after his coronation was to outlaw slavery?" said Matilda on one such day.

"Yes, I remember that. Many were not pleased," said Ecwyn.

"Why would the new king make a law that would upset so many in his kingdom?"

"Ah, well there are whispers that Wim was in love with a slave girl from the south," Ecwyn said. "The late King Edwin supposedly violated her, and so Wim vowed to purge slavery from Ardonn by whatever means necessary."

"They are rumours, nothing more," I interrupted.

Those rumours were, in fact, very true.

Ecwyn and Matilda got along quite well. They became good friends, and Matilda was happy in those two weeks before Winterlow.

I also allowed Dughlas to teach Matilda how to fight. Matilda watched Adalbert's warriors training in the yard with Dughlas some days and decided she wanted to learn too, Gods only know why. Initially I forbade it, but since Matilda had sworn no oath to me, I could not stop her from doing as she wished, although I could stop Dughlas from aiding her.

Eventually, though, I saw that there was probably no harm in it. Women should not fight, but these were strange times, and I had come to learn that strange things were happening every day somewhere in the world. I had Dughlas teach Philip how to fight every morning and every afternoon, and Matilda sometimes joined in with those training sessions. She was terrible, of course, but everyone is at first, and she learned fast.

When I found the time, I would walk with Philip through the castle and the forest nearby, or take him to the castle's library. I spent time teaching him about the Gods and the spirits that come into our world from the Otherworld, and the role those with the Gift must play in this world. I also taught him how to read.

Matilda wanted to search for insects in the woods, which I allowed as long as she stayed within a hundred feet of the castle and did not enter any sacred spaces. She collected so many critters that she had to clear out an entire bookshelf in her quarters to make room for all her new jars. Ecwyn even encouraged her interest by having a shipment of the materials Matilda needed to preserve the insects sent from Oldford.

It was not long before Winterlow came around. The first day of the season began like any other, but as evening drew near, Adalbert's servants began making preparations for the rituals and the feast. As the sun set, Adalbert's guests came into the keep with food as their contribution to the night's meal. The guests were mostly churls from the homesteads near Oldford, but there were some wealthy individuals from within Oldford itself. I suppose Adalbert did have some allies within the town.

I watched from the library window as the guests all crossed the castle's courtyard and entered the main hall, despite the cold wind and snow that battered them. A storm was coming.

I turned to hear a knock at the library door. "Who is it?"

"It is me," Matilda said. She was wearing a beautifully modest green woollen dress with long, loose sleeves. It was fitted tight around the torso, but at her waist the skirts puffed out.

"You look lovely," I said.

She blushed and made a curtsy. "It is Ecwyn's, but she let me borrow it." She wandered over to a pile of books I had on the desk in front of me and began tracing the spines with her finger, her sleeves hanging low from her wrists.

"Careful with those. Many of them are rare," I said.

She pulled her hand away. "And very old, by the looks of them." She turned to me and grinned. She did indeed look very beautiful, and despite the cold, a touch of warmth radiated from her face.

"Ecwyn found them in the cellar, locked away in some old chests. They are ancient compared with the ones kept in this library," I said.

Matilda looked fascinated. "I would like to have a read of them sometime. Anyway, Lady Ecwyn sent me to inform you that the celebrations are about to begin, so you should come down to the main hall now."

I nodded, packed up what I was doing, then headed through the castle to the feasting hall. It was crowded when we arrived, but two seats at the high table upon the dais had been reserved for Matilda and me. My seat was at the right of Adalbert, and that was significant. Before the Usurper's War, the Royal Godspeaker would sit in a seat to the right of the king's throne. Nowadays, the First Minister would sit to the right of the king, or on some occasions, his high priest. Adalbert's high priest was seated to my right.

Ecwyn was seated to the left of Adalbert's chair, which was traditionally the location of a lord's heir. This, like my positioning, was likely a display to the powerful men who found a place at Adalbert's tables.

Besides that on the dais, Adalbert's hall had four tables for the ordinary guests. These were already packed, and I spotted

Dughlas and Philip sitting down there talking with the other guests. Evergreen branches, wreaths, and even small trees decorated the walls and rafters, and the large firepit was raging. Matilda and I took our seats, with her sitting beside Ecwyn. Adalbert had not yet arrived, but Ecwyn was already seated, and we greeted each other.

Once all the guests had filled the hall, Adalbert finally made his appearance. He walked slowly to his high seat at the centre of the high table, sat down, and coughed. The lord glanced at me. "I see my daughter has put you in Lodulf's seat," Adalbert said, his voice hushed. Ecwyn looked over at me from the other side of her father and winked.

"Yes, My Lord," I said.

Adalbert nodded and raised his hand for silence. He waited for everyone to settle. "Welcome, everyone," he said. There were some mutters of thanks from around the hall. "I am glad that despite the weather tonight, you could all join me and my household for our annual Winterlow feast. There will be sacrifices, prayers, and feasting, as is custom. My temporary Godspeaker will now speak."

There was little charisma in the way he talked, and I noticed him suppress a cough once he finished speaking. I stood, unsure of what to say, since I had not known I would be doing this, and looked down on the guests staring up at me.

"Greetings all," I began. "As you know, Winterlow is a time for prayer, reflection, and worship. It is a time where we honour

our ancestors and Alcyn, the god of death and winter. We placate the spirits of the Otherworld as they leak into our world in this dark time. But let us not forget that Winterlow is a time for celebration! A time when we can remind the Gods that once again we have conquered the dying of the year and shall again see the birth of a new one. For many, winter brings hardship, and although we remember those who have died, we also celebrate those who still live. So, I bid you all enjoy the coming month and indulge in the festivities that Oldford has to offer."

There were some cheers from the audience, and many of the guests thumped the tables in agreement. I sat back down, and Lodulf the priest leaned over to me. "Good speech," he said. I thanked him. Lodulf was an old man. He had seen around sixty winters, was balding, but he had a thick silver beard and a mind full of wisdom. In the weeks I spent in Oldford I had come to like him.

Lodulf asked me how my search for Emrys was going, and I admitted I had found little information about the Immortal King. I told him that finding Ward would probably be the best lead, but I did not know how I would find him even if he still lived.

"My advice would be to seek those who knew him. People who were close to him," Lodulf said. I agreed that would probably be a good start. It seemed my quest would indeed take me to the Capital. "Ward would have had many friends in the Capital, though I advise caution, for he would have had twice as many enemies," Lodulf said.

I nodded and stared into the crowd. Lodulf knew that I sought
to prevent Emrys from being released, and the deeper I delved
into the lore regarding Emrys, the more my youthful hubris made
me believe I could — *should* — destroy Emrys forever and
prevent Aelda's prophecy from befalling. Finishing what
Godwin could not would bring me immense fame. My glory
would be immortalised in history and legend.

And the more I thought about it, the more it became clear that
Ward, if he lived, would be my best lead.

The guests talked and laughed for a little while as I sat deep in
thought, and breads, cheeses, and wines were brought to the
tables for the guests to pick at before the main feast following
the sacrifice. I spoke with Adalbert and Lodulf now and then,
and noticed Ecwyn eavesdropping on us as she watched the
guests.

Eventually, the doors at the front of the hall were pushed open,
and two of Adalbert's men hurried in, huddled in furs. They
closed the doors behind them, but not before a strong gust of
snow and wind blew through, its howl echoing throughout the
hall.

Alcyn, the Lord of Winterlow, had come to visit, and with him
rode his horde of dead men. They were here to receive our
sacrifice.

We all gathered in the woods behind the castle. A path lined with torches led us to a clearing, at the centre of which stood an enormous, leafless ash tree. A face had been crudely carved into the tree, and two torches stood on stakes at either side of it.

Adalbert led the procession to the clearing and was flanked by me and Lodulf. Ecwyn and Matilda followed, and behind them were the rest of the guests and Adalbert's warriors, servants, and courtiers. The slow, rhythmic beat of drums followed the procession while a woman sung a sombre tune. I could feel the presence of the Gods all around us.

Everybody crowded around the tree, at the edges of the clearing. All were hooded, for this was a sacred space, and despite the icy wind and snow battering them, they stood emotionless. Dark clouds rolled and tumbled above us, and lightning flashed, illuminating the sky and giving the appearance of great monsters battling above us, though oddly it neither rained nor snowed. The Gods were celebrating.

At the base of the tree was a stone slab — an altar — and beside that sat a large wooden bowl. The guests watched Adalbert intently as he knelt before the altar and called upon the Gods to look down on us. I felt them watching. Adalbert called out his prayers and asked that Alcyn spare us his wrath this winter. A crack of lightning split the sky and was followed by a deep grumble. Lodulf began to chant a hymn to the Gods while the drums rumbled and the woman from the procession hummed a wordless song.

And that was when it was brought before the tree. A pig,

traditionally the first sacrifice of Winterlow. A rope had been tied around its belly, and it was led by one of Adalbert's men into the clearing and up to the altar, unaware of its fate. The man came and stood beside Adalbert, keeping the pig close on its leash. It trembled and looked to be crying. Or perhaps that was just the snow that fell on its face.

I emerged from the crowd and approached the man with the pig. He handed me the leash, and I led the pig over to the stone slab by the tree. The singing woman handed me a bowl of water, with which I washed my hands and face. She bowed when I had finished.

Two more of Adalbert's men came forward, and the four of us lifted the pig onto the altar. It wriggled and squealed, but we managed to hold it in place atop the slab. The pig writhed and screamed. It kicked and swung its head, its eyes now wide with fear. Did it know its fate, or was this merely instinct? I gestured for another of Adalbert's men to help us hold it down.

I made the next step quick. I picked up the sacred blade and held it against the squealing animal's throat, and in one swift motion I brought it up and then there was nothing but the sound of howling wind and creaking trees. Adalbert declared his offering to Alcyn, and that was met with another flash of lightning and a clap of thunder.

I watched dark red blood flow swiftly from the beast's open throat and into the bowl. The Gods were pleased. I could feel it, and I am sure my guests could too, for many bowed their heads as a show of humility. Lodulf's hymn grew louder with the drums. The pig had stopped jerking, and what had been a gush became a trickle of blood.

Adalbert's men picked up the carcass and took it away. I then placed the blade down beside the altar, picked up the bowl now full of blood, and handed it to Adalbert. He placed the bowl on the altar then prostrated himself before the tree.

"You may now place your offerings on the altar," I said, turning to face the crowd. I gestured towards the great stone slab. and the guests began to place personal gifts of food and drink for their ancestors and the god Alcyn, while Lodulf engaged in a fierce singing match with the growling clouds.

I caught Matilda watching me from the crowd. She stared with a face betraying little emotion, deep in thought, though about what I could not tell. I knelt beside the altar, my eyes still locked with Matilda's. Neither of us could turn away. My heart was racing. Was it the Gods doing that, or something else? Ecwyn nudged Matilda, and she looked away, then I bowed my head and whispered quiet prayers to my ancestors.

I was the last to leave the clearing that night. Everyone else headed back to the castle after leaving their offerings, followed by Ecwyn, Matilda, and Adalbert, then Lodulf returned with the singing woman, who I learned later that night was Lodulf's concubine. But it was I who stayed in the cold the longest.

It seemed as if the feast had been going on for hours when I finally returned to the keep. Most of the men were already drunk, and people were digging into the various fruits and vegetables, fish, breads, and meats served by Adalbert. The guests shouted insults at each other, told jokes and tales, and boasted of their deeds.

I joined the others back up at the high table and filled my plate, but I did not drink, for I needed to have a clear head this night. Once I went to bed, I would dream and receive visions from the Gods. I needed to keep a clear head to interpret them and ensure they were not distorted. That was another aspect of my gift. The Gods could speak to anyone they chose, but only a few could understand them. Oneiromancy was an art all Godspeakers knew.

The pig we sacrificed was brought inside and cooked, and about midway through the feast it was served to the guests and we all took a piece. Adalbert had the first serving, of course, followed by Ecwyn.

Ecwyn also carried the sacred cup of mead around the hall, passing it to each of Adalbert's oathmen in turn along with any gifts Adalbert wished to give them. Passing of the cup was a rite typically reserved for the wife of a lord, but since Ecwyn's mother had died many years ago, that role was filled by Ecwyn herself.

After finishing my slice of roast pig, I went out to the castle wall for some air, looking out over the town. Lanterns hung from the walls, and a great bonfire roared in the square outside Oldford's town hall. The city folk would be celebrating Winterlow in their own way.

"They will be singing down there," Lodulf said. I turned to see the priest standing behind me. He wore his black wool and fur robes, as befits a priest during Winterlow. "If it were not for this storm, we would be able to hear them."

I nodded and looked back out over Oldford. "That bonfire should be outside the temple."

"Yes, but this is the way of the world now. We must adapt," Lodulf said. He came to stand beside me.

"Must we?"

We stared at each other for a second, and Lodulf chuckled. "You are young, Edward. I was like you were once. But now…"

"You think me foolish for loving the old ways."

"No, no," Lodulf laughed. "I think you idealistic. You have the fire of youth, but age will humble you, as it humbles all."

"Perhaps."

"When I was around your age, still a student at the temple down there, my friends and I were arrested for tossing manure at the mayor's house. We bought it from a hog farmer just outside town," Lodulf said. He chuckled. "The Aed had flooded that year, and the high priest petitioned for the mayor to fund a great sacrifice to Brim. Do you know what he did instead?"

"This is ancient history to me."

Lodulf laughed again. "He spent the town's budget buying a

166

country estate for his wife because the flood dirtied the street at her doorstep."

"What is the point of this story, Your Worship?"

"You are angry and prideful, like I was back then. You think you can save the world. I feel that your efforts to defeat Emrys will do little more to prevent this kingdom's destruction than the shit I threw at the mayor's house did to prevent him being elected for another term. Keep the old ways firm in your heart, Edward, but let the world run its course."

I had nothing to say. I only nodded and turned back to watch the bonfire in Oldford.

Lodulf sighed. "War is brewing, Godspeaker. Can you feel it too? Lords have been collecting oaths. For 'personal defence,' they say. The forges in the Capital have expanded, and the smiths are making more than nails and horseshoes. Tolls and taxes are increasing. The past eight years of peace have only been the interlude. A brief spot of calm before the storm resumes."

I opened my mouth to speak, but before I could, Matilda appeared behind us. She curtsied to Lodulf, and he bowed. "I must return to the feast," he said. "Do not stay out here long, you two. It is cold, and I fear it may snow soon."

I bid Lodulf farewell and greeted Matilda with a smile. "Grown tired of feasting, My Lady?"

Matilda smirked. "No. I just missed you."

"You missed me?"

"I mean I missed your tales and your jokes," she said. Her speech seemed a little slurred. She shivered.

"Are you cold?" I asked.

"Very." I removed my cloak and wrapped it around her shoulders, and she hugged herself beneath it while staring out at the town beside me. "What is it like? Killing an animal like that."

I thought for a moment, not expecting the question. "You feel absolute power," I said. "But it is also a humbling feeling. Your heart stops for a second as the blade scrapes along bone and you feel the beast's life force leaving its body. I do not enjoy it."

"Is it like killing a man?"

"No, but I will not speak of that. Forgive me, but I'd rather not be reminded of Osmund."

Matilda nodded and stared at the great fire in the town square. "Did your master teach you that? Sacrificing a pig?"

"Yes," I said.

"Was he a good man?"

"He made me into everything I am now. I'll let you decide whether that makes him a good man or not."

Matilda smiled. "I think he was a good man. What was his name again?"

"Brendan."

"Brendan." She repeated the name as if locking it into her memory. She watched the town for a few minutes and seemed to be building up the courage for something. It was the same look I had seen on the faces of men preparing to fight for the first time.

"Edward, I—" Matilda began, but before she could say anything more, she threw herself forward and emptied her dinner over the castle wall.

I shook my head and then pulled her hair back away from her face. I waited for her to finish. "Silly girl," I said.

"The pig was raw," she said. She leaned over the wall for another round.

Once Matilda had thrown up every last bit of food she had eaten and every drop of mead she had drunk, I took her to her room and helped her into bed. I went to find her a bucket, but when I returned she was out cold.

I left Matilda in bed and returned to the feast, joining in on the song and laughter and the tales and boasts. I had a good night, and as it grew late and the guests began to retire, I too went to bed.

Once alone in my quarters, I made myself comfortable in bed and shut my eyes. Slowly, I drifted off to sleep and received a series of dreams from the Gods.

The first dream began with an image of a mountain, and beneath that mountain was a hall. A great, vast hall built by a civilisation long gone. Within that hall stood three thousand horses and three thousand warriors. One of those warriors stepped forward. A grey dog followed him. He was their leader

— I do not know how I knew, but I just did, as is the way with dreams. He shook my hand, and the dream changed.

It was followed by a wild storm, raging and roaring, with fire raining down from the sky and thunder rumbling ceaselessly. Below the rolling clouds was a city, and that city was burning. I did not recognise it, but it had a tall bell tower in the centre that stood out among the rest of the buildings. The man from the first dream emerged from the city with his grey dog, smiled at me, and shook my hand again.

The dream changed, and now I was shown a grand seat. A throne. I recognised it immediately, for it was the royal throne in Ardonn's capital city. King Stephan's throne. On that throne sat a dead man, his flesh shrivelled and rotted away so that only his wrinkled skin, bones, and hair were left. He wore a fine suit of mail, and atop his head was a golden crown.

A young woman stood beside the throne wearing nothing but a loose coat of mail. Her legs and feet were bare, she was pale and had messy black hair. Blood dripped from her thin fingers and poured from her nose, her open mouth, and her empty eye sockets. She whispered my name, and at once I recognised her voice.

It was Matilda.

The man with the dog approached me from behind. I turned, and he was frowning this time. His dog came and stood at my feet, and the man shook my hand. He disappeared, and I awoke to the sound of birdsong. Light filtered through the window in my room.

I stared up at the ceiling, wondering what it had all meant. These dreams rarely made sense until the events they depict come to pass. But were they showing me the future or showing me what I must do? Perhaps both. Whatever the Gods wished to tell me, one thing was certain: I needed to find the man with the dog. Whoever he was, our fates had clearly been intertwined. I was almost certain he was related to King Emrys, but how?

I sought out Dughlas that morning. Until now I had kept our purpose from him, letting him believe we were only here until I could repair my home, but I decided now was the time to reveal the truth and beg his advice.

I found him in the castle courtyard. The storm from the night before had passed, but a thick layer of snow caked the ground. Dughlas was sparring with Philip using wooden swords, but Philip was almost knee-deep in the snow and could not stop himself from tripping. A few of Adalbert's men laughed as they watched.

"Dughlas, the poor lad can't fight in this," I said. He turned and laughed, and Philip saw the opportunity to strike the back of his knees, knocking him to the ground. "Well done, Philip. Always wait for the moment your opponent lets his guard down, then strike."

"Bastard," Dughlas said jovially. He threw a handful of snow at Philip, who dodged it.

"Did you enjoy your first night of Winterlow in Ardonn?" I

asked Philip.

He nodded. "Yes, master. It is very different from Trucilia back home."

"You honour the god Truci during this time, yes? You will have to tell me more about it later. Dughlas, I need to speak with you alone."

I sent Philip off to find Matilda so he could practice reading, and I took Dughlas over to the stables.

"Did you see something last night?" he asked. I nodded. "What was it?"

"I'm not certain. I think a legend is destined to wake from his slumber," I said.

Dughlas frowned. "What do you mean?"

"How much do you know about the legendary King Emrys?"

He shrugged. "Not much at all, I'm afraid. I've heard the name, but that's it."

And so I told Dughlas the legend that I had managed to piece together from my time reading in Oldford's library, before telling him about the conversation I had with Hakon in Oldford, and about what he wanted. I told him about the prophecy spoken to me by Aelda's ghost the night before we arrived in Oldford, and the dreams given to me by the Gods. I then revealed that I believed it was Hakon who had attacked my home earlier that winter, seeking my sword. He listened and nodded in thought as I spoke.

"So the Lady Ecwyn reckons Ward can lead you to Emrys?"

Dughlas said.

"Yes, that seems to be the best lead."

"And the Gods have warned you that you are connected to the release of Emrys?"

"Yes."

"So why pursue these leads? If I were you, I would be doing nothing."

"Doing nothing?"

"Yes. Think about it. If you go to Emrys's tomb, prison, whatever, then you're bringing the key with you. Isn't that what this Hakon fellow wants?"

"I suppose."

"If you want to stop Emrys from being released, find the man who wants to release him, not Emrys himself."

Dughlas was probably right, as usual. He had a simple mind, but sometimes simple minds come up with simple solutions. Perhaps I was overthinking my role in all this. Perhaps I should have done nothing.

"I was thinking that if I found Emrys's tomb, I could find some way to seal it forever or defend it against Hakon," I said.

Dughlas thought for a moment and then shook his head. "This is all futile. If Emrys is fated to be freed, as you have said, then that can't be avoided regardless of what you do," he said.

"That's true. But are the men who struggle against Fate, despite the futility of their struggles, not the most valiant? Even the Gods consider those who struggle, though they have lost all hope, to be of godly stock. And who's to say men cannot shape the fate of the world?"

"You sound like Brendan," said Dughlas. I smiled at that. "If you want to break the chains of Fate, I'll stand with you, as always. But if you want my advice, I say the best way to stop Hakon freeing Emrys is to kill Hakon, or failing that, destroy Godwin's sword."

I had thought about that. Of course I had. But I could find no trace of any man called Hakon who might be related to the man who had destroyed my home. He dressed well and had horses and men, so he must have had land somewhere. But where? I could ask around, but I would be stabbing in the dark. There were many nobles and even more wealthy free men throughout Ardonn with the name 'Hakon.' At least with Emrys I had leads.

As for destroying the sword, I quickly rejected that idea. If the sword was used to bind Emrys, its destruction could inadvertently unbind him. That was not a risk I was willing to take. Besides, the sword belonged to my master and was one of the few things of his I had left, not to mention the fact its supposed power kept me alive in a fight.

"I don't know how to find Hakon," I admitted.

"Why not let him come to you? He still needs your sword," Dughlas said.

I shook my head. "If I am going to kill Hakon, I need to be the hunter, not the hunted. He has at least enough men to destroy my home and slaughter my people, maybe more. I need to find him before he finds me." Little did I know Hakon knew exactly where I was.

"What about Ward?"

"What about him?"

"He may have connections to Hakon. How else could Hakon learn so much of Emrys unless he had access to royal secrets?"

I did not answer but gave the question some thought. Dughlas was right, of course. I needed to find Ward. I could seek to destroy Emrys, or seal him away for good, or simply kill Hakon to prevent his release — at least until some other man decided he would do the same — but regardless of the path I took, it was clear by now that the last Royal Godspeaker held the answers I needed.

The only problem was that he had supposedly been killed during the siege of the Capital nine years earlier.

I paced along the castle's walls, thinking. I knew then what I must do and where I must go. I would go north, to the capital, and begin my search for the late King Edwin's Godspeaker. That is where Fate was taking me. I gazed northwards. The Royal Way stretched far into the distance, disappearing into the low hills and fields that characterised the rich country around Oldford. I spied a fort on the horizon — one of the ancient ones — sitting atop a tall hill. I do not know why, but once I noticed that fort, a feeling of dread washed over me. Or perhaps that was just the breeze?

Regardless, I did not simply see a fort, as most would. I saw war on the horizon. I felt it in that moment, deep within my soul. War had begun far beyond those peaceful hills and fields.

The Gods were demanding more than the blood of pigs this winter.

7

Dawn

The month of Winterlow carried on more or less the same. Every evening, sacrifices were made as they had been done on First Night, and each night we feasted in honour of the dead and the Gods.

I told Matilda that I needed her help finding Ward, or any trace of him. She spent her days in Adalbert's library with Ecwyn looking for anything she could find about the last Royal Godspeaker, but they found nothing. I would sometimes come to the library to help or see what they had found, and often their conversations died the moment I entered the room.

I spent less time in the library than I would have liked during Winterlow, so I could not help much with the hunt for Ward. Although I was eager to find him, I had more immediate matters to attend to. Many of Oldford's citizens or peasants from the surrounding lands would come to Adalbert's castle during the day to seek my aid with whatever Otherworldly problems they had. Winterlow is a time when the dead wander this world, and so the common folk were always on edge — any strange sound or sight could spook them.

I saw about a dozen outside the walls each day who sought advice on a variety of problems: ghosts, revenants, witches, dwarves, odd dreams, and the like. Most of the issues sounded like superstitious nonsense, but I listened to every concern the people had and gave them the help they needed.

Some days I even went out to nearby homesteads and villages to deal with problems in person. Lodulf and Adalbert usually dealt with these things every Winterlow, but their ability when dealing with the Otherworld was nothing compared to mine. They did not have the Gift. Adalbert tried to convince me to work as his Godspeaker permanently, and although I was tempted, I had to decline. Fate had other plans for me.

When I was not dealing with commoners, I would sometimes walk the woods or the castle walls with Lodulf, discussing politics and matters pertaining to the Gods. Philip would sometimes join us on these walks to listen and learn.

I spent time with Philip, training him in the ways of our trade. He was surprisingly clever for his age, and I was growing fond of the boy. He knew a fair amount about his own gods and the various spirits that inhabit Luria.

I taught him the words we in Ardonn use for our spirits —

elves, dwarves, bogeys, and nixes, among others — and explained to him how they were not too different from the unseen beings that inhabited his homeland. One day, I was walking through the forest behind the castle with him, and he asked me whether our gods were different or the same. I thought about that for a moment.

"Can they not be both?" I asked. I did not expect an answer. Philip only looked at me, confused, and I chuckled. I would let him dwell on that question, for I felt it was important that he begin to learn that there are many mysteries in the world, and many of them remain forever unanswered. I enjoyed my time teaching Philip and hoped that was how my master felt when I was the boy's age.

But as each day passed, that feeling of dread I received atop the castle's wall on Winterlow's first day still haunted me, skulking in the back of my mind. I shared it with no one. I grew more and more anxious, and Dughlas noticed that each day I was spending more time up on the wall than I had the day before, staring gloomily to the north. He approached me on Winterlow's final day.

"You're waiting for something," he said. "I'm smart enough to know I shouldn't ask, but too curious not to. So, what are you waiting for?"

"War," I said.

Dughlas laughed. "Gods, you're miserable sometimes."

"The peace has been broken far to the north," I said. "I can feel it, as if the Gods themselves are warning me. I stand up here hoping to see a messenger."

"Could it be Emrys?"

"No. Hakon needs my sword to release him."

My hopes were not ill-founded, for a messenger did come, though he did not bring tidings of war — in fact, he knew nothing of it. Lud was my messenger, and he came with news for me alone.

"I came to the hall, lord," Lud said once he caught his breath. "But found it gone. Cubert and Egil said some bandits torched it, then told me I'd find you here."

"You saw Cubert and Egil?" I asked. I had not expected to ever hear of them again. They had deserted me, and I thought them long gone.

"Yes, lord, at the Rose."

I thought for a moment but decided those two were not worth my time. Oathbreakers brought their fate upon themselves, and I did not need to seek them out to punish them. The Gods would do that for me. My efforts were better off directed northwards. "What news do you bring, Lud?" I asked.

"A letter, lord, from your friend in the mountains." Lud handed me a scroll of fine parchment, tied with a purple ribbon and with a seal depicting a dragon.

"And you heard no news of war when you left?"

"No, lord. I encountered no trouble on my way here. Ardonn seemed peaceful enough."

I nodded and bid Lud head inside for some rest and ale. I was not comforted by what he had told me, because Lud often avoided the main roads and towns. If war had truly begun when I felt it had, Lud may have missed it entirely, and news of it would be far behind him.

I turned the small scroll in my hands. Perhaps this would have the answers. I headed for my quarters to read my letter in private, untied the purple ribbon, and popped open the wax seal once I was comfortably by the fire. I began to read.

Edward,

I have received your last letter. Regrettably, I have been unable to reply with my usual haste. I enjoy our conversations, but rebel activity has increased recently in the region, which has made letter-sending difficult. I am sure you understand.

What news, you ask? Well, Fate has decreed that I am to be married. I have been betrothed to the daughter of an important man nearby. I would have loved a king's daughter, but would it not be true to say that all men desire such a wife?

Her name is Amalie, and she is a pretty young lady with the most beautiful golden hair. She has seen fifteen winters, a virgin, and through our conversations I have already grown fond of her. I know you will probably be unable to make it to our wedding, but in case you find yourself in the area, we will be married at Petalsong this coming spring. I would very much like to meet you in person. Fate will bring us together one day, I am sure of it.

Besides that, business runs as usual. Your donations have been received in full, and for that I am eternally grateful. Your friendship and advice are all I could need in these times, and I shall tell you again that your wealth belongs to you, but I know this counsel will once more be ignored.

Our plans for the future are falling into place quite nicely, I must say. Each day I wake, I become more and more certain that our venture will succeed.

And now, I ask you, are all your matters well? I do hope you have a pleasant Winterlow. My prayers go out to you and your people in these troubling days.

I promise you, Edward, when we succeed in our aims, you shall want for nothing. I shall help find you a good wife, and once you have tired of working in partnership with me, you may retire with her and have a large family and live happily ever after. I swear it, before all the Gods and my ancestors.

Anyway, I must go now. Other matters call my attention. Best wishes to you, my friend, and happy Winterlow.

Your partner,

C.

I stared at the parchment and smiled. There was no news of war, but the letter had brightened my mood and instilled in me a renewed hope, as these letters always did. I placed it down on the small table beside the chair and then found some parchment to write my reply.

I wrote of Hakon and the attack on my home, though did not mention Emrys. I also told him of Matilda and my new apprentice. I wrote that I would be heading north to the Capital once Winterlow had ended and that our paths may cross in the near future. I wished my friend and his sister well and offered prayers for their efforts before closing off the message.

I then sought out Lud. I found him by the great fireplace in the castle's main hall and handed him my letter, sealed and tied with the same purple ribbon that had come with the letter I received.

"Rest here for a while, Lud," I said. "But once Winterlow ends, hasten back north and deliver this to our friend. And be wary on the road, for I sense there is danger near the Alps."

"I will take the winding side roads, lord, as always," Lud said.

"Good. Do not lose that letter, but keep yourself safe first. I can always write another letter, but I cannot write another Lud into existence. I am glad to see you."

"And you, lord. You've that look about you, but try not to do anything foolish."

I smiled, and at that a horn sounded outside, followed by shouting. Lud and I made our way outside to see what the fuss was about.

Lady Ecwyn stood on the ramparts above the gate with four armed men by her side, shouting at someone. Half a dozen archers pointed their bows down at whoever had appeared before Oldford Castle.

I climbed up the ramparts and stood by Ecwyn. She looked and me and smirked. "This is something you should have told us about when you arrived."

I looked down at the five horsemen who sat outside the gate. Three of them I had never seen before, but two I recognised. Gunn and Merewald, from Henton. Word must have come to them that I was staying in Adalbert's keep. They glared up at me.

"That is the Godspeaker our earl seeks," Merewald shouted. "Hand him over to us, please."

Ecwyn laughed. "And what will happen to us if I do not?"

Merewald said nothing, and Gunn rode forward a few paces. I heard the creak of bowstrings being pulled.

"Edward," said Gunn. He smiled up at me. "My da just wants his daughter back safe. No harm will come to you—"

Ecwyn spat down at him. "No harm will come to him regardless. Edward and Lady Matilda are under Lord Adalbert's protection now. The Earl of Henton would do well to remember the oath he swore to my father, and I would advise you not to break it on his behalf. Go home, men. Winter is no time for this sort of hunting."

She said not another word, only turned away, gave me a wink, then headed back to the keep with her bodyguards. The archers lowered their bows, and Merewald and his men turned away and headed back down the hill. Gunn stayed for a few moments, held up a hand, and I waved back. He then headed back down the hill with his companions.

It is truly a blessing to have powerful friends.

Once I was certain Gunn and his men were gone, I headed to the forest, following the torch-lined path to the sacred clearing where Winterlow sacrifices were made. I sat before the tree, wrapped in thick furs, and meditated.

The men from Henton would trouble us no more, but they were not our only troubles that winter.

I returned to the castle late that afternoon, just before sunset. It was growing cold, and that night would be the final night of Winterlow — the most important of all nights. On this night, the most valuable sacrifice would be given to Alcyn, and a feast would be had lasting through the darkness. We would stay up in vigil and await the sunrise so that we might greet the dawn of the new year.

Lady Ecwyn was in the main hall, giving orders to the servants as they prepared the feast. She smiled when she saw me. "Edward, my friend."

"My Lady. How is everything?"

"Oh, splendid. Everything has been perfectly organised. This year's feast will be one to remember. By the way, Matilda has been searching for you."

"What for?"

"I am not supposed to tell."

"All right, thank you, My Lady."

I left Ecwyn alone to continue preparing the Last Night

celebrations and headed up to my quarters. If Matilda needed me, she could find me there.

But once I got to my room, my stomach dropped, for it was I who found Matilda. She was standing beside the little table by the fireplace. In one hand she clutched a bouquet of winter flowers, and in the other she held the letter I had received earlier that day. She looked up from the parchment and smiled.

"What are you doing?" I demanded.

"Edward, I noticed you have been unhappy these past few days, so I wanted to cheer you up. I picked these flowers for you." Her smile faded when she noticed the anger on my face. I took a deep breath and stared at her. "Edward, I—"

"That letter is addressed to you, is it?" I said. Matilda flinched and opened her mouth to speak, but no words came out. She looked to be on the verge of tears, but anger boiled inside me. "Read the word at the top of the page."

"But…"

"Read it."

Matilda gulped and read my name slowly. "Edward."

"Edward," I repeated. "Not 'Matilda.'"

Matilda slumped her head and put the letter back down on the table. "I wanted to make you happy," she mumbled. "But then I saw your fancy letter and thought it was from the king, and I wanted to see why the king was writing to you."

I glared at her, and she stared down at her feet. She began to sob, and I watched as a tear fell to the fur rug. "I am sorry," she said.

"King Stephan would never write to me," I said. "You're a child. I regret taking you from Henton. You've been nothing but a burden and a pain. That letter is deeply personal, and you have no right to touch it. Get out." I pointed to the door and stood to the side. Matilda stared at me for a few moments, her eyes red and wet. Her face wore a look of total dismay.

"I said—" she began.

"Out! Go dig your pointy nose into someone else's business."

Matilda dropped the bouquet, put her hands over her mouth, and rushed out of the room. I was furious, partly with Matilda but mostly with myself. I should never have left that letter sitting out on the table, especially not with Adalbert's spies wandering the castle. Had I been too hard on her? I walked over to the flowers, now scattered over the rug, and scooped them up. They were indeed pretty. Some were even rare. I placed them down gently on the table and then tossed the letter into the fire. No one would see it now.

I sat before the fire for a while, watching the parchment burn. Matilda seemed to have no idea who the letter might have been from, or what it was about, which was a relief. But perhaps she would figure it out.

Not long after Matilda ran from my quarters, I received a knock at the door. It was Ecwyn, and she looked unhappy.

"What did you do?" she asked.

"Excuse me, My Lady?"

"I found Matilda heading for her quarters. She was in tears."

"I didn't do anything."

Ecwyn glided to the table and picked up the flowers. She admired them. "Matilda spent a long time in the woods picking these for you. She was wanting to brighten your mood. So, what did you do?"

"I yelled at her. She was reading a personal letter of mine."

"You are a cold man, Edward. I pity Matilda."

"Why do you pity her?"

"You are a fool if you cannot see it." Ecwyn put the flowers into a jug of water that sat by my bed. "Go apologise to her. Show her that there is still warmth in this bitter winter."

Ecwyn was right; I needed to apologise. I had wronged Matilda. I was foolish enough to leave that letter out for anyone to find, and she was only curious. Certainly, she was wrong to look, but her actions did not deserve my response.

Ecwyn left me alone, and I stared into the fire for a few moments longer, watching the last remnants of blackened parchment flutter up the chimney. I hated apologies, for I was prideful, but I owed it to Matilda. I had been very tense and irritable in those days, but that was no excuse for my reaction to her discovering the letter. I made my way to her room.

I stood outside for a few seconds. I knew she was in there, because I could hear her soft sobs from inside. I raised my knuckles to the door, paused, and then knocked three times.

"Come in," Matilda said. There was weakness in her voice. I

opened the door slowly and entered to see her lying on her side, on her bed, with her back to the door. I approached her and sat awkwardly for a little while, unsure of what to say. She just lay there in silence.

I looked around the room and spotted Matilda's insects. She had cleared more shelves of books and replaced them with jars of all sizes, and they were arranged neatly to showcase every single creature. She had clearly grown accustomed to Adalbert's generous hospitality the month past.

"Which insect is your favourite?" I asked, breaking the silence. She quickly rolled over and sat up, her eyes wide. I turned to her and gave a smile, and Matilda looked like she was about to cry. "Well?"

She said nothing, only got up from her bed and walked over to her shelf. She looked at her jars for a bit and then took one from the shelf and brought it over to me. I turned it in my hands while Matilda sat beside me, her arms folded over her chest.

The creature in the jar was an enormous moth, about the size of the palm of my hand. It was beautiful, with bright orange wings and black and red spots.

"I found it in the forest yesterday," Matilda said. "I have never seen it before, but I think it is quite pretty."

"It is," I said. I handed the jar back to her, and she placed it on her bedside table. Her eyes avoided mine. "Matilda, I want to say I am sorry. Sorry for how I treated you. You have been of great help to me lately, and it was unfair to repay that kindness in such a way."

She was silent for a long moment. Too long. I thought all hope
was lost, but then she shook her head. "No, I am sorry, Edward."
Matilda's eyes began to water, and her voice choked up. "Your
anger was justified. I looked at your private things and betrayed
your trust. And now you hate me." With those last few words,
two tears ran down her cheeks, and she shut her eyes tight.

"I don't hate you, Matilda. We all make mistakes. Will you
forgive my anger towards you?" I asked. She opened her teary
eyes and nodded. "Thank you. And thank you for those flowers.
They are very pretty."

Matilda forced a smile. Her feet shuffled. "Are you in danger?"

"Where did that question come from?"

"Dughlas told me you spend a lot of time waiting for
something up on the wall. And you have been very tense of late.
Something troubles you."

"Don't trouble yourself with my troubles. I will make sure you
are safe."

"But I want you to be safe too."

"I will be safe, I promise." I slowly, awkwardly, put my arm
around her shoulders. I had been with women plenty of times,
but now, just by putting my arm around Matilda, I felt strange. I
was nervous, wondering whether she would appreciate it. But
she did. Relief washed over me.

Matilda leaned in closer to me, and as she drew her head to my
chest, I put my other arm around her. We sat there for a while,

Matilda's head pressed against me with my arms around her. We said nothing. For some reason, I did not want this moment to end.

But it did, for we could not miss the Last Night celebrations.

I left Matilda alone so she could get ready, and I headed back to my quarters to change my clothes before heading down to the main hall. The coming night would be the longest of the year. The air was frigid, but it was deathly still. The first night of Winterlow had been wild, but this night was the complete opposite. The trees were still and the air was silent, so much so that the slightest noise echoed across the rolling hills around Oldford. The sky was void of clouds, which meant the night was a bright one, for the stars and the moon illuminated the land, their light reflected by the sparkling snow.

As the sun set, and all of Adalbert's guests made their way into the main hall, I sat in my seat at the high table. Philip was three seats to my right, since Ecwyn had given him a place at the high table for tonight. He was wrapped in a thick fur blanket and wore a fox-skin hat; the fire was raging, yet he was still cold. I laughed. "You don't get winters like this where you're from?"

Philip shook his head. "No, Master." He shivered. As we waited, Matilda came down. She looked beautiful, as always, and was wearing a thin black dress — presumably from Ecwyn — as well as one of the fur cloaks Adalbert had gifted me. She joined Philip and I at the high table.

"You're going to get cold wearing that dress," I said.

"I already am. But this will keep me alive, at least," Matilda said, stroking the fur. It was made from the coat of a black bear and was one of the finest cloaks I had ever worn. I had lent it to Matilda for the night. "It smells like you."

"It smells like bear," I said.

She shrugged. "What will you sacrifice tonight?"

"A horse."

"Not Lilly, I hope." She smiled at Philip. "You look cosy."

"I am not," he said.

"Do not complain too much. There are places far to the north that have no sunlight for days, and it is so cold that during winter people go blind because their eyes have frozen," Matilda said.

"And how could you possibly know that?"

"I read it."

I laughed. "Your eyes don't freeze up north."

She waved her hand as if to dismiss me. While we waited for the rest of the guests to fill the hall the three of us talked for a while about the south. Matilda was very curious about those lands and wanted to know all about Luria, of which Philip was quite proud. Once all the guests were in the hall, Adalbert and Ecwyn arrived, as did Lodulf, and speeches were made. Bread and cheese was eaten until the final sacrifice was ready, and then we all went outside and gathered in the sacred clearing, as we had done on First Night.

There Alcyn was appeased with Adalbert's finest mare. I silently prayed that Alcyn's desire for blood would be sated this winter, but I knew those prayers were in vain. The dread still lingered in my mind, but on this night, the Gods were silent.

Adalbert's guests all gathered in the main hall after the sacrifice. Ecwyn and I made speeches, thanking everyone for joining us that Winterlow and wishing them well in the coming year. The servants brought out a large barrel of mead, which had been blessed and prepared before the feast.

The mead was used in the ritual passing of the cup, which, as on First Night, Ecwyn carried out. She passed the mead cup around the hall three times to Adalbert's oathmen, followed by Lodulf, then me, and finally Adalbert. We all made toasts to our ancestors and the sovereign of winter, boasted of our deeds, and tossed insults at each other.

Once the third round had finished and the rite was over, Adalbert declared that all were now welcome to the mead, and the feast began. Men and women raced to the barrel to fill their cups, and within an hour, most of the guests were drunk. I admit, I was too.

The feast was glorious, as it always was on Last Night. The servants piled food onto the tables and then joined in with everyone else. As the night progressed, the tables emptied, so people were bringing in plates and bowls from the kitchen as they fancied. By midnight, twelve people had entered a state of vomiting and three had passed out. I even caught Adalbert smiling a few times.

Matilda also had more cups than she could handle. She spent most of the night flattering me and would not stop talking about things she had read or insects she had found, and she kept asking me to tell her about all the journeys I had been on, the places I had seen, and the women I had been with. Whenever I said something funny — and sometimes even when I said things that were not — she would start giggling and laughing and placing her hand on my arm or shoulder.

The mead ran dry very fast, and several hours after midnight Ecwyn locked the cellar to stop people bringing up more barrels of ale. Things calmed down in the early hours of the morning, but there was still fun and laughter flowing through the hall. Some of the men thought it would be amusing to get Philip drunk, so I had to keep checking on him whenever he went to be sick out in the courtyard. Whenever I returned to my seat, Matilda would be there waiting. She seemed to have no interest in anyone else.

Games and gambling took place once the food ran out. People played cards or draughts, and some wrestled or sparred out in the courtyard. Dughlas and Lud wrestled at one point in the night, and I placed bets on Dughlas. I lost that money.

Matilda challenged me to a fight too but said it should be in the forest so that no one would witness the humiliation of me losing to a lady. I rejected her challenge, of course, but she only laughed, called me a coward, and said that she would just go explore the forest instead. She jumped from her seat and bolted out the door.

That annoyed me. I did not think it was a good idea for people to be wandering the forest on Winterlow's nights, because it was a wild and untamed place with many malevolent spirits whose presence would only be strengthened that day. I had visited the forest on some evenings since we arrived in Oldford, and I had sensed those Otherworldly beings. I knew how to deal with them, but Matilda certainly did not.

Though she knew that, which was how she knew I would have to chase her.

I ran after her as she disappeared into the woods. It was not too dark due to the stars and the moon, but among the trees that light was absent, and the fact that both Matilda's hair and dress were black made her even harder to find. I went into the forest shortly after her, and although I could not see her, I could hear her giggling. I jogged through the trees, calling out to her. It was bitterly cold, and I was getting more and more frustrated with every step.

"Come find me!" she shouted, her voice echoing through the trees.

"Matilda, it's dangerous out here," I called back.

"You will just have to come find me then. Protect me from all the nasty spirits."

I could not figure out which direction she called from. It sounded as though there were thousands of her, calling from all directions. Could that have been the lack of wind causing an echo, or was it the tricks of the forest?

Her giggling fell silent.

"Matilda?" I said. In my half-drunken state, I failed to realise how deep I had gone into the woods. But now I did. The trees around me were wild and untamed. Undergrowth covered the ground, and it was hard to move without snapping branches. Matilda did not respond. There was nothing but silence. "Matilda, it's cold out here. Let's go back inside." Still nothing.

I turned sharply when I heard movement behind me. There was something in the bushes. Something heavy. I reached for my sword, but my heart dropped when my hand grabbed air. I had left the blade in the castle. There was more rustling, and a snarl. It was only a few feet away from me.

I backed away slowly. If this was a spirit, I would have sensed it long before I heard it. This had to be an animal of some kind. It growled again, the bushes hissed, and a shadow leaped from the trees. It threw itself at me, I yelled, and it pinned me to the ground. I prepared myself for death.

Then the beast began to giggle.

"Matilda," I breathed.

"Did I scare you?"

"No."

"I did. You are a liar," she said and then poked my nose. She sat on my belly, straddling me, with her hands pinning my shoulders. Her hair fell loose over her face, and she was breathing heavily. My heart was racing, though no longer due to fear.

"Why did you make me come out here?" I asked. She shrugged, and I let out a laugh. "You sure love your drink, young lady."

"I know," she said. I just shook my head and grinned. "I found a pond just over there. We should go for a swim," she said.

Before I could protest, she began to stand back up, but I grabbed her waist and pulled her back down. I rolled her over, laid her down on her back, and pinned her down as she had done to me. "No, it is freezing. We'll die within minutes."

She stared up at me, looking serious. Clouds of condensation puffed out of her mouth with every breath.

"I suppose," she said. Her eyes were locked onto mine, and she shuffled a bit but did not struggle. She shook her head to get the hair off her face.

"You look cold," I said.

Her eyes stared into mine, reflecting the light of the moon. "So do you."

I looked into Matilda's eyes, and in that moment I felt something strange. I must have had too much alcohol for one night.

I moved off her and sat down in the snow. "We should head back."

Matilda lay there for several moments, staring at me, then closed her eyes and nodded.

"Yes, I miss the fire already," she said. I stood up, brushed off snow, then helped Matilda stand. She brushed herself off, shook the cloak she was wearing, and I led her back through the dark woods to the castle. We had gone very deep. Fortunately, I could see the light of the castle, so we found our way back and returned to our seats to await the sunrise.

There were many hours left in that long night, but Matilda did not talk as much after that. She just kept sipping a tankard of water, seemingly lost in her own thoughts.

I left her alone and joined the men outside. We sparred to sober up and pass the time, and finally, after what seemed like forever, we began to see light appear in the east. We cheered, having successfully stayed up to witness the passing of the year, and soon the rest of the guests joined us all atop the castle's eastern wall to greet the sun as it came up over the horizon.

Winterlow was over. The year was over. The days to come would grow warmer and longer, and the nights would get shorter — but had I known what the coming year would bring, I would not have greeted it with such enthusiasm.

8

Northward

Two days after Winterlow I left Oldford with Dughlas, Philip, and Matilda riding by my side. I told Matilda I wanted her to stay in Oldford under Adalbert's protection, but she insisted on coming with us. She reminded me that she was a free noblewoman and had never promised me her obedience, but I had promised that I would show her the world.

Lady Ecwyn bid us farewell that morning. Apparently, Adalbert woke with a fit of coughing and was told by his physician to remain in bed. Ecwyn gave us two more horses for the road, along with enough provisions to last us until we reached Everlynn, and sent us on our way. She and Matilda said warm farewells, and she made us promise that we would visit sometime soon and write to her regularly.

Once Ecwyn and Matilda had embraced and said goodbye

more times than I could count, we headed off northward along the Royal Way. I sent Lud north a day earlier with my letter, telling him to look for me in the Capital once it was delivered. He would be travelling a lot faster than us, and it was unlikely we would catch up with him.

"So, we're heading to the Capital?" Dughlas asked once we were on the road.

"Yes. I want to track down Ward, if he's alive. We'll start where he supposedly died."

Dughlas nodded. "If you can get past the gates."

"Why would Edward not get past the gates?" Matilda asked.

"You haven't told her?" Dughlas said. I shrugged, and Dughlas tutted. "Two years ago — the last time Edward was in the Capital — King Stephan gave him one day to leave or be arrested for treason. How long were you banished for?"

"Eternally," I said.

"That's right. Forever and ever. Poor Edward."

"Gods, what did you do?" Matilda asked.

"When Stephan was crowned, he summoned all lords and landowners to swear fealty to him," I explained.

"And you did not?"

"I did not. I told him I would swear to Lord Adalbert, but never to a usurper's son. Apparently that was not enough for him."

"Splendid. I am travelling with a traitor."

"I'm no traitor. It was not me who joined my father in revolt against King Edwin."

"You are lucky you were not executed. So, how are we supposed to find Ward if we cannot enter the Capital?"

I thought about that for a while. I would probably just use an alias and hope no one recognised me. I had some fame in these parts of the kingdom, but in the north I was less known, so I could perhaps go unnoticed. Besides, the Capital was a big place. King Stephan was the least of my concerns.

Our more immediate concern was the men following us. We took no notice of them at first, but by midday it became clear that we were being tracked. I feared at first that it was Harold's men, but it soon became clear that Ecwyn's threats had worked. We would spy the occasional scout far behind us, riding a black horse and wearing a black cloak. I could not tell if it was one scout or many, nor could I tell how large his party was.

I thought it best to ignore him, or them, and judged based on the black clothes that they were the same men that had followed us from my home to Oldford weeks before. Had they been waiting all Winterlow for us to leave?

We rode all day, stopping infrequently with the hope that we could lose the men following us. Dughlas's horse carried sacks of food Ecwyn had given us, which he passed round for us throughout the day. Philip was not used to riding, having only learnt during our stay in Oldford, and Gods did he complain on that first day. He was always sore and said he would rather walk, but I had to tell him that would only slow us down.

We passed the occasional patrol or merchant caravan. Some of the merchants were from the south, and Philip liked to shout insults at them in his own language as we passed, as was customary in their land, or so he told me. They would shout back, though I could not understand them.

The landscape was beautiful. We were surrounded by cool, trickling streams, wide pastures and tall hills, quaint little hamlets and villages, ancient monuments, and the odd roadside burial mound. We also passed three forts, two of which were garrisoned. Oldford Castle was once one of these ancient forts, but because of its location it became a political centre and the seat of power for the kings and queens of the old kingdom of Aedonn. The soldiers who patrolled the Royal Way would stay in these places, rotating their posts.

Sweyn, one of my oathmen who died during the assault on my home, worked as a road guard for a year before coming into my service. He told me all about this tedious and tiresome job. The soldiers did indeed look grim standing up on the fort walls wrapped in blankets or huddled around fires.

We stopped that night at a place called Hili's Hamlet. It was a roadside inn, but the innkeeper owned the surrounding land, so the people living in the settlement that had popped up around the inn paid him rent. He earned a decent income from travellers and the rent his tenants paid.

The innkeeper's name was not Hili, but his grandfather's was, which was how the hamlet acquired its name. I had passed through many times before but never stayed, and I regretted that. Hili's grandson gave us warm beds and warm food, and the bard that lived there sang beautifully.

We left at dawn and carried on north. The next few days were very much the same. On our fourth day of riding, we were caught in heavy snowfall. We brought blankets with us, and they helped keep us somewhat warm. I was glad of the snow that day, however, because although it slowed us, it also covered our tracks.

"This is a good chance to take the side roads," Dughlas said.

"Aye, I agree."

Around midday, once we were sure we were not being watched, the four of us turned right and headed onto one of the beaten paths that wound through the hills and valleys to the east of the Royal Way. While not impossible, it would be difficult to track us along these roads during snowfall.

We stayed the night in a sorry, neglected tavern, and headed out the next morning once the skies had cleared. It took us two more days of following the side roads north, but we eventually made our way to Everlynn Forest. There was no sign of the scouts behind us now.

Everlynn Forest stretched for miles from end to end. It was owned by Lord Odo of Everlynn, the ruler of the city on the north side of the forest. Odo was a wealthy noble, not only because his city sat along the Royal Way, but also because he charged an enormous toll for protection to the merchant caravans that travelled through his forest. The place was notorious for its bandits. We stopped at the edge of the forest as the road we followed turned into little more than an old hunting track.

"This looks… Is it not safer to travel through here along the Royal Way?" Matilda asked.

"Not unless you want to pay for Odo's protection," I said.

"How much will it cost?"

"More than I am willing to pay. The Royal Way is a few miles to the west, and this track runs more or less parallel to it. I have used it before. It is popular among hunters, vagabonds, and other folk who cannot afford the tax."

"And bandits," Dughlas said.

"Yes. And bandits. I hope you all prayed for luck this morning."

I kicked my horse forward, and the others followed as I entered the snow-capped woods. I was hoping that whoever followed us assumed we would take the Royal Way, but I should have known better. The birds of the forest carried whispers of a larger group not far behind ours, and soon enough, after only several hours of riding through the woods, we spotted them.

"We're being followed again," Dughlas said to me.

"I know."

They made no effort to hide themselves now, and they travelled as one group. There were eight of them, I counted, and as the day went on, the horsemen inched closer and closer. How had they found us? I had my suspicions but did not voice them to the others. I could tell they were warriors, too. Dughlas and I both knew it would be foolish to turn and confront them. We were outnumbered.

"What will we do when they reach us?" Dughlas asked me.

"If they attack, we kill them. If they want to talk, we talk."

"If they wanted to talk, they would have done so already."

"My thoughts exactly. I may have an idea."

And so I told Dughlas my plan. The two of us could not possibly take on eight men, but perhaps we could take four at a time. He seemed to like my idea. Dughlas and I would ride off the path through the trees, while Matilda and Philip would ride hard northwards.

My hope was that their group would split. Dughlas and I would defeat those who chased after us, and then we would catch up to the others and defeat them before they could reach Matilda and Philip. Their horses were large and strong, but ours were nimble and better suited for the forest.

There was a chance this would work, but it would rely on my and Dughlas's sword-skill and Matilda and Philip's speed. Alternatively, our trackers could ignore Matilda and Philip and just follow me, but at least if that happened, the others would have a chance of escaping.

"On my command," I said to the others. "You two will follow the path. Ride with as much haste as your horses can give."

"Ride with us," Matilda said.

"No. I believe they are hunting me. If we ride with you, they will continue to hunt you."

"Let me fight with you. I can fight," Philip said.

I smiled at him. "You're right, you can fight. So, you need to protect Lady Matilda should she get into trouble."

I drew my sword, and Dughlas did the same. Glancing back at the men following us, I noticed them also drawing their swords. "Go! Now," I yelled. Matilda nodded and kicked her horse into a gallop, speeding off through the trees.

Philip hesitated. I nodded to him, and he shook his head, so I lifted my sword and slapped his horse's rump with the flat of the blade, sending him off after Matilda. I looked at Dughlas, and he looked at me, then I glanced back at the warriors behind us. They had kicked their horses and were growing nearer by the second.

Dughlas and I rode east. We could not ride side by side because the trees were too dense, and we had to weave our way around them, ducking under branches and leaping over fallen trunks. I felt the air rush through my hair and heard the sound of hoofbeats and snapping sticks behind me.

I glanced back and grinned. I did not know where the others were, but four from the group of warriors were on our tails. Our plan had worked. An arrow hissed past me and buried itself in the trunk of a thick ash. A sharp twig scratched my face. Another arrow thumped into the ground right in front of Lilly. I reared her, pointed my sword at the sky, and turned. I do not remember what exactly I yelled, but I recall shouting for Dughlas to join me before I invoked some god.

The next few moments happened very quickly. I pulled my shield from my back and charged Lilly forward. I picked my target — a bowman — and raised my sword high. He must not have been expecting me to turn and face him, for he turned his horse away and dropped his bow in panic. He drew his sword, but before he could strike I cut down into his shoulder. His blood spattered across my face and he cried as he fell from his horse.

The other three men were scattered, spread out among the trees. I heard a scream and spotted another of the black-dressed men tumble from his horse, an arrow in his chest. Dughlas was always good with a bow. I kicked my horse and charged at another man, but this one was ready. I could not see his face, for he wore a helmet. His sword was drawn, and he held his shield to block my incoming strike. As I sped past him, my blade thudded against the wood of his shield, the shock pulsing up my arm.

We turned to face each other, and he kicked his horse forward. He came at my right, I blocked his lunge with my shield, and he raised his sword to strike again, but I thrust at the opening, and the tip of my blade pierced mail. The man swore as I pulled away, and he kicked his horse in an attempt to ride off.

I turned to chase him, but an arrow whizzed through the trees. The black horse screamed as the arrow found its mark. It reared, throwing the man from his saddle, then sped off deep into the forest.

Dughlas pulled his horse up beside me and smiled. "I'd say

that counts as mine," he said. His breath was heavy.

I nodded. "You've always fought better on horseback."

"Better than you, it seems. What do we do with him?" He nodded down at the groaning man on the ground. He clutched at his gut where blood leaked from the tear in his mail.

"Leave him. We need to find the others."

The man yelled as we rode off, but I ignored him. Killing him would be a mercy but a waste of time. As for the fourth man, I did not see him die but learnt Dughlas had killed him too. We raced through the trees till we reached the path once more, then we followed it northwards as fast as our horses could take us.

Until we heard screams.

Matilda was calling my name, and I could hear a man shouting at her. We sped into a grove, where we found her and Philip up a tree surrounded by the other four men that had followed us. I could not see Matilda and Philip's horses, so they must have abandoned them in order to climb into the pine's branches. Philip was shouting insults, and one of the men had dismounted so he could climb after my companions. Matilda tossed a cone down at him.

"Edward!" she shouted.

The warriors turned to find us pulling our horses to a stop. Before they could react, an arrow from Dughlas's bow buried itself in the skull of one of the mounted warriors. I threw myself from my horse, and one of the horsemen turned to face me. Before he could attack, I sliced by blade across his horse's legs.

It reared and fell to the ground with a loud thud, pinning the rider beneath its weight. Without hesitation, I plunged my blade through his neck. He died quickly.

The next man — the one on foot — came at me with a cry. I blocked his strike, swung at him, he blocked, stabbed, I blocked, then before he could strike again, a large pine cone struck him on the head. He stumbled, so I used the opportunity to smack his blade aside with my shield and thrust my sword forwards. The blade buried itself in his chest. He gurgled, spat blood at my face, and it was then I recognised him.

It was Egil.

I pulled the sword from my old oathman's chest, and he fell to his knees before collapsing face down in the snow.

I turned sharply to a shout behind me. The fourth man, riding atop an enormous black stallion and dressed in a suit of fine mail, had charged his warhorse into Dughlas's and sent him toppling to the ground. He rolled, the warrior leapt from his horse, and ran at Dughlas.

Dughlas quickly stood and faced him, but the man with his heavy sword swung down with both hands at Dughlas, who lifted his sword — not his shield — to parry the blow. The shock went through Dughlas's arms, and he gave out a cry, falling back as the man's sword struck his face.

I sprinted to his aid, but the man turned just in time to parry my slash. I lunged, and he parried that too. His face was full of rage, his eyes were red, and veins were popping out of his bald head. He was huge, and fury had overcome him. He bore no shield but carried a sword so large, most men would struggle to wield it, and his dark steel mail looked very tough. *I could lose this*, I thought.

I made another thrust at him, but feinted, then brought my sword up and back down. He dodged, flicked my sword out of the way, and now it was his turn to go on the offensive. He slashed, I blocked, he slashed the other way, I blocked again, and he sliced once more. I dodged this time, rolled to the side, and he lunged his sword at me. I parried, but I lost my balance and fell. My arms were aching. A pine cone thudded onto the dirt at my feet. The warrior lifted his huge sword to bring it down upon me, but before he could strike he let out a gurgling cry and fell to his knee.

I wasted no time. I jumped back up, threw myself onto him and pinned him down, then put the tip of my sword at his throat and climbed to my feet.

"You've lost," I said, panting. The rush of battle had taken me over before, but now I had time to properly assess the situation. Philip had jumped from the tree, crawled over to my opponent, and stabbed his knife into the back of the man's leg before he could strike the killing blow. Dughlas lay a few feet away, holding his face.

But before I could do anything more, I heard Matilda gasp, my opponent chuckled, and I felt the prick of cold steel on the back of my neck.

"Looks like you missed one," the man on the ground said. I turned my head to look behind me and saw, with his sword pointed straight at me, the man I had left to die back in the woods. He had removed his helmet, revealing his identity.

"I believe you know this man," said the warrior at the tip of my weapon.

"I know this man," I said.

"Kill him, Cubert."

Cubert hesitated. He appeared to be thinking, deciding whether he should do as his new master commanded. He frowned and pressed the point of his blade slightly deeper into my neck. Cubert and I had been friends once. Brothers, even. Now here he was, betraying me, with sharp steel at my neck.

I turned my head back to look at the man I had on the ground. "If you kill me, Cubert, I kill your master."

The man on the ground only smirked. But that smirk quickly became a frown. I felt the prick of the blade disappear, and Cubert came around to my side. He threw his sword to the ground.

"I swore an oath to you, Edward. I know I deserted you, but I will not break that oath further by killing you," said Cubert.

"Treacherous bastard," said the warrior.

"Our orders were to take your sword," Cubert said. "We never had to kill you if we didn't need to. That was Leif's idea." He nodded at his master, who spat up at him.

I paused, staring at Leif, then looked back at Cubert. "Take it,"

I said. I handed my sword's hilt to Cubert, who stared at it with wide eyes.

"Lord, I…"

"Are these not your orders? Will your new master not reward you?"

Cubert hesitated for a very long while, while Leif and I just watched him. I knew he was tempted. Gods, he was tempted. I would not let him take it, of course, but I wanted to see what he would do.

He shook his head.

"That's the sword of Godwin, lord. It belongs to you," said Cubert.

I nodded and pointed it back at Leif's throat. "You will go back to whoever it is that sent you, Leif, and you will tell him that Edward will not be robbed so easily. Tell him if he wants my sword — or my life — he should come and take it himself. Understand?" I glared down at the man, who glared back at me, but finally he nodded.

I sheathed my sword and watched as he tried to reach for his blade. I kicked it aside, and he reluctantly limped over to his horse wounded and unarmed. He mounted and walked his stallion to me so I could smell its rank breath.

"You may have won this battle, Edward Corpse-Whisperer, but by all the Gods I swear you will not win this war," Leif said. He turned his horse, kicked it forward, and rode back south the way he had come.

What war would I not win?

"Good fight, eh?" Dughlas said. He had propped himself up against a tree and was holding a bloody rag to his face. He smiled as I approached him.

"I've never seen you defeated before," I said. "What happened?"

"The bastard nicked me with his sword." Dughlas pulled the rag away to show his bloodied face. A long, open cut ran down from his forehead to his lips, and I grimaced. His eye had been sliced open and I doubted he would be able to see through it again. Dughlas grinned through the pain.

"That's more than a nick. Does it hurt?" I asked.

"Just a bit."

I shook my head. "Your eye is practically gone, Dughlas."

"I've always thought one-eyed warriors were menacing."

"Only the good ones, so you're out of luck. We will need to dress that."

"Aye."

I turned to Philip, who paced around the tree. "Philip!"

"Yes, Master?" he called.

"Thank you for that. I probably would've died without you. Are you all right?"

"I am fine," he said. "It was no harder than killing the chickens back home."

I laughed. "Good lad, that's the spirit."

Matilda, looking a little green, rolled her eyes and tutted. "Farm boys…"

I opened my flask and gestured for Dughlas to sit back, then he pulled his hand away from his face and let me clean his gash. Matilda had brought with her a small flask of alcohol for treating wounds, and for that I was thankful. His scar was truly a gruesome sight and would need to be dealt with by a proper healer once we reached Everlynn. That was another two days through the forest, and I hoped Dughlas would last till then without his wound festering.

I tore a long, thin strip of linen from one of the cloaks of the men we killed and wrapped it tight around Dughlas's head. I was never good with fixing wounds, but I thought that — along with Matilda's alcohol — would be enough to keep him going for a few days.

The wound I had inflicted upon Cubert was less severe than I had thought. His mail had done its job well, so the wound was not very deep. I had Matilda wash the cut while I tended to Dughlas, and she wrapped Cubert's belly with clean cloth so it would not fester. She had some skill in tending wounds from when her father's men returned from hunting or fighting robber bands.

"You made the right choice, Cubert," I said once I had finished with Dughlas. "What will you do now?"

"I was hoping I could serve you again, lord. I know I broke my oath, but I want to right my wrongs. Ever since Egil and I left you in Oldford, I've had regrets," he said.

"You tried to kill me back there, before Dughlas shot your horse."

"I was just defending myself, lord. We meant only to take your sword."

I thought for a moment. Oathbreaking is a serious crime, but Cubert was a good man. He had been loyal until that night outside Oldford and served me faithfully. His sister had been killed during the attack on my home, and that must have been hard for him. I stared at Cubert, thinking. He could have killed me back then, when his sword was at my neck, but he did not. He disobeyed his orders in favour of me.

"You served a man named Hakon?" I asked.

"Yes, I did. He found me and Egil in Oldford after we deserted and offered us wealth and fame," said Cubert.

"He ordered the raid that ended your sister's life. Did you know that?"

"I did, lord. But when I swore to Hakon, I blamed you for Nell's death. It wasn't until we followed you from Oldford that I began to realise who was really at fault."

I nodded. "What can you tell me about Hakon or that man who led you?"

"Not much, lord. Hakon's the bastard brother of some nobleman, I know that much. But I did not get to speak to him after I swore my oath. Leif, on the other hand, is Hakon's most loyal thane. He led the attack on your home, lord."

I suspected that was the case. I recognised Leif from that day in Oldford when I first met Hakon. He was the big man that Hakon spoke to outside the Black Rose, and it was he who rode south out of the city. It seemed he was the man that did all of Hakon's dirty work. Work that would ruin the reputation of Hakon and his noble half-brother, whomever that might be.

Cubert seemed to be telling the truth, and his desire to redeem himself in my service appeared sincere. I allowed him to swear to me. This would be his last chance, I told him, and if he were to break his oath or prove disloyal once more, I would kill him without question.

If I am being honest, I probably would not have taken him back if I still had a hall, men, and money; but now all I had was one oathman, an apprentice, and a young lady accompanying me, along with what wealth I salvaged from the wreck of my home. If I were to hunt Hakon down and kill him, avenge my people, and prevent the return of the Immortal King that Queen Aelda prophesied, I would need help. I needed men.

And so Cubert was once again my oathman, loyal to our ends.

I did not tell him what our purpose was, only that we journeyed to the Capital for Godspeaker business. He did not ask questions and did not need to. We buried Egil that afternoon beneath the tree by which he died under a pile of river stones from a stream Matilda found nearby. He may have been an oathbreaker, but he was a fine warrior, and once upon a time he had been my friend. He deserved a proper burial. We said some prayers by his grave and moved on.

The horses gifted to Matilda and Philip by Lady Ecwyn were nowhere to be found, and I suspected they had either returned home or would become lost in these woods forever. I took Egil's black horse, given to him by Hakon, and I let Matilda ride Lilly. My new horse was called Brand, and he was a strong beast. Philip was too small to ride the horse left behind, so I had him share a saddle with Dughlas. They both complained.

We made camp at nightfall, then Philip and I caught us some rabbits to eat. I sat with Matilda by the fire after everyone else had gone to sleep, and we talked for a while. "Why did you not keep riding?" I asked.

"They were catching up to us. Neither Philip nor I are adept at riding through dense woods like this, but those men were."

"So you climbed a tree instead?"

"It seemed like a good idea at the time."

I chuckled. "Perhaps it was. At least you are both alive now. How does a lady even climb a tree?"

"I am not as useless as you think! I used to explore the woods with Gunn and Alia." Matilda frowned and sighed. "We lost the horses."

"I'm sure they will find their way home." I smiled at her, and she smiled back, though I could tell she was troubled by something. Could it be the death she witnessed? Did she feel guilty? I did not ask, but as I lay there under the stars after

Matilda had gone to sleep, I realised I should have.

We left early the next morning and headed farther along the track, and as I predicted, two days later we reached the forest's edge. Fortunately, neither Dughlas nor Cubert's wounds had festered, and Dughlas's eye socket appeared no worse. It still looked gruesome, but at least there was no pus. We emerged from the woods late one morning and felt the sun warm our faces once more. I rode ahead of my companions and stood atop a hill, looking back at them.

"Matilda, Philip," I called out. I pointed westwards. "If you look to the west, on the horizon, you will see the tall black towers of a great and ancient city. Welcome to Everlynn!"

I looked to the west and did indeed see the towers. The city rose up above the low hills, paddocks, and patches of woodland. Its snow-capped towers, famed for the darkness of the stones with which they are built, seemed to be competing with one another as they reached for the clouds. It was an ancient and glorious city and one of the most powerful in all Ardonn.

But as I gazed into the distance, a chill ran down my spine. My stomach dropped.

At the base of the towers, beneath the city's walls, I saw people. Hundreds upon hundreds of men had gathered, with almost as many tents and horses. Flags and banners fluttered in the breeze.

It was as I feared. This was an army, and these men, Everlynn's warriors, were marching to war.

9

March

Fate is a curious mistress. When poets and scholars tell the history of our world, they often focus on great kings and emperors and explain how the actions of one man have moulded and shaped their kingdoms into what they are today. But what the writers often neglect is the invisible hands of the Gods. Sometimes, the only thing needed to set the world ablaze is a spark. It is often difficult to see how something insignificant and ordinary such as light snowfall can lead the world into chaos.

Yet that was what had occurred over Winterlow. It all happened so fast, and most of the kingdom had no idea what had even occurred. The earl of a small town near the mountains far to the north had died at the age of eighteen when, after a little bit of snow, he slipped on the wet stone steps outside his keep and fell, hitting his head. He died instantly. He had been earl for only a few months, and he left no heir.

Lords die young all the time, and if they are childless, their titles and lands are often passed on to a distant cousin or some other relative. But as though the Gods were playing some cruel jest, when the Earl of Tillysburg cracked open his skull, his eldest cousins were identical twins.

There was no record of which twin was born first, and if there was, it could not be found. So the little town of Tillysburg had a succession crisis. Both twins had an equally justifiable claim to the town and its surrounding lands, but they could not come to an agreement.

The twins, Roger and Rainulf, then called on King Stephan for aid, each presenting him with their claims in the hopes of gaining his support. Stephan chose to remain neutral, believing it best that the locals resolve this matter themselves, but he sent a dozen housecarls to ensure peace. He suggested an election, but the brothers would have none of it.

Seeing that the king would not come to their aid, Roger decided to publicly pledge his allegiance to Carol the Pretender. A riot ensued, with Roger and Rainulf's supporters rising up to fight each other, and so the housecarls had to intervene.

They aided Rainulf, of course, in banishing Roger from Tillysburg. The king could no longer remain neutral, and so his housecarls declared Rainulf the legitimate earl and Roger a rebel and a traitor. Three days later, Roger returned to Tillysburg with several hundred warriors given to him by Carol.

They entered the city, slaughtered Rainulf and his supporters, and hung Rainulf from the bell tower.

But the real issue was when Roger's warriors executed all twelve of the king's men. The king could, in the interest of peace, tolerate the raids carried out by Carol's rebels, but when treasonous noblemen killed royal ambassadors in Carol's name, there was naught the king could do but go to war. If he did not crush the rebellion now, he would seem a coward and lose all claim to the throne his father usurped.

And so he went to war. The king was raising an army and summoning several of his nearby vassals to the capital, chief among these being Lord Odo of Everlynn, whose legendary army would make up almost a third of King Stephan's. They were preparing to march directly on Tillysburg and the Pretender; the town now served as his base alongside his mountain fortress.

All this had happened over the month of Winterlow.

I learned of these events the day my friends and I left the woods and arrived at Everlynn. Lord Odo's army had gathered outside the city's gates and was preparing to march the morning we arrived. Four soldiers rode to meet us as we approached the city and requested that we follow them into the camp. Behind all the pleasantries and the illusion of free will, I knew we were under arrest. This was war, and Odo could not risk any unnoticed infiltration.

The soldiers said nothing as they led us through the camp.

Tents were being dismantled and supplies loaded onto carts, while wives and mothers were saying their final farewells to their husbands and sons. Priests walked through the camp, blessing the soldiers, and bards sang songs to enthuse them.

Yet I sensed not a trace of fear among the men. These were soldiers — warriors — and war was their life. They welcomed the opportunity to crack some skulls and spill some guts. Many were veterans of the civil war and had fought for Odo, a supporter of Edwin who had been pardoned after the war. But now they marched to fight for the bastard son of the man who had usurped their king less than a decade earlier.

We arrived at a large, exquisite tent. I knew this would be Odo's tent, and my suspicions were confirmed when one of the soldiers escorting us announced who we were to meet. The flaps were pulled back, I told my friends to let me do the talking, and then we entered.

It was large, and though it was cold outside, it was warm inside. A fire pit had been dug in the centre, and its heat was bouncing back off the tent's thick walls. A makeshift dais with a small throne had been erected at the back. To its right there was a small dining area, and to its left was a table upon which sat a map and some figurines. Beside this was a mannequin holding Odo's armour, and beside that was a weapon rack holding his sword, his shield, and his long axe.

Gods, what a fearsome axe that was.

Odo and three other men stood around the table. Odo himself

was a formidable man. He made a name for himself during the Usurper's War and acquired a fearsome reputation in battle, and this renown only enhanced his imposing nature. I had never met him before, but the tales I heard about him were all true. He was tall, about a foot higher than most men. He had broad shoulders, thick muscles, and a rigid jaw covered in neatly trimmed black stubble. He had long, dark hair that had been pulled back behind his ears and allowed to fall to his back, and although he was in his thirties, there were already grey streaks in his glorious mane.

He looked up at me. His sharp, dark eyes met mine and almost bored into my soul. Then he smiled, and for a second he looked incredibly familiar. "Guests," he declared. His voice was deep but soft.

The men around his table all turned to look at me. I had no idea who two of them were —some courtiers or generals, I assumed — but I immediately recognised the third man. It was Hakon, dressed in mail and wearing a black cloak. A long, thin sword hung at his belt. He grinned at me, and winked, and I realised then where I had seen Odo's smile before.

"These are my generals," Odo said, gesturing to the men I did not know. "And this is my half-brother, Hakon." The three men all bowed their heads. "Who are you?"

I hesitated. There was no use lying with Hakon present, so I introduced myself and my companions, and they all bowed.

Odo gave us a friendly smile and then waved to his men. "Leave us." Once Odo's generals and bastard brother had left and we were alone with the lord, he went to sit in his throne. "Are you all spies?"

"No, My Lord," I said. "I haven't even any idea why you are assembling an army."

"You have not heard? The king has called us to war!" he said.

And that was when I learned of all that had happened in Tillysburg. Odo, realising we were ignorant of the situation, explained it all to us.

"If you are not spies, where have you all come from?" Odo asked.

"From Oldford, My Lord. We are travelling north to visit a friend of mine in the Capital," I said. That was not entirely a lie.

Odo frowned. "On what business?"

"Does a man need a reason to visit his friends?"

Odo shook his head and smiled. "Edward. Edward from Oldford. Your name sounds familiar," he said. He appeared to be lost in thought for a moment. "You mentioned that boy is your apprentice. What is your trade?"

"I deal with the Otherworldly, My Lord. I am one of the Gifted," I replied.

Odo raised his eyebrows and sat up in his seat. "Ah, of course. Slayer of the vampire of Oldford, immortalised in song. I want your friends to wait outside so that we may speak in private."

"She was a witch. And with all due respect, My Lord, it is cold outside."

"They can wait in my other tent. Guard!" A soldier entered.

"Take these four to my resting tent and give them whatever comforts they desire."

Matilda and I exchanged a look, and I nodded. The four of them followed the soldier outside, and I was now alone with Lord Odo.

"What did you want to speak about, My Lord?"

Odo stood up from his seat, went over to the dining table, then filled two goblets with wine. "I have use for someone like you. I will pay, of course." He handed me one of the goblets and took a sip from his own.

"I am sorry, My Lord, but I must reach the Capital as soon as I can."

"That makes two of us," Odo said. "The king has ordered that I travel north and join his army. That means we are both travelling north. You come with my army, and then we can part ways farther north. You take your payment and be on your way."

"What is it you want from me?"

Odo sighed and went to stand by the fire. "My son cannot sleep. He is plagued by horrible dreams, and my priest tells me it is the work of a foul spirit. The physicians have been no use, and priests do nothing but pray, though perhaps a Godspeaker can help."

"That sounds like a mara," I said.

"Can you banish it?"

"If it is a mara, then yes. What will my reward be?"

Odo thought for a moment. "Ten pounds of gold. And I will

happily conclude that you are not spies," he said with a smile, and I knew at that moment I had no option but to accept. If I refused, he would detain us. But I would not have refused the wealth he offered, even if I did have a choice.

"It should be easy enough. May I see your son?"

"Not yet. He rode ahead with the vanguard, but we will catch up with him by nightfall. You can see him then."

"Very well, My Lord. I will ride with your troops until your son is able to sleep properly again."

"Good, good!" Odo clapped and then rubbed his hands. "Now, we should prepare to leave. I would hate to miss the war. Go and join your friends again. Once you hear the horn blow three times, we will leave."

And so it was. A small northern town had some snow, an earl had died, a war had begun, and now my friends and I were bound to the service of one of the most powerful nobles in the kingdom.

Fate is a curious mistress indeed.

We received word that Odo's vanguard, led by his son William, had made camp on the outskirts of a small manor called Hariton. The rest of the army was to meet the vanguard there and make camp for the night, so my friends and I rode with Odo's oathmen all day long. It was around noon that Hakon brought his horse up beside mine and asked me to speak with him in private.

"It is good to see you again, Edward," Hakon said. We had moved aside from the rest of the army and sat on our horses as we watched the column move slowly along the Royal Way.

"I would be lying if I said the same about you," I replied.

"My heart breaks under the weight of your words."

"I encountered some of your men on the road here."

Hakon chuckled. "Ah, Leif. I was wondering if you had met him. I see you now have one of my men in your service."

"Cubert was my oathman first. You sent Leif to burn my home and slaughter my people, and then you sent him to kill me. Why?"

"You offend me, Edward."

"Your man took my friend's eye."

Hakon stared blankly at the marching army that passed by us. I could sense his anger, but he did well at hiding it. I suspected he was expecting to meet Leif in Everlynn with my sword and my head, but instead he had met me, which meant his warriors were dead. "It is nothing personal. I need your sword — the one you now wear at your belt, I assume. You would not sell it to me, so I was forced to take it. You and your men simply found yourselves in my way," Hakon explained.

"I cannot let you release Emrys. I travelled north to stop you, and I intend to do just that," I said.

A grin spread across his face. "I suppose I will have to kill you myself, then."

"I am under your brother's protection. He has a job for me."

"A pity. But mark me, Edward. Once you are released from this contract, I will not hesitate to glide a blade across your throat."

I did not respond to his threats. I kicked my horse and joined the army, leaving Hakon behind. He just sat on his horse and watched me. I wished I could have killed him then and there, but like me Hakon had the protection of the Lord of Everlynn. I would stay with Odo's army and banish whatever spirit plagued his son. Hakon's death would have to wait.

I did not see the wretch for the rest of the march that day. I suspected he rode with his own men. We arrived at Hariton just before sunset, and the army swiftly made camp. Dughlas and Cubert created a ring of stones for a fire, around which we erected the tents Odo had given us. Philip complained about Matilda's tent being with the rest of ours.

"The men should all have one fire for us to share, and Matilda should take her tent elsewhere and build her own fire," he told me.

"Why?" I asked.

"Because. We can talk about manly things like war, and politics, and ale." Philip was serious, and I laughed. Despite his moaning, I did not make Matilda move her tent, and she teased him relentlessly about having to camp alongside a woman.

After the tents had been erected and we ate our supper, I received a summons to come to Odo's tent for what I guessed would be my task. Philip needed a little taste of our trade, so I took him along with me. He was much happier after hearing that.

We walked through the camp to Odo's tent. Philip admitted that he missed his home and his family, but he was excited to learn about how to properly use his gift. He told me that once he finished his apprenticeship, he would go back to Luria and use his new skills to make his family richer. That warmed my heart.

When we reached Odo's tent, his guards ordered us to hand over any weapons we might be carrying. They let us inside, and we were welcomed by Odo. He handed us both a cup of wine.

"Edward! I have been waiting for you. And if I remember correctly, this is your apprentice?"

Odo stood towering above us. He was tall, taller than me, and was an imposing figure. His eyes were cold, but his smile was warm. I still did not know whether I could trust him.

"Yes, My Lord. He will be helping me," I said.

Odo nodded. "Good. Now, let me introduce you. This is my son, William." Odo turned and gestured to a young man, around eighteen or nineteen, standing at the back of the tent.

William gave me a tired smile and held up a hand in greeting. His grey eyes were heavy and had dark rings around them. He was pale and thin, wore a few days' worth of stubble, and had an unkempt mane of dark blonde hair that fell to his shoulders. William was handsome, though, and had the look of his father, though evidently none of his strength.

What caught my attention, however, was the woman standing beside him. She wore a plain, dark green dress, unusually modest for someone of her status, and although she looked to be of similar age to William, her long black hair had a strange streak of silver in it.

Her most striking feature, however, was her skin. It was the colour of chestnuts, like Philip's but much, much darker. I had only ever seen one person with skin like that before, and that was at the port in Tidegate, where I met an interesting man who had sailed from the lands to the west, across the sea. This woman did have that man's look. Not only did she have his skin, but she also had his high cheekbones, wide brown eyes, and sharp nose.

"And who is this?" I asked.

"She is my daughter-in-law. Eleni is her name," Odo said. Eleni stared at me with intense curiosity and then put her hand on William's arm and whispered something in his ear.

I turned back to Odo. "I will need to speak with your son about his problem before I can know how to fix it."

"Of course, of course. I have matters to attend to with my oathmen, so I will leave the four of you to it," Odo said. He clapped his hands and left the tent. Philip and I went over to William and his wife to introduce ourselves.

"Edward, yes?" William asked. His voice was tired.

"Yes, My Lord. And this is Philip."

William nodded and smiled at us, but it was clearly forced. Eleni gave a low curtsy. "Hello. Please, forget about your manners. My name is William, and I prefer that to 'My Lord,'" he said. "Come, take a seat."

William led us to the table and waited for us to sit before he too took a seat with a sigh. He downed the rest of his wine.

"Tell me about your dreams, then," I said.

William closed his eyes and tipped his head back. "Gods, I do not even know how to explain them," he groaned. "They started a fortnight ago and have plagued my sleep ever since. I have not slept at all in the last two days because I cannot bear to see…it again. I am tired." Eleni watched her husband with a look of deep concern, and she took his hand.

"Could you tell me a bit about this thing that you cannot bear to see? What happens when you sleep?"

"I can try," William sighed.

"That is good enough for me."

And so William told me about his dreams. He said he had horrifying visions of death and torment from which he struggled to wake, but when he did wake up in the dead of the night he found himself dreadfully cold and unable to move, so he would just lie there, frozen.

Though that was not the worst part. Shortly after he would wake, the evil spirits from his dreams surrounded his bed. I asked him if they did anything, but he said they just stood there watching him. Sometimes they whispered to him in a language he could not understand.

Then a creature would appear and straddle him as if to ride him the way a lover would. Sometimes this creature took the form of his wife, other times the form of his sister, and every now and then it would appear as a horrid dwarf-like man. My suspicions had been confirmed.

"This spirit that rides you sounds like a mara and would be the cause of your evil dreams," I told him. "Do you have mara in your country, Philip?"

Philip nodded. "We call them 'pressers.'"

"What does this mara want from me? Am I being punished?" William asked, wide-eyed.

"Punished? Have you done something wrong?" I asked. William shook his head. "Mara will sometimes be sent by Hefenstea to punish wrongdoers or warn those with ill fates, but most of the time they act in the service of Vylan and choose their victims on a whim. Do you speak while you dream or while this spirit rides you?"

He shrugged and looked to his wife.

Eleni nodded. "He speaks. I do not know the language." She spoke slowly, and her accent was very strong. Our language must have been new to her.

"Really?"

"That is what Eleni tells me," William said. "The only language I know is ours, as well as a little of Eleni's tongue. I do not know how I could speak any other."

I rested my chin in my hand, thinking. "It is quite rare for a person to *speak* to a mara. This is interesting."

"What does this mean? Why me?"

"I do not know. But what I do know is that I can banish your mara. I am sorry I cannot give you answers right away, William, but I will meditate on this. Try to get some sleep tonight. Mara grow stronger the wearier you are."

William nodded and squeezed Eleni's hand. She stared at me, as if wanting to say something, but then looked away. I finished the rest of my wine and stood.

"Thank you for what you have told me, and for the wine," I said. "We will speak more tomorrow, and I will see if I can cure you."

"My wife and I thank you, Edward. I hope that even if we do not banish this spirit, I will at least gain a new friend. Goodnight." William smiled, and I gave him a short bow. Philip and I left him alone with his wife and made our way back to where we were camped.

What William had told me was troubling, and all desire I had to sneak away from the camp and escape my bondage with Odo had gone. I had dealt with mara before, but William's case was unique and, frankly, much more severe than most others. I did not wish to tell William, but in most cases the mara only takes the form of the ugly dwarf or some unknown woman.

The fact that William spoke to his mara and that it would take the form of Eleni or his sister told me it was likely Hefenstea, goddess of vengeance, was inflicting some cruel punishment upon him.

But for what?

The next day was very much the same as the day before, except our column was larger. William and the vanguard rode with us, and the Earl of Hariton joined the army, adding an extra hundred or so soldiers. I estimated the entire army numbered at least one thousand strong, with the vanguard making up a quarter of that. This was by no means a large army, nor was it small. Besides, it was only needed to defeat a small group of rebels.

A housecarl I spoke to reckoned the entire force would triple in size once it had joined with the king at the Capital. "The king can raise around four thousand troops from his own lands," the warrior told me. "He will not bring them all, of course."

"Are other noblemen joining the army?" I asked.

"Some lesser nobles will bring their oathmen and a few hundred peasants. Together I'm guessing they'll make up one thousand. But the bulk of the force will comprise of Lord Odo and King Stephan's army."

Odo's men should not have been telling me details about his army. I was no spy, but to tell a stranger about a force's numbers was dangerous.

At around noon the army stopped marching so the soldiers could rest. There was light rainfall — the first I had seen this year. My companions and I found shelter under a large tree so we could stay relatively dry while we ate, but not long after we sat down we were approached by two warriors escorting Eleni. "Hello, Edward," she said.

10

Mara

William sat up in his bed, awaiting instruction. With Eleni and Philip's help, I had been preparing the ritual that would put William to sleep and allow me to banish the mara that possessed him. I brewed a potion of sorts out of a mixture of wine and a special type of mushroom found around animal droppings that I had Philip collect for me. "Tell me again about this ritual," William said.

"Once Eleni has returned from the physician with the herbs I need, I will get you to drink this concoction I have made, we will burn the herbs, and then you will inhale the smoke," I explained. "The smoke will induce the nightmares you are having and trap you within the dream state. The mara will need to expend a lot of energy to wake you up this time, and that will weaken it."

"This sounds…safe."

"You're in good hands. The drink will make your dreams more vivid but will loosen the mara's hold so you may speak to me while it torments you. I will not be able to see the mara, so I will need you to tell me when it appears."

William sighed. I could tell he was fearful, but I was confident in my ability to banish this spirit. I had dealt with beings far worse in my time. William was about to speak, but Eleni entered and interrupted him. She wore her large, plain cloak again because the rain had returned. Eleni carried a small bag and smiled as she came in.

"I have the plants," she said. She handed me the bag, and I poured the herbs out into an empty bowl.

"Thank you," I said. "You kept them dry, yes?"

"Yes."

I began crushing the herbs and mixing them together. I asked Eleni to fetch me a large match, which I would use to burn the herbs and create smoke.

"Is there anything I need to do, master?" Philip asked. He sat by the fire, keeping it burning.

"When I say so, put out the fire and wait outside with Lady Eleni," I replied. I did not want Philip present once the mara appeared because he was still untrained in the using of his Gift, which could have been more an obstacle than a boon. He wanted to watch but understood why he could not.

Everything was now ready. William was comfortable and prepared to sleep, the mushroom concoction was made, and the herbs were ready to burn. I handed William the cup and instructed him to down it all. He grimaced but managed to swallow all of it.

"Out, everyone," I said.

Philip emptied a jug of water over the fire. It hissed. I took a deep breath and put a rag over my mouth while the other two left the tent. I pressed the match against the mixed herbs, and they started to smoke and catch. I held them out to William and told him to breathe it all in. He took three long, deep breaths. One. Two. Three.

"It won't take long, My Lord."

Sure enough, William's eyes fluttered and his breathing softened. He drifted off to sleep. I waited in silence, meditating, listening to the soft patter of rain on the roof of the tent and the last gasps of breath made by the fire's embers, along with the occasional laugh or shout from somewhere in the camp. I made a few quiet prayers and let my mind focus as I sat in darkness. William would dream soon, and with those dreams would come his tormentor.

Before long he began to mumble.

"William," I whispered, moving over to his side. "Can you hear me?"

He muttered something but aside from that made no response. I sat back and waited. William twitched and shivered while whispering and mumbling incoherently. He was dreaming now, and soon the mara would come. It would take a lot of strength for it to break into William's mind and feed on his nightmares this time. I would have the upper hand.

Or so I thought.

"Ed—Edward," William said. "Edward, I cannot move."

"Calm yourself, I am here, my friend. Trust in the Gods," I said. I put a hand on William's arm and squeezed. His body was like ice. It was dark, but despite that I could see William trembling.

"She is here," he said.

A cold chill crept up my spine. "What form does it take?"

"A girl. I do not know her." His voice was a whisper, as though he feared the spirit would hear him.

"Describe her."

"Her skin is pale. She is thin. Her eyes glow blue, and her hair is black as night. She has the wings of a moth—"

I shuddered. "That will do, William. Can you touch her?"

"She sits on my chest. I cannot move."

"Ask her name."

I heard William mumble something. I did not understand, but it seemed he spoke another language, some harsh and guttural tongue. Then he spoke to me. "She will not reply. She only stares."

And at that, my blood ran cold. It was as I feared. William was ruled by a mara sent by the Avenger. Lesser mara — the Thorns in the service of Vylan — would never refuse to offer their names. They were proud spirits and wanted their victims to

246

know exactly who haunted their sleep.

I had banished many mara both before and after my master's death, and each time they had revealed their names. I needed a name so I could banish the mara. The charm required it. "Do not take your eyes off of her, William," I said.

I reached into the pouch at my belt and pulled out a small iron trinket. It was little more than a bent rod, but it had hidden power. I placed it in William's hand and closed his fist tight around it.

"She is watching you," William warned. I felt the air turn cold. Very cold. The tent flapped and shook. I fell back, picked up my sword, and clambered to my feet. I held the hilt with both hands and pointed the blade in William's direction.

I must admit, my spirits were shaken in that moment. I was afraid. What calmness I did have was now gone, and my heart was racing. I could hear the blood pumping in my ears, beating like the drums of death.

"Begone, monster," I yelled. "Begone, foul spirit! Go back to the world in which you belong. You are henceforth banished from here, vile slave of Hefenstea. Return to your mistress. Begone!"

That was no proper incantation. I made it up as I went, since I was at a loss for what to say. I was hoping beyond all hope that this mara would be like those I had faced before, but I should have known better. The incantation was false, and of course, it did not work.

And then came the screaming. At first I thought it was in the tent, or near it, but as it grew louder, I knew it was in my head. Or was it? I dropped my sword and fell to my knees, my hands pressed against my ears in vain.

I knew those screams. I do not know how I knew, but I did. They were the cries of my mother in her final moments. She died in childbirth, bringing me into the world, and for that I had never been able to forgive myself. I never knew my mother or her voice, only her screams of anguish as she tore and bled and died. A second voice began to wail in my head, and it spoke to me.

"My Lady has a message for you, Edward the Gifted. Edward the Doomed," the shrill voice cried. "She bids me tell you this world shall be smitten by your own action, and only that which you do not intend can save it. The Lady of Night advises you keep the Earl of Henton's daughter close. She shall be your light in the darkness you have forged. She shall be your light. She shall be your light."

Fear gripped my heart and coursed through my veins. I shouted over the voice and over the screams. "Alcyn, Hefencyn, Lufi, Hildafol. Oh Gods, do not forsake me. Carry this creature away," I prayed. Tears ran down my cheeks.

"She shall be your light. Your light…" The voice faded. The screams stopped. The violent shaking of the tent's walls ceased, and soon all I could hear was the light tapping of rain.

Then William began to snore. I reached down, shaking, and found my sword. My knuckles turned white as I gripped the hilt.

It was over.

I climbed back to my feet and wiped my face with my sleeve. My heart was still racing, but relief now washed over me. The spirit was gone, and the night was once again calm, though how I banished it I did not know. Had my fearful pleas roused pity in the hearts of the Gods, or had the mara finished its business?

I sheathed my sword and headed back outside. Eleni and Philip stood there and turned as they heard the tent's flaps open. In the torchlight, I could see the worry on their faces.

"A vicious wind came over us," Lady Eleni said. "We heard shouting from inside. Is my husband…?"

"William is sound asleep, My Lady. My job here is done."

Eleni sighed, and a weary smile came to her lips. "You have my eternal gratitude, Edward. There is no word in your tongue or mine that can express the thanks you deserve."

"Lord Odo's gold will be thanks enough. Forgive me, My Lady, but I am exhausted. I must bid you goodnight."

"Of course. We should speak tomorrow, so William and I may thank you properly."

I nodded and stood aside for the lady. She entered her husband's tent, and I turned to Philip. He opened his mouth to speak, but I shook my head. He nodded. We walked silently back to where we were camped, where we found Matilda sitting alone by the fire, wrapped in furs. She was wet, her black hair matted down. The fire coughed and sputtered as it struggled against the light rainfall. I bid Philip goodnight and sat on the stool beside

Matilda. She was shivering.

"It's late and miserable, My Lady. You should be in your tent," I said.

"I could not sleep, and the fire shields me from the worst of the cold," said Matilda. "I find comfort in gentle, night-time rain like this. It is like the soft tears of Hefenstea, weeping for what she has lost."

I said nothing, only stared into the flames, watching them flicker and hiss and toss sparks into the air. I thought about what had happened in the tent. What I had heard and felt. I took a deep breath, and my eyes began to water. The shock was disappearing. I started to sob.

"Edward?" Matilda said.

I put my face in my hands and wept. "Osmund was right. I'm cursed."

I had worn a tough face for Philip and Eleni since I left William's tent, partly because my experience there had left me numb and confused. But now, for some reason, my strength had failed, and I let out all my fear and despair. Matilda slowly put her arms around me and pulled me close, and I cried into her shoulder. She said nothing, I said nothing, and we sat there shivering in the cold and wet by a dying fire for a very long time.

"We will die out here soon," Matilda said after a while, breaking the silence.

I nodded. "I'll light a fire in my tent. We can warm ourselves inside."

We went into my tent, I pushed my bedroll as close to the side as possible, and cleared a space on the floor to light a fire. My tent was not large, like William's, but there was enough room for the two of us. It was also dry, aside from a small leak by the entrance. The tent quickly filled with smoke, so I opened the flap a crack to let it escape. I was beginning to warm already, and Matilda and I removed our cloaks and placed them by the fire.

"Do you mind?" I asked. I started undoing my tunic, which was also soaked. Matilda shook her head, and I stripped down to my pants.

Matilda took the fur blanket I slept under and wrapped it around herself. She shuffled and wriggled, and I frowned, then she tossed her wet dress from under the blanket. She wrapped the fur around her tightly and stared into the fire. She glanced at me every so often, but aside from that we just sat there for some time as we dried off.

"Forgive me for my show of weakness," I said.

Matilda shook her head. "I cannot judge you for it. I do not know what a Godspeaker must face."

"Something happened in that tent," I said. "It was no ordinary mara that possessed William. I believe it was sent by the Gods, but I do not know why."

"What happened?"

"I cannot explain it. It could be mere coincidence, but I believe the mara appeared to William as you for some reason, though you had the wings of a moth. And I heard my mother screaming."

"I do not understand."

I did my best to explain the details. My fear had gone, but now I was once more puzzled and haunted by a sense of dread. The Gods and their servants only appear fearsome to those they are punishing. What had I done, or what was I to do, to earn their wrath?

Matilda tried to understand, but I could tell it confused her as much as it confused me. I felt fear begin to grow in my heart once more, so I shook my head and stopped talking. Matilda took the hint. "Tell me about those scars," she said.

I looked down at the numerous scars that decorated my upper body and pointed to the long, wretched one on my breast. "You have probably heard about this one," I began. "When I fought the witch in Oldford, she swung a lumber axe at me. My mail took most of the blow, but my ribs took the rest."

I moved my finger to one on my right shoulder. "This one was an arrow. Bandits would raid my lands every so often, and my oathmen and I would fight them back each time." I smiled a little. "Cubert saved my life that day."

I pointed to the scar on my left arm. "During another skirmish against raiders, I blocked a blow from a hammer with an old shield. The wood splintered and stuck in my arm. It was a bitch to remove. Pardon my tongue."

Matilda chuckled. "What about that one?" She nodded to the mark at the side of my abdomen.

"A pig gored me while I was hunting. Fortunately, it was not deep," I said.

Matilda cringed. Her hair was dry now but was all messy and knotted. We locked eyes for a moment and then she looked away. I noticed her face turn red. "You know," Matilda began, "when I first met you, and while we stayed in Oldford, I believed you were some great warrior. Untouchable. Undefeated. Travellers from Oldford would speak of your deeds and make you sound almost godlike. Stories always make the heroes out to be perfect."

"And do you still think that?"

Matilda shook her head. "I know you are brave. I know you have skill with a blade. But you are nothing like the travellers and merchants make you seem. Your body is evidence of that."

"Only the good warriors have scars. The bad ones don't live to bear them."

Matilda smiled. "The stories also do not tell of your temper. They do not tell of your coldness or of your pride. Stories of your deeds tell of Edward the Gifted, but you sit before me as Edward the Man. Edward the Flawed."

"I am sorry I do not live up to your expectations."

"No, you exceed them. I much prefer this Edward. My favourite poems and tales are those that tell of the hero's imperfections."

I nodded. "Perhaps you are right. When I tell my children and my children's children of my adventures, I will try to tell them of my failings. And of yours, Lady of Henton."

Matilda smiled but said nothing. She glanced at my scars once more and then stared back into the flames. We sat again in silence for a time, listening to the little fire crackle, the rain fall against the tent, and the drops of water dripping through the leak and into the small puddle it had made beneath it.

I pulled on a shirt once I was dry, and after a while I began to notice Matilda struggling to keep her eyes open. Without a word, she lay down on her side by the fire, curled up under my fur blanket. It did not take her long to fall asleep.

I rolled up one of my other shirts and lifted her head gently, putting the shirt underneath to act as a pillow. She did not wake. I watched her and the fire and the rain deep into the night. I was thinking about the mara again, and of my mother. Was she watching me from wherever she was? Did I make her proud? I hoped so.

I did not realise how long I sat there until I heard a lone bird sing in the distance. The night was slowly drawing to an end. The fire had died down, and Matilda was deep in sleep. I decided I should get a few hours of rest before the army marched again at daybreak, so I lay down on my bedroll and closed my eyes. I must have been the last in camp to fall asleep.

The rain did not pass before dawn the next day, so the army departed in a miserable mood. It was little more than drizzle, but it still made us cold and wet. The ground was muddy and sloshed under our feet, and everyone knew this would slow us down. The Royal Way had fallen into disrepair here, and the paving had long ago degraded into the dirt.

As the army began its march and my companions and I were packing up our things to load back onto the wagon, William approached us with an escort of six housecarls. He sat upon a beautiful white stallion in a shining suit of mail. Draped over his shoulders was a thick woollen cloak dyed a deep blue, fastened by a white-gold brooch in the shape of a hare — William's personal emblem.

He smiled at me as he approached, and despite the rain, he was cheerful. The dark circles around his eyes were gone, and there was colour in his cheeks. His hair was combed back behind his ears but otherwise fell loose. He had the look of a brave young warrior off to make a name for himself in war, like in the heroic tales of old. "A fine morning, is it not? I do love the scent of grass in the rain," William said. He dismounted, and we clasped each other's forearms. "Edward, I wish to thank you for—"

"It was my pleasure, but I would rather not talk about it," I said. He frowned but nodded.

"I have a message for the lady who travels with you," William said. "My wife wishes to travel with her in the carriage today. She says a noblewoman should not be made to ride on horseback in this weather, and I must say I agree."

"I am sure she will be grateful for that offer," I replied. "She and Dughlas are watering their horses at the moment, but I will send for her. Cubert!"

Cubert turned away from helping Philip load the wagon and came over to me. "Yes, lord?"

"Go and fetch Matilda, and take her to Lady Eleni's carriage, if she so wishes. I would also have you ride alongside it today."

"As you wish, lord."

"You two, go with him," William said. He pointed to two of his warriors and sent them off with Cubert.

Philip came to stand beside me. William thanked him for his help with the mara, and Philip nodded, but he was in a sorry state. His nose was runny, and he frequently sniffled, and I feared he had come down with a cold. That was often the case when southerners travelled north during the colder months. He had wrapped himself in thick leathers and furs, but they did little to protect him.

"Can I ride in the cart with Matilda too?" he asked me.

I looked at William and raised my eyebrows, and he nodded. "You are in no state to ride today, little Lurian," he said. I nodded for him to go, ruffled his curly locks, and he followed Cubert and William's warriors. "I am feeling much better today, Edward. As if I have been born anew. Tell me, did you sleep well, my friend?"

"I slept well," I replied.

"Excellent. I will make sure the payment my father promised gets to you. Will you allow me to ride with you today?"

"It would be my pleasure. May I ask why you're wearing your mail and not travelling with your wife?" I continued packing up the last of our gear.

William threw the cloak off his arms and began to help. "Well, it allows me to get used to it, plus my men will feel like I am one of them. I am to be the Lord of Everlynn one day, so I should learn to lead."

"You are making a fine example already, if I may say so."

William laughed. "You may."

We finished loading our gear onto the transport wagon. The wagons carried the essentials that could not be carried in bags or on horses, and they lumbered along behind the army, dragged by strong mules. The carriages carrying noblemen and their women and children also travelled with this part of the army, and today this would include Matilda and Philip, though I feared the wet weather would muddy the ground too much and slow the wagons significantly.

I introduced William to Dughlas, and he was quite impressed by my oathman's new scar, calling him a "fearsome-looking man." William was right — Dughlas did look fearsome. Even without his patched eye and the gruesome scar running down his face, his long, bright hair and beard, broad shoulders, and tall stature were menacing. He had bought a new coat of mail from Odo's quartermaster, which he now wore under his cloak and tied at the waist with a thick leather belt. I would not want to fight him.

"This is a man I want as a friend," William said to me before turning his attention back to Dughlas. "May I ask how…"

Dughlas chuckled. "Some bandits attacked us on the way here from Oldford, and I missed a parry during the fight, so my opponent scratched my face. Nothing too major." He loved bragging about his new scar. I had already heard him tell the story in all its gory details to dozens of the soldiers we travelled with.

He had his wound tended to, as did Cubert, on the day we arrived at Lord Odo's camp. I admit, the healers did a much better job at fixing it than I had. He had even developed a liking for Gyde, the woman who patched him up. She had to remove the eyeball, and during the surgery Dughlas screamed so loud I reckoned he could be heard from all the way in Erila. I later discovered he had been with her while I banished William's mara.

Once William and Dughlas stopped chatting, we all mounted our horses and joined the column. We were among the first to leave that morning, so we were at the front of the marching army. My fears regarding the wagons came true; they were bogged down by the mud and trundled along slowly. Three of my friends were all the way at the other end with them, and that made me uneasy.

The march this day was much merrier than one would expect in such weather, because William was constantly passing jokes down the line and sharing tales and songs. He even knew a ballad about me and my fight with the witch in Oldford, although the song insisted it was a vampire.

His housecarls accompanied us, and they sang along with William. He made the most of the day, and he seemed an entirely different person now that his Otherworldly tormentor was gone. Despite the rain and the cold and the muddy slush we travelled through, William was happy. But that slush meant the wagons and carriages lagged far behind.

"I am always urging my father to post more soldiers to the wagon train," William told me. "But he insists it would be unnecessary. 'The rebels are in the north,' he says, 'and our wagons are in the south.'" He lowered his voice and pulled a face, and his men laughed.

"Why don't you put your own men at the back?" Dughlas asked him.

"Oh, I do. I have a dozen oathmen guarding my wife's carriage. But most of the men I command are technically my father's. I have only a small retinue."

A calm voice spoke up behind us. "I agree with you, William. It would be wise to leave a portion of the soldiers with the carriages. They are left vulnerable to attack if they are unprotected." We all turned to see who had spoken.

"Thank you, Uncle. Perhaps you can convince my father to guard the wagons," William replied. We had been approached by Hakon, and he flashed me a cruel smile.

"I have tried. Your father is stubborn, unfortunately," Hakon said. "Why are you not with your wife, Nephew?"

"I wish to ride with my friends today."

"You should be with your wife."

"Are you with yours, Uncle?"

Hakon scoffed and turned his horse away from us. He rode off back down the column.

"What was that about?" Dughlas asked.

"I hate my uncle," William said. "He is a spineless, scheming fool. And a bastard. I am certain he wishes me dead so he can succeed my father."

"Do you have no other brothers?" I asked.

William chuckled. "I have seven sisters, but no brothers. Legally, Anora should succeed my father if I were to die, but Hakon has more men and wealth than she."

"Sword and Silver: the two lords Law must kneel to."

William only nodded. We rode on, despite the weather. Lord Odo, whom I did not get to see that morning, apparently insisted we march through the rain so we could reach the Capital on time. William continued to talk with us for a while, and I got to know him and his men better.

Our conversation was cut short when we heard horns. Battle horns, coming from the rear of the marching column. We could hear the beating of hooves and the hammering of boots, and there was a sudden confusion rushing down the line. Men and women began shouting, and William, Dughlas, and I all turned our horses and drew our swords, as did the warriors that rode with us. "What is happening?" William asked.

"The rear is under attack!" a soldier shouted. Without hesitation, William kicked his horse and sped off down the line, followed by his men. Dughlas and I glanced at each other, and a wave of fear washed over me. Matilda, Philip, and Cubert were at the rear.

I knew this would happen. I knew it in my gut the moment I woke to the sound of rain. The wagons would be slowed considerably, and it left them vulnerable. War was not often waged that early in the year for reasons like this, but ill luck had forced King Stephan's hand.

I kicked my horse and rode with haste down the column, followed by Dughlas. The air rushed past my face, cold and hard, and my mind had gone empty. I thought only of one thing: reaching the wagons to defend my companions. I had failed to defend those I had sworn to protect when my home was attacked, and I would be damned if I failed now.

There was confusion along the whole column, with men shouting and warriors rushing back and forth, unsure of what to do or where to go. Panic had struck this army.

As I reached the rear of the column, some soldiers were rushing to fight off the attackers, raiders mounted on horseback wearing black cloaks and hoods to conceal their identity. There were perhaps only a few dozen, but they struck hard and fast and in the confusion managed to slay twice their number. Help had come too late.

I pulled the reins and reared Brand, pausing momentarily to assess my surroundings. His hooves skidded through the mud. Many of the raiders were already fleeing now that the army was coming to its senses, but some remained. I saw William and his oathmen cutting down those that stayed behind, and Cubert fought with them.

Eleni's carriage had a broken wheel, and its horses had broken free and escaped. The driver was pinned to the carriage with a spear through his chest. The dozen or so men that guarded the carriage were either dead or wounded, and amongst the mess lay Eleni.

Almost without thinking, I turned Brand sharply to the left and lifted my sword, parrying an incoming blow from the raider that chose to attack me. A poor choice. Brand butted the raider's horse with his head, and it reared back with a cry. I turned my horse further and with one sideways cut opened my assailant's chest. He died screaming and gurgling as he slid from his horse and landed on the muddy road with a splash.

I turned back around in time to notice Dughlas thrust his blade through another of the raiders who had made an attempt to strike my rear. I gave him a quick nod. The rest of the raiders realised that they would only die if they continued to fight, so they too rode off to join their comrades, but William was not going to show mercy so easily. His wife had been assaulted, and he wanted vengeance, so he raced after the raiders to ride them down.

"Go with them," I shouted to Dughlas. He nodded and rode off to join William in his chase. I threw myself down from my horse and ran over to Eleni. She was unconscious, so I lifted her, propping her up against the carriage's good wheel.

She groaned. It appeared there was no permanent damage. A nasty gash in her forehead was bleeding down her face, and she only opened one eye when I said her name. Her lip was also broken, and her nose bled.

"William?" she said.

"No, it's Edward," I said. I knelt down and looked Eleni in the eye, and she slowly opened her other one. Her eyeball was red.

"Edward," she mumbled. "They came out of nowhere."

"Where is Matilda?" I snapped.

She winced. "They took her. And Philip too. I tried to stop them, but… I cannot fight."

With those words, utter despair fell over me. I was a fool. I knew there would be danger on this journey, but against reason I brought Matilda and Philip along anyway. I sat there, and the world seemed to freeze.

Eleni put her arms around me and kept saying she was sorry over and over again, but I just ignored her. I knew who those men were. I recognised their black cloaks and their noble dress. They were no ordinary bandits, and they had attacked the wagons for one purpose. Robbers would have targeted gold and material wealth, but this was personal.

Matilda and Philip would become bait and I, honour-bound to

stay true to the oath I swore to Liviu and the promise I had made to Matilda, would have no choice but to walk into the trap that was set for me.

My enemy had won.

11

Captive

Once Eleni was safe, I raced as hard as I could to catch up to William and his men. I was too late, however. I met them as they returned, unsuccessful, having slain some of the raiders, but many had escaped. Philip had not been saved.

Fortunately, Matilda had been rescued. She rode with Dughlas as the warriors returned from their chase, jumped down from his horse, and ran to embrace me.

"The daring lass managed to wriggle free, though not before showing her captor how hard a lady can bite," Dughlas explained.

Matilda nodded with tears in her eyes. "I went for a bit of a tumble, but I am all right." She smiled and looked down at her muddy dress.

William sped to his wife's aid and helped tend to her head

wound. She was only dazed; after a few days rest she would be well again. Other soldiers and the healers were now coming to help the wounded while I spoke to Dughlas and Cubert about our next move.

"It was Hakon. I know it. I want to go after them," I said.

"He'll want you to do that. You're safer with his brother's army," said Dughlas.

"No. I swore an oath to Philip's father, Livi. I swore that he would be safe as long as he is apprenticed to me. I am sure Brendan would do the same."

Dughlas nodded and then turned as William approached us. "Edward, my friend, I am sorry. Your apprentice…"

"I need to find him. Forgive me, but we must part ways."

William understood well enough and offered us advice. He told us where he had chased them and the direction in which they fled, and he insisted we accept his aid. I would not take his men, but I gladly accepted his offer of food and provisions. I also had Dughlas find Matilda a change of clothes, something more suitable for travelling than the dresses she had brought with her from Oldford.

We bid farewell to William and Eleni, and they thanked me once again for helping them with the mara. I introduced Matilda to William and asked if she was the girl the tormentor appeared as the previous night. He insisted that although they looked similar, Matilda was not the girl. That made me at least somewhat relieved — but if it was not Matilda, then who? My question would have to remain unanswered.

As soon as we were able, we went off on our way. We followed the tracks of a number of horses through the countryside and the empty meadows and grasslands to the east of the royal road. This area of the kingdom was miserable. It rained frequently; in the wet months it was often flooded, and the ground was always muddy.

The fields were grim, with no crops and few livestock. The grass was grey and the trees twisted and bare. In the distance we could see tall hills lining the horizon to the east at the edge of that flat, wet land — but only barely, for there was a constant shroud of mist in that country. William told us that if we rode northeast for about a week from the place we were attacked, we would arrive in Tillysburg, but the tracks we followed appeared to be taking us eastwards, so eastwards we went.

"Hakon knows you care for Philip and Matilda," Cubert said to me as we rode.

"How?"

"Egil. He and I didn't think it'd matter, but I guess Hakon has made use of that knowledge."

"What else did you or Egil tell him about me?"

"Not much else, lord."

I did not blame Cubert. This was my fault, and I should have known better. I should have kept my friends safe. There was only one course of action now. We would hunt down Hakon's men, rescue Philip, and if Hakon was with them, I would kill him. Even if I had sworn no oath to Livi, I would still have followed Philip's captors because I had grown fond of the boy. He reminded me of myself.

The air was still as we travelled. There was no wind, and our voices echoed. This was a dreary land. Folk called it the Mireland, and I could see why, though it once had a different name, now forgotten. In the days before the Unification, the Mireland was home to a petty kingdom, but all memory of it had faded into its mists. It was now home to a dejected and neglected people who made a living scraping whatever crops they could from the boggy earth.

Just before nightfall, we found a small village, ironically called Greensted, and decided it would be a good idea to rest and continue our search the next day. I wanted to keep going through the night, but the others convinced me we needed our rest, and we would barely be able to see the tracks in the dark anyway. The owner of the inn reassured us that we were right to stay there, since vampires and dead men wandered the fields of this country at night. Perhaps that was true, or perhaps it was just a lie to attract more patrons. We rented the last two vacant rooms, and I retired immediately. The others stayed downstairs for a drink and some food.

The room was small, but it was better than sleeping outside in the cold. The floorboards creaked, and there was a small hole in the corner by the roof, letting in a draft. On the wall opposite the door was a window, and there was a bed on each side. An armchair sat beneath the window beside a small end table, on which sat a single candle.

I lit the candle and opened the shutters to let the moonlight in then sat down in the chair and stared outside. The window faced towards the east, and I could make out the silhouettes of tall hills against the starry sky. I suspected that was where Philip was being taken. Hakon's men could lose us in those hills, so we had to catch them while we still followed on low, flat land. I prayed they would not harm him.

"Edward?" Matilda poked her head into the room. She opened the door slowly and then entered and sat on the bed opposite me. She held a tankard in one hand and a steaming bowl in the other. "Mushroom soup and warm wine," she said, placing the food and drink on the end table. I ignored it. "Dughlas and Cubert are sharing the other room, so that means we are together tonight." I nodded, said nothing, and kept staring into the night. "Edward, I am sorry."

I turned my head slowly to look at her, and for a few moments I stared into her big blue eyes. They were wet. "I feel so useless," I mumbled before looking back out the window. I rested an arm on the table, and I felt Matilda's gentle hand rest on mine. She squeezed it.

"It is not your fault. We will find him," she assured me. I nodded and clenched my jaw. It was very dark with the room only lit by the candle and the dim moonlight. The flickering flame made Matilda's eyes glisten.

"You've stuck by me through all of this, when you could have easily returned home. Why?" I asked.

"You promised me an adventure when you stole me away from Henton."

"I remember," I said.

Matilda pulled something from under her shirt, and it shimmered like a star as moonlight shone faintly through the window. "Do you remember giving me this on the night we left?"

I could not help but smile. "The moth pendant. You wear it."

"Of course I do. It reminds me of the promise you made me."

"It seems so long ago that I first met you, but it really wasn't."

"A lot has happened since. And what an adventure it has been."

"Do you remember how close we were to being caught by your father's guards?"

"Yes! If we had been a few moments too slow, they would have seen us for sure."

"And your mother — my heart almost stopped for good when she appeared."

Matilda laughed. I turned my attention to the food she had brought me. I did not realise how hungry I was, but now it hit me, and it felt like my stomach was tied in a knot. I had not eaten all day.

"Edward…" Matilda began. She looked away.

"What is it?"

"I noticed, when we were in Oldford, you were quite close with Ecwyn. She said you two are just friends, but I was wondering about it. Are you…?"

"Am I what?"

"Do you love her?"

I laughed and shook my head. "No, Ecwyn is right. We became close while I stayed in Oldford with my master, many years ago."

"Oh. Good."

"Good?"

"It is quite beautiful out there, if you think about it." Matilda looked out at the fields surrounding Greensted. It was indeed beautiful.

We spent the rest of the night chatting about trivial, pointless things, distracting ourselves from the reality of our situation, and I admit for a few hours I almost forgot my despair over Philip and just enjoyed Matilda's company, as if nothing else mattered.

A harpist played a soft, melancholy tune downstairs, and the melody floating up to our room filled me with wistful sadness. We could hear the occasional cow lowing in the distance, its deep, sad sound echoing across the hills and pastures. Sometimes another cow responded, as if they were speaking to one another. I liked to think they were, and I wondered what, in the dead of the night, cows would talk about.

The harpist continued to play. His songs were all sorrowful. Sometimes he sang in a strange but pretty tongue, though that just made the songs more beautiful.

"What language is that?" Matilda asked.

I pointed out the window. "There is a land to the east beyond the mountains on the borders of our kingdom. It is full of hills and lakes and rivers, and the spirits are almost as numerous as the people. The harpist is singing in the language of those people."

"Have you ever been there?"

"No, but I have heard it is beautiful, and legend says the land was created by the elves. Dughlas was born there, did you know?"

"I think he mentioned it once or twice. Can you understand the harpist?"

I nodded. "A little. He sings of the tragedy of Erian and Erianwen."

"I do not know that tale."

"Really? It is a legend from Lakeland," I explained. "In days long past, a girl named Erianwen disappeared one night, taken while dancing in a grotto with some fairies. Her twin brother, Erian, set out into the woods to rescue her. He journeyed into the Otherworld and faced the Fairy-King, all so he might see his sister once again."

"And did he? See his sister?"

I smiled. "He did. He found Erianwen dancing with the fairies and had to overcome three trials to save her. But it was all for naught. Erianwen died before they could leave the Otherworld, slain by Erian's own blade. '*And it is said, as poor Wen bled, her brother rose seas with the tears he shed. Though not for her end did he lament, which all mortals must face once we're spent, but for the passing of his twin's sweet smile as she sailed for the fairy-folk's isle. Hence her warm laughter Erian would ne'er hear 'mongst the oaks and birches again. And sing by the ancient grotto she'd ne'er, for the fair Erianwen does dance, dance, dance with the fairies forever.*'" I looked towards the east, to the far-off homeland of the ill-fated twins.

"What happened to Erian?" Matilda asked.

I shrugged. "Who can say? Some suggest he still wanders the Otherworld, unable to leave his sister behind. Others say he found his way out but that upon his return to this world, millennia had passed and all that Erian knew and loved was gone."

"And what do you think?"

"I believe he is still out there. Alone. Afraid. A doomed man till the very end."

We listened as the harpist finished his song. It was indeed a sad tune. After a while, Matilda asked me once more about my travels and the lands I had seen. I told her some more, trying to recall the stories I had already told her in the past. I told her about my adventures in the south and in the north beyond the Northern Alps, and about the time I went across the sea to the Glacier Cape — a land full of dwarves and ice and headlands made of rock as pale as snow. Matilda loved to hear of my adventures; the lands beyond her home fascinated her. I told her that although new lands are beautiful and full of wonder, my travels had only strengthened my love for my homeland.

After our conversation died we sat in silence for a few moments before Matilda sighed. "It is not fair," she said.

"What is not fair?"

"I was thinking about Lilly, and the danger I have put her in. Do you regret killing horses in battle?"

I smiled. "Yes, but we do what we must in the heat of combat. If challenged by a rider with shield, mail, and helm, one must find his weakness. Often, that weakness is the horse."

"I understand." Matilda stared out into the night. "The world is cruel, sometimes."

I said nothing. Matilda began to doze off at around midnight, so we went to bed. She fell into a deep sleep almost as soon as I blew out the candle, but I left the shutters open, and in the moonlight I could just make out Matilda's face. I lay on my side, watching her sleep. She looked so peaceful, and from across the room I could hear her mumbling in her dreams. I struggled to sleep, as I did most nights, and after several hours I lay on my back and wondered if I would get any rest before sunrise. At that moment, I heard a soft patter on the windowsill. I looked up to see a very large, white moth staring straight at me.

"Hello," I whispered. It fluttered across the room and landed on the shelf by the door. It stared at me, and I stared back, and I began to drift into a dreamless sleep. I do not know how long the moth stayed, but I had a strange feeling it sat on that shelf watching me until dawn.

My despair had almost vanished the next day. I was now determined — vengeful, even — but confident we would find Philip. After a night's rest and a big breakfast, my mood had lifted.

That is, until we realised we had lost the tracks. It had rained while we slept, and that rain had turned the ground into sludge. The tracks were gone, and I wondered how we would find Philip now.

We decided to ask around the village to determine if anyone had seen horsemen wearing black passing through with a young boy. We split up and spent about an hour finding whatever information we could. No one seemed to have seen Hakon's men come through this way, and I began to lose hope once more, not to mention the fact that I struggled even speaking to the peasants at all, for the superstitious folk of the countryside feared people like me. We often show up where Shadow dwells, and some see this darkness as a result of our presence, rather than our presence as a result of the darkness. It was not always like this, my master once said.

Matilda had better luck. "Edward, I found them," she shouted. She came to a stop and paused for a moment to catch her breath. "I found them."

"Where?"

Matilda pointed eastwards. "A farmer I spoke to said that last night a company of horsemen dressed in black, with a southerner, came to his home asking for a place to stay. He said the boy barely spoke except to say 'yes' and 'no,' and it made the farmer uneasy. He let them stay in his barn, and during the night he went to spy on them."

"And? What did he see?"

"They were drinking and talking, and the boy was drinking and eating too, but not with the men. They seemed unhappy, apparently. They said it was dishonourable to take a child and could not wait to hand him over to their lord once they reached Mudhill."

"Mudhill?"

"The farmer said it is an old wooden fort about a day's ride from here. It is occupied by outlaws. They call the man in charge the 'Muddy Earl.' These lands belong to some old thane, but their true ruler is the man in Mudhill."

We wasted no time in riding east. I thought if we hurried we might be able to catch them before they arrived at Mudhill.

It was a difficult journey that day, however. Our horses struggled through the mud, and even though we travelled along what the locals called a road — it was barely that — there were points on our journey where we had to dismount and walk so the horses would not sink. The mist was thicker that day, so we could barely see more than a few yards ahead of us. Matilda

hated it. She complained that she had never seen mud like this
before, and all the while Dughlas and Cubert teased her
mercilessly. The leather pants Dughlas had found for her were
made for travelling, but she nevertheless rolled them up above
her knees so they would not get too dirty. She took her boots off
too and hung them from her horse.

"It feels so disgusting," she moaned as we waded through a
layer of thick sludge. "It is oozing between my toes."

I laughed. "Put your boots back on then."

"They will get dirty. Why can they not just build a proper
bloody road?"

"You're a snob, Tilly." Dughlas chuckled. "Did you not get
dirty searching for bugs in Oldford's woods?"

Matilda scowled at him. "I do not mind dirt if I know I will be
able to wash soon afterwards. Edward, can you carry me?"

"You're joking…"

"Please?"

"Fine, come on then." I crouched down so Matilda could hop
on my back. She squelched over, put her hands on my shoulders,
jumped up and then wrapped her arms and legs around me while
I held on to her thighs. Cubert and Dughlas were hysterical.

"Take note of this, men," I said. "This is heroism."

"I've heard many stories of gods and heroes, but none of them
carry women on their backs through the mud," Cubert said.

"That's because a real hero would never bring a lady to a place
like this," Dughlas said. I glared at both of them, and they soon

calmed down.

We carried on, treading through the mud until our horses could carry us again. It seemed as if it would take us days to reach Mudhill at the rate we were travelling, and I hoped the farmer Matilda spoke to took into account the mud when he said it was a day's ride from Greensted. It did not help that we could barely see ahead of us. We had to keep getting down from our horses every hour or so, and each time I had to carry Matilda on my back. She was very light, but she made it hard to wade through the mud, which at some points almost went up as far as my knees. Eventually, I lost my balance and slipped, sending me and Matilda tumbling down into the sludge.

Matilda screamed and sat up, caked in mud. It was all through her hair and all over her clothes and stained half her face. She was horrified. She flicked her head to the side and, for a second, I thought she was going to kill me. Instead, she threw herself on top of me and pinned me to the muddy ground. I could feel it seeping through my clothes.

"I hate you, I hate you, I hate you," Matilda snarled. Her hair was dripping wet, and brown water trickled down her face. I could not help but laugh. She clenched her teeth together and sucked air in and out, but then she started giggling too, and that turned into laughter.

Soon we were both laughing, and I threw her off me and down into the mud. Matilda gasped, then scooped up a large chunk of it and threw it at me. I flicked some mud back at her, then she lunged forward, laughing, and tackled me. She sat on top of me, her breath heavy.

"You two all right?" Cubert asked. He and Dughlas were grinning over us now.

"No. Edward dropped me," Matilda said.

"There's a hillfort just up ahead," Cubert said.

"Is it Mudhill?" I asked. I sat up, and Matilda climbed to her feet.

"Well, it's a wooden fort on a hill surrounded by mud," Dughlas said. "I'd say so."

And so it was. Though the trek there was hard and messy, we had made it to Mudhill at last. But would Philip be here? Would Hakon? Or were we too late?

As evening drew near, the four of us sat on our horses before Mudhill's gate. The fort stood atop a hill that rose up out of the flat, muddy countryside. The base of the hill was surrounded by a shallow, empty moat, but there was no palisade protecting the thatched huts of the men and their families who lived here. We rode across the narrow bridge over the moat without trouble and then rode up the hill past dishevelled villagers with dirty faces and tattered clothes.

Behind the palisade walls I could just make out the roof of what I assumed to be the keep of the leader of these outlaws, the Muddy Earl. Two men sat on the ramparts above the gate, watching us. They looked tired and miserable. Night was drawing near, and a sullen drizzle fell. I would have hated to live in this country. Even when it was not raining, the sky was always grey and the ground was always wet. We waited outside the gate while one of the guards informed their leader of his guests.

"Where're you folk from?" a guard called down.

"Oldford," I called back.

"Gods, you've come a long way, haven't you?"

"We have."

The guard turned around, spoke to someone behind him, then nodded. "What's your business in the Mireland?"

"We wish to pledge service to your lord."

"Now what in the world happened that would lead you to make that choice?"

I made no response. Shortly after, the gate opened up for us, scraping against the mud behind it. "Come on through," the guard said.

Another guard approached with a large box. "Your weapons," he commanded. Dughlas and I glanced at each other. We were hesitant. "You'll get 'em back. If we wanted to kill you, we would've done it already."

I supposed that was true, so we reluctantly placed our weapons in the box.

"How much for the lass?" one of the men asked. He ogled Matilda.

"She's not for sale," I snapped.

"All right, all right. I was only asking."

The guard who had greeted us led us through the courtyard, past a smithy and a stable and what appeared to be a barracks. Some warriors were training outside while others were drinking and laughing and placing bets on two cocks fighting in a ring. The keep itself sat at the back of the courtyard and was made out of wood and brick. It was shoddy and ill-maintained — the perfect home for outlaws and outcasts. We were led to a large wooden door, and the guard pushed it open and welcomed us inside.

We entered and found ourselves in what looked to be a games room. It was large and had numerous tables for playing draughts, cards, or various other games. At one side of the room was a large fireplace with two long benches and an armchair. In that armchair sat a huge, muscled man with a belly that hung over his belt, a bushy red beard with streaks of grey, and a shaved head. He had a pot of ale in his hand, and he burped as we came in. The guard gestured for us to take a seat at the benches by the fire.

"Welcome to Mudhill, the Mountain of the Gods," the big man said. "I am told you wish to die for me." His voice was gruff and slurred, but he spoke like a nobleman. He had clearly not always been an outlaw. The four of us sat down opposite him, with the fire to our left.

"Yes, that's right," I said.

"Tell me your names then," the man said. He waved his guard

away. "Leave us."

"My name is Edmund. These are my friends, Darryl, Frank, and Milburga," I said, pointing to each of my companions.

"Edmund?" The man thought for a few moments. He snorted. "You can drop the lies, Edward of Winterhome. I knew you would come. Besides, I recognised you the moment you walked in here. You are the spitting image of your father."

My heart skipped a beat. "You know my father?"

"Aye, I know him. You look like your sister as well, though far less pretty."

"Who are you?"

"The peasants in these lands — my lands — call me the Muddy Earl, but I have a feeling you already know who I am."

The Muddy Earl was right. I did have my suspicions. I had them as soon as I saw him, and his recognition of me only confirmed them. Folk like us — the Gifted, that is — often feel a sense of familiarity with one another, even if we have never met. It would seem like I was facing an outlaw holed up in a broken fort atop a muddy hill, but I knew he was much more than that.

"How did you know we were coming, Ward?"

He smirked. "Hakon. I believe you know him. He left here earlier this morning and headed northwards, though not before warning me that his men were being tailed by none other than Edward of Winterhome."

"I am Edward of Oldford now."

"Until recently, I have heard."

So there he was, the last Royal Godspeaker. He told me everything then. Hakon had lands loaned to him by his half-brother a little way to the west of Everlynn, and with those lands he housed and funded his band of several hundred oathmen. He and his men were zealots, fixated on some radical notion of creating a holy kingdom from the ashes of a world devoured by war, but Ward cared little for that. Ward's only concern nowadays was wealth, and Hakon was very generous with that. He had paid Ward for information years earlier.

What information, you may ask? The location of the resting place of Emrys, along with the proper rites needed to open it, so all Hakon now desired was my sword. Godwin's sword. The same sword used to lock Emrys within his prison all those years ago.

Why Hakon needed this information, Ward did not care to ask, but he put the pieces together and suspected that Hakon intended to use Emrys as the spark that would light the fires of war. Philip was merely bait to lure me in so that I would bring Godwin's sword to a place where he could take it. And what reason did Ward have to stop him? None. In fact, for a small handful of silver it was Ward who told Hakon of the current bearer of that ancient blade.

"How do you know so much about Emrys?" I asked.

Ward stood and stretched. "When I was Edwin's Godspeaker, I had access to the vast stores of information held in the Royal Secrecy. It holds everything one would need to know about how

Emrys was entombed and how to release him. And that brings me to why I was hoping you would come. Wait here.”

The four of us waited in silence while Ward left the room. He was gone only for a few moments and then returned with a small wooden lockbox decorated with the symbol of a golden dragon. “This box will change your life,” said Ward.

“What is inside?” I asked.

“When Edwin charged me with the defence of the Capital, he made me swear that should the city fall, I would save this little box, which was locked up tight in a room within the Secrecy only the king had access to. He said that nothing else is more important than preventing the Usurper from opening that box. Many, including the pretender Carol, believe I fled the city to save my own hide, when in truth I fled to save this box. For years I did not open it, but curiosity eventually got the better of me. It is yours now.”

Ward held the box out for me, but as I reached for it, we were startled by a crash, the sound of horses and the shouts of men, followed by the deep groan of a war horn. *Arooooooo. Aroo, aroo, arooooo.*

“What in the Heavens is going on out there?” Ward shouted. The keep’s door swung open, and the guard that led us in burst through, panting.

“Lord, they’re here,” he said.

“Who?”

“The Moun—”

"Shit. Fucking weasels." Ward turned to me. "You. I need every man who can use a blade. I am the only one who knows the secret in this box, so help me, and I will tell you what was inside." At that, Ward hurled the lockbox into the fireplace, and we watched for a moment as it burned. I was dumbfounded. Ward turned back to his man. "You know what to do. Kill them all."

"What is going on?" I asked.

"We are under attack. I knew this day would come. It seems my time as an outlaw is finally coming to an end. Follow me. I will get you your weapons."

Ward marched outside, and Cubert, Dughlas, and I followed. Ward wore no armour. He had no time to put any on, so he would be fighting in nothing but his shirt and pants. He picked up a large, two-headed axe that rested against the wall beside the door. It was then that I realised Matilda was following us.

"Stay here," I said. "You cannot fight."

"The earl said he needed every man who can use a blade," said Matilda.

"True. But you're not a man."

"Why do you doubt me?"

I put my hands on her shoulders and looked into her eyes. "I do not doubt your bravery, but I don't want you to die."

"Nor do I want you to die, Edward, but why must I be safe while you are not? Why must the men fight while the women cower?"

"I won't have this argument with you here. Stay inside."

Matilda opened her mouth to protest but then sighed and nodded. "Be safe."

Cubert, Dughlas, and I went after Ward, who led us to the palisade gate. He handed us our weapons and, when he picked up my blade, admired it for a moment.

"This is Godwin's sword. The sword of my ancestor. Do not dishonour it, Edward of Winterhome," he said. He handed me the sword and then shouted for us to follow him up to the ramparts. We climbed the steps to the top of the palisade, where I took a few moments to see what was happening.

We were indeed under attack. There were about one hundred warriors assaulting the fort on Mudhill, I estimated, and those warriors were all clad in mail and wielding swords, spears, shields, and bows. Yet they carried no banners. The warriors had crossed the moat with no resistance, and many were now raging through the narrow streets around the huts, looting and burning the settlement. The ones that were not pillaging stood at the base of the palisade throwing javelins or shooting arrows, and there was a group of around two dozen warriors ramming the gate with a felled tree.

On our side I guessed there were about three dozen. We may have been able to hold out against the assailants, but they were burning down the homes of the men defending Mudhill, their wealth was being stolen, and their women and children were being slaughtered. The men were demoralised and knew that the longer they fought, the longer their families would suffer.

Every few seconds, the men with the tree would roar and charge at the gate in an attempt to smash through, and on our side we had our strongest men bracing the gate with beams, poles, spears, and whatever else they could find. They grunted and yelled every time the ram crashed against it.

Cubert, Dughlas, and I stood on the palisade above the gate with Ward. One of Ward's men came running to us with a big bag of javelins, and Ward demanded that we start hurling them down onto the attackers. He handed me one, I leaned over the palisade, and immediately found a target.

I did not hesitate, cleared my mind of the fact that this man was a person, and with all my strength I threw the javelin down. A split-second later his ribcage cracked open. He screamed and fell to his knees, then one of his comrades kicked him out of the way so they could make another charge at the gate.

He died, face down in the mud, with an iron point protruding from his back.

Dughlas threw a javelin just after me, but it missed and was buried in the mud. The warrior Dughlas was aiming for took it, looked up at Dughlas, and tossed it back. It stuck in the palisade wall.

"Shit aim," Cubert yelled.

"Him, or me?" Dughlas asked. Cubert only laughed and then tossed another javelin over the wall.

We continued throwing spears from the wall with Ward and

his men. We killed a few of the warriors, but they were good at dodging and their shields were strong, and the ones we killed were quickly replaced by men who grew tired of pillaging and came to help their friends at the gate. Men were screaming and shouting on both sides. Everything was happening so fast. The sun had not yet set, but there was barely any light besides that from the burning huts due to the thick clouds, and to make matters worse, it soon began pelting down rain. It was so heavy, we could hardly hear the cries of those we fought beside.

But we did hear the terrible creaking noise below us, followed by a thundering crash. The gate had been torn from its hinges, the wooden posts holding up the ramparts snapped, and the whole structure collapsed down into the mud. We all fell, and time seemed to slow for a while.

I eventually landed in the mud with a splash and lay there dazed. I could hear screams and the splashing of mud, and the clash of steel on steel, or steel on wood, or steel on bone. I turned my head to see Dughlas help Cubert up, and the two of them ran through the mud to the newly formed gap in the palisade. Ward's men were forming a wall of shields in the breach, but it would not be long before that too was broken.

"Edward!" Someone was shouting my name. "Edward, get up lad." I felt someone help me up, and I snapped back to my senses. Time went back to normal, and Ward stood over me.

"We should retreat back to the keep," I yelled over the deafening thunder of rain.

"No," Ward shouted. He pulled my sword out of the mud and handed it to me. "They'll just burn us out. I would rather make my stand here and die like a man than fall back and die screaming as flames tear the flesh from my bones."

Ward was right. I thought to ask him what these men wanted, but he turned to join his own men in their final stand at the breach.

"Push! Push them back," one man shouted.

"Kill them all," cried another. I saw Ward shouting as he entered the fray, lifting his axe and swinging it down over the shield wall. That was a formidable weapon and was splitting open helmet and skull alike, then flicking back blood as he brought it up over his head. I found Cubert and Dughlas at the front of the shield wall. Their own shields were locked together with those of Ward's men, and they were now jabbing and thrusting their swords through the gaps in the wall.

That was a desperate, brutal fight. I had never been in a struggle like that before, and I could not shake the thought that this was where I would die. Songs and tales make shield walls sound glorious, but now that I was in one, I discovered it was nothing like the stories. It was cramped, and I was overpowered by the strong stench of sweat, blood, and shit. One of Ward's men died beside me, and I quickly took his place. The man was pulled back out of the fight by his comrades, and I knelt in his spot, holding the shield tight.

"If we die here," Cubert said, "I want to be the first to toast

Edward the Gifted while we feast at the Table of the Slain."

"If we die here, Cubert, know that your oath has been fulfilled," I said.

"Thank you, lord. But instead of dying, let's give the Gods a victory to sing about."

I smiled and poked my sword through the wall. I felt the grinding feeling as my blade sliced through flesh and scraped against bone. A man screamed in front of me and fell down as he clutched his leg, then I made another thrust at his face, killing him instantly. Bodies were piling up against our wall, but we were quickly losing men. Archers on the other side were launching volleys over the palisade, killing our men at the back. Ward noticed we were losing.

"Pull back," he yelled. "We'll box them in."

I knew what he meant, and his men did too. The shield wall folded inwards all at once, and the attackers piled in through the breach, tripping over bodies and each other, thinking we had retreated. But we were not retreating. About two dozen of the attackers were surrounded on three sides by Ward's warriors, and what had looked like a retreat had been a trick. We closed in on them, slicing and lunging. We were like a wolf's jaw, and we made a bloodbath.

But now our defences were broken. Ward ordered us to fight to the death, and that we did. The attackers poured in through the breach, and men on both sides died in the vicious melee that ensued. I still had my shield, so I put my mind to work. Block,

slice. Block, lunge. Block, slice. Block, block, parry. All I could
think about was the fighting. The killing. I did not even
remember why I was fighting. I tried to count how many I killed,
but I lost track. I felt myself struck multiple times by swords and
spears, but the pain was dulled by the rush of the battle.

And indeed it was a rush. Soon enough, I heard a yell and the
sound of a horn. The fighting stopped. I looked around to see we
were surrounded by our enemies. I saw Cubert lying face down
in the mud. His mail was drenched in his own blood, and my
heart sank. Dughlas had three spears pointed at him, and his
shield was broken in half, so he threw his sword down into the
mud, realising it was over. The few warriors left on our side did
the same, and I felt a blade poke at my back. I dropped my
weapon, placed my hands behind my head, and fell to my knees.

Only Ward remained fighting. His face and hair were caked in
blood, and he stood a few yards away, swinging his great axe.
No one dared get close to him. He was shouting insults and
taunting them, insulting their mothers and their wives and their
sisters and their daughters.

One man tried to approach him from behind, but Ward swung
his axe around and smashed it right through his enemy's shield
and sliced down his arm. The man screamed and collapsed, and
Ward brought the axe up above his head to finish the brave man
off, but another man behind him lunged a spear into his calf.

Ward groaned, the axe fell from his hands, and he dropped to
his knee. A dozen warriors leapt on him and pinned him in the

mud. The attackers all gave a triumphant shout.

The rain started to die down. It was over. We were prisoners.

12

King

I sat in the damp, dark, cellar of Mudhill's keep with Dughlas, eight other warriors, and the Muddy Earl. We had lost the battle outside and were dragged down here whilst the enemy decided what to do with us.

We were cold, wet, and bloody. I had two large gashes, one on my leg and another on my shoulder. My chest ached with every breath, and my head was thumping. I had not noticed these injuries during the rush of battle, but now that I was sitting in the quiet cellar with ten other defeated men, the pain had arrived.

Dughlas was injured too. An axe had smashed his shield in two and cut into his arm. It was a nasty wound. Cubert was not with us, for he had fallen during the battle. I wished I had died with him, but I knew that I would meet him again soon enough. Still, the pain of knowing he was gone stung worse than my wounds.

Ward also had numerous cuts on his body but the spear wound in his leg was the worst. Drenched in mud and blood, he would likely die from infection within the next few days. He was in a sorry state, refused to speak, and had the look of a man who had already given up on life.

We were all shivering. The warriors guarding the cellar had given us blankets, but they did little to shield us from the cold. We could not even drink Ward's ale and wine to warm our bellies because our captors had raided the cellar and taken everything, and they were now upstairs in the keep celebrating their victory, gorging themselves on Ward's food and drink. All we had to sustain ourselves was the rainwater trickling down through leaks in the cellar and the stale bread that one of the guards brought to us.

"Dinner's ready, lads," he taunted, opening the cellar door. "This is your last meal in this world, so make sure you savour it."

He threw a large bucket of round lumps of bread on the floor, and the men all scrambled for their share. Only Ward and I remained disinterested. He just sat in the corner, wrapped in a blanket and staring at the floor, his teeth chattering. I leaned against a post with my legs crossed.

"Guard," I called as he was closing the door. He turned and glared at me. "There was a girl up there. Where is she now?"

"Matilda? She your lass?"

"She's my friend. May I speak to her?"

The guard chuckled. "No. She's a comely thing, though, isn't she?" he jeered. I clenched my jaw. "The boys are all taking turns on her upstairs. She looks to have a pretty little arse. I might have a go myself soon."

I shot up and lunged at the door, but the guard backed away and swung it shut. I slammed my fist against the hard oak door and cursed the man. He laughed as he walked away. I turned around to the men surrounding the bucket, stuffing bread into their mouths.

"Next time he comes back, I say we kill him," I said. Some of the men murmured in agreement.

"And then what?" Dughlas asked. "Escape? Retake the fort?"

"Rescue Matilda."

"So that's all that matters, is it? Your damsel in distress?"

"I made a promise, and gods damn me if I don't keep it."

Dughlas shrugged and turned his attention to a piece of bread he was picking at. I went to slump back down against the post and hugged my legs. My wounds were sore, and I was freezing.

"It is hopeless," Ward mumbled from his corner.

"What is?" asked one of his men.

"Saving the girl. Getting out of here. It is all hopeless." Ward lifted his head and stared at the ceiling. He grimaced, and I could tell his wounds were hurting him. "They are going to execute us all tomorrow morning."

"Then why not die fighting? Let's kill the guard and break out of here," I said.

Ward snorted. "It will barely be a fight. I want to at least die with dignity and go to my death willingly, not flailing about half naked like some mad jester." Some of his men nodded. Ward was right. Any escape attempt would be futile. We might have been able to kill the guard, but we would be cut down the moment we left the cellar. We would die like fools. At least if we were executed, our deaths would be clean.

I sighed and leaned my head back against the post. Could this be it? Would I die on my knees in the mud atop some irrelevant northern hill? We all die and join our ancestors in the afterlife to boast of our glory and guide our children and descendants. I would have been content dying on Mudhill and joining the slain in their halls but for the fact Matilda was upstairs being violated by dozens of warriors, and that ignited a wild fury within me.

The ancient wisemen — those who were said to have spoken to the Gods — taught us that is one of the three unforgiveable crimes, along with oathbreaking and kinslaying. How could fate have led me to be sitting there helpless while my friend I promised to protect suffered and the Gods' laws were broken?

I could not die yet.

I also thought of Philip. He was still out there, taken by Hakon and his men. If Hakon learned of my death, what would happen to Philip? His bait would be useless, and I somehow doubted Hakon would spare Philip's life in that case. I could not fail everyone who relied on me. I knew then that if I were to die and meet my forebears, I would face them with shame.

No, I could not give up yet. If I could not save the world, I could at least try to save my friends.

I tried to speak to Ward about a plan to escape. When that failed, I asked about the lockbox he burned, or about the location of Emrys's tomb, which he had not yet revealed to me. He was in no mood to talk. He only stared at the ceiling in silence, and thus it seemed Ward's secret would die with him come morning, along with every man that now sat in that cellar. Yet even that near to the end, I refused to accept that I had failed.

The leader of the force that attacked Mudhill was a man named Arne. He was short but stocky, in his mid-thirties, and he presented himself well. His blonde hair was tied back in one long braid, and he was clean-shaven save for a moustache, the ends of which hung below his chin and were tied with colourful beads.

Arne ordered me and the other prisoners out of the cellar, into the courtyard, then up onto the section of the ramparts that was still intact. We all lined up, our wrists tied, and the chains rattled as we shivered in the cold morning air. There was light snowfall that morning, and the sky was a dark grey. Arne stood up with us on the ramparts, standing beside one of his warriors, who carried a long, sharp axe.

He also had two white hound puppies following him everywhere he went, and they now sat at his feet. He was wearing his war gear: a fine mail coat, a decorated helmet he held under his arm, and a long sword that hung at his belt. We prisoners all stared at him.

"Let's make this quick and clean, men," Arne said. A crowd stood beneath the ramparts in the courtyard, watching. Most were Arne's men, but some were Ward's servants and the families of the warriors that lived there.

Without invitation, one of the prisoners stepped forward, knelt down in front of Arne's executioner, and bowed his head. Arne looked at him for a moment and then nodded and stood back. The executioner lifted his axe and brought it down swiftly. The prisoner's head dropped to the wood with a thud, and his body fell sideways, blood spurting from his open neck.

The executioner kicked the body down off the ramparts and into the mud, then picked up the head and showed it to the crowd. Most of them cheered, Arne's hounds yapped, and the head was thrown over the palisade and down into the ruins of the village below.

I felt terrible. I was cold, and my wounds, my chest, and my head were groaning with pain. On top of that, like most of the prisoners, I had not slept the night before. I tried to think of something, anything, that I could do to avoid the axe, but deep down I felt it was over. I had failed to find Philip. I had failed to stop Hakon unleashing chaos on the land. I had failed to bring a good death to Dughlas. I had failed Cubert, who had foolishly retaken his oath to me in Everlynn Forest.

But the worst pain was the knowledge that I had failed

Matilda. I had allowed her to suffer and face humiliation at the hands of these brutes, and by now she was likely dead. I allowed my final thoughts to be ones of hopeless vengeance.

I watched as another man lost his head and had it tossed over the palisade. Two headless bodies now lay in the mud below us, slowly being buried by snow. "Does anyone wish to go next?" Arne asked.

"Aye." Ward stepped forward, his head held high. He limped, he was shivering, and his beard was wild, but he seemed prepared to meet his death. He stood a pace in front of Arne, towering over him, and the two men stared at each other for a few moments. Ward turned and knelt and then looked at me. "You shall live past this day," he said. He gave me a quick nod and smiled. I looked forward to joining the Muddy Earl in the halls of the dead very soon.

"I have waited a long time for this moment, Ward," Arne said.

Ward turned to him. "Do me the honour of swinging the axe yourself, then," he said. Arne stared at him and then took the axe from his executioner. He positioned himself and raised the axe above his head.

"Long live the Kingdom of Ardonn," Ward shouted. He glanced at me. "Long live the *true* king."

The axe came down, and Ward slumped sideways. His head rolled down from the ramparts and landed with a splash in the mud below. Arne pushed his body down with it and then handed the axe back to the executioner. "Next," he said.

I took a deep breath and made one step forward, but felt a hand on my chest. It was Dughlas, and he shook his head. "I wouldn't stand to see you die, Boss." He grinned, and I noticed a tear forming in his eye. I responded with a sad smile. Memories of our adventures together began to run through my mind, and my eyes began to water. I felt comfort in the fact that we would soon share one more.

"You stupid bastard," I said. He laughed, I started laughing too, and we embraced.

"I don't have all morning," Arne called.

Dughlas pulled away from me, nodded, then turned and walked over to Arne. He dropped to his knees, facing the crowd, and bowed his head. "I come to you, my ancestors," he said.

The executioner shuffled his feet and steadied himself, then began to lift his axe. I could not watch, so I looked away and felt a tear run down my cheek. Or perhaps that was a flake of snow melting on my face.

"Stop this now!" someone screamed. It was a woman. I snapped my head in the direction of the voice and saw Matilda standing at the door to the keep, a look of horror on her face. She was barefoot, her hair was loose and wild, and she wore only a nightgown. Everyone turned to look — the men in the crowd all turned, the prisoners all turned, Dughlas lifted his head, and Arne's puppies started yelping.

"What is the meaning of this?" Arne growled.

The executioner lowered his axe. At that moment, a man burst from inside the keep, panting, with blood trickling down his forehead. He stood beside Matilda, bent over to catch his breath for a few seconds, then stood back up.

"Greyham, I told you to guard her," Arne yelled.

"She escaped, lord," the man beside Matilda said.

"How?"

"She hit me with a chair, lord."

Arne rolled his eyes, and some of the warriors in the crowd laughed.

"Do not kill that man," Matilda said.

"My Lady—" Arne stared.

"I said do not kill that man."

"He is a traitor, My Lady."

"He is no traitor. This is Dughlas, a loyal oathman and companion to Edward Godspeaker of Oldford."

"What?" Arne frowned and looked down at Dughlas, puzzled. He gestured for the executioner to step back.

Matilda then pointed at me. "And that, Arne, is Edward."

Arne and his executioner stared at me. The crowd below went silent and started whispering among themselves. The two puppies watched me, unmoving. "Is this true?" Arne asked, his mouth hanging open. I nodded, and Arne immediately went down on one knee. "I am sorry, I did not know…"

I just looked at Arne, confused. I admit I had no idea what was happening. Arne's men all stared up at the scene on the ramparts in similar confusion. The other prisoners all turned to look at me, frowning, and I noticed Dughlas grinning.

"The king will wish to speak with you," Arne mumbled. He turned his head to his men. "Kneel, you bastards. This is Edward, the heir of Godwin and the Sacred Champion of our King Carol, the true Lord of Ardonn."

Without hesitation, all of Arne's men went down and put one knee into the mud. It was then that I finally understood. These men were Mountaineers, the warriors and soldiers loyal to Carol the Pretender. Rebels. They had come to Mudhill to punish Ward and his followers for fleeing the Capital in its hour of need and refusing to support the young Carol's cause, and in doing so had accidentally stumbled upon their spiritual champion.

I then understood why Fate had brought me there.

I sat on a chair in one of the bedrooms of Mudhill's keep. One of Arne's healers was washing and stitching my wounds. She had already stitched the wound on my leg, and now she was fixing my shoulder. I winced as she stuck a needle through the skin.

"Sorry," she muttered. The healer bit her lip, focussing as she slowly slid the needle and thread through my flesh. Matilda sat on the end of the bed across from me, watching the healer do her work.

"Will he be all right?" Matilda asked.

"The wounds don't look infected," she replied, her attention fixed on my shoulder. "What worries me is his chest. If the ribs are broken, the marrow could leak into his blood, and that'll not end well." Matilda frowned and twisted her mouth.

"Tell me what happened last night," I said to Matilda.

"I waited inside the keep whilst the battle raged outside. Some of Ward's servants came to join me, but none of us spoke much. They said we would lose, and I suppose they were right," she began. "When the fighting stopped, some of the men came into the keep and told us to stay put. Shortly afterwards, Arne came in with his dogs, and he immediately noticed that I was not a servant. He asked who I was, so I told him, and he treated me as a noblewoman should be treated. I was given a room, fresh clothes, food and all that, but I was put on guard. Arne came and visited me after I had washed and told me he was an oathman in the service of the king, and I begged him to release you. He said he would consider it but that you were a traitor and deserved to die."

"Did you not tell him who I was?"

"No. I only told him your name was Edward and that you were one of my bodyguards, but that is all. I worried that if he knew your identity, he would never release you. I thought he served King Stephan."

I smiled, for that was clever of her. "Why did you tell him the truth this morning, then?"

"Last night, I noticed Arne wore a dragon emblem on his belt. I thought nothing of it then, but when I awoke this morning I realised I had seen that emblem before — on Ward's lockbox and the seal on the letter you received in Oldford. I made the connections and some risky guesses and then hastened to tell Arne you were on his side. That was when I saw them ready to execute Dughlas."

"Thank you, Matilda. I owe you my life," I said. She blushed and shook her head. "One of the guards made it seem like you were mistreated. Is this true?"

Matilda frowned. "No, I was treated rather well."

I sighed, relieved. Matilda had been entirely unharmed. The healer cut the thread and tied it, completing the stitch. She then started pressing my chest, and Matilda looked away.

"Does it hurt to breathe?" the healer asked.

I nodded. "A little."

The healer pressed my chest in different spots, trying to feel if there was a break. She ran her fingers along each of my ribs, frowning. "I can't feel a break," she said. "It's probably just bruised. I think you will be okay. Just don't get into any fights for a few weeks."

"That's a relief," I said.

The healer smiled. "Are you a farmer?"

"Not really. Why?"

She shrugged and started washing her bloody hands in a bucket. "You have the chest of a farmer. Broad and tough. I can tell you work often."

"Why are you making this observation?" Matilda asked.

"You should try to rest for a while instead, Edward, and avoid work," the healer said.

I thanked her and stared out of the window. It was late morning now, and the snow was still falling. Ash fell from the sky too, because Arne's men had burned down most of the huts around the fort, and so smoke billowed above the keep and overpowered the stench of death.

I heard men outside cleaning up the bodies, piling them all at the base of the hill. The pile would be burned when we left the keep, and that was soon. Arne did not want to linger here for much longer. I wondered how Dughlas was. The rest of Ward's warriors had been executed, but Arne had spared Dughlas because he was my companion. He had been hurt badly too, but the healer assured me he would recover. He always healed fast.

I mourned for Cubert. His body would likely be among the others, piled up and waiting to be burned. But I could take comfort in the fact that he died a warrior's death.

At that moment, there was a knock at the door, and Arne entered. His puppies ran into the room ahead of him and leapt up onto the bed to pounce on Matilda. She laughed and fell back, and the puppies started licking her face as she ruffled their fur.

"His Lordship gave them to me as a Winterlow gift," Arne said. "His blacksmith's bitch gave birth to a litter, but he did not want the puppies. Is Edward healed, Louisa?"

"He is, lord," the healer replied.

"Good. We can be off soon then. Edward, I have sent a rider ahead to Tillysburg to inform His Lordship of what happened here and that you will be coming with us. I am sure the king will be eager to meet his champion."

"I never knew I was so famous among Carol's men," I said.

Arne laughed. "The king is always talking about you. He tells us all how well you guard his realm from Otherworldly threats and of how you work for the betterment of his subjects' souls. He believes you are Godwin reborn."

I knew Carol planned to make me his Royal Godspeaker should he reclaim the throne his father had lost, but I never realised how important I was to him. It seemed as though Carol already thought of me as his champion, just as Godwin had been the champion of King Carol the Great all those centuries ago. I had never met the Pretender, but now I was going with Arne and his men to meet him.

Arne told me that after Roger had overthrown his brother and become the Earl of Tillysburg, Carol took his army from the fort in the mountains and marched to support Roger, who had pledged fealty to Carol. Carol now ruled his small kingdom from Tillysburg and was preparing for the war King Stephan was bringing. So, we were going to Tillysburg, and from there I would set out to find Philip. I still worried about him, but I was hopeful now.

Arne had come to this room to give me fresh clothes, return my weapons, and tell me to prepare to leave. Matilda and I packed our things and made ready to ride north, and we then met with Dughlas. He was sore, but he was strong, and I was confident he would live. His left arm was in a sling, mangled from the axe blow, and he had a fractured ankle which gave him a limp.

We joined Arne in the courtyard outside the keep, and he returned our horses to us. I mounted Brand, then Matilda and I followed Arne and his men out of the broken gate, back down the hill, and through the ruined, scorched village. A wagon followed, pulled by two mules, and Arne's dogs sat in that with the healer Louisa, Dughlas, and some other wounded men.

We rode past the pile of bodies outside the hillfort, and some men dismounted to set it ablaze. It was an awful smell, and some of the men even vomited as we passed it. I noticed Ward's bald, bearded head among the pile of bodies. His eyes were wide open, giving me an empty stare. I am sure Cubert was in that pile as well, but I did not see him.

I bowed my head as a show of respect and carried on north with the rest of Arne's warriors. I held no animosity towards Arne and his men for slaying my friend. We were warriors and had all fought bravely and fairly. Cubert had fallen in honourable combat and was now drinking and feasting with his ancestors.

It was shortly after we left Mudhill that the tiredness hit me. I struggled to keep my eyes open and at one point almost slid from my saddle. Arne did not want to stop till nightfall because he knew the local nobles would see the smoke at Mudhill and send men to investigate. I was glad of Arne's hastiness, for I wished to reach Philip as soon as I could, though the riding took its toll.

Matilda insisted that I let her ride Brand for me so I could rest. I reluctantly agreed.

She sat in the front of my saddle and tied her horse to mine with a rope so it would not wander off. Matilda took the reins and rode Brand onwards while I put my arms around her, rested my head on the back of her shoulder, and drifted off to sleep.

It was a week-long ride from Mudhill to Tillysburg, and it both rained and snowed frequently. The pain in my chest lessened, and it no longer hurt to breathe. My shoulder and leg still hurt, but they were healing nicely. Dughlas's wounds were healing too, and Louisa assured him that it was unlikely infection would set in at this point. He even managed to ride his own horse on the seventh day.

"Have you heard the tale of how Tillysburg earned its name?" he asked as he rode at my side.

"Can't say that I have," I said.

"I have," said Matilda.

I raised my eyebrows. "A tale you two know, but which I do not. That's a first."

"One of the men told it to me," said Dughlas. "But go on, Tilly, let's hear your version of it."

Matilda smiled and cleared her throat. "Tillysburg was named in honour of Matilda Meatcleaver, the woman I am named after. She was the daughter of the Lord of Everlynn during the War of

Betrayals nearly two centuries ago, but the way she acted, one would think she was his son.

"When Everlynn fell to Hemma's forces, Matilda fled the city with several hundred warriors and made her way to a hillfort near the Alps. Hemma's army followed her, and there she made a final stand.

"She held them off for months, with her warriors killing eight times their number, until eventually they were betrayed and the fort was infiltrated. Matilda stood her ground on the bridge to the keep, and it is said she slew forty men single-handedly before they managed to cut her down. Her enemies had such respect for her that when they captured the fort, they named it in her honour. Tillysburg." Matilda looked proud when she finished telling her story.

"That's not how I heard it," said Dughlas. "The man I spoke to said nothing about a betrayal, and that Matilda fell in a duel, not after defeating forty men."

"Well, your version is wrong," Matilda barked. Dughlas smirked. "At any rate, Matilda was a fierce and noble woman, and I am glad to share her name."

"How did she earn the title of 'Meatcleaver'?" I asked.

"It was her sword. They say it was so large, one swing of it could cleave a man in half," said Matilda.

I grinned. It was a rare thing for a woman to fight in battle, and rarer still for one to become so legendary, but I had seen and heard of stranger things.

We arrived at Tillysburg in the afternoon of the final day of our journey. It sat upon a low, wide hill, and a small fort rose above the buildings in the centre of the town at the highest point. Beside that castle stood a tall bell tower.

A high wooden wall surrounded the outer edge of the town, but it was in a state of disrepair. Numerous gaping holes could be spotted, rendering the wall more or less useless. Men were filling the gaps with freshly cut logs, barrels, and anything else they could find to patch them up. War was coming, and they anticipated a siege. Stephan would be lucky if he could catch Carol here. I remember feeling that this town looked eerily familiar, though I could not place where I had seen it before.

As Arne's small army approached the gates, they were slowly pulled open for us to enter. An archer above the gate waved down to us, and Arne waved back. "The king is in the town hall," the archer called. We entered Tillysburg, and the gates closed behind us with a loud groan.

The houses inside the walls were mostly made of wood, though some upper-class homes had brick and stone. It was not shoddy, though, and the buildings were well maintained. If I had to pick one word to describe the town, I would simply use 'brown.' The streets were bumpy and made from cobblestone, so we had to leave our horses in the huge stable at the gate. Only the wagon came with us.

Dughlas struggled to walk along the cobbles, so he sat with the other wounded men and Arne's dogs in the wagon. Matilda walked beside me through the town, and Arne walked ahead of us at the front of his column. As we walked, women threw flowers down onto the warriors from the windows, and people cheered as we passed. Some women wept, for they had lost their loved ones in the attack. I felt guilty, for I knew I had killed some of them.

Matilda stopped suddenly and turned, and I looked to see what had halted her. She was staring at a large wooden temple, which was now surrounded by scaffold on which builders worked to repair the sacred building. But what had caught Matilda's eye was the scene in the square outside it.

"By Hefenstea…" she whispered.

My blood ran cold. In front of the temple were eight tall gibbets rising high above the square, from which naked men were hanging by their feet. Their skin was blue, they were castrated, their guts hung down from open bellies, and their eye sockets were empty. Flies buzzed around them, drawn to the rotten stench. One of Arne's men noticed us staring at the scene before us.

"Traitors to the king are hanged or beheaded," he said and then nodded at the hanging men. "But traitors to the Gods suffer a fate far worse."

I realised then who those men were. They were priests. Men who had likely maintained and performed rites in the temple outside which they now hung. Carol must have had them executed when he arrived in the city, because many priests these days spewed false words about the Gods and rejected the old dynasty in favour of the new. I took Matilda's arm and pulled her along, leaving the priests to rot.

We saw a similar scene when we arrived at the town hall, but the men on the gibbets here were only hung by the neck. Arne told me they were the town's wealthiest men, along with the mayor, who had been punished for refusing to support Carol or for aiding the usurper Wim during the war.

The town hall itself was impressive. It was three storeys tall, with exquisite carvings and niches displaying statues and beautiful windows. Attached to that building was the bell tower that rose up above the town. A half-rotten corpse in fine clothes hung from the top of that tower, and I assumed that was Rainulf, the earl's twin brother. So much death in such a little town.

To the north, rising above the wooden houses, was Tillysburg's small stone fort flying the town's white banners. Arne's warriors all waited outside the town hall while he led Matilda and I inside.

He took us into the council chamber, which had tiered seating along the left and right walls. At the opposite end to the doors was a high dais on which sat a throne. The throne was backed against a wall, from which hung four tall banners. They were a deep purple, and a golden dragon was emblazoned on each one.

About a hundred men sat in this chamber, and we could hear them roaring with laughter even before we entered. Two warriors stood at the door and bowed to us, and in the middle of the room stood a young man dressed in a fine grey woollen tunic woven with golden threads.

He wore tall black boots, black gloves, and a rich purple cloak was draped over his shoulders. He was blonde, clean-shaven, and his wavy hair, which fell halfway down his neck, was cut sharply at an even length. He was incredibly handsome, and even without that simple iron crown atop his head I would have known he was Carol the Pretender.

Carol was holding some pieces of parchment and addressing the audience. The scene at first looked as though Carol was reciting a comedy, but I quickly realised he was reading legal proposals sent across the land by King Stephan to the nobility.

"And hear this one," he said. "The 'good king's' council wishes to enforce his laws throughout the kingdom by planting his own men in the lands of the nobility and revoking the traditional rights of Ardonn's lords. Does the bastard really think he can keep men from joining my cause with such edicts?"

This was the first time I had heard Carol speak, and I immediately liked him. His accent was elegant and noble, he was charismatic, and his voice alone sounded as though it was touched by the Gods. It was high but commanding. Calm but firm. The men in the chamber all laughed when he finished, and he bore a handsome grin.

"Lord King, forgive me," Arne said. He bowed, and Carol turned to us. The hall went silent. I bowed too, and Matilda made a low curtsy. We stood straight again, and Arne opened his mouth to speak, but Carol raised a hand to silence him.

"You are Edward," he said, gazing at me from across the hall. I bowed my head low. "By all the Gods, you are finally here…"

The hall was silent. I kept my head down and heard his footsteps echo as he made his way over to me. He lifted my chin, and I noticed the dark makeup he wore around his eyes. He smiled as our eyes met. They were a bright blue, like the sky at dawn, and they shone like jewels. He threw his arms around me, and as he pulled away I fell to one knee.

"I am at your service, Lord King," I said.

He looked down at me and smiled. "And I am at yours, Edward of Oldford. My friend."

The Gods were smiling. The king and his champion had finally met, and our plan for this kingdom was ready to be set in motion.

"That throne is my right," Carol told me. "My fathers have held that seat for eight hundred years. That bastard Stephan sits on *my* throne and rules *my* kingdom, and now you tell me that a dead man also lays claim?"

Carol and I were sitting alone together in a study high up in the town hall's tower. He was pacing back and forth in front of the fireplace while I sat in a chair beside the hearth. His crown was now sitting on the desk, and he had removed his cloak. Carol had dismissed his council after my arrival and insisted we talk in private. I told him everything that had happened since I arrived in Henton and warned him that a noble named Hakon was planning to release the legendary Immortal King.

"No, Lord King. I am telling you that a man who never died will try to claim it," I said. I watched the pretender pace with a cup of wine in his hand.

"Yes, yes, of course. I know the legend of Emrys. He is my ancestor, you know."

"I did know, Lord King. Many will follow Emrys. He will represent for many a return to the old order and a better age. There are many in your kingdom who see no hope in neither you nor Stephan. Hakon believes Emrys is Alcyn incarnate, come to chastise and reforge the world in the fires of war, and he will convince many of that lie."

Carol turned on his heel, smiled, and came to sit in the chair beside mine. He leaned in close. "According to legend, my ancestor King Carol the Great, whose name I bear, fought side by side with your predecessor Godwin, and the two of them sealed Emrys away inside a mountain. But we both know deep down that it was Godwin who did all of the work."

"I do not see how that is relevant, Lord King."

"Ah, but it is, do you not see?" Carol tipped back the rest of his wine, placed the cup down on the chair's arm, then took my hand in both of his. "You are Godwin's heir! I wager that Fate has brought you and I together to defeat Emrys once and for all, and then we shall return my kingdom to glory."

"If you insist, Lord King."

"I do insist, Edward. I shall provide you with whatever help you need to hunt down this Hakon character and rescue your apprentice, but should Emrys be freed, you will have my army at your back, and the two of us will fight this immortal warlord side by side. And please, call me Carol. 'Lord King' is only necessary in public. More wine?"

I nodded, then Carol stood and marched over to the table, where he poured us both another cup.

The Pretender was strangely excited about the prospect of Emrys being released from his imprisonment. Emrys would bring chaos, but Carol was confident that history would repeat itself and that he and I would be able to swiftly defeat him, just as Godwin and Carol the Great had done three centuries ago. Carol loved the old poems and legends about his royal ancestors, and so he would not let a chance to relive those go to waste. And besides, Carol was yet untested, and such a victory would prove his worth and earn greater support for his rebellion.

I was not as enthusiastic about Emrys, however. I only wanted to find Philip and prevent more warfare and bloodshed. Nevertheless, it seemed violence was inevitable in those days. Those who did not pick a side were doomed to suffer the chaos.

Alongside the desire to relive old tales, Carol did have good reason to concern himself with Emrys, who, never having technically died, had a claim to at least a sizeable chunk of the Kingdom of Ardonn. It was a shaky claim, but a claim nonetheless.

His real lure, which would sway many men into supporting him, was what he represented: change. It would mean Carol would lose supporters to the Immortal King, not to mention that the land he wished to rule would be devastated by Emrys's rampaging horde. The fear of that devastation alone would be enough to drive many to swear oaths to Emrys.

"Do you believe I was justified in my treatment of the priests? I trust you saw them as you passed the temple," Carol asked me as he handed me a full cup of wine. He sat back down and looked into the fire.

"I am not sure it is my place to judge," I responded.

"Your place is where your king puts you, and I put you at my side as my highest spiritual advisor and guardian of all the souls of my realm. This is a matter which concerns you," he said. He flashed me a friendly smile.

"Well, I do think we need to do away with the false priests that poison this kingdom," I explained. "But executing them on the spot may be a bit rash. In the future I would advise giving priests a chance to turn back to truth, and if they refuse, then they should be made an example of. If they preach treason, punish them as traitors. If they preach lies, let them keep their lives, but strip them of their titles. In ancient times the king was head of their order, and thus it should be your right to revoke their privileges."

Carol nodded slowly. "I will trust you, my friend. I appreciate your counsel."

"I would also advise against mutilating them, even if they do preach treason against you. Such treatment will not sit well with their followers, of which there are many."

"Thank you, Edward. And what of those merchants? Did they deserve their fate?"

"They did, Lord King — I mean, Carol. They were traitors and deserve a traitor's death."

Carol smiled and took a sip of his wine. "We have much work to do, Edward. The false king marches on us as we speak, and with him comes the army of the Lord of Everlynn. We must go to war, and I need you at my side, but I cannot ask you to fight with me until you have rescued your apprentice."

"Thank you, Carol."

He reached over and placed a gentle hand on my arm. "Enough of this grim talk. Tell me, my friend, how were your Winterlow celebrations this year?"

And so I told Carol about Winterlow, then the two of us talked for hours and hours until late into the evening. I was growing fond of him — he was a likeable young man, after all — and he filled me with new hope for the future. This man was descended from the Gods, and if he was successful, I knew in my heart and soul that Ardonn would prosper.

He was not even king yet, but Carol already acted like he ruled all of Ardonn, and he treated both the men and women loyal to him and those loyal to Stephan as his own people. He would make a good king, far better than Stephan or his father, and I was glad to be his champion.

Several hours before midnight, Carol informed me that he needed to attend to private business with Roger, the Earl of Tillysburg. Carol had arranged for me, Matilda, and Dughlas each to have our own personal bed chambers in the town hall, and he escorted me to mine.

The room was small but comfortable, and it served its purpose. It had a double bed with rich silk sheets and an otter-fur quilt, an ornate dresser, and a small fireplace beside the bed with a little dining table next to it. Carol told me that I would have servants to attend my every need. He also said that supper would be brought up to me, and there was a selection of fresh clothes for me to choose from in the dresser. After ensuring I was settled, Carol left for his meeting with the earl.

I threw myself down onto the bed and let out a sigh. I realised then that I had not taken a proper sleep since Oldford. I could have fallen into a dream right then and there, but I was hungry, and the night was still young. I tend to stay awake late into the night because the days are always busy, and the night gives me time for contemplation.

Shortly after Carol left, however, there was a knock at the door. A servant had brought me supper, as promised, and I asked him to place it on the table by the fire. It was roasted duck baked into a pie and came with a tall bottle of red wine. Louisa, the healer, accompanied the servant. I had asked for her to help me re-dress my wounds and make sure they were healing properly.

Once the servant placed my meal on the table, only he left. Louisa stayed behind, though she did more than simply check my wounds. She was good, we enjoyed each other, and she helped to take my mind off Philip for a time, but as I lay beside her while she slept, I stared up at the ceiling, wondering why that felt like a betrayal.

Why did I feel so guilty? I could not shake these thoughts, and I struggled to sleep. A slight nausea lurked in the pit of my stomach. I wondered if it was the duck that made me feel that way, but looking back, I know it was far more.

13

Messenger

My companions and I stayed in Tillysburg for several weeks before Louisa told us we were fit to travel again. Thankfully Dughlas's eye socket gave him no trouble, and our injuries healed nicely. I wanted to leave as soon as I could to resume my hunt for Philip, who since his capture had always occupied a place in my mind, but I understood it would have been futile if we succumbed to unhealed wounds before we found him.

Carol was kind enough to send his own men in search of my apprentice. Three parties of his best trackers went searching for any sign of Hakon and his men, but each time they returned with nothing. The thought of Philip and my failure to protect him gnawed at me, but the events of those few weeks kept me busy enough to prevent the anxiety and guilt from driving me mad.

I met Lud, my friend and messenger, in Tillysburg a few days after we arrived. We exchanged stories of our journeys to the town over a few pots of ale, and I gave him a letter I had written to deliver to Lady Ecwyn. I promised I would write to her, and write to her I had. I wrote a lot, since it kept my mind distracted, and when I exhausted all I had to say, Lud took my letters south.

Dozens of free men and outlaws poured into the town every day to swear oaths to Carol. Some of these men had seen many winters, and many had fought for Edwin during the civil war, but there was also a mass of young warriors eager for adventure and the chance to prove themselves in battle by serving Ardonn's true king.

I also suspected some were criminals and bandits, men outlawed by Stephan who saw a chance for forgiveness in Carol. Not all of these men came to fight for Carol. Many would fight for themselves.

When Matilda and I first left Henton, she feared the rumours of rebels who would hide out in the woods awaiting Carol to raise the banner and call them to war, and during my stay in Tillysburg I discovered those rumours had indeed been true.

With the rebels coming to Tillysburg to serve Carol, we also received news from across the kingdom that raids were being carried out frequently against King Stephan's supporters in Carol's name. Matilda worried for her family, and so Carol issued a decree protecting Henton from the havoc his supporters were wreaking throughout the country. I hoped his followers would listen.

Each day, more traitors were uncovered and either executed or banished as part of Carol's purge. Despite his firm rule, Carol had great support from both the peasantry and the nobility, and many of the old rights, privileges, and laws were restored.

The town's craftsmen were once again able to form guilds, trade was no longer monopolised by a few wealthy merchants, and the peasants were able to openly practice folk customs previously outlawed by corrupt priests. The purpose of these customs was often to keep harmful spirits at bay, and a lot of my work came about due to neglect of such customs.

It was the merchants who suffered most of all under Carol's new regime, and many of them were tried as traitors and faced the noose. There seemed to be a new widow weeping every day beneath the gibbets in the town square.

The month of Dawning began about a week after we arrived in Tillysburg, and it was under that new moon that Carol summoned me to a small grove outside the town. A stream trickled through it, cutting the grove in two, and on a little island in the centre of the stream sat a large, dark boulder. I arrived there to find seven housecarls with helmets hiding their faces, and Carol, who was kneeling and praying before the boulder.

One of the housecarls stopped me at the edge of the grove and made me wait in silence until Carol had finished. The king held up a long, bent dagger, then dropped it into the stream. He mumbled something as the dagger sank to the bottom.

"This is a holy place," he said. He stood, brushed his knees, and gestured for me to join him.

"It is, Lord King. I can feel it," I said.

Carol smiled. "I have summoned you here because I require an oath from you, and what better place to swear an oath than in a temple built by the Gods in their forging of the world?"

I nodded, and he gestured for me to kneel. Drawing my sword, I went down on one knee and stuck the point into the earth. I held the hilt with both hands and bowed my head. I still remember the oath word-for-word to this day, because I have always regretted breaking it.

"My King," I began. "My Lord Carol, rightful ruler of Ardonn. I offer you my sword, my life, and my soul. Before the spirits of this grove, before the Gods, before these men, and before you, I swear this oath of fealty and pledge my eternal loyalty to you. Should I fail to keep and uphold this oath, I pray that these warriors and the men of your kingdom strike me down, or better, you do, and may my ancestors banish me from their halls for bringing dishonour to their name."

Carol placed his hand gently on my head when I finished, and I looked up at him. He was grinning. "Beautiful words, very beautiful. I accept your oath, Edward of Oldford, and shall hold you to it. These seven men here will remember it. Stand," he said. I stood.

Carol placed his hands on my shoulders and winked. He put his arm around me and led me back to the town while the housecarls followed behind us, out of earshot.

We did not see as much of Carol as I would have liked during our time in Tillysburg, because when he was not administering justice against traitors, he was preparing Tillysburg's defences for the coming war. He anticipated a siege, though I heard from Arne that all of Carol's commanders were advising him to meet Stephan in open battle.

Carol felt that victory would likelier be found behind Tillysburg's walls, not outside them, and apparently he would not budge on this idea. The disagreement with his commanders was causing some tension, especially between Carol and Roger, Tillysburg's earl.

Carol's soldiers, however, were much more enthusiastic about a siege than they were about marching to face Stephan. I suppose they thought, like Carol, that they would have a better chance at victory with the help of Tillysburg's walls.

Carol spent many hours wandering the town's ramparts and visiting the barracks and camps, checking the defences and inspiring his men with hope and courage. I talked to many of the warriors in Tillysburg, and they all spoke of how they loved the young Pretender.

When we did see Carol, it was mostly during the many debates held within the town hall that Dughlas and I were allowed to sit in on. It was during one such debate that a new factor in the war emerged, which would force Carol to reconsider his war plan, and which changed my life and the future of Ardonn forever.

The debate was one surrounding the contentious issue of

slavery, and just as it came to a close, the council chamber's doors burst open and Earl Roger marched in. He was red-faced and panting. A dirty, bloodied warrior followed, also out of breath. They had clearly come here from Roger's keep in a hurry, and the blood-covered soldier startled everyone in the chamber. He left a trail of mud behind him on his way in.

"Lord King," Roger said, bowing. He was tall and broad-shouldered, in his late twenties, with dark brown hair tied back in a loose ponytail, a sharp face, and a layer of stubble.

"Earl Roger," Carol said. The look on his face showed he was awaiting an explanation for the interruption.

"This man is a messenger from your fortress in the mountains. He has some information for you."

Carol inhaled deeply and froze for a second. "Out! Everyone, get out," he said. We all rose from our seats and made our way out of the hall, but Carol looked at me and held out his hand, indicating that Dughlas and I were to stay.

The messenger turned to leave, but Roger grabbed his arm and held him where he was. Within seconds, the chamber was empty aside from myself, Dughlas, Roger, Carol, and the bloodied warrior. "Lord King, I—" the messenger began. He limped forward.

"What is it? What happened?" Carol said.

Dughlas and I gave each other a concerned glance, and the messenger fell to his knees. "We lost it," the man mumbled.

"You *what*?"

The fort was attacked, Lord King. They came out of nowhere in the middle of the night. We tried to hold them off, but we were caught off guard. Forgive me." The messenger bowed his head, and a tear fell to the stone floor.

"I left Baldric in command of the fort. Is he alive?" Carol asked.

"Yes, Lord King. They are holding him prisoner, with the princess. They killed everyone else."

"How did this happen? Was no one patrolling the pass?"

"We had twenty men patrolling the pass, Lord King."

"So why were you caught off guard? There is something you are failing to tell me, man."

I watched the messenger shiver and saw more tears fall from his face. His muddy knees had dirtied the stone, and dried blood had matted his hair. He looked up at the king and bowed his head again.

The messenger explained to Carol what had happened, and although Carol made his best efforts to retain his composure, we could all tell he was furious. Baldric was one of Carol's oathmen who had apparently helped the young king escape the Capital when it fell to Wim's forces.

Carol trusted Baldric and left him in charge of his mountain fortress while he ruled from Tillysburg. The defence of that fortress was crucial, not only because of its strategic value, but also because Carol had left his sister — his only heir — at that fortress in case Carol were to die while fighting Stephan.

The previous day, however, was little Clodild's ninth name day, and she apparently insisted Baldric throw her a celebration. Every man posted to that fortress was ordered to partake in the celebrations. Why Baldric would agree to that vexed Carol, but I had suspicions there was more at fault here than a child's name day party.

"So, Baldric has failed me. I should pray that the men who attacked my fortress will save me the trouble of disciplining him. But Clodild…" Carol said. He turned away from the messenger, lost in thought. The messenger stood, wiped his tears away, and looked at his king with sorrow.

Roger stepped forward. "Young man, you said they killed everyone else, but clearly you are an exception. Why?"

"They spared me, lord. They even gave me a horse and bandaged my wounds," said the messenger.

"Why?" Carol asked, turning back to the man.

"Their leader told me that I was to carry a message. I'm supposed to find a man called Edward and tell him that his Lurian is waiting for him. He said you would know who I'm talking about."

When the messenger said those words, everything seemed to slow down, and my heart sank. Carol turned his head to look over at me, and his jaw dropped. Carol's fortress had been attacked and captured by Hakon and his men.

Both Carol and I immediately understood why. The fortress, which had been occupied by Carol's ancestors and passed down through his line to him, was not protecting a mountain pass, as was commonly thought, but was guarding a legend.

And now Hakon had it.

It took great effort convincing Carol not to march his army back to the mountains to retake his fortress and rescue his sister. Roger and I explained to him that if he did so, Stephan and Odo would trap him there — that is, if he was able to recapture the fort, which would cost hundreds of his own men and possibly his sister's life.

Roger's scouts had reported that the usurper's army was only a few days' march away, and if he retreated now, the war would be over. Carol did not tell Roger what the messenger had meant, and so Roger believed that the fortress was taken as part of Stephan's war plan. He suggested paying a ransom for Clodild's release, but no ransom was offered. It was not gold Hakon desired.

"Our only hope now is to meet Stephan on the field. We choose the ground that gives us the advantage and beat the king in one swift move," Roger advised. Carol had summoned several of his top strategists, including Arne, and we were now discussing what Carol's response to the loss of his fort should be.

"Earl Roger is right, Lord King," Arne said. "If we can play the offensive and beat the usurper in one big battle, then his men will lose heart and the nobles hidden away in their castles will emerge and support us. But if you go back to the fort, it will look like cowardice, and bouncing back and forth between here and there will make you seem confused. No one will support you then."

"Do you all think war is some kind of game?" Carol snapped. His advisors all bowed their heads. Only Roger and I looked at him. "How big did you say Stephan's army was, Edward? Three thousand men? We have little more than one third of that, and many of them will die if we engage our enemies in battle. They are not pieces on a draughts board. They are brothers, husbands, fathers, and sons."

"And how many will die if we besiege your fort?" Roger asked.

Carol clenched his jaw and looked to me for advice.

I shrugged. "I know little about strategy and war. But Lord King, I urge you to let me go to the fort alone. I will make the enemy leave, and then all you need to do is decide whether to stay here or march on Stephan."

"And how could you possibly do that?" Roger retorted.

"I know the man who leads them. I think I can make some kind of arrangement with him."

Roger opened his mouth to argue, but Carol raised a hand and he went quiet. "I trust you, Edward. I will allow you to go, but please do not fail me. I cannot beat Stephan if I am threatened from the west as well as the north," Carol said. "And please, save my sister. Should I die, Clodild is the last of the Eomundson line."

The other men began to protest, but Carol kept his hand up, raised his eyebrows, and looked each of them in the eye one by one, shutting them up.

Roger turned to me and gave a quick nod. "Do not fail, Godspeaker. Remember, it is my town and her citizens that are under threat."

It is all Ardonn under threat, I thought. I bowed, and Carol dismissed me from his war council. I went up to the higher levels of the town hall to find my friends and tell them I was going north, alone. Carol's fort was about a day or two's ride from Tillysburg, and I planned to leave immediately and ride as fast as possible, even through the night if I needed to.

It would be a hard ride, through hills and up into the mountains, and Brand would hate me for it, but the fate of all hung in the balance. The fate of myself, the fate of my friends, and the fate of Ardonn.

The Gods were watching me closely now, placing bets on my every decision. It was possible that I would fail and that Emrys would be released and ride to ravage the kingdom, but I had to try.

Neither Dughlas nor Matilda were in their rooms, and I did not have time to search elsewhere, so I immediately began to pack my things. I got changed out of the clothes I was wearing and put on something warmer and more suitable for hiking.

I stared at my sword for a moment, wondering whether I

should take it. A wise man would leave it behind, for why would any with his wits about him bring the one thing Hakon needed into an obvious trap? Yet a wise man I was not. I was young, hardly an experienced warrior, and in those days I did not want to imagine combat without that lucky Edin-forged blade in my hand. I clipped both dagger and sword to my belt, packed the rest of my tools and belongings into a bag, then headed for the door.

But the moment I opened it, I came face-to-face with Matilda, standing in the doorway. Her smile turned into a frown. "Where are you going?"

"Away," I said.

I took a step forward and tried to get past her, but she put her arm against the doorframe and stopped me. She stared up into my eyes. "Where are you going?"

"I'm to rescue Philip. Hakon has captured Carol's fort, and Philip is there, along with Carol's sister. Will you let me pass?"

Matilda only stared at me as she processed what I had said. She took a deep breath. "You mean to go alone."

"Yes."

"You may die."

"I *will* die, be it tomorrow or in a hundred years. But Carol's fort has been guarding Emrys's tomb this whole time. I have to stop Hakon."

Without another word, Matilda threw her arms around me and buried her head in my chest. She knew there was no point in arguing and that I would never let her come along. Or perhaps she was tired of travelling.

Whatever the case may have been, she accepted that we were parting ways. She was saying goodbye for what may be the last time. I held her close, and the moment seemed to last forever. I did not want to let go. I had to conjure great will to pull myself away.

"Where is Dughlas?" I asked.

Matilda wiped her eyes. "We were looking around the markets. I forgot my coin purse, so I came back here to get it when I heard you in your room."

"Go and tell him where I have gone. I will come back, Matilda. I won't say goodbye, for we will see each other again."

"Is that a promise?"

"It is a promise," I said. I did not know if I was telling the truth. Matilda nodded and then looked down at her feet.

"Edward, I just want to say…" she began.

I held my finger to her lips. "No more words. Two nights, then we will see each other again." I smiled, kissed her forehead, and pushed past her.

I did not turn back as I walked through the hallway and down the stairs. I needed to go, and if I had turned, or if Matilda had said one more word, I may not have been able to. I felt her standing there watching me as I left her behind, and my heart felt as though it was twisting up in knots.

I headed for the stables and mounted Brand. I guided him to the gate, kicked his side, cracked the reins, and the two of us raced north.

Would I see Matilda again?

I was fortunate. The skies were clear and there was little wind, so the weather was not an obstacle on my ride to the mountains. The hills were, though, but Brand was a strong horse and he could handle it. I pushed him hard that afternoon, but I was sure he would forgive me.

Night fell, but I kept riding. I had to pause to let Brand catch his breath every so often, and I let him drink whenever we found a stream or a pond, but I could not stop for long. The air turned bitterly cold very fast, and the enormous silhouettes of the mountains loomed above me like great giants. The moonlight reflected off their snowy peaks.

As we rode farther and farther uphill, the soil grew colder and harder, the trees grew sparser, and patches of snow dotted the ground. It also got windier, and in the distance I could hear the mountain passes howling like wolves.

It was around midnight when I found another stream, and I let the poor, tired Brand quench his thirst while I dismounted and rummaged through my bag to find him an apple. He eagerly munched on it. I stroked his neck, and he snorted his thanks.

But then I heard another noise. Something in the distance, getting closer and closer.

I shushed Brand, crouched low, then crept forward several

paces to hide behind a boulder, squinting south into the distance. It was downhill, so was coming from the same direction I had come from, but I could barely see anything. The light from the moon and stars was all I had to guide me.

The sound was muffled by the echoes coming from the mountain pass to the north, but as it grew louder I realised it was hoofbeats. One horse, it sounded like. It moved with great haste.

I eased my sword from its sheath, taking care not to make a sound, for any noise I made would have echoed downhill. I crept back to Brand, my heart beating faster and faster, but before I could mount, the stranger's horse skidded to a stop right behind me. I was too slow.

I spun around, and clutching my sword in both hands, I gave a yell and swung at the man atop the horse.

With blinding speed he drew his sword and parried my blow and then spurred his horse forward and kicked me in the chest with his boot. I fell backwards and dropped my sword, stunned.

"You pigshit," the man growled. He jumped down from his horse and walked over to me. I could see only a shadow standing over me. He sheathed his sword, crouched down, and reached out his hand. "Do you know how hard I had to ride to catch up with you?"

I recognised the voice. It was Dughlas, and as my eyes focussed I saw him grinning, looking down at me with his one eye. I grabbed his hand, and he pulled me back to my feet.

"I told Matilda I was going alone," I said. I should have been angry, but I was somewhat glad that I now had company. I was beginning to wonder if riding through the mountains alone at night was a good idea.

"You really think I would have let you do that? Besides, she made a pitiful effort at stopping me," he said. I chuckled, and he patted me on the chest. "Didn't kick you too hard, did I? I forgot your ribs were sore."

"I'm fine. Water your horse, and we'll leave in a minute."

"You don't want to rest?"

"No. Not here, at least."

And so Dughlas fed his horse and let him drink, and we filled our waterskins. We wasted no time in mounting again and heading deeper into the mountains. The air was certainly thinner up there, so we had to ride a little slower to ensure that the horses would not collapse from exhaustion. We rode for a few more hours, and although I wanted to keep going, the horses were beginning to protest. We had to find somewhere to rest, and so we chose a small outcrop to camp under.

Despite the sparsity of trees here, Dughlas managed to find a few pieces of deadwood, so we made a small fire under our natural shelter and huddled close to it, wrapped in our cloaks. Although we had fur and fire, we were still shivering.

"I am grateful you followed me," I said.

"And I'm grateful you left. I was beginning to get sick of that stinking town."

"I don't know if I can stop Hakon. I feel it may all be

hopeless," I confessed.

Dughlas sighed and shrugged, then patted me on the shoulder with his big, gloved hand. "Have faith, Edward. All things happen for a reason. Even if we lose, at least we know we were the good guys."

"Are we, though?"

"Of course. Edward, you are the most selfless, noble, and pious person I've ever met. You may seem reserved and lacking in empathy, but deep down I can see that you care immensely for the Gods, the land, and your people. And your friends. Who else would beat their horse to death riding into the mountains on a cold Dawning night?"

I chuckled, and a small rush of hope went through me. The tiredness hit me, so I decided to try to get some sleep. I lay down beside the fire, wrapped in fur, with my bag as a pillow. Dughlas stayed awake, and I quickly fell asleep to the melody of the whistling mountains. As I drifted, I pictured a chorus of elves singing softly to me in a warm, green wood, and then darkness.

I slept until dawn and was woken by Dughlas nudging my shoulder. I yawned, sat up, and found myself face-to-face with a spear. I lifted my hands and looked over at Dughlas, who also had a spear pointed at him. Three men stood before us, dressed in black. They were grinning.

"Edward, I presume?" one of the men asked. I nodded slowly, and they pulled their spears away. One of them kicked snow over the embers of our fire. "Our lord has been expecting you. You want an escort?"

"Do we have a choice?" I asked.

"We're going to the same place, are we not? Might as well go together."

Reluctantly, Dughlas and I packed up our things and mounted our horses. Brand was feeling much better after his rest, and surprisingly, the men did not confiscate our weapons.

We followed them up into the mountains and through the pass, which at some points was so narrow we could spread our arms and touch both sides at the same time. The pass was never wide enough for more than a dozen men marching abreast, and so any army coming this way would have a hard time. The men escorting us had to yell to talk to each other because the wind gushing through the passage was unbearably loud.

It was only a few more hours of riding through the pass to Carol's fortress, and by the time we arrived it was late morning. The fortress was immense and looked virtually impenetrable. It was backed by a sheer rock cliff built into the mountain centuries ago. The stronghold's stone bricks were large, dark, and heavy, presumably made using the cold rock dug from the surrounding mountains.

There was something unusual about this fortress, however — it seemed to be turned inside out. It had two walls, but where usually the inner wall would be higher than the outer wall, this fort had it backwards. The defences also seemed to be facing into the fort, rather than facing outside. It was built as though it was defending against an enemy within, and I supposed that would be true if Hakon was right about the location of Emrys.

Still, even if it was attacked from the outside, the formidable walls would take thousands to conquer if it was properly defended, and I imagine it could survive over a year with only twenty men on its walls. Hakon never should have been able to capture this place in one night.

The roof of the fort's massive keep could be spotted peeking over the top of the walls. This would have housed Carol and his leading men when they lived here, but now it was home to Hakon and his henchmen.

Warriors dressed in black patrolled the outer wall, and a lone black banner with the emblem of a silver snake fluttered high above us. As we approached the iron gates, they opened one after the other to let us through, scraping against stone and causing the chains that lifted them to groan under their weight. Our escort led us inside the fortress as the gates closed behind us.

Once through, we found ourselves in a large courtyard packed with tents. Hakon's men watched as we rode through, curious and excited. We stopped outside the keep's enormous double door, and standing there before us in his rich garments and a thick black bearskin cloak was the man I had been hunting. Hakon. Our escort dismounted, bowed to him, then led their horses away to rest.

"Friends. I have been expecting you," Hakon said. He had the air of a man who knows he has won.

"We aren't your friends," I snapped, quickly dismounting. Dughlas followed suit, and we put our hands on our swords. A crowd was beginning to form around us, so killing Hakon right now was out of the question.

Hakon looked genuinely offended. "Edward, please. I offer an opportunity to make some coin in these trying times, and you repay me by killing some of my best men. I forgave you for that out of the kindness of my heart, but now, when I offer you the comfort of my new home and extend to you the gesture of hospitality, you spit on me and threaten me."

"Where is Philip?" I growled.

"He is here, resting."

"Bring me to him."

"Calm down, Edward. I can tell you are distressed, but he is unharmed. We have treated him nicely, in fact, as we do with all our guests."

"I don't believe you," I said.

Hakon shrugged and then pointed towards me. "Why not ask him yourself?"

I turned, and there, standing behind me, was Philip. He was wrapped in leather and fur and appeared unhurt, but he looked a lot more miserable than he was the last time I saw him. He ran to stand between me and Dughlas. I put my arm around him and drew my sword. Dughlas tousled his curly hair. "I told your father I would keep you safe, didn't I?"

"Yes, so I won't tell him what happened," Philip said.

I smirked but then frowned again at the sound of steel scraping leather. I looked back to Hakon, and some of his men had drawn their weapons and stood close by him, including a large, bearded, middle-aged man in fine mail. He wore a heavy wolfskin cloak, which was pinned together at the shoulder by a golden brooch in the shape of a dragon. I assumed from the brooch that this was Baldric and thus confirmed my suspicions that he had betrayed Carol. At what price Baldric sold this fortress to Hakon, I could only guess.

"Where is the princess Clodild?" I said. I glanced at the man with the brooch when I said her name, and he looked away.

"Princess?" Hakon said. His men laughed. "Edward the Rebel, I see. She is inside."

"Take me to her."

"I cannot do that, I am afraid. She is being prepared."

"Prepared for what?"

"The sacrifice, of course. The blood of Emrys is required to unlock this prison, and that blood flows through Clodild's veins. It was his descendent, after all, that married King Eomund, the founder of our kingdom. We will kill the girl, and when Emrys is restored to his rightful throne, little Clodild will be remembered as the self-sacrificing saviour of our kingdom."

My heart sank. As Hakon grinned at me, his wicked plans now crystal clear, I bent over and emptied my belly into the snow.

"What's your plan?" Dughlas whispered to me.

We were being led by Hakon and two hundred of his men into an underground passage beneath the keep. The entrance to the passage had been concealed by a wall, but that wall had been knocked down and opened up to a damp, cold hallway, about six horses wide and three men tall. The hallway was sloped slightly and seemed to go on down forever into the darkness. Some of the men carried torches, but even they emitted little light.

As we marched down beneath the mountain, Hakon and his men chanted slow, melancholic songs from the times before Ardonn was unified. I can recall this passage:

> *The King that did die,*
> *'Neath a mountain does lie.*
> *For centuries he sleeps,*
> *While the darkness creeps.*
> *While the darkness creeps,*
> *O'er the land while he sleeps.*
> *But the King soon shall rise,*
> *And all he'll chastise.*
> *He will usher in the night,*
> *Gone is the light.*
> *Gone is the light,*
> *'Till the end of the night.*

My master taught me the ancient tongue, so I could understand the words and what they meant, but I doubted many of these men did. The songs were haunting and gave me chills, but at least they drowned out the sounds of the rats that scurried past our feet.

Dughlas, Philip, and I walked side by side amongst all the men so that we could not try anything against Hakon's wishes. He even let us keep our weapons in some proud display of the power he had over us, for it would be futile of us to use them then, though I knew I would be forced to give up my sword soon enough.

Hakon himself was the only man on a horse, and he rode with Clodild in his saddle ahead of the marching men, leading the way into the darkness. It was difficult to breathe down there, and I began to grow weary, but we kept on moving.

A worry crept into the back of my mind, telling me that all had been in vain. I had hastened to this fortress out of anger and desperation, but I had no real plan for how I was going to save Philip and Clodild, let alone retake the entire fort myself.

I was foolish. I thought that perhaps I could bargain with Hakon, but all I had done was fall into his trap and bring him what he needed: Godwin's sword. It appeared that any luck that weapon did possess had finally run out. What chances I had were quickly disappearing. I needed a plan soon.

"I've got nothing," I whispered back to Dughlas.

He grunted. "Let's just see what happens first. We might have to improvise, like you did with the vampire. You're good at that."

I smiled. I loved Dughlas. He always knew how to lift my spirits, even in the darkest of times. We could be marching through the deepest, darkest depths of the Pits, but Dughlas would still be cracking jokes.

We marched for what seemed like forever. I thought that this tunnel would never end, but eventually we came out into an enormous chamber. It was circular, the roof was three storeys high, and the floor could have fit thousands of men. As the procession entered the chamber, it diverged and the men all spread out along the walls.

Hakon, who had left his horse in the tunnel, stood in the centre of the hall with Clodild. Her hands were tied behind her back, and her mouth was stuffed with a rag. Her eyes were red and her cheeks wet. In the middle of the chamber, in front of Hakon, was a large stone bowl that seemed to be carved into the floor.

An offering bowl.

And then I noticed, stretching from the floor to the ceiling, a large archway. It was at the end of the chamber opposite the passage and looked to be sealed up by bricks carved by giants. I did not notice it earlier because it looked just like the rest of the chamber's wall, but once my eyes had adjusted to the dark I could see its outline clearly. As we entered the chamber, Hakon beckoned to me.

"Welcome, everyone," he called out, his eyes fixed on mine.

He pulled a long knife from his belt and pointed it at Clodild's chest. Her breathing quickened. She watched me with panicked eyes. The chamber went silent, and the singing stopped. Not even the rats made a sound.

"Today, with the help of Edward, we will release the incarnation of the Dead-God from his mountain prison. He shall ride forth in the body of Emrys once more and chastise this world for abandoning the Gods." Hakon held out his hand to me, but I did not move.

I only shook my head.

"Your sword, Edward?" Hakon said. I do not know why I said what I said next. I was out of ideas, and it seemed that the only chance I had to save Ardonn now was to kill Hakon. I would not be able to save Philip or Dughlas or Clodild, but I might be able to prevent the release of Emrys. Gods, I was a fool for bringing that sword.

"I will duel you for it," I said.

"What?"

"I challenge you to a hazeling. If I win, then the Gods do not favour you, and your task is not meant to be. I will take my sword and the princess and go free. If you win, you can take the sword from my corpse."

"It would be foolish for me to accept this challenge, Edward."

"Foolish? Are you a nobleman, Hakon, or some slave girl's bastard?"

Hakon flinched, and I heard some murmurs among the crowd.

I had challenged Hakon's honour, and were he to refuse this fight, he would lose all but his life. And so he accepted. "I will nominate a champion to fight in my name. Leif."

And so Leif, the tall man who had attacked us in Everlynn forest, emerged from the crowd and stood by his lord. He had a limp, but he would still probably have a better chance at beating me than Hakon. I had come to learn that Hakon was no warrior.

"Let me fight him," Dughlas said. I turned around, and Dughlas stepped forward.

"This is my fight," I said.

"Hakon has put forward a champion, so it's only fair that you do too. I want to fight him."

"For revenge?"

"For justice. He took my eye, and so I'll take his life."

"But your arm is still wounded, and your ankle has not fully healed."

Dughlas laughed. "Leif has a chance then."

I thought about it for a few moments and then nodded. I did not want to appear a coward, but Dughlas was insistent. His honour depended on avenging the loss of his eye. I could not deny him this.

I insisted my oathman use Godwin's sword, for he needed all the luck he could get, but Dughlas refused. He knew his own blade better. Before I could protest, Dughlas approached Leif and drew his weapon. Hakon stepped back out of the way, pulling Clodild with him, and I went to stand beside Philip. The ground was ready for the duel that would seal Ardonn's fate.

"Make it quick, Dughlas," I said.

"Don't I always?" With a smile and a roar, Dughlas leapt towards Leif, and the two men clashed, parrying each other's blows.

Every man in the room was silent as we watched the two warriors dance. They spun and twirled and ducked and dodged, blocking and parrying every swing and lunge of the blade. Dughlas was taunting Leif, and Leif taunted back, as each tried to enrage the other, drawing out a wrong move.

Despite his limp and his size, Leif seemed quite nimble, and Dughlas struggled to find an opening, but slowly Leif began to grow tired. Dughlas noticed too, and so instead of trying to hurt Leif, he started toying with him, egging him on and forcing him to keep his leg moving.

Leif was red-faced and panting now, but Dughlas seemed to be completely fine. In fact, he did not seem bothered by his injuries at all. He was smiling as he whirled in circles around Leif, tapping his opponent's longsword with the tip of his own as if inviting him to strike.

Leif was making heavy swings at Dughlas, but the weight of his sword and his limp meant Dughlas could easily dodge them. He even began to laugh as his long golden hair flicked back and forth. He was a warrior, but he looked like a dancer.

Then Dughlas's teasing was over. Leif was tired, and his morale was quickly dropping. I could see beads of sweat reflecting the torchlight, and the veins were popping out of his bald head. Leif grunted and attempted to lunge at Dughlas, but Dughlas only knocked the blade aside, and then with the flick of his wrist, Dughlas brought his sword up towards Leif's head.

Just in time, Leif jerked backwards so the top of the blade only scraped his chin. An arch of blood streamed from his face, and he stumbled back, holding his new wound. Dughlas took a step back to catch his breath. "Should I finish him, Edward?" he called.

"I told you to make it quick," I said. My hope had been renewed. Dughlas smiled and then went to fulfil his promise.

He jumped forward, lifted his sword up above his head, and Leif lifted his to block. But Dughlas feinted, and instead of striking above the head, he quickly brought his sword back down and around and cut into Leif's thigh. Even standing several yards away I could hear steel meet bone, and Leif let out a mighty roar. He lifted his blade to counter Dughlas, but Dughlas pulled away just in time. He backed up slowly, and Leif followed, enraged.

In his fury, Leif made a foolish, clumsy lunge, but Dughlas stepped aside, grabbed Leif's arm, and brought his elbow down onto it, snapping the bone in two. Leif cried out and his sword fell to the ground, but then he swung with his left arm and hooked Dughlas in the face.

Dughlas stepped back and spat out some blood, but before he could react, Leif threw himself at Dughlas and tackled him to the ground. His sword went skating across the cold stone, and the two men began to wrestle. Leif, however, was stronger and bigger than Dughlas, and he managed to pin my oathman to the ground.

He was beating him now. Again and again and again he hammered Dughlas, flicking blood up with his fist whenever he pulled back to punch again. Dughlas's face became a bloody mess, and whenever Dughlas tried to hit back, Leif simply swatted his arm out of the way.

"Get up, Dughlas," I shouted. He appeared not to hear me, and I shouted again.

Hakon smiled at me. "Finish the job, Leif."

Leif grunted and reached for Dughlas's blade. He held it up with two hands, pointing the blade down at Dughlas's chest. Dughlas had lost. He would die, pierced by his own sword. Leif yelled in triumph, but just as he was about to thrust steel through Dughlas's heart, I shouted. "Stop this!"

Leif paused, and Hakon frowned at me. He held a hand up to Leif.

"It is over. Your man has won," I said. Tears were forming in my eyes. "You can have Godwin's sword. You can have the princess. But please, let my man live."

Hakon grinned. "You have lost, then?"

"I have lost."

Dughlas turned his head to look at me. I looked into his eye and saw sorrow. Anguish. He knew he had failed me, but it was I who failed him. I should have fought Leif myself, but now it was over. I drew my sword and tossed it to the ground.

"Let him live, Leif. I want this dog to see what his master has done. Bring me the blade," said Hakon.

Leif obeyed and left Dughlas lying there. I went to him and helped him sit up. His head was limp, and blood poured from his open mouth and nose, but he would live.

"I can walk," he mumbled. Dughlas tried to stand but fell to his knees. "I just need a moment."

"We shall continue the ritual," Hakon said.

He held my sword — Godwin's sword — in front of his face, admiring it, then beckoned to two men in the crowd. They came forward, took Clodild by the arms, and dragged her to the bowl, then pushed her to her knees. Her screams, muffled by the rag in her mouth, echoed throughout the chamber.

The two men held her head down over the bowl. I stood, and Dughlas slowly climbed to his feet. The two of us watched in horror. It was just like the pig I helped sacrifice in Oldford during Winterlow, except this was no pig but a little girl instead. A child.

Clodild would not stop squealing. Hakon approached her and held the edge of my blade at her throat. She was bawling her eyes out, writhing and wriggling in vain, but the men held her tight. Philip came and held my arm, and Dughlas shut his eye.

Yet Clodild did not die. I do not know whether Hakon changed his mind, or if he was merely tormenting the girl, but he moved the blade away from her throat and in one swift motion cut across her cheek with the tip. Clodild fainted. The men held her head in place as blood trickled from her open gash into the bowl.

"The blood of Emrys is needed to open the prison," Hakon said. "But not a lot. Let that scar be a reminder to you, little Clodild, of what you have done for this country. You shall be rewarded in this life and honoured long after your death."

He watched as drops of blood continued to fall into the bowl, but as they began to slow, Hakon nodded, satisfied that he had enough. The men pulled Clodild away, and her eyes fluttered open. She seemed dazed for a few moments, but when she remembered where she was, she began to struggle and scream again.

One of the men clapped her on the back of the head, and she went limp once more.

"What now, lord?" Leif said.

"We wait," said Hakon.

And so we waited for what seemed like an eternity. I watched the giant archway. Nothing was happening, and the hall was silent. Hakon stared at the archway too. We all did. None of us knew what to expect. Was Emrys merely fiction after all?

But then we began to hear a rumble. It was soft at first and seemed distant, but it grew closer and louder, and eventually it was deafening. Some of Hakon's men bolted for the tunnel and fled, but many stayed, and Hakon began to laugh. The stone blocks that sealed the archway were beginning to shake, and then as if by magic they crumbled into dust. A cloud of dust shrouded

the archway, the rumbling stopped, and the chamber went silent
again.

Then we heard the slow, steady clap of a single horse walking
on stone. It echoed around the chamber, and my blood ran cold.
My intuition was screaming at me, urging me to run, to abandon
everything. But I stood frozen, staring at the cloud of dust in the
open archway.

Then I saw it. The outline of a man on a horse. He emerged
from the dust, and Hakon with all his men fell to their knees.

I could see the man clearly now. He sat upon an imposing grey
horse. He wore a suit of dark steel mail and had broad shoulders
and a rugged, menacing face. His grey hair was long and wild
and fell down to his waist, and his grey, wispy beard grew to his
chest.

In front of him, sitting in the saddle, was a grey puppy, and the
man stroked its fur as he rode forward. I remember thinking
about how odd that was, but the thought was overshadowed by
the darker forces radiating from this man.

He was not holding the horse's reins, and it seemed to be
guided by his mind alone. Instead, in his other hand, he held a
leaf-bladed, gilded sword. His horse entered the room slowly,
and he looked around at everyone on the floor.

He smirked. The horseman came to the blood bowl and stared
down into it for a moment, then looked up, and his eyes locked
onto mine. Like everything else about him, his eyes were grey.
Cold. A shiver crept through me. The mere sight of this man,

knowing who he was yet not knowing what he might do, was enough to fill the hearts of even the mightiest heroes with terror.

I shivered with fear, for I could sense the doom he would bring. It seemed as if all my courage had fled.

"Godwin," the man said. His voice was an eerie mix between a hiss and a groan. "I did not expect to see you here again."

"I am not Godwin. I am Edward, his successor," I replied. The man was speaking the ancient tongue, so I replied in that.

"Ah. You…feel like him. Tell me, Heir of Godwin, why have you released me?" I pointed at Hakon, who had his face to the floor in prostration. The man on the horse looked puzzled.

"This man freed you," I said in my own language.

Hakon looked up, and the horseman laughed. "So you are his tool, then?" he said, turning back to me.

Before I could respond, Hakon stood and scurried over to the horseman, bowing his head. He held out a piece of parchment. "My Lord Emrys, I am but a messenger. This letter is for you," he said. He was a completely new man now, and I could almost smell the fear on him.

Emrys reached down from his horse and plucked the letter from Hakon's hand. "Oh? I cannot read your language. Edward, would you translate this for me?" I slowly walked over to him and took the parchment, unfolded it and began reading, translating its contents into the ancient tongue. Hakon glared at me.

As I read the letter, my heart sank. Hakon was right; he was just an instrument. The levels of treachery at play here were far more complex than I thought. I read the words out loud to Emrys, doing my best to translate. He closed his eyes as if the sound of my voice was a soothing song.

King Emrys. I beseech you on behalf of all people in this land. We are betrayed by a man who calls himself king, but he is nothing more than a puppet. If you are reading this letter, it is because you have been freed by a pawn in my game.

But what is my plan, you may ask? I wish to overthrow our false 'king' and put the rightful ruler back on the throne. That ruler is you, Lord Emrys. I offer you my loyalty and the throne of Ardonn, and all you must do to claim it is head south from your prison until you reach a town called Tillysburg, occupied by another false claimant to the throne. Ignore him, for he is weak.

Once you reach this town, head west until you encounter an army. You must slaughter any man who does not fight under a blue banner, and just like that, you will have your kingdom.

After we have annihilated the false king's army, we will discuss our next steps.

Now, the man you likely see grovelling before you is my brother. He believes he will ride alongside you to glory, but he is a fool and a bastard. He wishes to take what rightfully belongs to my son and will no doubt use you for his own gain. I do not need him anymore, so you may put him and his men out of their misery.

I had spoken in the ancient tongue, but everyone else in the room understood the name at the end. Lord Odo. He had orchestrated this plan all along. He was the architect. I had thought Hakon was the leader of this fanatical plot, but in truth Hakon was as much a pawn as I was.

In the past, mortal lords had allied themselves with Emrys in his attempted conquests, but did Odo really want to put Emrys on the throne? Or did he simply want to use the Immortal Horde to claim it for himself? When I met Odo, he did not strike me as a man who cared much for legends, or legitimacy. He had the air of a man who believed power resided in wealth and arms.

There were murmurs among the crowd. Emrys began to hum, then he smiled at me.

"A tempting offer. Perhaps I shall go and visit this man called Odo," he said. He looked back down at Hakon, who had prostrated himself at the horse's feet. "You are a rat, and I hate rats. I will not dirty my blade with your filth. Your men, on the other hand, will die."

Emrys pulled a hollowed goat's horn from his belt and blew into it. Its droning sound echoed through the chamber, and with its noise I heard the sound of hundreds of hoofbeats coming from beyond the archway.

In an instant, hundreds of warriors on horseback streamed out of the cloud of dust and immediately began cutting down Hakon's men. The screaming was terrible, and the men all began to flee in an attempt to escape the wrath of the Immortal Horde.

The horsemen seemed to pour endlessly into the chamber, and they all laughed and whooped with glee as they slaughtered Hakon's screaming men. Hakon was wailing in despair, pulling at his hair and pacing back and forth. Leif tried to flee, but he was too slow. Emrys's horsemen rode him down like the rest of Hakon's warriors, and he died on the spot.

I grabbed Philip and ran to check on Clodild, who was now awake and crying. She was terrified. I put my arm around Philip and my body over the princess to shield her, and when I turned my head I saw Emrys sitting up on his horse above me. I could smell the beast's breath.

"You and your friends here will be safe," he shouted down to me. The sound of horses, laughter, and dying men was deafening. I could hardly hear him. "But tell me, what year is it?"

"Eleven nineteen," I yelled back.

Emrys nodded. "I have been entombed for three centuries," he yelled. I noticed a flash of anger appear on his otherwise emotionless face.

"What will you do?"

"Take what is mine. We will meet again, Edward, Heir of Godwin. I am in your debt."

Before I could reply, Emrys's horse leaped over me, and he

galloped away with his riders, who were now rushing into the tunnel to ride down any who had escaped. The screams were still going, and I knew they would haunt my dreams for years to come. These were not merely the cries of dying men, but those of men who knew absolute fear and desperation.

I helped Clodild sit up and hugged her tight, holding her for what seemed like hours as hundreds of avenging immortal horsemen rode from their prison and out into the world once more. I held Clodild while Dughlas and Philip crouched beside me until the last of the horsemen went through the tunnel and the trembling roar of hooves ceased.

We were now alone in the cold, quiet dark.

I had lost.

14

War

Once it was clear that Emrys and his horde were gone, the four of us made our way back up through the tunnel in the dark. Clodild had stopped crying now and was silent. I carried her on my back.

I had taken my sword back from Hakon and thought about killing him with it, but I felt disgusted by his miserable state so I spared him the dignity of death. We could hear his muffled sobs echoing up from the chamber where Emrys had humiliated him and slaughtered his men. The stench of death was intense, but it lessened the farther up the passage we went.

The sun was setting when we left the fort, and the mountains cast a long shadow over us. The lifeless bodies of Hakon's men lay all over the fort's courtyard and walls, and some were scattered along the mountain pass. Emrys had killed them all.

We found our horses tied up in the fort's courtyard, so we mounted and rode through the night with haste to Tillysburg.

Dughlas was badly hurt and still seemed a little dizzy, but he assured me he could ride, so he and Philip shared a saddle while I rode with Clodild, her arms wrapped tight around me.

We followed the tracks left behind by the Immortal Horde, but they seemed to have unnatural speed and were far ahead of us. I could only hope that Carol had remained in Tillysburg as he had planned, rather than march west to meet Stephan.

The journey south was much easier and much faster than the journey north. Brand moved fast downhill this time. He was a little more enthusiastic about this journey than that of the day before.

We rode in the light of the full moon, which marked the festival of Middlespring. In gentler times, folk would be gathered together for feasting and merriment, but Fate had other plans for us on this day.

We only stopped twice to let the horses rest and drink. The first time, Brand was drinking from a stream while I washed Dughlas's blood from my hands.

"Hello," Clodild said. This was the first time I had heard her speak. I turned to see her standing behind me, wrapped in a fur cloak we found in the fortress.

"My Lady," I said.

"Who are you? Why did you save me?"

"My name is Edward of Oldford. Your brother sent me to

rescue you."

"Are you the man who talks to elves?"

I grinned. "I am. I'm a Godspeaker."

"Wow."

"I heard it was your name day just recently. How old are you, My Lady?"

"I am nine, I think. What about you?"

"I'm about twenty."

"Wow, that is old. Thank you for saving me, Lord Edward." Clodild wrapped her arms around my neck and hugged me.

"Do I get a hug too, Lord Edward?" Philip asked with a smirk. He had come to stand by me with Dughlas, whose face was now cleaned of blood but was badly bruised. His nose was broken and a tooth was missing.

"I see you lost none of your cheek while Hakon held you captive." I grinned. "It is good to see you again, lad. I am sorry for what happened."

"That is all right. It was an adventure, and you came to find me in the end."

"I swear to you, it won't happen again. Are you ready to keep going?" I said. Philip nodded.

"Aye, we should hurry. Tilly and Tillysburg are in danger," Dughlas said.

I agreed, and so we mounted our horses and sped south.

We stopped to rest again a couple of hours before dawn, and that was when we discovered we were too late. Off in the distance, coming towards us up the dirt path, was a long line of about three hundred people.

We first spotted their torches, but then we could see the people themselves. They were in a hurry, and I could tell immediately that they were refugees. They must have come from Tillysburg, which meant Emrys had stopped to attack the town, as I had feared. They would not have needed to besiege it, because the decrepit state of Tillysburg's walls would mean they could just pour right through into the streets.

I paused to watch them and then kicked the horse and sped off downhill to meet the line.

"Halt!" the man at the head of the column shouted as we approached. It was Arne. His sword was drawn, his armour broken and bloodied, and he looked like a mess.

I pulled Brand to a stop and threw myself down from him, holding my hands up. "It's me. Edward."

Arne sheathed his sword. "What news from the fort?"

"The men who captured it are all dead, slaughtered by the warlord Emrys and his band. I could not stop them." I bent over and put my hands on my knees, panting. Clodild stayed in the saddle.

"*The* Emrys? From the legends? Gods…" Arne shook his head.

"Where are you all going?"

"East. There is an ancient, abandoned fort some days that way, called Giant's Rest by the locals. Tillysburg is in flames. Hundreds of horsemen just attacked out of nowhere."

"That was Emrys and his men. Where is Carol?"

"He marched west yesterday with Earl Roger and left me in charge of the city's defence."

"Then I need to warn him. Is Matilda—"

Arne opened his mouth to speak, but before he said anything, a woman called my name. Running towards me along the line, holding her dress up to her knees, was Matilda. I breathed a sigh of relief to know she was alive, and it felt as though a weight I did not know was there had been lifted from my shoulders. She was smiling, though her hair was messy, her dress was torn, and her legs were covered in mud. But she was alive. She threw herself into my arms.

"You kept your promise," Matilda said.

"I must go again, Matilda. Carol is marching to war, and I need to warn him of the danger he truly faces."

Matilda's smile turned into a frown. She nodded. "I see you rescued Philip and Carol's sister."

"Yes, but I could not stop Hakon. I was a fool, Matilda. It is all my fault."

"No. You saved two lives today. You did what you felt needed to be done."

"But how many more will die?"

Matilda shook her head. "You cannot save everybody. One day, I will tell my children of this story, and they will know Edward Godspeaker as a hero."

Before I could respond, Clodild climbed down from my horse

and came to stand beside me. She put her hand in mine, then Arne went to his knee.

"Princess Clodild, I thank all the Gods that you are alive," he said.

Clodild nodded. "The elf-friend saved me. Can he be my housecarl?"

"You will have to ask your brother, My Lady, once he meets us at Giant's Rest. Come, we must go now."

Clodild looked up at me as if for approval, and I nodded. She hugged me again and then went and took Arne's hand. He helped her up onto his horse, and she gave me a wave. I waved back.

"Dughlas, Philip," I said. "Go with the refugees to Giant's Rest. Neither of you will be any help in the battle to come, but should this old fortress need defending, they will need every able man and woman."

"Aye, Boss. I'd wish you luck, but you probably don't need it," Dughlas said. He flashed a smile and gave what must have been a wink.

"Arne, look after them. Farewell," I said. Arne nodded, and I could tell he was eager to get his column moving again. Dughlas and Philip rode to join Clodild among the refugees, and I walked back to Brand alone.

I put my boot in the stirrup, grabbed the saddle, and just as I was about to pull myself up, Matilda called my name again and came running over to me. Arne tipped his head back in frustration, and I put my foot back down and turned to her.

"What is it?" I asked.

Without saying a word, she put my head in both her hands, stood up on her toes, and pressed her lips against mine. I did not know what to do or how to feel, so I just put my hands on her waist and kissed her back.

It seemed to last forever, though it only lasted a few seconds. Her lips tasted like soot and ash, but no kiss had ever before been sweeter. Matilda pulled away, and I stared into her beautiful blue eyes. She was teary, but she smiled and blushed.

"That was for luck," she said. Matilda took my hand and put something cold in my palm, then closed my fingers around it. "And this is so you remember to come back. No goodbyes. Now go and fulfil your oath, Edward of Winterhome."

And at that she turned away and joined the column again. Arne gave a command, and the refugees resumed their march.

I pulled myself up onto Brand and caught one last glimpse of Matilda watching me as the column marched eastwards. I sat gazing on them for a while, wondering if I would ever see her again, then turned Brand back south. I opened my fist and saw what Matilda had given me.

It was a thin silver chain, and attached to that chain was a little pendant in the shape of a moth.

I smelt it before I saw it. Burning. Burning wood and burning corpses. The sun was still below the horizon, but as dawn approached, and as I rode closer to Tillysburg, I could see a thick black cloud rising over the hills.

But the horror truly struck me when the town came into view. At first it was a glow on the horizon, but as the town appeared over the hills, I saw the flames and the burning buildings. The town hall's bell tower stood gasping for air, drowning in a sea of flames. Roofs had collapsed and walls had tumbled down onto the streets. The keep and the temple — the two buildings made of stone — were the only ones spared.

As I neared Tillysburg I could hear screams and moans, the shrieking of horses, and the laughter of greedy men. But what struck me most was not the flames. It was not the screams or the killing or the terror. What made my blood run cold was that I had seen this before in the vision I had received during Winterlow. The Gods' prophecy had come true, yet only now did I understand. Now, when it was all too late. I had recognised Tillysburg when I first arrived, but I could not figure out where I had seen it until that moment.

Several large wagons piled high with chests were being dragged by horses from a great wound in the town's wall, led by some of Emrys's men. This would have been their plunder, but what a horde of immortal horsemen needed wealth for, I could only guess.

They also led a long line of people from the gates. Many of them were women and children, but there were some men. The wagons and the prisoners were being led south, and as I approached along the northern road, three horsemen veered away from the group and rode towards me.

I drew my sword. The horsemen came to a halt a few yards away. One of the horsemen, a man on a grey horse, came forward. He wore an elaborate gilded helmet with a horrifying faceplate depicting a snarling wolf. His face was hidden, but his long grey beard and the puppy in his saddle revealed his identity.

"Emrys," I said.

"Edward," he said. Emrys removed his helmet and scratched his dog behind the ear. He was grinning at me.

"What have you done?" I spoke in his language.

"I have pillaged this town. I need wealth, and we cannot exactly earn it honestly," he replied. His voice betrayed little emotion. The two warriors he brought with him chuckled, but he silenced them with a hiss. "Have you come to collect your share of the plunder?"

"No, I have come to find my friends."

"Ah, your friends. How charming. I apologise, but your friends are likely slaves now. Or dead."

"What is that for?" I asked, pointing to his dog. I spoke in my language this time, and I noticed it made Emrys wince.

"My men and I cannot touch the ground until this little dog jumps from my saddle, lest all the years we have lived pass us by in a single moment," Emrys explained. So the legends were true. Emrys was cursed, and it seemed the puppy was the only way to save him.

"Then why do you need to raid and pillage this land?" I asked.

"Because I can also break this curse if I once again wear the crown of my ancestors. And thus, I go to war against this man who calls himself 'Stephan' and join forces with Odo of the letter."

And that was where I spotted Odo's first mistake. In the legends, whenever Emrys emerged he had subsequently gone to war with whomever the king was at the time, and so Odo must have taken this to mean that Emrys desired the kingdom of Ardonn.

But now it became clear to me. Emrys cared little for the kingdom. All he wanted was the crown, and he had fought the kings for that crown. In ancient times, that crown had symbolised the king's divinity and his right to rule, but that meaning had been forgotten to all but a few, Odo included.

Emrys would lead his horde to destroy Stephan, and Odo would betray his king, but what they did not realise was that when Stephan's father usurped the throne and became Ardonn's ruler, he had a new crown forged with gold and fur and gemstones.

The crown of the ancients, the crown Emrys desired, was made from simple iron and decorated with a single piece of amber, and it sat atop the head of Carol the Pretender. I chose to withhold that last piece of information from Emrys.

"That crown was destroyed when Stephan's father took the throne. Only the dog can free you from you curse," I said. "I beg you, Emrys. Do not ride west. You will be fighting for nothing. Stay here, and I will see if I can help you."

I saw Emrys think for a moment, considering my offer, and then he smiled. "I appreciate your concern, Heir of Godwin, but I do not trust you. I shall defeat this army for Odo, and if the crown of this false king does not free me from the chains of this curse, I will retreat to the woods and await your aid. But tell me, why are you so concerned with where I march?"

"Because my friend leads an army against Stephan and Odo."

"Ah, yes. The folk of this town have spoken of this Carol fellow. My descendant, I have heard."

"Yes, he is."

"He desires my crown. I shall slaughter him with all the rest."

"But he will not expect you," I replied, hoping to trigger some sense of honour. I was anxious now, and Emrys could tell.

"Then you had better go and warn him," Emrys said. He grinned at me and then pulled something from inside his big grey cloak. It was a leather pouch, and he tossed it to me. "This is for freeing me from that accursed tomb."

I caught the pouch and was surprised by its weight. Emrys bowed his head, he and his companions turned their horses, and they rode off to join the rest of his men in the burning town.

I opened the pouch and saw it was filled to the brim with gold coins. They were minted during Stephan's reign, so they must have been taken from Tillysburg that night. I tossed it away, throwing it as far as I could, then sped off westwards.

I had to reach Carol before Emrys did, or all would be lost.

A few miles west of Tillysburg was the battlefield where the Pretender had chosen to make a stand against Stephan. I heard the two armies as I approached: the sound of horns, the beating of drums and feet, and the yelling of men giving and receiving orders. I climbed to the top of a ridge that ran from north to south, and from there I had a view of the entire field. I did not know much about military strategy, but I could tell the moment I arrived that Carol had chosen well.

The ground Carol had chosen was a flat plain stretching for many miles to the south and west, but in the north the plain began to incline and grow into a hill. The hill stretched along the northern edge of the plain for about a mile or so. Westwards, the hill began to veer north, and eastwards it connected to the ridge I was sitting atop, which guarded the eastern edge of the plain and would have been far too steep for an army to climb without sustaining severe casualties.

Carol had positioned his army atop that northern hill, facing south, so that if Stephan wished to attack him he would need to either climb that hill and attack from the west or south or climb the ridge and then turn and attack from the east. It would have been impossible to go around the back, since Carol was guarded by the mountains to the north.

Stephan, seeing no other option, positioned his army at the

bottom of the incline. I could see then that Stephan, combined with Odo's army, led a force that outnumbered Carol's nearly three to one.

The armies faced each other, taunting and yelling, inciting the other to attack. Stephan did not want to suffer the penalty of attacking uphill, but Carol did not want to leave his position of safety atop it. However, the positions of both sides would not matter if Emrys charged his horde from the east and attacked the flanks of both armies.

Based on his letter, Odo seemed to think Carol would hide behind Tillysburg's walls so he could be dealt with later, yet I doubted the Pretender's presence on this battlefield would make little difference when faced with Emrys's horde.

I suspected that Odo was now hoping Emrys would join the battle once the two forces had engaged so that Odo could turn and attack from the west, and Emrys would attack from the east, outflanking both Stephan and Carol and decimating both forces. The art of warfare was not in numbers, but in outsmarting and outmanoeuvring your enemies.

I turned Brand and hastened north along the ridge, then headed west along the hillside. Ahead I could see the long shadows of the ridge behind me stretching across the battlefield, and light touched the treetops in the distance. I could feel the sun begin to warm my back. Dawn was here, and the sun was beginning to rise. A party of warriors rode out from Carol's army to meet me. They recognised me and escorted me to Carol.

The Pretender was in an open tent at the back of his army, in council with his strategists and commanders. He was in his war gear. A purple cape was folded over his shoulders, and a longsword hung at his belt. He wore his crown. Carol smiled as I entered the tent, and I gave a short bow.

"Edward," he exclaimed. "I was praying you had survived."

"Lord King, I—"

Carol raised his hand. "I heard. I know about Tillysburg."

"I am sorry, Lord King."

Before Carol could respond, Earl Roger slammed his fist on the table. "You failed us all, Edward. So much for being 'Gifted.'" His face was bright red, and he glared at me until he was back-handed by Carol.

"When we win this battle, Roger, and I have my kingdom back, you will be compensated for the loss of your town. Do not let your sense of self-importance allow you to forget your place, Earl," Carol said. Roger bowed his head and mumbled an apology. "And what of my sister? Did you rescue her?"

"I did, Lord King. She is safe with your man Arne and is heading with the Tillysburg refugees to Giant's Rest."

"Then you have brought honour to your name, Edward. I cannot thank you enough, but once we have crushed this usurper, I will try."

"As you say. But I must warn you. Emrys will be heading this way with around three thousand cavalrymen, and Lord Odo plans to turn on Stephan once he arrives," I said.

shield wall that was now forming and fell in beside Roger.

"You let him go," Roger said as I locked my shield in place. We all stared through the gaps at the wall William was now forming in front of us. "Back up," Roger called. "Slowly now."

We all backed up in unison, and William's wall slowly followed us. Dozens and dozens of corpses lay in between both forces, and William's men now had to walk over their dead to get to us.

I could see now that we were losing the battle, and Roger had called us back with the slim hope that we could win. To our left, the battle was still raging on, but some of our men were already beginning to run, and to our right, Odo's forces were slowly pushing against Carol's, which now faced west instead of south.

"We're losing our right flank," I said to Roger.

"I know," he said. At that, William's shield wall began moving towards ours, but then they stopped. In the distance we heard warhorns, hundreds of them trumpeting from over the hills. William's forces paused, and every man turned to the east to see what the noise was.

And that was when we saw them.

There were hundreds of them, all on horseback, lined up along the ridge to the east. Our left unit, still fighting Stephan's troops, also spotted them. Their commander sounded his horn, and they bolted, retreating farther up the hill towards Carol. Their last remnants of hope had been shattered, and they were now fleeing for their lives.

Stephan's cavalry chased them down, but his infantry ignored them, and the soldiers who were previously fighting Carol's troops turned their attention to the east. Stephan must have realised that the horsemen on the ridge were not his allies, because his troops to our left had now formed a long wall of spears to counter this new threat.

But then we heard more horns to our right. I looked over, peeking through the gaps in our shield wall, and saw that Odo was betraying his king. He had kept half of his troops in reserve while the other half fought our right unit, but those reserve troops were now attacking Stephan's left flank.

Roger's shield wall and William's shield wall stood facing each other, unsure of what to do next. I felt the ripples of confusion flow through our men, and I guessed the same was happening to our enemy. Odo was supposed to be fighting with Stephan, not against him, so this new turn of events would have shocked everyone.

"I will hold William here for as long as I can. Get the king to safety," Roger said to me. "This battle is lost."

Roger was probably right, but I just stared at him, agape. I did not want to believe it.

"Go," he barked. I nodded and pushed back through the men behind me, threw my shield down, and pulled off my helmet, then sprinted off uphill. We had enemies to our south, to our west, and now to our east.

The Gods were about to have their fun.

"I will *not* leave my men to these animals," Carol said. For the first time since I had met him, he was angry with me.

"If you stay, you will die," I said.

Carol scoffed, and his advisors all exchanged glances. I had begged him to retreat with whatever men he could back to his fortress or to Giant's Rest. The battle was lost, and his generals all agreed with me. The men from the left unit who had routed regrouped at the top of the hill around Carol, guarding him, but I could sense their uncertainty. If we fled the field, many of those men would lose faith in Carol and go back to their homes. If we stayed, many would die.

"Remind me again, Edward. Who is the king?" Carol asked. He glared down at me from atop his horse.

"You are, Lord King."

"Indeed. And that means I choose whether to stay or go. And I wish to stay and die with my men."

"Then do not stay up here, My King," one of Carol's strategists said. "If you wish to show your men that you will die with them, at least do so on your own terms. Lead these men back into the fight."

Carol pursed his lips and looked over the battlefield, thinking. Roger and William's shield walls still faced each other, locked in a stalemate. The force around Carol was swelling, being bolstered by men who had fled or retreated but regrouped back at the top of the hill.

The battle at the western edge of the field was still raging, with Carol's and Stephan's forces now fighting side by side against Odo, who was slowly pushing them back. And in the east, atop the ridge, the Immortal Horde grew larger and larger as more horsemen arrived from Tillysburg, while the other half of Stephan's forces stood facing them, waiting for the imminent slaughter. The warriors around Carol were all looking up at him, awaiting his orders.

Carol nodded and pointed to an archer. "You there, go and tell Earl Roger that I command him to pull back and then come around to Lord Odo's left flank. He should come up the hill, go across, and then bring his men back downhill to strike," Carol ordered.

The archer bowed and sprinted off downhill to Roger's shield wall. Carol looked over his bloodied, beaten, and dishevelled men, then sighed.

"You are often told by those above you that the fate of this kingdom rests with me," Carol began. His voice was raised so all could hear. "But the men who say this are wrong! The fate of Ardonn lies not in my hands, but in yours. Our kingdom's heart beats in your chests. Her arms carry your swords, and she defends herself with your shields. Your ancestors forged this kingdom with their strength and tempered her steel with their own blood, and now, today, you brave men must do the same.

"The men you see on that ridge to the east wish to take from you everything you hold dear and tear our country apart. They wish to slaughter your brothers and sons and violate your daughters and wives. So, let us stop them! Let us show them what it means to have the Gods on our side."

Carol drew his sword from its sheath and threw himself down from his saddle, and the warriors around him all cheered. Even his cautious advisors were smiling. The sunlight gleamed off his blade. "I may be your king, but I am not your ruler. Brothers, today I am your leader. Will you follow me?"

With those last words, Carol's soldiers all drew their weapons, thrust them into the air, and cried a resounding "yes." Carol was grinning.

Roger must have received Carol's message, for he was beginning to withdraw back up the hill to make a move on Odo's flank. William's wall stood firm for a while, but they must have seen that Roger was no longer a threat, because they too withdrew, going back downhill.

But in the east, we heard a warhorn blowing. It was low and long — one great hum to signal the coming of our doom. My blood ran cold, and my muscles seemed to freeze at the sound.

The three thousand horses began to stomp their hooves, and soon after, the long line of immortal riders moved forward, coming slowly down the steep hill from atop the ridge.

"Captains," Carol shouted. "Get your men moving. We will form a wall in front of the usurper's men. Let us hope Stephan knows his real enemy today. Go!"

Without hesitation, the bedraggled warriors atop the hill sprinted down with their king at their side, screaming, filled with passion and fury. I ran with them, sword in hand, and Carol ran at my side.

I was afraid. Terrified.

Yet I could not help but smile. I would die beside my king. My friend. The horses started to gallop, hoping to catch us before we could brace ourselves, and we sprinted faster and faster, the wind tearing at our faces. Many men were throwing down their shields or pulling off their helmets so they could move faster.

We made it, but only just. The first men to arrive in front of Stephan's line began to form a shield wall, and bit by bit it widened, extending along the bottom of the eastern hill. We could hear the enemy horses screeching and their riders growling and shouting, and the clatter of shield locking against shield, and the rumble of hoof against earth. I fell into the shield wall, behind two rows of men, and Carol came in beside me. Neither of us had shields, so we stood behind those men who were forming the wall.

"Brace yourselves, men. Today we save our kingdom," Carol shouted. He punched me on the arm and laughed. "Are you ready, Edward?"

"I hope so," I said.

He grinned at me. "We will win today. I can feel it."

I said nothing, but deep down I too had a feeling that we would win. Was it a message from the Gods, or was I merely inspired by Carol's presence? We would soon find out. The horsemen came closer and closer, speeding down the hill, and eventually the only thing we could hear was the thunder of hooves.

Then I heard another sound. Carol heard it too. It was a warhorn, blowing from behind us. "To their flanks," a man shouted.

Carol and I both turned, and many of the men in the back rows did too, and a feeling of dread washed over us. Stephan's forces, only half a dozen yards behind us, all turned and ran to the sides of our wall. Half went left, while the other half went right. Carol had taken a great risk by forming his wall in front of Stephan's line, and now we were about to pay the price.

We would be surrounded on three sides.

But I was wrong. Upon reaching our flanks, Stephan's men did not turn and face us. They did not begin cutting through the line to crush us between both halves. Instead, Stephan's men faced eastwards and formed their own walls alongside ours. The two kings both united against a third. This was not at all what Odo had hoped for.

And then the chaos began.

There was a great roar, like the world itself was being torn asunder. The shields thundered, and the men screamed as hundreds upon hundreds of horses smashed into the wall of spears and shields.

Riders were thrown from their saddles over the wall and landed with a thud on the other side, writhing and moaning as time caught up with them and they dissolved into thin air. The horses all cried out in pain as they collided with our wall, and they all toppled in front of our men. A shield wall would halt ordinary cavalry, but these beasts were fearless, driven on by the sheer will of their riders. Blood sprayed everywhere, and our wall held as horses crashed against us like waves breaking against a cliff face.

But it could not hold forever. Our line broke in one spot farther along to the left, and horses began pouring through. Before we could react, it broke again farther along, and then once again to the right. It was not long before Emrys's riders were breaking through and surrounding us.

Carol shouted orders, some horns were blown, and the entire shield wall was dismantled in an instant. The last of the enemy's horsemen rode past us, cutting men down as they went, and then they all came around for another go.

This was the true meaning of chaos. Horses were charging from all sides. Men were screaming in panic. The stench of death clogged our nostrils. And it all happened so fast. Men who fought for Carol and men who fought for Stephan were now fighting side by side for Ardonn, and they were dying not as enemies, but as brothers, cut down by Emrys and his horde.

Yet no man fled. We stood our ground, ducking and dodging, stabbing and cutting, slaying horse and man alike. We fought hard, knowing we would likely die but content that it would be for something great. I was separated from Carol shortly after the wall of shields collapsed, and I hoped by all the Gods that he would not die.

It did not take long for our men to figure out that the riders would die if they touched the ground. They would have been confused and bewildered by this strange sorcery, but they did not let that stop them from fighting. Instead, it only increased their zeal. We were striking at the horses now, spearing their sides or slicing at their legs, constantly ducking and rolling to avoid the downward cuts of the ancient blades.

Horsemen came toppling from their beasts all around us, turning to dust as they hit the earth, and riderless horses were galloping among the chaos in confusion. My ears were ringing, howling. The sound of steel against steel, the sound of bones being snapped and armour being crushed, the sound of dying horses and men, and the sound of warhorns blowing surrounded me. I was in a sea of death.

And then I was knocked flat on my back, the air kicked out of me. My sword flew from my hands. A horse had rammed into me and thrown me to the ground, then it turned and started to charge again, kicking up dirt. I rolled to the side, only just dodging it, then rolled back the other way again to avoid the heavy hooves of another horse. I fumbled for a spear resting in the dirt and then crawled back to my feet.

The horse that tried to trample me stopped. It was large and grey, and I immediately recognised the man sitting atop it. I recognised his terrifying faceplate first, but then I saw the leaf-

shaped blade and the puppy and heard his deep, hollow laugh.
He was staring down at me from his horse, which had several
arrows and broken spears protruding from its mail coat.

"I hope you understand that you will die today, Edward,"
Emrys shouted in my own tongue.

"Maybe. But not by your hand."

Emrys growled, and his horse lunged forward. I lunged too,
and at the last moment, before Emrys's blade cut my skull open,
I held my breath and jumped to the side, thrusting the spear at
the beast. The shock rippled up the spear as it broke through the
horse's armour, sending a wave of pain through my arms, and
with a scream I was thrown back. The grey horse reared, with the
spear stuck several inches in its chest, but Emrys held on.

I heard a yell, and then Carol appeared out of nowhere and cut
at Emrys's leg. The warlord growled and then swung his sword
around and smashed the side of his head with the pommel. Carol
twisted and fell, and the iron crown flew from his head and
landed in the trampled grass.

I found a spear while Emrys had his attention turned to Carol,
and I took that opportunity to thrust it with all my strength at the
warlord. He noticed me just in time and spun his horse around.
The spear missed its mark but its tip pierced the horse's mail
coat instead, scraping along broken steel, then without hesitation
I yanked the weapon free.

The animal screeched as blood squirted from behind the mail,
and Emrys lost control of the beast. It reared, pushing back at me

and sending me tumbling, then it charged off through the battle with Emrys holding on for dear life.

The entire time, the small grey puppy managed to stay on the saddle and seemed completely unmoved by the events going on around it.

I picked up my sword and sprinted over to Carol, who was lying on his back with his hand on his head, groaning.

"Carol, can you hear me?" I shouted.

He just moaned. His eyes were clenched shut, and blood was pouring from the side of his skull, soaking his hair. I looked around at the chaos and quickly swung my blade to the side to cut at the legs of an oncoming horse. The beast fell forward with a cry, flipped onto its back, and the rider went rolling across the ground as he faded into dust. I put my arms under Carol's and lifted him, then he coughed and puked up both his breakfast and blood.

I spotted a horse standing without a rider several feet away from us. A mangled skeleton lay at its feet, reaching up with its bony hand gripping the reins. I dragged Carol over to the horse and with a great heave lifted him up into the saddle, then I kicked the dead hand away from the reins and handed them to Carol. He coughed up more vomit.

"We have…won," he groaned.

I frowned at him but then turned around and saw that Carol was right. Emrys was atop his grey horse galloping back up the hill. He was blowing his horn again and again, and his horsemen were beginning to pull away from the battle. They were fleeing back east, and our men started cheering as they realised one by one what Carol had seen. Some men chased after them but could not outrun the horses.

"Let us do the rest," I shouted, turning back to Carol. He nodded slowly, leaning forward awkwardly in the saddle, and I slapped the horse's rump with the flat of my blade. With a whinny it raced off north away from the last of the fighting. I was panting, and relief washed over me.

But then the sound of more horns echoed from the west. My heart sank. Although we had routed Emrys, the battle was not yet over.

On the other side of the field, Odo's men were being pushed backwards, but they were holding firm. They were outflanked and outnumbered, but even so, some of Stephan and Carol's men dropped their weapons and gave up the fight. The men were exhausted. I grabbed the reins of a horse as it ran past me, pulled myself up into the saddle, then pointed my sword to the west at the battle still raging.

"The Gods tell me we must finish this," I shouted. Many of the men who were celebrating their victory over Emrys turned to look at me. "Let's not disappoint them."

The men all shouted in agreement, and I kicked my horse. Once again, we charged into battle.

A stalemate had occurred at the other end of the battlefield. The army of Everlynn was now one mass as William had brought his forces to join his father's, but they were surrounded.

They had formed a large shield wall in the shape of a half-circle, and so the combined forces of Stephan, Roger, and Carol had done the same. Neither shield wall wanted to attack the other. Odo was outnumbered, but his warriors were famed even beyond Ardonn for their skill and ferocity in battle.

The men I led to join the new wall had just defeated the legendary Immortal Horde, and they thought of themselves as heroes, but the men who had been fighting Odo were tired and demoralised.

The battle was not over, and victory was far from certain. Emrys may have fled the field, but Odo still stood firm. The men from both sides yelled insults and curses at each other, but the taunting could not entice anyone to attack.

However, the warriors who had faced Emrys's horde were now drunk on victory and blood, and they wanted another taste. Screaming, cheering, and shouting, they all joined the encirclement, and many of them pushed past and threw themselves at Odo's wall, hacking and jabbing at their shields. They must have believed themselves invincible.

But they were not.

Within seconds, those same men were cut to pieces and now lay dead at the base of Odo's shield wall. The stalemate began once more. Everything went silent. I could hear the breathing of the man beside me and the occasional clatter of weapons and armour, but no one moved and no one spoke. I could smell death and fear. My heart was racing.

"Archers, ready," a commander shouted.

All of the archers around me pulled back away from the wall, lined up, and readied their bows. They were given the command to aim and then loose a volley. The arrows went whizzing up into the air, and then a volley came from Roger's troops, and more volleys from other parts of our half-circle. Iron and death rained on Odo's forces, but the shields held above their heads protected them and the arrows were barely effective. The volleys kept coming and seemed to go on forever.

After some time, the arrows ceased, and there was a mighty cheer from among Odo's men. Then the tension began once again. Both sides just watched each other, waiting for the other to make a move.

I could not stand it any longer. I pushed past the men in front of me and then opened up our wall and stepped out in front of it. I saw the men behind Odo's wall shuffle, eager for me to be close enough to kill.

"Odo," I shouted. I wanted everyone to hear me. "Odo! I killed your brother, Hakon, and now I come to kill you. Face me, or face your ancestors a coward."

I was challenging him to single combat. Like in the old tales about legendary warriors and heroes, I was going to duel a man between two armies. By declaring I had killed Hakon — which was a lie, of course — I was letting all his men know that if he denied my challenge, not only would he be a coward, but he would also be dishonouring the bond of kinship, and his refusal to avenge his brother would mean many would not want to follow him ever again.

I heard shuffling from behind the wall, and then the front parted and Odo stepped out. He wore a coat of thick mail and a crested helmet with a visor over his eyes. He carried no shield but instead wielded a large bearded axe in both hands.

I gulped, and he stomped over to me. Behind the holes in his visor, his cold eyes burned through to my soul. His face raged red with fury.

"I wanted to kill you the moment I laid eyes on you," Odo said. He gave a short bow. I was going to die.

"Gods help me," I whispered, taking three paces backwards.

"Freeing that horseman was clearly not worth the effort. But once I am done with you, I will deal with the usurper's son and the boy pretender."

I gave a yell and charged at him. He growled, and as I lunged he swung his axe and parried, then stepped to the side. The way he moved that axe made it seem weightless. I could see how he earned his fame. I turned and tried another lunge, but this time I feinted and swung my blade up. He dodged that with ease and stepped back. We circled each other for a few moments.

Odo laughed. It was his turn to attack. He brought the axe up above his head and sliced low at my legs, but I jumped back just in time. He pressed forward, swinging the axe up with a loud grunt, down again, then to the side and back the other way.

I dodged each swing, but only by a hair. Not only was he incredibly strong, but Odo was also fast, and were his axe any lighter I would probably have been cleaved in two. Men on both sides shouted encouragement or insults, but Odo and I ignored them. We were focussed.

"You are quick, boy. But it will not save you," Odo said. He swung his axe and I dodged, but before I could react he jabbed it forward, and I felt it connect with my gut. It pushed me onto my behind and knocked the air out of me, and I crawled backwards as Odo made another swing down. I rolled and then threw myself back to my feet.

Odo's swing at me buried his axe into the ground, and that gave me a few seconds to strike. I slashed at Odo — a stupid move. My blade met his mail, but it only slid off, and Odo barely seemed to notice. He smacked my sword aside and pulled his axe from the ground. I lunged, he parried that, I sliced again, he dodged, I lunged, he parried.

Before I could make another move, Odo thrust the axe again, and it was my turn to dodge. We went away at each other like this for a while, but then death approached. I cut at Odo's leg, hoping to disable him, but he had iron in his boots. My sword only struck metal.

Odo brought the shaft of his axe up to my face and knocked me back, then without hesitation he swung his axe over his head.

I tried to move but felt the axe rip through mail and slice through the flesh of my shoulder. It did not cut deep, but the shock rushed through my whole body. I dropped my sword and collapsed with a cry.

Odo was laughing as he brought the axe up again to finish me, but instinct kicked in. I did not leap for my sword, but instead I leapt for Odo's leg. I hugged it, tackling him to the ground. Odo struck my back with his axe, but the blow was weak.

Odo and I tumbled to the ground, and before he could do anything, I pulled myself on top of him and drew my knife from its sheath. I stabbed down at Odo's throat, but he grabbed my wrist with both hands and held it in place. We struggled. I used all my strength, gritting my teeth to overcome the pulsing pain in my shoulder, and Odo used all of his.

But Odo was stronger, and my strength gave way. He pushed my wrist up, smashed the butt of my knife into my face, then swung at my jaw with his fist, and my head snapped back. I swallowed a tooth. Odo pushed me back and pinned me down. My whole face was aching, and the world appeared to spin. The shouts of the men in the shield walls seemed distant and muffled.

Odo wasted no time wrapping his fingers around my neck and squeezing. Hard. I gasped for air, but Odo's clench only tightened. I tried to gasp again, but no air went in. I felt the veins in my head pumping hard and fast, then I started to hear a sound in my ears like gushing waterfalls. The world seemed to spin.

I pulled at Odo's hands, trying to pry his fingers away from my neck, but he was far too strong. Death smiled at me. My sight blurred. The light began to fade. I clawed at Odo's face, but then my hands fell to my side and the world went dark.

One moment I was lying on the cold, muddied earth, surrounded by warriors and strangled by a mail-clad nobleman, and the next moment I found myself floating on a raft in a gentle, endless ocean. It was chilly but not uncomfortable. I could not move, so I just lay on my back staring up at the clear blue sky.

And then I felt something press against my lips. It was ice-cold but soft. A kiss. But who was kissing me? Then a voice whispered my name. A woman. She lay beside me, but I could not see her. She spoke softly into my ear.

"What are you doing?" the woman asked.

"Dying."

"Do not do that."

"That is not for me to decide."

"Who told you that?" I recognised the voice. It was Aoife, the elf that watched over the woods near my home. But why, and how, was she here?

"Where am I?"

"Home is the last thing many men think of before they die," Aoife said.

"This is not my home; this is the ocean."

"Where is your home, Edward?"

I opened my mouth to answer, but I realised I would be wrong. I lived in the house near Oldford, but that was now a pile of scorched rubble. I grew up on a farm near Winterhome, but I had not seen that since Brendan took me away, so that was not my home either. I had no home.

"Why are you here?" I asked.

"You summoned me here. You could have stayed with me, Edward. We could have made a home together in my forest. That is all you want in this world, is it not? A home to call your own."

"Yes."

"If you die now, you will have no home. You will wander forever, bound to no one."

"Who are you, really?"

"I am Aoife. But I think you have figured out by now that Aoife is much more than an elf."

"Take me with you, Aoife," I said.

She giggled. "Perhaps one day, my darling Edward. But not today. You have a promise to fulfil."

"A promise?"

Without another word, Aoife brought her cold, gentle hand to my neck and then slowly pulled something from inside my shirt. She plucked it from my neck and placed it in my hand. It was the moth pendant I had given to Matilda, and which she had given to me. "You cannot take this to the world of the dead," Aoife said.

"How can I return it?" I asked. I felt Aoife's icy breath against my ear.

"Take the dagger from Odo's belt," she whispered.

And just like that, the raft, the ocean, and Aoife were gone. I found myself staring up at Odo's face once more and felt the pain in my throat and torso and the slow, dull thudding in my skull. Everything was spinning, and for a second I forgot where I was.

But then I remembered and quickly fumbled for Odo's dagger. Without hesitation, I pulled it out and with every ounce of effort I had left, I thrust it up under the mail at Odo's groin. I felt it pierce thick leather, but then I heard a crunch and felt the horrible feeling of steel sliding through flesh and muscle.

Hot blood poured over my hand, the air rushed back into my lungs, and I watched as Odo reared back, screaming. I held on to the weapon and pulled it from Odo's groin, and he collapsed and fell onto his back, writhing and moaning.

I tried to stand, but the world seemed to flip up on itself, and I collapsed to the ground again. I heard shouting and the thundering of feet, and for a few moments my vision darkened.

But as light returned, I caught a glimpse of the screaming Lord Odo being pulled away by his men. I too was being pulled back, and as I was dragged away, Carol and Stephan's warriors rushed past me and threw themselves at Odo's shield wall.

The man who pulled me away from the fight sat me up and said something to me, but I did not hear. All I noticed was a breach appear in Odo's wall. Then another. And then another. Bit by bit, shield by shield, Odo's wall fell apart and his men were slaughtered like pigs.

Some tried to fight. Young fools. The smarter ones ran. They dropped their swords, spears, shields, and axes and ran for their lives. What remained of Carol and Stephan's cavalry thundered past us and rode Odo's men down. It was madness. It was death. Alcyn's thirst for blood this season had finally been sated.

I watched as a large stallion carrying the wounded Lord of Everlynn sped from the chaos and raced southwards. Some of Carol's horsemen tried to chase him, but they quickly gave up.

At the same time, a blue banner emblazoned with a white hare was torn and fell to the ground, and from the madness and death stumbled a bloody, ragged warrior with a cloak of blue.

He fell to his knees, chased by one of Stephan's men, but he turned and thrust his sword up into his assailant's belly. Stephan's man died, the blue-cloaked warrior crawled over to me, and before the man guarding me could react, the warrior removed his glove and threw it into my lap.

"I yield. End it," he said. I only stared at him. "End it!"

I snapped back to my senses. William. It was William. He had crawled from the fight to surrender to me, and now he looked up and pleaded for the slaughter to stop. His comrades — his friends — were being put to the sword, and William only wanted it all to end.

I took William's glove in my hand and looked him in the eyes. They were red and wet with tears.

"These men are out of my control," I said. William squeezed his eyes shut, rolled onto his back, and let out a scream. He screamed at the sky, cursing the Gods and his father. The slaughter continued until there were none left to kill.

The battle was over.

I sat up on Brand atop the ridge above the battlefield, my hand pressed against my swollen jaw, watching over the mess. My shoulder still ached unbearably, but it had been stitched up and bandaged by one of Stephan's battlefield healers. So much violence, so much death, and for what? It seemed as though it was all for nothing. Emrys had fled, Odo had escaped, while Stephan and Carol were back where they began.

The field was littered with the dead or dying, and men from Stephan and Carol's armies were helping each other collect their fallen comrades for burial. Some of the wives and children of the men who fought had come over from the camps a few miles away to find their loved ones among the living, or among the corpses.

The soldiers who were not helping to collect bodies were standing in the middle of the plane, facing each other. In between them was a tent, and inside that tent, Carol and Stephan discussed peace.

I heard a person approach me, but I did not turn to see who it was. The man came up beside me and looked out over the field.

"I believe this belongs to your king," he said. I turned to see William, bloodied and dishevelled, but smiling. He was holding out a bent iron crown, and I took it from him, turning it over in my hands.

"The ancient crown of Ardonn," I said. I then began to laugh. All of that death had been for a cheap piece of ancient iron. "You know, this probably isn't even the original."

William began to laugh too, and for a while the two of us stood up on that ridge, chuckling.

"What do you think will happen?" I asked, nodding to the big tent down below.

"There will be peace for a few years, but Carol will gain more and more support once news of today's events spreads through the kingdom and beyond, so I doubt that peace will last. I suspect Stephan will have no choice but to let Carol retain control over Tillysburg and the lands around it. The earl, Roger, died in battle. He left no heirs."

That news struck me. I was not fond of Roger, but he was a good man nonetheless, and loyal to Carol. He did not deserve to die, but few men who lay on the field that day did.

"I suppose I am your prisoner now," William said.

"Well, you gave me your glove. Do you want to go free?"

"Will you let me?"

I shrugged. "You'd be worth a pretty penny."

"True. All I want right now is a cold drink and the embrace of my wife, but I suppose it is better to be a hostage than to be dead. What about you? Will you go to that girl you were with?"

"Girl?"

"The black-haired one. I cannot recall her name."

"Oh. Her name is Matilda. I suppose I will go back to her. I made a promise, after all."

"And what then?"

"Spring is here, and Carol will be getting married soon, to his betrothed from beyond the Alps. I think I will stay up in the north for that, so my friends and I can rest a while. There is nothing more I can do about Emrys, so I will leave that problem to the men with the armies. I'm already tired of war. I guess after the wedding I will go to Everlynn and ransom you to your father, then head back to Oldford and continue hunting ghosts and witches."

"And vampires," William said with a smile. I smirked. "I think I am glad to be your prisoner, Edward. I did not know my father's plans, and if I did, I hope I would not have agreed to them. I do not want any part in his little rebellion. As for you, I do not believe your part in the wars to come is at an end. Your fate is certainly tied up with it all."

"I hope you are wrong."

"So do I, my friend, so do I."

I smiled at William, and a tear came to my eye. Despite the hardship, the pain, and the chaos, I had gained a new friend. For that I was grateful, and it almost made the death worth it.

And William was right — my fate was bound to Emrys and the events to come. There was no doubt about that. But what part I would play, I could not yet tell. Carol and Stephan would make peace, but Odo would retreat to Everlynn and likely raise another army to wage war against Stephan while Emrys and the Immortal Horde, despite their humiliating defeat, would rampage in whatever part of the kingdom they saw fit.

I did not know what fate had planned for me, and although I wished never to see Emrys again, I knew deep down that I could not avoid him.

The Gods love poetry. Three centuries ago, my predecessor Godwin fought side by side with Carol's ancestor and bound Emrys inside a mountain tomb, but now he was free. How poetic it would be that the heir of Godwin and the heir of Carol the Great should defeat the Immortal King once and for all.

No man or god is immune to Fate's capricious pen — our lives and our stories have already been written, and all we in this world can do is follow along, line by line, and hope for the best from our final pages.

Or perhaps I am wrong. Perhaps we are free to forge our own destinies, as Aoife once told me. Whichever is the case, I knew I would not know peace until Emrys was dead.

That much was certain.

Edward's saga, and that of all Ardonn,
will soon continue…

The Noble Families of Ardonn

The Eomundson Kings

Family currently headed by **Carol**, known as *the Pretender*.

Who is the son of King Edwin of Ardonn, known as *the Fifth*, who was married to Lady Elfswith of Winterhome, daughter of Lord Wulfstan of Winterhome, and also fathered Clodild.

Who was the son of King Edwin, known as *the Fourth*, who also fathered Lady Alhilda, wife to Lord Adalbert of Oldford.

Who was the son of King Francis, known as *the Feeble*, who was married to Elain, known as *the Weaver*.

Who was the son of King Ermenwulf, who was married to Lady Eadburg.

Who was the great-grandson of King Edmund, known as *the Child*, who was married to Lady Melisende of Everlynn.

Who was the son of King Francis, known as *the Second*, who was married to Lady Hemma and who also fathered Queen Hemma, known as *the Traitor*, wife to King Tanred of Erila; and Cwenhild, Clodild, and Edwina.

Who was the son of King Francis, known as *the First*.

Who was the son of King Carol, known as *the Great*, who unified the Twin Kingdoms, who was married to Lady Aleanor and also fathered Carol, known as *the Younger*, who was married to Edith, Godwin's daughter.

Who was the son of King Edgar.

Who was descended from King Adalwulf, known as *the Good-Healthed*.

Who was the son of King Edwulf.

Who was the great-great-grandson of King Eomund, founder of the Eomundson dynasty, who was the first King of Ardonn from among the Exiles, and who married Lady Eirwen of Ardonn, descendent of King Emrys; and who legend tells was the son of Lita, the daughter of Morenlea and Hefencyn.

Who was the son of Adalwer, King of the Black Coast, who also fathered Eored, founder of the Eoredson dynasty, who was the first King of Aedonn from among the Exiles.

The Eoredson Kings and Lords of Oldford

Family currently headed by **Lord Adalbert of Oldford**, who was married to Lady Alhilda and who fathered Lady Ecwyn.

Who was the son of Lord Godred, known as *the Mild*.

Who was the son of Lord Elwin.

Who was the son of Lord Godred, known as *the Lesser*, who also fathered Earl Adalstan, known as *the Cowherd*, who fathered Lady Alia, who was married to Earl Odhelm of Henton, who fathered Earl Harold, who was married to Eleanor and who fathered Gunn, Alia, and Matilda.

Who was the son of Lord Godred, known as *the Oathbreaker*, self-styled King of Aedonn.

Who was the descendent of King Godheart of North-Aedonn, later Lord of Oldford, known as *the Kneeler*, for it was he who yielded the Kingdom of Aedonn to King Carol *the Great*.

Who was the son of Queen Aelda of Aedonn, known as *the Fair* and *the Cruel*, who was married King Godheart of Beglen and who also mothered King Elwulf of West-Aedonn, known as *the Coward*; and King Cured of South-Aedonn, later Lord of Beglen, known as *the Hammer*.

Who was the daughter of King Elwulf, known as *Wolfsbane*, who married Lady Hilda of Bullhorn.

Who was the descendent of King Eored, founder of the Eoredson dynasty, who was the first King of Aedonn from among the Exiles; and who legend tells was the son of Lita, the daughter of Morenlea and Hefencyn.

Who was the son of Adalwer, King of the Black Coast, who also fathered Eomund, founder of the Eomundson dynasty, who was the first King of Ardonn from among the Exiles.

The Usurper Kings

Family currently headed by **King Stephan of Ardonn, previously Lord of Tidegate**, known as *the Bastard*, who is married to Lady Bebbe of Winterhome, daughter of Lord Wulfstan of Winterhome, and who fathered Lord Wim of Tidegate, known as *the Young*.

Who was the son of Lord Wim of Tidegate, later King of Ardonn, known as *the Usurper*, who remained unmarried until death.

Who was the descendent of Cedwin, who was the first Lord of Tidegate from among the Exiles, known as *the Tidebringer*.

The Lords of Everlynn

Family currently headed by **Lord Odo of Everlynn**, who is married to Lady Eadswith and who fathered William, who married Lady Eleni, daughter of Sealord Tripho of Cavoucara; and Anora, Arlette, and five other daughters.

 Who was the great-grandson of Lord Elmore of Everlynn, known as *the Peacemaker*.

 Who was a descendent of Richard, known as *the Foreign-Lord*, who was the first Lord of Everlynn from among the Erilans and who also fathered Lady Melisende, wife to King Edmund *the Child* of Ardonn.

 Who was the son of King Rubert of Erila, who also fathered King Tanred of Erila, also later King of Ardonn, who married Queen Hemma *the Traitor* of Ardonn.

Acknowledgements

While the name "Jason Malone" may be on the cover of this novel, I am by no means the only one deserving of credit for it. Although I did most of the writing and editing, I have a whole legion of people who deserve recognition.

I would first and foremost like to thank my mum and dad, for their undying support and praise, without whom even the first word of this book could not have been written, let alone the last. I am incredibly lucky to have the privilege of being their son, and am eternally grateful for all they have done to help me tell this story.

Secondly, I would like to thank Sophie, whose support has been immeasurable. Sophie has stood by me from day one, has suffered through numerous drafts, provided feedback, listened to my ramblings, and most importantly, has kept me writing even in moments of the most intense doubt. She instilled in me the confidence and drive to keep going, and without her I also could not have brought this story to completion. For that I will always be thankful.

I also wish to extend my gratitude to those who read through my drafts, giving suggestions, feedback, and reviews which have played a big part in shaping the final version of this tale: Mackenzie, Tony, Ella-Maree, Campbell, Breanne, Ruby, and my brother Harrison. And for their continued support, I am grateful to Joshua, James, Ashton, and the rest of my family. Their help has meant more than I think they realise, and I will always be thankful for them.

On top of this, special mention should be given to Allister Thompson, my editor, and Lena Yang, who designed the cover of this book.

And, of course, special thanks should be given to you, the reader, for making it through to the end of this novel. I sincerely hope you enjoyed it, and invite you to stay tuned for the sequel, in which Edward's adventures shall continue…

I must also thank the goddess Frīge, my divine patron and muse, who provided the inspiration for this story and all others I have written. Truly, it cannot be said that these stories are my own, as I am merely the pen with which their true author writes.

Enjoy the Immortal King?

Consider leaving a review on Amazon!

Want to be notified when new stories from Ardonn are released?
Subscribe to the free exclusive mailing list now on…

www.talesfromardonn.com

Follow the author on @talesfromardonn

Or facebook.com/talesfromardonn